GREAT STORIES BY
Chekhov

Translated by Constance Garnett

*Edited, with an introduction,
by David H. Greene*

Published by
DELL PUBLISHING CO., INC.
750 Third Avenue
New York 17, N.Y.

The stories in this volume are translated by Constance Garnett and reprinted by permission of The Macmillan Company:

"Misery" and "In Exile," from THE SCHOOLMISTRESS AND OTHER STORIES, copyright 1918 by The Macmillan Company, renewed 1948 by David Garnett.

"A Problem" and "The Kiss," from THE PARTY AND OTHER STORIES, copyright 1917 by The Macmillan Company, renewed 1945 by Constance Garnett.

"A Father" and "My Life," from THE CHORUS GIRL AND OTHER STORIES, copyright 1920 by The Macmillan Company, renewed 1947 by David Garnett.

"Ward No. 6," from THE HORSE STEALERS AND OTHER STORIES, copyright 1921 by The Macmillan Company, renewed 1949 by David Garnett.

"The Darling," from THE DARLING AND OTHER STORIES, copyright 1916 by The Macmillan Company, renewed 1944 by Constance Garnett.

"Peasants," from THE WITCH AND OTHER STORIES, copyright 1918 by The Macmillan Company, renewed 1946 by Constance Garnett.

First printing—January, 1959
Second printing—May, 1963
Third printing—February, 1965
Fourth printing—February, 1966
Fifth printing—July, 1967

Printed in U.S.A.

Contents

Introduction

By DAVID H. GREENE

SINCE E. M. Forster once defined a novel as "a prose fiction of a certain length," one cannot blame less distinguished theorists in such matters for a reluctance to be any more specific. Aristotle's dictum about tragedy being "of a certain magnitude" is just as vague and has been infinitely more intimidating. What bothers me about Forster's definition is not his vagueness—he was vague only in not specifying the length about which he was otherwise so certain—but his leaving no apparent room for any distinction between the novel and the short story, or worse still in implying that the only thing which distinguishes one from the other is length. Since Forster is himself a practitioner of both forms, the definition reveals more about his own practice than about either the novel or the short story. Besides, everyone knows that the short story is short, if it is anything, and that the novel is longer than the short story. The only real difficulty here is when you try to define the length of one without reference to the other.

Other distinguished practitioners have fortunately insisted upon more valid distinctions between the short story and the novel and between the short story and other forms of narrative, like the yarn. But they, too, tend eventually to collapse into ambiguities, and the conclusion one is forced to draw is that since nobody has any difficulty in saying what the modern short story is there is not much point in worrying about what it is not.

Many people will agree that the man who is chiefly responsible for the modern short story being what it is, is Anton Chekhov (1860-1904). With the kind of egotism acceptable only in great creative artists he wrote in 1888, before his best work was yet done, "Everything I have written will be forgotten in five or ten years; but the road I have laid down will endure—therein lies my only achievement as a writer." What that road was we can learn from other pronouncements he made about his work and his habits of work, for to study his career as a writer is to study the evolution of the literary form he may be said to have invented.

All the facts seem to have been in his favor—even the unhappy ones. First, he was lazy—though one has to take his frequent application of the word to himself with a grain of salt—and the short story is the lazy man's dish, to be prepared or consumed in one sitting or thereabouts. Second, his older brother was a short story writer, and Chekhov was provided with a living model in his own home. Third, he had to be fed, so he began writing short stories because there was a paying market for them in the Russia of his day. Since the magazines he wrote for did not pay well he had to sell a good many stories to support the large family his father was incapable of supporting. His apprenticeship, which began when he was only twenty, was therefore prolific. Before he was twenty-five Chekhov had published almost three hundred stories. Before he was twenty-seven he had written three hundred more. Such impressive experience, one is tempted to think, would have made even a writer of mediocre talent a master of the form.

Necessity in Chekhov's case was the mother of facility. "I can't remember a single story," he wrote, "on which I spent more than one day, and I wrote my stories just as newspaper reporters write their notices of a fire—mechanically, half-consciously, with little thought of my readers or myself." Chekhov was fond of deprecating his early work, much of which was merely facile. But four of the stories I have selected for this volume were written during the period I have described as his apprenticeship; and one of them ("Misery"), which Chekhov classified among his "unimportant trifles," is now rightly considered a classic.

Other remarks which Chekhov made about his early work, however, quickly dispel the impression that he wrote mechanically and without conscious design. In 1883 he complained to the editor of a magazine which published only stories of one hundred lines, "I get a subject for a story and sit down to write it, but the thought of one hundred lines and no more interferes with my writing from the very start. I condense as much as I can and keep cutting it down, sometimes (as my literary sense warns me) to the detriment of my subject and (above all) to the story's form. Having strained and compressed it, I begin to count the lines, and having counted 100, 120, 140 . . . I begin to get frightened and I don't send it. Very often I have to re-write the ending of a story in a hurry and send you something I should not ordinarily have liked to send you. As soon as I go over the fourth page of small note-paper I begin to be assailed by doubts."

Although he protested against the limitations of brevity the experience was obviously valuable for a man who was to work exclusively in the short story and in the drama, where length is so rigidly prescribed by the form. He wrote to a friend who was starting her career, in 1886, what must have seemed to her to be mere advice, but it was actually a lesson he had learned through necessity. "Write a story at one go . . . and don't forget that brevity is the mother of all virtues especially if you write for the popular press, and the best way to check that is by your note-paper (the same as I am writing on now). The moment you come to page 8-10 stop!"

But brevity and facility were not all, it would appear from advice he gave to his brother a year later. "Don't invent sufferings which you have not experienced and don't paint landscapes you have not seen, for a lie in a story is a hundred times more boring than in a conversation." If there is one uncontrovertible observation that can be made about Chekhov's work it is that he practiced what he was preaching—he gathered his materials directly from the life he knew, even if his vision seemed to focus more on the minor cracks of life's surface than on the great crevices which Dostoyevsky and Tolstoy preferred to explore. One of Chekhov's friends has recorded his saying, "I will describe life to you truthfully, that is, artistically, and you will see in it what you have not seen before—its divergence from the norm, its contradictions."

Despite the fact that Chekhov always insisted upon the seriousness of his work, even of his comedy, some readers have mistakenly assumed that his light-handedness, his air of quiet detachment, reveals a frivolousness in his art which makes it anything but the criticism of life so dear to the heart of the traditionalist. But from the very beginning of his career Chekhov never considered his work as anything but an attempt to capture something of life's meaning. "A small story," he wrote apologetically to one of his editors, "containing a good plot and an effective protest is, so far as I am able to observe, read with pleasure or, in other words, is not dull. Besides, a good word uttered on behalf of a thief at Easter will not ruin your journal. And, to tell you the truth, it is not so easy to chase after humor . . . you just can't help trying to be serious occasionally."

There are other facts which fortuitously combined to make Chekhov the kind of artist he became and which explain why the short story in his hands became what it did. Chekhov's genius, for example, was essentially a dramatic one—as his success in writing plays proves—and he quickly learned that it was a dramatic talent he was exploiting in his short stories. He wrote his brother, to whom he was always giving advice, "The best thing of all is not to describe the emotional state of your characters; you ought to try to make it clear from their actions. Neither should you have too many characters. The center of gravity should be two: he and she . . ." When Chekhov wrote this in 1886 he had yet to write his first play or even to think about himself as a dramatist, but he was speaking as only a dramatist would have spoken. He also advised his brother not to be subjective, which one might think a strange bit of advice to give when subjectivity was to become the hallmark of the modern novel. "Subjectivity," Chekhov wrote, "is a dangerous thing."

His failure as a novelist also made him aware of the peculiar talents he was bringing to the short story, for the same talents would not suffice in the novel. Chekhov wrote two novels and started a third, which he never finished. He destroyed all three manuscripts. In 1888 he wrote to a friend, "Before sitting down to a write a novel I must train myself to communicate ideas freely in a narrative form." Some months later he wrote again, "I don't think I shall be able to master the technique of the novel. I am still weak so far as that is concerned, and I feel that I am making a great number of big mistakes." It is clear that in his own view, at least, what was balking him was the necessity of using a purely narrative technique. In a novel one could not depend on the mere actions of the characters to do all the work. Some story-telling was necessary, and Chekhov was not really a story-teller.

If the short story in our time seems thin-blooded, plotless, more like lyric poetry than prose fiction because of its introspection, more like the drama than lyric poetry because of its penetrating but evanescent insights into human character—what Stephen Dedalus called *epiphanies*—it is because this is the road Chekhov laid down for us. It was the only possible road, given his limitations and his genius.

January, 1959

Misery

"TO WHOM SHALL I TELL MY GRIEF?"

THE TWILIGHT of evening. Big flakes of wet snow are whirling lazily about the street lamps, which have just been lighted, and lying in a thin soft layer on roofs, horses' backs, shoulders, caps. Iona Potapov, the sledge-driver, is all white like a ghost. He sits on the box without stirring, bent as double as the living body can be bent. If a regular snowdrift fell on him it seems as though even then he would not think it necessary to shake it off. . . . His little mare is white and motionless too. Her stillness, the angularity of her lines, and the stick-like straightness of her legs make her look like a halfpenny gingerbread horse. She is probably lost in thought. Anyone who has been torn away from the plough, from the familiar gray landscapes, and cast into this slough, full of monstrous lights, of unceasing uproar and hurrying people, is bound to think.

It is a long time since Iona and his nag have budged. They came out of the yard before dinner-time and not a single fare yet. But now the shades of evening are falling on the town. The pale light of the street lamps changes to a vivid color, and the bustle of the street grows noisier.

"Sledge to Vyborgskaya!" Iona hears. "Sledge!"

Iona starts, and through his snow-plastered eyelashes sees an officer in a military overcoat with a hood over his head.

"To Vyborgskaya," repeats the officer. "Are you asleep? To Vyborgskaya!"

In token of assent Iona gives a tug at the reins which sends cakes of snow flying from the horse's back and shoulders. The officer gets into the sledge. The sledge-driver clicks to the horse, cranes his neck like a swan, rises in his seat, and more from habit than necessity brandishes his whip. The mare cranes her neck, too, crooks her stick-like legs, and hesitatingly sets off. . . .

"Where are you shoving, you devil?" Iona immediately hears shouts from the dark mass shifting to and fro before him. "Where the devil are you going? Keep to the r-right!"

"You don't know how to drive! Keep to the right," says the officer angrily.

A coachman driving a carriage swears at him; a pedestrian crossing the road and brushing the horse's nose with his shoulder looks at him angrily and shakes the snow off his sleeve. Iona fidgets on the box as though he were sitting on thorns, jerks his elbows, and turns his eyes about like one possessed, as though he did not know where he was or why he was there.

"What rascals they all are!" says the officer jocosely. "They are simply doing their best to run up against you or fall under the horse's feet. They must be doing it on purpose."

Iona looks at his fare and moves his lips. . . . Apparently he means to say something, but nothing comes but a sniff.

"What?" inquires the officer.

Iona gives a wry smile, and straining his throat, brings out huskily: "My son . . . er . . . my son died this week, sir."

"H'm! What did he die of?"

Iona turns his whole body round to his fare, and says:

"Who can tell! It must have been from fever. . . . He lay three days in the hospital and then he died. . . . God's will."

"Turn round, you devil!" comes out of the darkness. "Have you gone cracked, you old dog? Look where you are going!"

"Drive on! drive on! . . ." says the officer. "We shan't get there till to-morrow going on like this. Hurry up!"

The sledge-driver cranes his neck again, rises in his seat, and with heavy grace swings his whip. Several times he looks round at the officer, but the latter keeps his eyes shut and is apparently disinclined to listen. Putting his fare down at Vyborgskaya, Iona stops by a restaurant, and again sits huddled up on the box. . . . Again the wet snow paints him and his horse white. One hour passes, and then another. . . .

Three young men, two tall and thin, one short and hunchbacked, come up, railing at each other and loudly stamping on the pavement with their goloshes.

"Cabby, to the Police Bridge!" the hunchback cries in a cracked voice. "The three of us, . . . twenty kopecks!"

Iona tugs at the reins and clicks to his horse. Twenty kopecks is not a fair price, but he has no thoughts for that. Whether it is a rouble or whether it is five kopecks does not matter to him now so long as he has a fare. . . . The three young men, shoving each other and using bad language, go up to the sledge, and all three try to sit down at once. The question remains to be settled: Which are to sit down and which one is to stand? After a long altercation, ill-temper, and abuse, they come to the conclusion that the hunchback must stand because he is the shortest.

"Well, drive on," says the hunchback in his cracked voice, settling himself and breathing down Iona's neck. "Cut along! What a cap you've got, my friend! You wouldn't find a worse one in all Petersburg. . . ."

"He-he! . . . he-he! . . ." laughs Iona. "It's nothing to boast of!"

"Well, then, nothing to boast of, drive on! Are you going to drive like this all the way? Eh? Shall I give you one in the neck?"

"My head aches," says one of the tall ones. "At the Dukmasovs' yesterday Vaska and I drank four bottles of brandy between us."

"I can't make out why you talk such stuff," says the other tall one angrily. "You lie like a brute."

"Strike me dead, it's the truth! . . ."

"It's about as true as that a louse coughs."

"He-he!" grins Iona. "Me-er-ry gentlemen!"

"Tfoo! the devil take you!" cries the hunchback indignantly. "Will you get on, you old plague, or won't you? Is that the way to drive? Give her one with the whip. Hang it all, give it her well."

Iona feels behind his back the jolting person and quivering voice of the hunchback. He hears abuse addressed to him, he sees people, and the feeling of loneliness begins little by little to be less heavy on his heart. The hunchback swears at him, till he chokes over some elaborately whimsical string of epithets and is overpowered by his cough. His tall companions begin talking of a certain Nadyezhda Petrovna. Iona looks round at them. Waiting till there is a brief pause, he looks round once more and says:

"This week . . . er . . . my . . . er . . . son died!"

"We shall all die, . . ." says the hunchback with a sigh, wiping his lips after coughing. "Come, drive on! drive on! My friends, I simply cannot stand crawling like this! When will he get us there?"

"Well, you give him a little encouragement . . . one in the neck!"

"Do you hear, you old plague? I'll make you smart. If one stands on ceremony with fellows like you one may as well walk. Do you hear, you old dragon? Or don't you care a hang what we say?"

And Iona hears rather than feels a slap on the back of his neck.

"He-he! . . ." he laughs. "Merry gentlemen. . . . God give you health!"

"Cabman, are you married?" asks one of the tall ones.

"I? He-he! Me-er-ry gentlemen. The only wife for me now is the damp earth. . . . He-ho-ho! . . . The grave that is! . . . Here my son's dead and I am alive. . . . It's a strange thing, death has come in at the wrong door. . . . Instead of coming for me it went for my son. . . ."

And Iona turns round to tell them how his son died, but at that point the hunchback gives a faint sigh and announces that, thank God! they have arrived at last. After taking his twenty kopecks, Iona gazes for a long while after the revelers, who disappear into a dark entry. Again he is alone and again there is silence for him. . . . The misery which has been for a brief space eased comes back again and tears his heart more cruelly than ever. With a look of anxiety and suffering Iona's eyes stray restlessly among the crowds moving to and fro on both sides of the street: can he not find among those thousands someone who will listen to him? But the crowds flit by heedless of him and his misery. . . . His misery is immense, beyond all bounds. If Iona's heart were to burst and his misery to flow out, it would flood the whole world, it seems, but yet it is not seen. It has found a hiding-place in such an insignificant shell that one would not have found it with a candle by daylight. . . .

Iona sees a house-porter with a parcel and makes up his mind to address him.

"What time will it be, friend?" he asks.

"Going on for ten. . . . Why have you stopped here? Drive on!"

Iona drives a few paces away, bends himself double, and gives himself up to his misery. He feels it is no good to appeal to people. But before five minutes have passed he draws himself up, shakes his head as though he feels a sharp pain, and tugs at the reins. . . . He can bear it no longer.

"Back to the yard!" he thinks. "To the yard!"

And his little mare, as though she knew his thoughts, falls to trotting. An hour and a half later Iona is sitting by a big dirty stove. On the stove, on the floor, and on the benches are people snoring. The air is full of smells and stuffiness. Iona looks at the sleeping figures, scratches himself, and regrets that he has come home so early. . . .

"I have not earned enough to pay for the oats, even," he thinks. "That's why I am so miserable. A man who knows how to do his work, . . . who has had enough to eat, and whose horse has had enough to eat, is always at ease. . . ."

In one of the corners a young cabman gets up, clears his throat sleepily, and makes for the waterbucket.

"Want a drink?" Iona asks him.

"Seems so."

"May it do you good. . . . But my son is dead, mate. . . . Do you hear? This week in the hospital. . . . It's a queer business. . . ."

Iona looks to see the effect produced by his words, but he sees nothing. The young man has covered his head over and is already asleep. The old man sighs and scratches himself. . . . Just as the young man had been thirsty for water, he thirsts for speech. His son will soon have been dead a week, and he has not really talked to anybody yet. . . . He wants to talk of it properly, with deliberation. . . . He wants to tell how his son was taken ill, how he suffered, what he said before he died, how he died. . . . He wants to describe the funeral, and how he went to the hospital to get his son's clothes. He still has his daughter Anisya in the country. . . . And he wants to talk about her too. . . . Yes, he has plenty to talk about now. His listener ought to sigh and exclaim and lament. . . . It would be even better to talk to women. Though they are silly creatures, they blubber at the first word.

"Let's go out and have a look at the mare," Iona thinks. "There is always time for sleep. . . . You'll have sleep enough, no fear. . . ."

He puts on his coat and goes into the stables where his mare is standing. He thinks about oats, about hay, about the weather. . . . He cannot think about his son when he is alone. . . . To talk about him with someone is possible, but to think of him and picture him is insufferable anguish. . . .

"Are you munching?" Iona asks his mare, seeing her shining eyes. "There, munch away, munch away. . . . Since we have not earned enough for oats, we will eat hay. . . . Yes, . . . I have grown too old to drive. . . . My son ought to be driving, not I. . . . He was a real cabman. . . . He ought to have lived. . . ."

Iona is silent for a while, and then he goes on:

"That's how it is, old girl. . . . Kuzma Ionitch is gone. . . . He said good-by to me. . . . He went and died for no reason. . . . Now, suppose you had a little colt, and you were own mother to that little colt. . . . And all at once that same little colt went and died. . . . You'd be sorry, wouldn't you? . . ."

The little mare munches, listens, and breathes on her master's hands. Iona is carried away and tells her all about it.

1886

A Father

"I ADMIT I have had a drop. . . . You must excuse me. I went into a beer shop on the way here, and as it was so hot had a couple of bottles. It's hot, my boy."

Old Musatov took a nondescript rag out of his pocket and wiped his shaven, battered face with it.

"I have come only for a minute, Borenka, my angel," he went on, not looking at his son, "about something very important. Excuse me, perhaps I am hindering you. Haven't you ten roubles, my dear, you could let me have till Tuesday? You see, I ought to have paid for my lodging yesterday, and money, you see! . . . None! Not to save my life!"

Young Musatov went out without a word, and began whispering the other side of the door with the landlady of the summer villa and his colleagues who had taken the villa with him. Three minutes later he came back, and without a word gave his father a ten-rouble note. The latter thrust it carelessly into his pocket without looking at it, and said:

"*Merci.* Well, how are you getting on? It's a long time since we met."

"Yes, a long time, not since Easter."

"Half a dozen times I have been meaning to come to you, but I've never had time. First one thing, then another. . . . It's simply awful! I am talking nonsense though. . . . All that's nonsense. Don't you believe me, Borenka. I said I would pay you back the ten roubles on Tuesday, don't believe that either. Don't believe a word I say. I have nothing to do at all, it's simply laziness, drunkenness, and I am ashamed to be seen in such clothes in the street. You must excuse me, Borenka. Here I have sent the girl to you three times for money and written you piteous letters. Thanks for the money, but don't believe the letters; I was telling fibs. I am ashamed to rob you, my angel; I know that you can scarcely make both ends meet yourself, and feed on locusts, but my impudence is too much for me. I am such a specimen of impudence—fit for a show! . . . You must excuse me, Borenka. I tell you the truth, because I can't see your angel face without emotion."

A minute passed in silence. The old man heaved a deep sigh and said:

"You might treat me to a glass of beer perhaps."

His son went out without a word, and again there was a sound of whispering the other side of the door. When a little later the beer was brought in, the old man seemed to revive at the sight of the bottles and abruptly changed his tone.

"I was at the races the other day, my boy," he began telling him, assuming a scared expression. "We are a party of three, and we pooled three roubles on Frisky. And, thanks to that Frisky, we got thirty-two roubles each for our rouble. I can't get on without the races, my boy. It's a gentlemanly diversion. My virago always gives me a dressing over the races, but I go. I love it, and that's all about it."

Boris, a fair-haired young man with a melancholy immobile face, was walking slowly up and down, listening in silence. When the old man stopped to clear his throat, he went up to him and said:

"I bought myself a pair of boots the other day, father, which turn out to be too tight for me. Won't you take them? I'll let you have them cheap."

"If you like," said the old man with a grimace, "only for the price you gave for them, without any cheapening."

"Very well, I'll let you have them on credit."

The son groped under the bed and produced the new boots. The father took off his clumsy, rusty, evidently second-hand boots and began trying on the new ones.

"A perfect fit," he said. "Right, let me keep them. And on Tuesday, when I get my pension, I'll send you the money for them. That's not true, though," he went on, suddenly falling into the same tearful tone again. "And it was a lie about the races, too, and a lie about the pension. And you are deceiving me, Borenka. . . . I feel your generous tactfulness. I see through you! Your boots were too small, because your heart is too big. Ah, Borenka, Borenka! I understand it all and feel it!"

"Have you moved into new lodgings?" his son interrupted, to change the conversation.

"Yes, my boy. I move every month. My virago can't stay long in the same place with her temper."

"I went to your lodgings, I meant to ask you to stay here with me. In your state of health it would do you good to be in the fresh air."

"No," said the old man, with a wave of his hand, "the woman wouldn't let me, and I shouldn't care to myself. A hundred times you have tried to drag me out of the pit, and I have tried myself, but nothing came of it. Give it up. I must stick in my filthy hole. This minute, here I am sitting, looking at your angel face, yet something is drawing me home to my hole. Such is my fate. You can't draw a dung-beetle to a rose. But it's time I was going, my boy. It's getting dark."

"Wait a minute then, I'll come with you. I have to go to town to-day myself."

Both put on their overcoats and went out. When a little while afterwards they were driving in a cab, it was already dark, and lights began to gleam in the windows.

"I've robbed you, Borenka!" the father muttered. "Poor children, poor children! It must be a dreadful trouble to have such a father! Borenka, my angel, I cannot lie when I see your face. You must excuse me. . . . What my depravity has come to, my God. Here I have just been robbing you, and put you to shame with my drunken state; I am robbing your brothers, too, and put them to shame, and you should have seen me yesterday! I won't conceal it, Borenka. Some neighbours, a wretched crew, came to see my virago; I got drunk, too, with them, and I blackguarded you poor children for all I was worth. I abused you, and complained that you had abandoned me. I wanted, you see, to touch the drunken hussies' hearts, and pose as an unhappy father. It's my way, you know, when I want to screen my vices I throw all the blame on my innocent children. I can't tell lies and hide things from you, Borenka. I came to see you as proud as a peacock, but when I saw your gentleness and kind heart, my tongue clave to the roof of my mouth, and it upset my conscience completely."

"Hush, father, let's talk of something else."

"Mother of God, what children I have," the old man

went on, not heeding his son. "What wealth God has bestowed on me. Such children ought not to have had a black sheep like me for a father, but a real man with soul and feeling! I am not worthy of you!"

The old man took off his cap with a button at the top and crossed himself several times.

"Thanks be to Thee, O Lord!" he said with a sigh, looking from side to side as though seeking for an ikon. "Remarkable, exceptional children! I have three sons, and they are all like one. Sober, steady, hard-working, and what brains! Cabman, what brains! Grigory alone has brains enough for ten. He speaks French, he speaks German, and talks better than any of your lawyers—one is never tired of listening. My children, my children, I can't believe that you are mine! I can't believe it! You are a martyr, my Borenka, I am ruining you, and I shall go on ruining you. . . . You give to me endlessly, though you know your money is thrown away. The other day I sent you a pitiful letter, I described how ill I was, but you know I was lying, I wanted the money for rum. And you give to me because you are afraid to wound me by refusing. I know all that, and feel it. Grisha's a martyr, too. On Thursday I went to his office, drunk, filthy, ragged, reeking of vodka like a cellar . . . I went straight up, such a figure, I pestered him with nasty talk, while his colleagues and superiors and petitioners were standing round. I have disgraced him for life. And he wasn't the least confused, only turned a bit pale, but smiled and came up to me as though there were nothing the matter, even introduced me to his colleagues. Then he took me all the way home, and not a word of reproach. I rob him worse than you. Take your brother Sasha now, he's a martyr too! He married, as you know, a colonel's daughter of an aristocratic circle, and got a dowry with her. . . . You would think he would have nothing to do with me. No, brother, after his wedding he came with his young wife and paid me the first visit . . . in my hole. . . . Upon my soul!"

The old man gave a sob and then began laughing.

"And at that moment, as luck would have it, we were eating grated radish with kvass and frying fish, and there was a stink enough in the flat to make the devil sick. I was lying down—I'd had a drop—my virago bounced out at

the young people with her face crimson. . . . It was a disgrace in fact. But Sasha rose superior to it all."

"Yes, our Sasha is a good fellow," said Boris.

"The most splendid fellow! You are all pure gold, you
and Grisha and Sasha and Sonya. I worry you, torment you,
disgrace you, rob you, and all my life I have not heard
one word of reproach from you, you have never given me
one cross look. It would be all very well if I had been a
decent father to you—but as it is! You have had nothing
from me but harm. I am a bad, dissipated man. . . . Now,
thank God, I am quieter and I have no strength of will, but
in old days when you were little I had determination, will.
Whatever I said or did I always thought it was right. Sometimes I'd come home from the club at night, drunk and ill-
humoured, and scold at your poor mother for spending
money. The whole night I would be railing at her, and
think it the right thing too; you would get up in the morning
and go to school, while I'd still be venting my temper upon
her. Heavens! I did torture her, poor martyr! When you
came back from school and I was asleep you didn't dare to
have dinner till I got up. At dinner again there would be a
flare up. I daresay you remember. I wish no one such a
father; God sent me to you for a trial. Yes, for a trial!
Hold out, children, to the end! Honour thy father and thy
days shall be long. Perhaps for your noble conduct God
will grant you long life. Cabman, stop!"

The old man jumped out of the cab and ran into a tavern.
Half an hour later he came back, cleared his throat in a
drunken way, and sat down beside his son.

"Where's Sonya now?" he asked. "Still at boarding-
school?"

"No, she left in May, and is living now with Sasha's
mother-in-law."

"There!" said the old man in surprise. "She is a jolly
good girl! So she is following her brother's example. . . .
Ah, Borenka, she has no mother, no one to rejoice over
her! I say, Borenka, does she . . . Does she know how I am
living? Eh?"

Boris made no answer. Five minutes passed in profound
silence. The old man gave a sob, wiped his face with a rag
and said:

"I love her, Borenka! She is my only daughter, you know,

and in one's old age there is no comfort like a daughter.
Could I see her, Borenka?"

"Of course, when you like."

"Really? And she won't mind?"

"Of course not, she has been trying to find you so as
to see you."

"Upon my soul! What children! Cabman, eh? Arrange
it, Borenka darling! She is a young lady now, *delicatesse,
consommé,* and all the rest of it in a refined way, and I
don't want to show myself to her in such an abject state.
I'll tell you how we'll contrive to work it. For three days
I will keep away from spirits, to get my filthy, drunken
phiz into better order. Then I'll come to you, and you shall
lend me for the time some suit of yours; I'll shave and have
my hair cut, then you go and bring her to your flat. Will
you?"

"Very well."

"Cabman, stop!"

The old man sprang out of the cab again and ran into a
tavern. While Boris was driving with him to his lodging he
jumped out twice again, while his son sat silent and waited
patiently for him. When, after dismissing the cab, they
made their way across a long, filthy yard to the "virago's"
lodging, the old man put on an utterly shamefaced and
guilty air, and began timidly clearing his throat and click-
ing with his lips.

"Borenka," he said in an ingratiating voice, "if my virago
begins saying anything, don't take any notice . . . and behave to her, you know, affably. She is ignorant and impudent, but she's a good baggage. There is a good, warm
heart beating in her bosom!"

The long yard ended, and Boris found himself in a dark
entry. The swing door creaked, there was a smell of cooking
and a smoking samovar. There was a sound of harsh voices.
Passing through the passage into the kitchen Boris could
see nothing but thick smoke, a line with washing on it, and
the chimney of the samovar through a crack of which
golden sparks were dropping.

"And here is my cell," said the old man, stooping down
and going into a little room with a low-pitched ceiling, and
an atmosphere unbearably stifling from the proximity of the
kitchen.

Here three women were sitting at the table regaling themselves. Seeing the visitors, they exchanged glances and left off eating.

"Well, did you get it?" one of them, apparently the "virago" herself, asked abruptly.

"Yes, yes," muttered the old man. "Well, Boris, pray sit down. Everything is plain here, young man . . . we live in a simple way."

He bustled about in an aimless way. He felt ashamed before his son, and at the same time apparently he wanted to keep up before the women his dignity as cock of the walk, and as a forsaken, unhappy father.

"Yes, young man, we live simply with no nonsense," he went on muttering. "We are simple people, young man. . . . We are not like you, we don't want to keep up a show before people. No! . . . Shall we have a drink of vodka?"

One of the women (she was ashamed to drink before a stranger) heaved a sigh and said:

"Well, I'll have another drink on account of the mushrooms. . . . They are such mushrooms, they make you drink even if you don't want to. Ivan Gerasimitch, offer the young gentleman, perhaps he will have a drink!"

The last word she pronounced in a mincing drawl.

"Have a drink, young man!" said the father, not looking at his son. "We have no wine or liqueurs, my boy, we live in a plain way."

"He doesn't like our ways," sighed the "virago."

"Never mind, never mind, he'll have a drink."

Not to offend his father by refusing, Boris took a wine-glass and drank in silence. When they brought in the samovar, to satisfy the old man, he drank two cups of disgusting tea in silence, with a melancholy face. Without a word he listened to the virago dropping hints about there being in this world cruel, heartless children who abandon their parents.

"I know what you are thinking now!" said the old man, after drinking more and passing into his habitual state of drunken excitement. "You think I have let myself sink into the mire, that I am to be pitied, but to my thinking, this simple life is much more normal than your life. . . . I don't need anybody, and . . . and I don't intend to eat humble pie. . . . I can't endure a wretched boy's looking at me with compassion."

After tea he cleaned a herring and sprinkled it with onion, with such feeling that tears of emotion stood in his eyes. He began talking again about the races and his winnings, about some Panama hat for which he had paid sixteen roubles the day before. He told lies with the same relish with which he ate herring and drank. His son sat on in silence for an hour, and began to say good-bye.

"I don't venture to keep you," the old man said, haughtily. "You must excuse me, young man, for not living as you would like!"

He ruffled up his feathers, snorted with dignity, and winked at the women.

"Good-bye, young man," he said, seeing his son into the entry. *"Attendez."*

In the entry, where it was dark, he suddenly pressed his face against the young man's sleeve and gave a sob.

"I should like to have a look at Sonitchka," he whispered. "Arrange it, Borenka, my angel. I'll shave, I'll put on your suit . . . I'll put on a straight face . . . I'll hold my tongue while she is there. Yes, yes, I will hold my tongue!"

He looked round timidly towards the door, through which the women's voices were heard, checked his sobs, and said aloud:

"Good-bye, young man! *Attendez."*

1887

The Kiss

AT EIGHT O'CLOCK on the evening of the twentieth of May all the six batteries of the N—— Reserve Artillery Brigade halted for the night in the village of Mestechki on their way to camp. At the height of the general commotion, while some officers were busily occupied around the guns, and others, gathered together in the square near the church enclosure, were receiving the reports of the quartermasters, a man in civilian dress, riding a queer horse, came into sight round the church. The little dun-colored horse with a fine neck and a short tail came, moving not straight forward, but as it were sideways, with a sort of dance step, as though it were being lashed about the legs. When he reached the officers the man on the horse took off his hat and said:

"His Excellency Lieutenant-General von Rabbeck, a local landowner, invites the officers to have tea with him this minute. . . ."

The horse bowed, danced, and retired sideways; the rider raised his hat once more and in an instant disappeared with his strange horse behind the church.

"What the devil does it mean?" grumbled some of the officers, dispersing to their quarters. "One is sleepy, and here this von Rabbeck with his tea! We know what tea means."

The officers of all the six batteries remembered vividly an incident of the previous year, when during maneuvers they, together with the officers of a Cossack regiment, were in the same way invited to tea by a count who had an estate in the neighborhood and was a retired army officer; the hospitable and genial count made much of them, dined and wined them, refused to let them go to their quarters in the village, and made them stay the night. All that, of course, was very nice—nothing better could be desired, but the worst of it was, the old army officer was so carried away by the pleasure of the young men's company that till sunrise he was telling the officers anecdotes of his glorious past,

taking them over the house, showing them expensive pictures, old engravings, rare guns, reading them autograph
letters from great people, while the weary and exhausted
officers looked and listened, longing for their beds and
yawning in their sleeves; when at last their host let them
go, it was too late for sleep.

Might not this von Rabbeck be just such another?
Whether he were or not, there was no help for it. The
officers changed their uniforms, brushed themselves, and
went all together in search of the gentleman's house. In
the square by the church they were told they could get to
his Excellency's by the lower road—going down behind the
church to the river, walking along the bank to the garden,
and there the alleys would take them to the house; or by
the upper way—straight from the church by the road which,
half a mile from the village, led right up to his Excellency's
barns. The officers decided to go by the upper road.

"Which von Rabbeck is it?" they wondered on the way.
"Surely not the one who was in command of the N——
cavalry division at Plevna?"

"No, that was not von Rabbeck, but simply Rabbe and no
'von.'"

"What lovely weather!"

At the first of the barns the road divided in two: one
branch went straight on and vanished in the evening darkness, the other led to the owner's house on the right. The
officers turned to the right and began to speak more softly.
. . . On both sides of the road stretched stone barns with
red roofs, heavy and sullen-looking, very much like bar-
racks in a district town. Ahead of them gleamed the windows of the manor house.

"A good omen, gentlemen," said one of the officers. "Our
setter leads the way; no doubt he scents game ahead of
us! . . ."

Lieutenant Lobytko, who was walking in front, a tall
and stalwart fellow, though entirely without mustache (he
was over twenty-five, yet for some reason there was no sign
of hair on his round, well-fed face), renowned in the brigade for his peculiar ability to divine the presence of
women at a distance, turned round and said:

"Yes, there must be women here; I feel that by instinct."

On the threshold the officers were met by von Rabbeck himself, a comely looking man of sixty in civilian dress. Shaking hands with his guests, he said that he was very glad and happy to see them, but begged them earnestly for God's sake to excuse him for not asking them to stay the night; two sisters with their children, his brothers, and some neighbors, had come on a visit to him, so that he had not one spare room left.

The General shook hands with everyone, made his apologies, and smiled, but it was evident by his face that he was by no means so delighted as last year's count, and that he had invited the officers simply because, in his opinion, it was a social obligation. And the officers themselves, as they walked up the softly carpeted stairs, as they listened to him, felt that they had been invited to this house simply because it would have been awkward not to invite them; and at the sight of the footmen, who hastened to light the lamps at the entrance below and in the anteroom above, they began to feel as though they had brought uneasiness and discomfort into the house with them. In a house in which two sisters and their children, brothers, and neighbors were gathered together, probably on account of some family festivity or event, how could the presence of nineteen unknown officers possibly be welcome?

Upstairs at the entrance to the drawing-room the officers were met by a tall, graceful old lady with black eyebrows and a long face, very much like the Empress Eugénie. Smiling graciously and majestically, she said she was glad and happy to see her guests, and apologized that her husband and she were on this occasion unable to invite *messieurs les officiers* to stay the night. From her beautiful majestic smile, which instantly vanished from her face every time she turned away from her guests, it was evident that she had seen numbers of officers in her day, that she was in no humor for them now, and if she invited them to her house and apologized for not doing more, it was only because her breeding and position in society required it of her.

When the officers went into the big dining-room, there were about a dozen people, men and ladies, young and old, sitting at tea at the end of a long table. A group of men wrapped in a haze of cigar smoke was dimly visible behind their chairs; in the midst of them stood a lanky young man with red whiskers, talking loudly in English, with a burr. Through a door beyond the group could be seen a light room with pale blue furniture.

"Gentlemen, there are so many of you that it is impossible to introduce you all!" said the General in a loud voice, trying to sound very gay. "Make each other's acquaintance, gentlemen, without any ceremony!"

The officers—some with very serious and even stern faces, others with forced smiles, and all feeling extremely awkward—somehow made their bows and sat down to tea.

The most ill at ease of them all was Ryabovich—a short, somewhat stooped officer in spectacles, with whiskers like a lynx's. While some of his comrades assumed a serious expression, while others wore forced smiles, his face, his lynx-like whiskers, and spectacles seemed to say, "I am the shyest, most modest, and most undistinguished officer in the whole brigade!" At first, on going into the room and later, sitting down at table, he could not fix his attention on any one face or object. The faces, the dresses, the cut-glass decanters of brandy, the steam from the glasses, the molded cornices —all blended in one general impression that inspired in Ryabovich alarm and a desire to hide his head. Like a lecturer making his first appearance before the public, he saw everything that was before his eyes, but apparently only had a dim understanding of it (among physiologists this condition, when the subject sees but does not understand, is called "mental blindness"). After a little while, growing accustomed to his surroundings, Ryabovich regained his sight and began to observe. As a shy man, unused to society, what struck him first was that in which he had always been deficient—namely, the extraordinary boldness of his new acquaintances. Von Rabbeck, his wife, two elderly ladies, a young lady in a lilac dress, and the young man with the red whiskers, who was, it appeared, a younger son of von Rabbeck, very cleverly, as though they had rehearsed it beforehand, took seats among the officers, and at once got up a heated discussion in which the visitors could not help taking part. The lilac young lady hotly asserted that the artillery had a much better time than the cavalry and the infantry, while von Rabbeck and the elderly ladies maintained the opposite. A brisk interchange followed. Ryabovich looked at the lilac young lady who argued so hotly about what was unfamiliar and utterly uninteresting to her, and watched artificial smiles come and go on her face.

Von Rabbeck and his family skillfully drew the officers into the discussion, and meanwhile kept a sharp eye on their glasses and mouths, to see whether all of them were drinking, whether all had enough sugar, why someone was not eating cakes or not drinking brandy. And the longer Ryabovich watched and listened, the more he was attracted by this insincere but splendidly disciplined family.

After tea the officers went into the drawing-room. Lieutenant Lobytko's instinct had not deceived him. There were a great many girls and young married ladies. The "setter" lieutenant was soon standing by a very young blonde in a black dress, and, bending over her jauntily, as though leaning on an unseen sword, smiled and twitched his shoulders coquettishly. He probably talked very interesting nonsense, for the blonde looked at his well-fed face condescendingly and asked indifferently, "Really?" And from that indifferent "Really?" the "setter," had he been intelligent, might have concluded that she would never call him to heel.

The piano struck up; the melancholy strains of a waltz floated out of the wide open windows, and everyone, for some reason, remembered that it was spring, a May evening. Everyone was conscious of the fragrance of roses, of lilac, and of the young leaves of the poplar. Ryabovich, who felt the brandy he had drunk, under the influence of the music stole a glance towards the window, smiled, and began watching the movements of the women, and it seemed to him that the smell of roses, of poplars, and lilac came not from the garden, but from the ladies' faces and dresses.

Von Rabbeck's son invited a scraggy-looking young lady to dance and waltzed round the room twice with her. Lobytko, gliding over the parquet floor, flew up to the lilac young lady and whirled her away. Dancing began. . . . Ryabovich stood near the door among those who were not dancing and looked on. He had never once danced in his whole life, and he had never once in his life put his arm round the waist of a respectable woman. He was highly delighted that a man should in the sight of all take a girl he did not know round the waist and offer her his shoulder to put her hand on, but he could not imagine himself in the

position of such a man. There were times when he envied
the boldness and swagger of his companions and was inwardly wretched; the knowledge that he was timid, round-
shouldered, and uninteresting, that he had a long waist and
lynx-like whiskers deeply mortified him, but with years he
had grown used to this feeling, and now, looking at his
comrades dancing or loudly talking, he no longer envied
them, but only felt touched and mournful.

When the quadrille began, young von Rabbeck came
up to those who were not dancing and invited two officers
to have a game of billiards. The officers accepted and went
with him out of the drawing-room. Ryabovich, having nothing to do and wishing to take at least some part in the
general movement, slouched after them. From the big
drawing-room they went into the little drawing-room, then
into a narrow corridor with a glass roof, and thence into
a room in which on their entrance three sleepy-looking footmen jumped up quickly from couches. At last, after passing
through a long succession of rooms, young von Rabbeck
and the officers came into a small room where there was a
billiard table. They began to play.

Ryabovich, who had never played any game but cards,
stood near the billiard table and looked indifferently at the
players, while they in unbuttoned coats, with cues in their
hands, stepped about, made puns, and kept shouting out
unintelligible words.

The players took no notice of him, and only now and
then one of them, shoving him with his elbow or accidentally touching him with his cue, would turn round and
say *"Pardon!"* Before the first game was over he was weary
of it, and began to feel that he was not wanted and in the
way. . . . He felt disposed to return to the drawing-room
and he went out.

On his way back he met with a little adventure. When he
had gone half-way he noticed that he had taken a wrong
turning. He distinctly remembered that he ought to meet
three sleepy footmen on his way, but he had passed five or
six rooms, and those sleepy figures seemed to have been
swallowed up by the earth. Noticing his mistake, he walked
back a little way and turned to the right; he found himself
in a little room which was in semidarkness and which he
had not seen on his way to the billiard room. After stand-

ing there a little while, he resolutely opened the first door
that met his eyes and walked into an absolutely dark room.
Straight ahead could be seen the crack in the doorway
through which came a gleam of vivid light; from the other
side of the door came the muffled sound of a melancholy
mazurka. Here, too, as in the drawing-room, the windows
were wide open and there was a smell of poplars, lilac, and
roses. . . .

Ryabovich stood still in hesitation. . . . At that moment,
to his surprise, he heard hurried footsteps and the rustling
of a dress, a breathless feminine voice whispered "At last!"
and two soft, fragrant, unmistakably feminine arms were
clasped about his neck; a warm cheek was pressed against
his, and simultaneously there was the sound of a kiss. But
at once the bestower of the kiss uttered a faint shriek and
sprang away from him, as it seemed to Ryabovich, with disgust. He, too, almost shrieked and rushed towards the gleam
of light at the door. . . .

When he returned to the drawing-room his heart was
palpitating and his hands were trembling so noticeably that
he made haste to hide them behind his back. At first he was
tormented by shame and dread that the whole drawing-
room knew that he had just been kissed and embraced by a
woman. He shrank into himself and looked uneasily about
him, but as he became convinced that people were dancing
and talking as calmly as ever, he gave himself up entirely
to the new sensation which he had never experienced before in his life. Something strange was happening to him.
. . . His neck, round which soft, fragrant arms had so lately
been clasped, seemed to him to be anointed with oil; on his
left cheek near his mustache where the unknown had kissed
him there was a faint chilly tingling sensation as from peppermint drops, and the more he rubbed the place the more
distinct was the chilly sensation; all of him, from head to
foot, was full of a strange new feeling which grew stronger
and stronger. . . . He wanted to dance, to talk, to run into
the garden, to laugh aloud. . . . He quite forgot that he was
round-shouldered and uninteresting, that he had lynx-like
whiskers and an "undistinguished appearance" (that was
how his appearance had been described by some ladies
whose conversation he had accidentally overheard). When
von Rabbeck's wife happened to pass by him, he gave her

such a broad and friendly smile that she stood still and looked at him inquiringly.

"I like your house immensely!" he said, setting his spectacles straight.

The General's wife smiled and said that the house had belonged to her father; then she asked whether his parents were living, whether he had long been in the army, why he was so thin, and so on. . . . After receiving answers to her questions, she went on, and after his conversation with her his smiles were more friendly than ever, and he thought he was surrounded by splendid people. . . .

At supper Ryabovich ate mechanically everything offered him, drank, and without listening to anything, tried to understand what had just happened to him. . . . The adventure was of a mysterious and romantic character, but it was not difficult to explain it. No doubt some girl or young married lady had arranged a tryst with some man in the dark room; had waited a long time, and being nervous and excited had taken Ryabovich for her hero; this was the more probable as Ryabovich had stood still hesitating in the dark room, so that he, too, had looked like a person waiting for something. . . . This was how Ryabovich explained to himself the kiss he had received.

"And who is she?" he wondered, looking round at the women's faces. "She must be young, for elderly ladies don't arrange rendezvous. That she was a lady, one could tell by the rustle of her dress, her perfume, her voice. . . ."

His eyes rested on the lilac young lady, and he thought her very attractive; she had beautiful shoulders and arms, a clever face, and a delightful voice. Ryabovich, looking at her, hoped that she and no one else was his unknown. . . . But she laughed somehow artificially and wrinkled up her long nose, which seemed to him to make her look old. Then he turned his eyes upon the blonde in a black dress. She was younger, simpler, and more genuine, had a charming brow, and drank very daintily out of her wineglass. Ryabovich now hoped that it was she. But soon he began to think her face flat, and fixed his eyes upon the one next her.

"It's difficult to guess," he thought, musing. "If one were to take only the shoulders and arms of the lilac girl, add the brow of the blonde and the eyes of the one on the left of Lobytko, then . . ."

He made a combination of these things in his mind and so formed the image of the girl who had kissed him, the image that he desired but could not find at the table. . . .

After supper, replete and exhilarated, the officers began to take leave and say thank you. Von Rabbeck and his wife began again apologizing that they could not ask them to stay the night.

"Very, very glad to have met you, gentlemen," said von Rabbeck, and this time sincerely (probably because people are far more sincere and good-humored at speeding their parting guests than on meeting them). "Delighted. Come again on your way back! Don't stand on ceremony! Where are you going? Do you want to go by the upper way? No, go across the garden; it's nearer by the lower road."

The officers went out into the garden. After the bright light and the noise the garden seemed very dark and quiet. They walked in silence all the way to the gate. They were a little drunk, in good spirits, and contented, but the darkness and silence made them thoughtful for a minute. Probably the same idea occurred to each one of them as to Ryabovich: would there ever come a time for them when, like von Rabbeck, they would have a large house, a family, a garden—when they, too, would be able to welcome people, even though insincerely, feed them, make them drunk and contented?

Going out of the garden gate, they all began talking at once and laughing loudly about nothing. They were walking now along the little path that led down to the river and then ran along the water's edge, winding round the bushes on the bank, the gulleys, and the willows that overhung the water. The bank and the path were scarcely visible, and the other bank was entirely plunged in darkness. Stars were reflected here and there in the dark water; they quivered and were broken up—and from that alone it could be seen that the river was flowing rapidly. It was still. Drowsy sandpipers cried plaintively on the farther bank, and in one of the bushes on the hither side a nightingale was trilling loudly, taking no notice of the crowd of officers. The officers stood round the bush, touched it, but the nightingale went on singing.

"What a fellow!" they exclaimed approvingly. "We

stand beside him and he takes not a bit of notice! What a rascal!"

At the end of the way the path went uphill, and, skirting the church enclosure, led into the road. Here the officers, tired with walking uphill, sat down and lighted their cigarettes. On the farther bank of the river a murky red fire came into sight, and having nothing better to do, they spent a long time in discussing whether it was a camp fire or a light in a window, or something else. . . . Ryabovich, too, looked at the light, and he fancied that the light looked and winked at him, as though it knew about the kiss.

On reaching his quarters, Ryabovich undressed as quickly as possible and got into bed. Lobytko and Lieutenant Merzlyakov—a peaceable, silent fellow, who was considered in his own circle a highly educated officer, and was always, whenever it was possible, reading *The Messenger of Europe*, which he carried about with him everywhere—were quartered in the same cottage with Ryabovich. Lobytko undressed, walked up and down the room for a long while with the air of a man who has not been satisfied, and sent his orderly for beer. Merzlyakov got into bed, put a candle by his pillow and plunged into *The Messenger of Europe*.

"Who was she?" Ryabovich wondered, looking at the sooty ceiling.

His neck still felt as though he had been anointed with oil, and there was still the chilly sensation near his mouth as though from peppermint drops. The shoulders and arms of the young lady in lilac, the brow and the candid eyes of the blonde in black, waists, dresses, and brooches, floated through his imagination. He tried to fix his attention on these images, but they danced about, broke up and flickered. When these images vanished altogether from the broad dark background which everyone sees when he closes his eyes, he began to hear hurried footsteps, the rustle of skirts, the sound of a kiss—and an intense baseless joy took possession of him. . . . Abandoning himself to this joy, he heard the orderly return and announce that there was no beer. Lobytko was terribly indignant, and began pacing up and down the room again.

"Well, isn't he an idiot?" he kept saying, stopping first before Ryabovich and then before Merzlyakov. "What a fool and a blockhead a man must be not to get hold of any beer! Eh? Isn't he a blackguard?"

"Of course you can't get beer here," said Merzlyakov, not removing his eyes from *The Messenger of Europe*.

"Oh! Is that your opinion?" Lobytko persisted. "Lord have mercy upon us, if you dropped me on the moon I'd find you beer and women directly! I'll go and find some at once. . . . You may call me a rascal if I don't!"

He spent a long time in dressing and pulling on his high boots, then finished smoking his cigarette in silence and went out.

"Rabbeck, Grabbeck, Labbeck," he muttered, stopping in the outer room. "I don't care to go alone, damn it all! Ryabovich, wouldn't you like to go for a walk? Eh?"

Receiving no answer, he returned, slowly undressed, and got into bed. Merzlyakov sighed, put *The Messenger of Europe* away, and extinguished the light.

"H'm! . . ." muttered Lobytko, lighting a cigarette in the dark.

Ryabovich pulled the bedclothes over his head, curled himself up in bed, and tried to gather together the flashing images in his mind and to combine them into a whole. But nothing came of it. He soon fell asleep, and his last thought was that someone had caressed him and made him happy— that something extraordinary, foolish, but joyful and delightful, had come into his life. The thought did not leave him even in his sleep.

When he woke up the sensations of oil on his neck and the chill of peppermint about his lips had gone, but joy flooded his heart just as the day before. He looked enthusiastically at the window-frames, gilded by the light of the rising sun, and listened to the movement of the passers-by in the street. People were talking loudly close to the window. Lebedetzky, the commander of Ryabovich's battery, who had only just overtaken the brigade, was talking to his sergeant at the top of his voice, having lost the habit of speaking in ordinary tones.

"What else?" shouted the commander.

"When they were shoeing the horses yesterday, your Honor, they injured Pigeon's hoof with a nail. The vet put on clay and vinegar; they are leading him apart now. Also, your Honor, Artemyev got drunk yesterday, and the lieutenant ordered him to be put in the limber of a spare gun-carriage."

The sergeant reported that Karpov had forgotten the new cords for the trumpets and the pegs for the tents, and that their Honors the officers had spent the previous evening visiting General von Rabbeck. In the middle of this conversation the red-bearded face of Lebedetzky appeared in the window. He screwed up his short-sighted eyes, looking at the sleepy faces of the officers, and greeted them.

"Is everything all right?" he asked.

"One of the horses has a sore neck from the new collar," answered Lobytko, yawning.

The commander sighed, thought a moment, and said in a loud voice:

"I am thinking of going to see Alexandra Yevgrafovna. I must call on her. Well, good-bye. I shall catch up with you in the evening."

A quarter of an hour later the brigade set off on its way. When it was moving along the road past the barns, Ryabovich looked at the house on the right. The blinds were down in all the windows. Evidently the household was still asleep. The one who had kissed Ryabovich the day before was asleep too. He tried to imagine her asleep. The wide-open window of the bedroom, the green branches peeping in, the morning freshness, the scent of the poplars, lilac, and roses, the bed, a chair, and on it the skirts that had rustled the day before, the little slippers, the little watch on the table—all this he pictured to himself clearly and distinctly—but the features of the face, the sweet sleepy smile, just what was characteristic and important, slipped through his imagination like quicksilver through the fingers. When he had ridden a third of a mile, he looked back: the yellow church, the house, and the river, were all bathed in light; the river with its bright green banks, with the blue sky reflected in it and glints of silver in the sunshine here and there, was very beautiful. Ryabovich gazed for the last time at Mestechki, and he felt as sad as though he were parting with something very near and dear to him.

And before him on the road were none but long familiar, uninteresting scenes. . . . To right and to left, fields of young rye and buckwheat with rooks hopping about in

them; if one looked ahead, one saw dust and the backs of
men's heads; if one looked back, one saw the same dust
and faces. . . . Foremost of all marched four men with
sabers—this was the vanguard. Next came the singers, and
behind them the trumpeters on horseback. The vanguard
and the singers, like torchbearers in a funeral procession,
often forgot to keep the regulation distance and pushed a
long way ahead. . . . Ryabovich was with the first cannon
of the fifth battery. He could see all the four batteries moving in front of him. To a civilian the long tedious procession
which is a brigade on the move seems an intricate and unintelligible muddle; one cannot understand why there are
so many people round one cannon, and why it is drawn
by so many horses in such a strange network of harness, as
though it really were so terrible and heavy. To Ryabovich it
was all perfectly comprehensible and therefore uninteresting. He had known for ever so long why at the head of
each battery beside the officer there rode a stalwart noncom,
called bombardier; immediately behind him could be seen
the horsemen of the first and then the middle units. Ryabovich knew that of the horses on which they rode, those on
the left were called one name, while those on the right were
called another—it was all extremely uninteresting. Behind
the horsemen came two shaft-horses. On one of them sat
a rider still covered with the dust of yesterday and with a
clumsy and funny-looking wooden guard on his right leg.
Ryabovich knew the object of this guard, and did not think
it funny. All the riders waved their whips mechanically
and shouted from time to time. The cannon itself was not
presentable. On the limber lay sacks of oats covered with a
tarpaulin, and the cannon itself was hung over with kettles,
soldiers' knapsacks, bags, and looked like some small harmless animal surrounded for some unknown reason by men
and horses. To the leeward of it marched six men, the
gunners, swinging their arms. After the cannon there came
again more bombardiers, riders, shaft-horses, and behind
them another cannon, as unpresentable and unimpressive
as the first. After the second came a third, a fourth; near the
fourth there was an officer, and so on. There were six batteries in all the brigade, and four cannon in each battery.
The procession covered a third of a mile; it ended in a
string of wagons near which an extremely appealing

creature—the ass, Magar, brought by a battery commander from Turkey—paced pensively, his long-eared head drooping.

Ryabovich looked indifferently ahead and behind him, at the backs of heads and at faces; at any other time he would have been half asleep, but now he was entirely absorbed in his new agreeable thoughts. At first when the brigade was setting off on the march he tried to persuade himself that the incident of the kiss could only be interesting as a mysterious little adventure, that it was in reality trivial, and to think of it seriously, to say the least, was stupid; but now he bade farewell to logic and gave himself up to dreams. . . . At one moment he imagined himself in von Rabbeck's drawing-room beside a girl who was like the young lady in lilac and the blonde in black; then he would close his eyes and see himself with another, entirely unknown girl, whose features were very vague. In his imagination he talked, caressed her, leaned over her shoulder, pictured war, separation, then meeting again, supper with his wife, children. . . .

"Brakes on!" The word of command rang out every time they went downhill.

He, too, shouted "Brakes on!" and was afraid this shout would disturb his reverie and bring him back to reality. . . .

As they passed by some landowner's estate Ryabovich looked over the fence into the garden. A long avenue, straight as a ruler, strewn with yellow sand and bordered with young birch-trees, met his eyes. . . . With the eagerness of a man who indulges in daydreaming, he pictured to himself little feminine feet tripping along yellow sand, and quite unexpectedly had a clear vision in his imagination of her who had kissed him and whom he had succeeded in picturing to himself the evening before at supper. This image remained in his brain and did not desert him again.

At midday there was a shout in the rear near the string of wagons:

"Attention! Eyes to the left! Officers!"

The general of the brigade drove by in a carriage drawn by a pair of white horses. He stopped near the second battery, and shouted something which no one understood. Several officers, among them Ryabovich, galloped up to him.

"Well? How goes it?" asked the general, blinking his red eyes. "Are there any sick?"

Receiving an answer, the general, a little skinny man, chewed, thought for a moment and said, addressing one of the officers:

"One of your drivers of the third cannon has taken off his leg-guard and hung it on the fore part of the cannon, the rascal. Reprimand him."

He raised his eyes to Ryabovich and went on:

"It seems to me your breeching is too long."

Making a few other tedious remarks, the general looked at Lobytko and grinned.

"You look very melancholy today, Lieutenant Lobytko," he said. "Are you pining for Madame Lopuhova? Eh? Gentlemen, he is pining for Madame Lopuhova."

Madame Lopuhova was a very stout and very tall lady long past forty. The general, who had a predilection for large women, whatever their ages, suspected a similar taste in his officers. The officers smiled respectfully. The general, delighted at having said something very amusing and biting, laughed loudly, touched his coachman's back, and saluted. The carriage rolled on. . . .

"All I am dreaming about now which seems to me so impossible and unearthly is really quite an ordinary thing," thought Ryabovich, looking at the clouds of dust racing after the general's carriage. "It's all very ordinary, and everyone goes through it. . . . That general, for instance, was in love at one time; now he is married and has children. Captain Wachter, too, is married and loved, though the nape of his neck is very red and ugly and he has no waist. . . . Salmanov is coarse and too much of a Tartar, but he had a love affair that has ended in marriage. . . . I am the same as everyone else, and I, too, shall have the same experience as everyone else, sooner or later. . . ."

And the thought that he was an ordinary person and that his life was ordinary delighted him and gave him courage. He pictured *her* and his happiness boldly, just as he liked. . . .

When the brigade reached their halting-place in the evening, and the officers were resting in their tents, Ryabovich, Merzlyakov, and Lobytko were sitting round a chest having supper. Merzlyakov ate without haste and, as he munched deliberately, read *The Messenger of Europe,* which he held on his knees. Lobytko talked incessantly and kept filling up his glass with beer, and Ryabovich, whose head was confused from dreaming all day long, drank and said nothing. After three glasses he got a little drunk, felt weak, and had an irresistible desire to relate his new sensations to his comrades.

"A strange thing happened to me at those von Rabbecks'," he began, trying to impart an indifferent and ironical tone to his voice. "You know I went into the billiard-room. . . ."

He began describing very minutely the incident of the kiss, and a moment later relapsed into silence. . . . In the course of that moment he had told everything, and it surprised him dreadfully to find how short a time it took him to tell it. He had imagined that he could have been telling the story of the kiss till next morning. Listening to him, Lobytko, who was a great liar and consequently believed no one, looked at him skeptically and laughed. Merzlyakov twitched his eyebrows and, without removing his eyes from *The Messenger of Europe,* said:

"That's an odd thing! How strange! . . . throws herself on a man's neck, without addressing him by name. . . . She must have been some sort of lunatic."

"Yes, she must," Ryabovich agreed.

"A similar thing once happened to me," said Lobytko, assuming a scared expression. "I was going last year to Kovno. . . . I took a second-class ticket. The train was crammed, and it was impossible to sleep. I gave the guard half a rouble; he took my luggage and led me to another compartment. . . . I lay down and covered myself with a blanket. . . . It was dark, you understand. Suddenly I felt someone touch me on the shoulder and breathe in my face. I made a movement with my hand and felt somebody's elbow. . . . I opened my eyes and only imagine—a woman. Black eyes, lips red as a prime salmon, nostrils breathing passionately—a bosom like a buffer. . . ."

"Excuse me," Merzlyakov interrupted calmly, "I understand about the bosom, but how could you see the lips if it was dark?"

Lobytko began trying to put himself right and laughing at Merzlyakov's being so dull-witted. It made Ryabovich wince. He walked away from the chest, got into bed, and vowed never to confide again.

Camp life began. . . . The days flowed by, one very much like another. All those days Ryabovich felt, thought, and behaved as though he were in love. Every morning when his orderly handed him what he needed for washing, and he sluiced his head with cold water, he recalled that there was something warm and delightful in his life.

In the evenings when his comrades began talking of love and women, he would listen, and draw up closer; and he wore the expression of a soldier listening to the description of a battle in which he has taken part. And on the evenings when the officers, out on a spree with the setter Lobytko at their head, made Don-Juanesque raids on the neighboring "suburb," and Ryabovich took part in such excursions, he always was sad, felt profoundly guilty, and inwardly begged *her* forgiveness. . . . In hours of leisure or on sleepless nights when he felt moved to recall his childhood, his father and mother—everything near and dear, in fact, he invariably thought of Mestechki, the queer horse, von Rabbeck, his wife who resembled Empress Eugénie, the dark room, the light in the crack of the door. . . .

On the thirty-first of August he was returning from the camp, not with the whole brigade, but with only two batteries. He was dreamy and excited all the way, as though he were going home. He had an intense longing to see again the queer horse, the church, the insincere family of the von Rabbecks, the dark room. The "inner voice," which so often deceives lovers, whispered to him for some reason that he would surely see her . . . And he was tortured by the questions: How would he meet her? What would he talk to her about? Had she forgotten the kiss? If the worst came to the worst, he thought, even if he did not meet her, it would be a pleasure to him merely to go through the dark room and recall the past. . . .

Towards evening there appeared on the horizon the familiar church and white barns. Ryabovich's heart raced. . . . He did not hear the officer who was riding beside him and saying something to him, he forgot everything, and looked eagerly at the river shining in the distance, at the roof of the house, at the dovecote round which the pigeons were circling in the light of the setting sun.

When they reached the church and were listening to the quartermaster, he expected every second that a man on horseback would come round the church enclosure and invite the officers to tea, but . . . the quartermaster ended his report, the officers dismounted and strolled off to the village, and the man on horseback did not appear.

"Von Rabbeck will hear at once from the peasants that we have come and will send for us," thought Ryabovich, as he went into the peasant cottage, unable to understand why a comrade was lighting a candle and why the orderlies were hastening to get the samovars going.

A crushing uneasiness took possession of him. He lay down, then got up and looked out of the window to see whether the messenger were coming. But there was no sign of him.

He lay down again, but half an hour later he got up and, unable to restrain his uneasiness, went into the street and strode towards the church. It was dark and deserted in the square near the church enclosure. Three soldiers were standing silent in a row where the road began to go down-hill. Seeing Ryabovich, they roused themselves and saluted. He returned the salute and began to go down the familiar path.

On the farther bank of the river the whole sky was flooded with crimson: the moon was rising; two peasant women, talking loudly, were pulling cabbage leaves in the kitchen garden; beyond the kitchen garden there were some cottages that formed a dark mass. . . . Everything on the near side of the river was just as it had been in May: the path, the bushes, the willows overhanging the water . . . but there was no sound of the brave nightingale and no scent of poplar and young grass.

Reaching the garden, Ryabovich looked in at the gate. The garden was dark and still. . . . He could see nothing but the white stems of the nearest birch-trees and a little bit of the avenue; all the rest melted together into a dark mass. Ryabovich looked and listened eagerly, but after waiting for a quarter of an hour without hearing a sound or catching a glimpse of a light, he trudged back. . . .

He went down to the river. The General's bathing cabin and the bath-sheets on the rail of the little bridge showed white before him. . . . He walked up on the bridge, stood a little, and quite unnecessarily touched a sheet. It felt rough and cold. He looked down at the water. . . . The river ran rapidly and with a faintly audible gurgle round the piles of the bathing cabin. The red moon was reflected near the left bank; little ripples ran over the reflection, stretching it out, breaking it into bits, and seemed trying to carry it a-way. . . .

"How stupid, how stupid!" thought Ryabovich, looking at the running water. "How unintelligent it all is!"

Now that he expected nothing, the incident of the kiss, his impatience, his vague hopes and disappointment, presented themselves to him in a clear light. It no longer seemed to him strange that the General's messenger never came and that he would never see the girl who had accidentally kissed him instead of someone else; on the contrary, it would have been strange if he had seen her. . . .

The water was running, he knew not where or why, just as it did in May. At that time it had flowed into a great river, from the great river into the sea; then it had risen in vapor, turned into rain, and perhaps the very same water was running now before Ryabovich's eyes again. . . . What for? Why?

And the whole world, the whole of life, seemed to Ryabovich an unintelligible, aimless jest. . . . And turning his eyes from the water and looking at the sky, he remembered again how Fate in the person of an unknown woman had by chance caressed him, he recalled his summer dreams and fancies, and his life struck him as extraordinarily meager, poverty-stricken, and drab. . . .

When he had returned to the cottage he did not find a single comrade. The orderly informed him that they had all gone to "General Fontryabkin, who had sent a messenger on horseback to invite them. . . ."

For an instant there was a flash of joy in Ryabovich's heart, but he quenched it at once, got into bed, and in his wrath with his fate, as though to spite it, did not go to the General's.

1887

A Problem

THE STRICTEST MEASURES were taken that the Uskovs' family secret might not leak out and become generally known. Half of the servants were sent off to the theatre or the circus; the other half were sitting in the kitchen and not allowed to leave it. Orders were given that no one was to be admitted. The wife of the Colonel, her sister, and the governess, though they had been initiated into the secret, kept up a pretence of knowing nothing; they sat in the dining-room and did not show themselves in the drawing-room or the hall.

Sasha Uskov, the young man of twenty-five who was the cause of all the commotion, had arrived some time before, and by the advice of kind-hearted Ivan Markovitch, his uncle, who was taking his part, he sat meekly in the hall by the door leading to the study, and prepared himself to make an open, candid explanation.

The other side of the door, in the study, a family council was being held. The subject under discussion was an exceedingly disagreeable and delicate one. Sasha Uskov had cashed at one of the banks a false promissory note, and it had become due for payment three days before, and now his two paternal uncles and Ivan Markovitch, the brother of his dead mother, were deciding the question whether they should pay the money and save the family honour, or wash their hands of it and leave the case to go for trial.

To outsiders who have no personal interest in the matter such questions seem simple; for those who are so unfortunate as to have to decide them in earnest they are extremely difficult. The uncles had been talking for a long time, but the problem seemed no nearer decision.

"My friends!" said the uncle who was a colonel, and there was a note of exhaustion and bitterness in his voice. "Who says that family honour is a mere convention? I

don't say that at all. I am only warning you against a false
view; I am pointing out the possibility of an unpardonable
mistake. How can you fail to see it? I am not speaking
Chinese; I am speaking Russian!"

"My dear fellow, we do understand," Ivan Markovitch
protested mildly.

"How can you understand if you say that I don't believe in family honour? I repeat once more: famil-y honour fal-sely un-der-stood is a prejudice! Falsely understood! That's what I say: whatever may be the motives for
screening a scoundrel, whoever he may be, and helping him
to escape punishment, it is contrary to law and unworthy
of a gentleman. It's not saving the family honour; it's civic
cowardice! Take the army, for instance. . . . The honour of
the army is more precious to us than any other honour, yet
we don't screen our guilty members, but condemn them.
And does the honour of the army suffer in consequence?
Quite the opposite!"

The other paternal uncle, an official in the Treasury, a
taciturn, dull-witted, and rheumatic man, sat silent, or
spoke only of the fact that the Uskovs' name would get into
the newspapers if the case went for trial. His opinion was
that the case ought to be hushed up from the first and not
become public property; but, apart from publicity in the
newspapers, he advanced no other argument in support
of this opinion.

The maternal uncle, kind-hearted Ivan Markovitch, spoke
smoothly, softly, and with a tremor in his voice. He began
with saying that youth has its rights and its peculiar temp-
tations. Which of us has not been young, and who has not
been led astray? To say nothing of ordinary mortals, even
great men have not escaped errors and mistakes in their
youth. Take, for instance, the biography of great writers.
Did not every one of them gamble, drink, and draw down
upon himself the anger of right-thinking people in his young
days? If Sasha's error bordered upon crime, they must remember that Sasha had received practically no education;
he had been expelled from the high school in the fifth
class; he had lost his parents in early childhood, and so
had been left at the tenderest age without guidance and
good, benevolent influences. He was nervous, excitable,
had no firm ground under his feet, and, above all, he had

been unlucky. Even if he were guilty, anyway he deserved indulgence and the sympathy of all compassionate souls. He ought, of course, to be punished, but he was punished as it was by his conscience and the agonies he was enduring now while awaiting the sentence of his relations. The comparison with the army made by the Colonel was delightful, and did credit to his lofty intelligence; his appeal to their feeling of public duty spoke for the chivalry of his soul, but they must not forget that in each individual the citizen is closely linked with the Christian. . . .

"Shall we be false to civic duty," Ivan Markovitch exclaimed passionately, "if instead of punishing an erring boy we hold out to him a helping hand?"

Ivan Markovitch talked further of family honour. He had not the honour to belong to the Uskov family himself, but he knew their distinguished family went back to the thirteenth century; he did not forget for a minute, either, that his precious, beloved sister had been the wife of one of the representatives of that name. In short, the family was dear to him for many reasons, and he refused to admit the idea that, for the sake of a paltry fifteen hundred roubles, a blot should be cast on the escutcheon that was beyond all price. If all the motives he had brought forward were not sufficiently convincing, he, Ivan Markovitch, in conclusion, begged his listeners to ask themselves what was meant by crime? Crime is an immoral act founded upon ill-will. But is the will of man free? Philosophy has not yet given a positive answer to that question. Different views were held by the learned. The latest school of Lombroso, for instance, denies the freedom of the will, and considers every crime as the product of the purely anatomical peculiarities of the individual.

"Ivan Markovitch," said the Colonel, in a voice of entreaty, "we are talking seriously about an important matter, and you bring in Lombroso, you clever fellow. Think a little, what are you saying all this for? Can you imagine that all your thunderings and rhetoric will furnish an answer to the question?"

Sasha Uskov sat at the door and listened. He felt neither terror, shame, nor depression, but only weariness and inward emptiness. It seemed to him that it made absolutely no difference to him whether they forgave him or not; he had

come here to hear his sentence and to explain himself
simply because kind-hearted Ivan Markovitch had begged
him to do so. He was not afraid of the future. It made no
difference to him where he was: here in the hall, in prison,
or in Siberia.

"If Siberia, then let it be Siberia, damn it all!"

He was sick of life and found it insufferably hard. He
was inextricably involved in debt; he had not a farthing
in his pocket; his family had become detestable to him; he
would have to part from his friends and his women sooner
or later, as they had begun to be too contemptuous of his
sponging on them. The future looked black.

Sasha was indifferent, and was only disturbed by one
circumstance; the other side of the door they were calling
him a scoundrel and a criminal. Every minute he was on
the point of jumping up, bursting into the study and shouting in answer to the detestable metallic voice of the Colonel:

"You are lying!"

"Criminal" is a dreadful word—that is what murderers,
thieves, robbers are; in fact, wicked and morally hopeless
people. And Sasha was very far from being all that. . . .
It was true he owed a great deal and did not pay his debts.
But debt is not a crime, and it is unusual for a man not to
be in debt. The Colonel and Ivan Markovitch were both
in debt. . . .

"What have I done wrong besides?" Sasha wondered.

He had discounted a forged note. But all the young men
he knew did the same. Handrikov and Von Burst always
forged IOU's from their parents or friends when their allow-
ances were not paid at the regular time, and then when they
got their money from home they redeemed them before
they became due. Sasha had done the same, but had not
redeemed the IOU because he had not got the money which
Handrikov had promised to lend him. He was not to blame;
it was the fault of circumstances. It was true that the use of
another person's signature was considered reprehensible;
but, still, it was not a crime but a generally accepted dodge,
an ugly formality which injured no one and was quite harmless, for in forging the Colonel's signature Sasha had had
no intention of causing anybody damage or loss.

"No, it doesn't mean that I am a criminal . . ." thought
Sasha. "And it's not in my character to bring myself to

commit a crime. I am soft, emotional. . . . When I have the money I help the poor. . . ."

Sasha was musing after this fashion while they went on talking the other side of the door.

"But, my friends, this is endless," the Colonel declared, getting excited. "Suppose we were to forgive him and pay the money. You know he would not give up leading a dissipated life, squandering money, making debts, going to our tailors and ordering suits in our names! Can you guarantee that this will be his last prank? As far as I am concerned, I have no faith whatever in his reforming!"

The official of the Treasury muttered something in reply; after him Ivan Markovitch began talking blandly and suavely again. The Colonel moved his chair impatiently and drowned the other's words with his detestable metallic voice. At last the door opened and Ivan Markovitch came out of the study; there were patches of red on his lean shaven face.

"Come along," he said, taking Sasha by the hand. "Come and speak frankly from your heart. Without pride, my dear boy, humbly and from your heart."

Sasha went into the study. The official of the Treasury was sitting down; the Colonel was standing before the table with one hand in his pocket and one knee on a chair. It was smoky and stifling in the study. Sasha did not look at the official or the Colonel; he felt suddenly ashamed and uncomfortable. He looked uneasily at Ivan Markovitch and muttered: "I'll pay it . . . I'll give it back. . . ."

"What did you expect when you discounted the IOU?" he heard a metallic voice.

"I . . . Handrikov promised to lend me the money before now."

Sasha could say no more. He went out of the study and sat down again on the chair near the door. He would have been glad to go away altogether at once, but he was choking with hatred and he awfully wanted to remain, to tear the Colonel to pieces, to say something rude to him. He sat trying to think of something violent and effective to say to his hated uncle, and at that moment a woman's figure, shrouded in the twilight, appeared at the drawing-room door. It was the Colonel's wife. She beckoned Sasha to her, and, wringing her hands, said, weeping:

"*Alexandre,* I know you don't like me, but . . . listen to me; listen, I beg you. . . . But, my dear, how can this have happened? Why, it's awful, awful! For goodness' sake, beg them, defend yourself, entreat them."

Sasha looked at her quivering shoulders, at the big tears that were rolling down her cheeks, heard behind his back the hollow, nervous voices of worried and exhausted people, and shrugged his shoulders. He had not in the least expected that his aristocratic relations would raise such a tempest over a paltry fifteen hundred roubles! He could not understand her tears nor the quiver of their voices.

An hour later he heard that the Colonel was getting the best of it; the uncles were finally inclining to let the case go for trial.

"The matter's settled," said the Colonel, sighing. "Enough."

After this decision all the uncles, even the emphatic Colonel, became noticeably depressed. A silence followed.

"Merciful Heavens!" sighed Ivan Markovitch. "My poor sister!"

And he began saying in a subdued voice that most likely his sister, Sasha's mother, was present unseen in the study at that moment. He felt in his soul how the unhappy, saintly woman was weeping, grieving, and begging for her boy. For the sake of her peace beyond the grave, they ought to spare Sasha.

The sound of a muffled sob was heard. Ivan Markovitch was weeping and muttering something which it was impossible to catch through the door. The Colonel got up and paced from corner to corner. The long conversation began over again.

But then the clock in the drawing-room struck two. The family council was over. To avoid seeing the person who had moved him to such wrath, the Colonel went from the study, not into the hall, but into the vestibule. . . . Ivan Markovitch came out into the hall. . . . He was agitated and rubbing his hands joyfully. His tear-stained eyes looked good-humoured and his mouth was twisted into a smile.

"Capital," he said to Sasha. "Thank God! You can go home, my dear, and sleep tranquilly. We have decided to pay the sum, but on condition that you repent and come with me tomorrow into the country and set to work."

A minute later Ivan Markovitch and Sasha in their great-coats and caps were going down the stairs. The uncle was muttering something edifying. Sasha did not listen, but felt as though some uneasy weight were gradually slipping off his shoulders. They had forgiven him; he was free! A gust of joy sprang up within him and sent a sweet chill to his heart. He longed to breathe, to move swiftly, to live! Glancing at the street lamps and the black sky, he remembered that Von Burst was celebrating his name-day that evening at the "Bear," and again a rush of joy flooded his soul. . . .

"I am going!" he decided.

But then he remembered he had not a farthing, that the companions he was going to would despise him at once for his empty pockets. He must get hold of some money, come what may!

"Uncle, lend me a hundred roubles," he said to Ivan Markovitch.

His uncle, surprised, looked into his face and backed against a lamp-post.

"Give it to me," said Sasha, shifting impatiently from one foot to the other and beginning to pant. "Uncle, I entreat you, give me a hundred roubles."

His face worked; he trembled, and seemed on the point of attacking his uncle. . . .

"Won't you?" he kept asking, seeing that his uncle was still amazed and did not understand. "Listen. If you don't, I'll give myself up tomorrow! I won't let you pay the IOU! I'll present another false note tomorrow!"

Petrified, muttering something incoherent in his horror, Ivan Markovitch took a hundred-rouble note out of his pocket-book and gave it to Sasha. The young man took it and walked rapidly away from him. . . .

Taking a sledge, Sasha grew calmer, and felt a rush of joy within him again. The "rights of youth" of which kind-hearted Ivan Markovitch had spoken at the family council woke up and asserted themselves. Sasha pictured the drinking-party before him, and, among the bottles, the women, and his friends, the thought flashed through his mind:

"Now I see that I am a criminal; yes, I am a criminal."

Ward No. 6

IN THE HOSPITAL YARD there stands a small lodge surrounded by a perfect forest of burdocks, nettles, and wild hemp. Its roof is rusty, the chimney is tumbling down, the steps at the front-door are rotting away and overgrown with grass, and there are only traces left of the stucco. The front of the lodge faces the hospital; at the back it looks out into the open country, from which it is separated by the grey hospital fence with nails on it. These nails, with their points upwards, and the fence, and the lodge itself, have that peculiar, desolate, God-forsaken look which is only found in our hospital and prison buildings.

If you are not afraid of being stung by the nettles, come by the narrow footpath that leads to the lodge, and let us see what is going on inside. Opening the first door, we walk into the entry. Here along the walls and by the stove every sort of hospital rubbish lies littered about. Mattresses, old tattered dressing-gowns, trousers, blue striped shirts, boots and shoes no good for anything—all these remnants are piled up in heaps, mixed up and crumpled, moldering and giving out a sickly smell.

The porter, Nikita, an old soldier wearing rusty good-conduct stripes, is always lying on the litter with a pipe between his teeth. He has a grim, surly, battered-looking face, overhanging eyebrows which give him the expression of a sheep-dog of the steppes, and a red nose; he is short and looks thin and scraggy, but he is of imposing deportment and his fists are vigorous. He belongs to the class of simple-hearted, practical, and dull-witted people, prompt in carrying out orders, who like discipline better than anything in the world, and so are convinced that it is their duty to beat people. He showers blows on the face, on the chest, on the back, on whatever comes first, and is convinced that there would be no order in the place if he did not.

Next you come into a big, spacious room which fills up the whole lodge except for the entry. Here the walls are painted a dirty blue, the ceiling is as sooty as in a hut without a chimney—it is evident that in the winter the stove smokes and the room is full of fumes. The windows are disfigured by iron gratings on the inside. The wooden floor is grey and full of splinters. There is a stench of sour cabbage, of smoldering wicks, of bugs, and of ammonia, and for the first minute this stench gives you the impression of having walked into a menagerie. . . .

There are bedsteads screwed to the floor. Men in blue hospital dressing-gowns, and wearing nightcaps in the old style, are sitting and lying on them. These are the lunatics.

There are five of them in all here. Only one is of the upper class, the rest are all artisans. The one nearest the door—a tall, lean workman with shining red whiskers and tear-stained eyes—sits with his head propped on his hand, staring at the same point. Day and night he grieves, shaking his head, sighing and smiling bitterly. He rarely takes a part in conversation and usually makes no answer to questions; he eats and drinks mechanically when food is offered him. From his agonizing, throbbing cough, his thinness, and the flush on his cheeks, one may judge that he is in the first stage of consumption. Next him is a little, alert, very lively old man, with a pointed beard and curly black hair like a Negro's. By day he walks up and down the ward from window to window, or sits on his bed, cross-legged like a Turk, and, ceaselessly as a bullfinch whistles, softly sings and titters. He shows his childish gaiety and lively character at night also when he gets up to say his prayers—that is, to beat himself on the chest with his fists, and to scratch with his fingers at the door. This is the Jew Moiseika, an imbecile, who went crazy twenty years ago when his hat factory was burnt down.

And of all the inhabitants of Ward No. 6, he is the only one who is allowed to go out of the lodge, and even out of the yard into the street. He has enjoyed this privilege for years, probably because he is an old inhabitant of the hospital—a quiet, harmless imbecile, the buffoon of the town, where people are used to seeing him surrounded by boys and dogs. In his wretched gown, in his absurd night-cap, and in slippers, sometimes with bare legs and even without trousers, he walks about the streets, stopping at the gates and little shops, and begging for a copper. In one place they will give him some kvass, in another some bread, in another a copper, so that he generally goes back to the ward feeling rich and well fed. Everything that he brings back Nikita takes from him for his own benefit. The soldier does this roughly, angrily turning the Jew's pockets inside out, and calling God to witness that he will not let him go into the street again, and that breach of the regulations is worse to him than anything in the world.

Moiseika likes to make himself useful. He gives his companions water, and covers them up when they are asleep; he promises each of them to bring him back a kopeck, and to make him a new cap; he feeds with a spoon his neighbor on the left, who is paralyzed. He acts in this way, not from compassion nor from any considerations of a humane kind, but through imitation, unconsciously dominated by Gromov, his neighbor on the right hand.

Ivan Dmitritch Gromov, a man of thirty-three, who is a gentleman by birth, and has been a court usher and provincial secretary, suffers from the mania of persecution. He either lies curled up in bed, or walks from corner to corner as though for exercise; he very rarely sits down. He is always excited, agitated, and overwrought by a sort of vague, undefined expectation. The faintest rustle in the entry or shout in the yard is enough to make him raise his head and begin listening: whether they are coming for him, whether they are looking for him. And at such times his face expresses the utmost uneasiness and repulsion.

I like his broad face with its high cheek-bones, always pale and unhappy, and reflecting, as though in a mirror, a soul tormented by conflict and long-continued terror. His grimaces are strange and abnormal, but the delicate lines traced on his face by profound, genuine suffering show intelligence and sense, and there is a warm and healthy light in his eyes. I like the man himself, courteous, anxious to be of use, and extraordinarily gentle to everyone except Nikita. When anyone drops a button or a spoon, he jumps up from his bed quickly and picks it up; every day he says good-morning to his companions, and when he goes to bed he wishes them good-night.

Besides his continually overwrought condition and his

grimaces, his madness shows itself in the following way also. Sometimes in the evenings he wraps himself in his dressing-gown, and, trembling all over, with his teeth chattering, begins walking rapidly from corner to corner and between the bedsteads. It seems as though he is in a violent fever. From the way he suddenly stops and glances at his companions, it can be seen that he is longing to say something very important, but, apparently reflecting that they would not listen, or would not understand him, he shakes his head impatiently and goes on pacing up and down. But soon the desire to speak gets the upper hand of every consideration, and he will let himself go and speak fervently and passionately. His talk is disordered and feverish like delirium, disconnected, and not always intelligible, but, on the other hand, something extremely fine may be felt in it, both in the words and the voice. When he talks you recognize in him the lunatic and the man. It is difficult to reproduce on paper his insane talk. He speaks of the baseness of mankind, of violence trampling on justice, of the glorious life which will one day be upon earth, of the window-gratings, which remind him every minute of the stupidity and cruelty of oppressors. It makes a disorderly, incoherent potpourri of themes old but not yet out of date.

2

Some twelve or fifteen years ago an official called Gromov, a highly respectable and prosperous person, was living in his own house in the principal street of the town. He had two sons, Sergey and Ivan. When Sergey was a student in his fourth year he was taken ill with galloping consumption and died, and his death was, as it were, the first of a whole series of calamities which suddenly showered on the Gromov family. Within a week of Sergey's funeral the old father was put on his trial for fraud and misappropriation, and he died of typhoid in the prison hospital soon afterwards. The house, with all their belongings, was sold by auction, and Ivan Dmitritch and his mother were left entirely without means.

Hitherto in his father's lifetime, Ivan Dmitritch, who was studying in the University of Petersburg, had received an allowance of sixty or seventy roubles a month, and had had no conception of poverty; now he had to make an abrupt change in his life. He had to spend his time from morning to night giving lessons for next to nothing, to work at copying, and with all that to go hungry, as all his earnings were sent to keep his mother. Ivan Dmitritch could not stand such a life; he lost heart and strength, and, giving up the university, went home.

Here, through interest, he obtained the post of teacher in the district school, but could not get on with his colleagues, was not liked by the boys, and soon gave up the post. His mother died. He was for six months without work, living on nothing but bread and water; then he became a court usher. He kept this post until he was dismissed owing to his illness.

He had never even in his young student days given the impression of being perfectly healthy. He had always been pale, thin, and given to catching cold; he ate little and slept badly. A single glass of wine went to his head and made him hysterical. He always had a craving for society, but, owing to his irritable temperament and suspiciousness, he never became very intimate with anyone, and had no friends. He always spoke with contempt of his fellow-townsmen, saying that their coarse ignorance and sleepy animal existence seemed to him loathsome and horrible. He spoke in a loud tenor, with heat, and invariably either with scorn and indignation, or with wonder and enthusiasm, and always with perfect sincerity. Whatever one talked to him about he always brought it round to the same subject: that life was dull and stifling in the town; that the townspeople had no lofty interests, but lived a dingy, meaningless life, diversified by violence, coarse profligacy, and hypocrisy; that scoundrels were well fed and clothed, while honest men lived from hand to mouth; that they needed schools, a progressive local paper, a theatre, public lectures, the co-ordination of the intellectual elements; that society must see its failings and be horrified. In his criticisms of people he laid on the colors thick, using only black and white, and no fine shades; mankind was divided for him into honest men and scoundrels: there was nothing in between. He always spoke with passion and enthusiasm of women and of love, but he had never been in love.

In spite of the severity of his judgments and his nervousness, he was liked, and behind his back was spoken of affectionately as Vanya. His innate refinement and readiness to be of service, his good breeding, his moral purity, and his shabby coat, his frail appearance and family misfortunes, aroused a kind, warm, sorrowful feeling. Moreover, he was well educated and well read; according to the townspeople's notions, he knew everything, and was in their eyes something like a walking encyclopedia.

He had read a great deal. He would sit at the club, nervously pulling at his beard and looking through the magazines and books; and from his face one could see that he was not reading, but devouring the pages without giving himself time to digest what he read. It must be supposed that reading was one of his morbid habits, as he fell upon anything that came into his hands with equal avidity, even last year's newspapers and calendars. At home he always read lying down.

3

One autumn morning Ivan Dmitritch, turning up the collar of his greatcoat and splashing through the mud, made his way by side-streets and back lanes to see some artisan, and to collect some payment that was owing. He was in a gloomy mood, as he always was in the morning. In one of the side-streets he was met by two convicts in fetters and four soldiers with rifles in charge of them. Ivan Dmitritch had very often met convicts before, and they had always excited feelings of compassion and discomfort in him; but now this meeting made a peculiar, strange impression on him. It suddenly seemed to him for some reason that he, too, might be put into fetters and led through the mud to prison like that. After visiting the artisan, on the way home he met near the post office a police superintendent of his acquaintance, who greeted him and walked a few paces along the street with him, and for some reason this seemed to him suspicious. At home he could not get the convicts or the soldiers with their rifles out of his head all day, and an unaccountable inward agitation prevented him from reading or concentrating his mind. In the evening he did not light his lamp, and at night he could not sleep, but kept thinking that he might be arrested, put into fetters, and thrown into prison. He did not know of any harm he had done, and could be certain that he would never be guilty of murder, arson, or theft in the future either; but was it not easy to commit a crime by accident, unconsciously, and was not false witness always possible, and, indeed, miscarriage of justice? It was not without good reason that the agelong experience of the simple people teaches that beggary and prison are ills none can be safe from. A judicial mistake is very possible as legal proceedings are conducted nowadays, and there is nothing to be wondered at in it. People who have an official, professional relation to other men's sufferings—for instance, judges, police officers, doctors—in course of time, through habit, grow so callous that they cannot, even if they wish it, take any but a formal attitude to their clients; in this respect they are not different from the peasant who slaughters sheep and calves in the backyard, and does not notice the blood. With this formal, soulless attitude to human personality the judge needs but one thing—time—in order to deprive an innocent man of all rights of property, and to condemn him to penal servitude. Only the time spent on performing certain formalities for which the judge is paid his salary, and then—it is all over. Then you may look in vain for justice and protection in this dirty, wretched little town a hundred and fifty miles from a railway station! And, indeed, is it not absurd even to think of justice when every kind of violence is accepted by society as a rational and consistent necessity, and every act of mercy—for instance, a verdict of acquittal—calls forth a perfect outburst of dissatisfied and revengeful feeling?

In the morning Ivan Dmitritch got up from his bed in a state of horror, with cold perspiration on his forehead, completely convinced that he might be arrested any minute. Since his gloomy thoughts of yesterday had haunted him so long, he thought, it must be that there was some truth in them. They could not, indeed, have come into his mind without any grounds whatever.

A policeman walking slowly passed by the windows: that was not for nothing. Here were two men standing still and silent near the house. Why were they silent? And agonizing days and nights followed for Ivan Dmitritch. Everyone who passed by the windows or came into the yard seemed to him a spy or a detective. At midday the chief of the police usually drove down the street with a pair of horses; he was going from his estate near the town to the police department; but Ivan Dmitritch fancied every time that he was driving especially quickly, and that he had a peculiar expression: it was evident that he was in haste to announce that there was a very important criminal in the town. Ivan Dmitritch started at every ring at the bell and knock at the gate, and was agitated whenever he came upon anyone new at his landlady's; when he met police officers and gendarmes he smiled and began whistling so as to seem unconcerned. He could not sleep for whole nights in succession expecting to be arrested, but he snored loudly and sighed as though in deep sleep, that his landlady might think he was asleep; for if he could not sleep it meant that he was tormented by the stings of conscience —what a piece of evidence! Facts and common sense persuaded him that all these terrors were nonsense and morbidity, that if one looked at the matter more broadly there was nothing really terrible in arrest and imprisonment—so long as the conscience is at ease; but the more sensibly and logically he reasoned, the more acute and agonizing his mental distress became. It might be compared with the story of a hermit who tried to cut a dwelling-place for himself in a virgin forest; the more zealously he worked with his axe, the thicker the forest grew. In the end Ivan Dmitritch, seeing it was useless, gave up reasoning altogether, and abandoned himself entirely to despair and terror.

He began to avoid people and to seek solitude. His official work had been distasteful to him before: now it became unbearable to him. He was afraid they would somehow get him into trouble, would put a bribe in his pocket unnoticed and then denounce him, or that he would accidentally make a mistake in official papers that would appear to be fraudulent, or would lose other people's money. It is strange that his imagination had never at other times been so agile and inventive as now, when every day he thought of thousands of different reasons for being seriously anxious over his freedom and honor; but, on the other hand, his interest in the outer world, in books in particular, grew sensibly fainter, and his memory began to fail him.

In the spring when the snow melted there were found in the ravine near the cemetery two half-decomposed corpses —the bodies of an old woman and a boy bearing the traces of death by violence. Nothing was talked of but these bodies and their unknown murderers. That people might not think he had been guilty of the crime, Ivan Dmitritch walked about the streets, smiling, and when he met acquaintances he turned pale, flushed, and began declaring that there was no greater crime than the murder of the weak and defence-less. But this duplicity soon exhausted him, and after some reflection he decided that in his position the best thing to do was to hide in his landlady's cellar. He sat in the cellar all day and then all night, then another day, was fearfully cold, and waiting till dusk, stole secretly like a thief back to his room. He stood in the middle of the room till day-break, listening without stirring. Very early in the morning, before sunrise, some workmen came into the house. Ivan Dmitritch knew perfectly well that they had come to mend the stove in the kitchen, but terror told him that they were police officers disguised as workmen. He slipped stealthily out of the flat, and, overcome by terror, ran along the street without his cap and coat. Dogs raced after him bark-ing, a peasant shouted somewhere behind him, the wind whistled in his ears, and it seemed to Ivan Dmitritch that the force and violence of the whole world was massed to-gether behind his back and was chasing after him.

He was stopped and brought home, and his landlady sent for a doctor. Doctor Andrey Yefimitch, of whom we shall have more to say hereafter, prescribed cold compresses on his head and laurel drops, shook his head, and went away, telling the landlady he should not come again, as one should not interfere with people who are going out of their minds. As he had not the means to live at home and be nursed, Ivan Dmitritch was soon sent to the hospital, and was there put into the ward for venereal patients. He could not sleep at night, was full of whims and fancies, and disturbed the patients, and was soon afterwards, by Andrey Yefimitch's orders, transferred to Ward No. 6.

Within a year Ivan Dmitritch was completely forgotten

in the town, and his books, heaped up by his landlady in a sledge in the shed, were pulled to pieces by boys.

4

Ivan Dmitritch's neighbor on the left hand is, as I have said already, the Jew Moiseika; his neighbor on the right hand is a peasant so rolling in fat that he is almost spherical, with a blankly stupid face, utterly devoid of thought. This is a motionless, gluttonous, unclean animal who has long ago lost all powers of thought or feeling. An acrid, stifling stench always comes from him.

Nikita, who has to clean up after him, beats him terribly with all his might, not sparing his fists; and what is dreadful is not his being beaten—that one can get used to—but the fact that this stupefied creature does not respond to the blows with a sound or a movement, nor by a look in the eyes, but only sways a little like a heavy barrel.

The fifth and last inhabitant of Ward No. 6 is a man of the artisan class who has once been a sorter in the post office, a thinnish, fair little man with a good-natured but rather sly face. To judge from the clear, cheerful look in his calm and intelligent eyes, he has some pleasant idea in his mind, and has some very important and agreeable secret. He has under his pillow and under his mattress something that he never shows anyone, not from fear of its being taken from him and stolen, but from modesty. Sometimes he goes to the window, and turning his back to his companions, puts something on his breast, and bending his head, looks at it; if you go up to him at such a moment, he is overcome with confusion and snatches something off his breast. But it is not difficult to guess his secret.

"Congratulate me," he often says to Ivan Dmitritch; "I have been presented with the Stanislav order of the second degree with the star. The second degree with the star is only given to foreigners, but for some reason they want to make an exception for me," he says with a smile, shrugging his shoulders in perplexity. "That I must confess I did not expect."

"I don't understand anything about that," Ivan Dmitritch replies morosely.

"But do you know what I shall attain to sooner or later?"

the former sorter persists, screwing up his eyes slily. "I shall certainly get the Swedish 'Polar Star.' That's an order it is worth working for, a white cross with a black ribbon. It's very beautiful."

Probably in no other place is life so monotonous as in this ward. In the morning the patients, except the paralytic and the fat peasant, wash in the entry at a big tub and wipe themselves with the skirts of their dressing-gowns; after that they drink tea out of tin mugs which Nikita brings them out of the main building. Everyone is allowed one mugful. At midday they have soup made out of sour cabbage and boiled grain, in the evening their supper consists of grain left from dinner. In the intervals they lie down, sleep, look out of window, and walk from one corner to the other. And so every day. Even the former sorter always talks of the same orders.

Fresh faces are rarely seen in Ward No. 6. The doctor has not taken in any new mental cases for a long time, and the people who are fond of visiting lunatic asylums are few in this world. Once every two months Semyon Lazaritch, the barber, appears in the ward. How he cuts the patients' hair, and how Nikita helps him to do it, and what a trepidation the lunatics are always thrown into by the arrival of the drunken, smiling barber, we will not describe.

No one even looks into the ward except the barber. The patients are condemned to see day after day no one but Nikita.

A rather strange rumor has, however, been circulating in the hospital of late.

It is rumored that the doctor has begun to visit Ward No. 6.

5

A strange rumor!

Dr. Andrey Yefimitch Ragin is a strange man in his way. They say that when he was young he was very religious, and prepared himself for a clerical career, and that when he had finished his studies at the high school in 1863 he intended to enter a theological academy, but that his father, a surgeon and doctor of medicine, jeered at him and declared point-blank that he would disown him if he became a priest. How far this is true I don't know, but Andrey Yefimitch himself has more than once confessed that he has never had a natural bent for medicine or science in general.

However that may have been, when he finished his studies in the medical faculty he did not enter the priesthood. He showed no special devoutness, and was no more like a priest at the beginning of his medical career than he is now.

His exterior is heavy, coarse like a peasant's, his face, his beard, his flat hair, and his coarse, clumsy figure, suggest an overfed, intemperate, and harsh innkeeper on the highroad. His face is surly-looking and covered with blue veins, his eyes are little and his nose is red. With his height and broad shoulders he has huge hands and feet; one would think that a blow from his fist would knock the life out of anyone, but his step is soft, and his walk is cautious and insinuating; when he meets anyone in a narrow passage he is always the first to stop and make way, and to say, not in a bass, as one would expect, but in a high, soft tenor: "I beg your pardon!" He has a little swelling on his neck which prevents him from wearing stiff starched collars, and so he always goes about in soft linen or cotton shirts. Altogether he does not dress like a doctor. He wears the same suit for ten years, and the new clothes, which he usually buys at a Jewish shop, look as shabby and crumpled on him as his old ones; he sees patients and dines and pays visits all in the same coat; but this is not due to niggardliness, but to complete carelessness about his appearance.

When Andrey Yefimitch came to the town to take up his duties the "institution founded to the glory of God" was in a terrible condition. One could hardly breathe for the stench in the wards, in the passages, and in the courtyards of the hospital. The hospital servants, the nurses, and their children slept in the wards together with the patients. They complained that there was no living for beetles, bugs, and mice. The surgical wards were never free from erysipelas. There were only two scalpels and not one thermometer in the whole hospital; potatoes were kept in the baths. The superintendent, the housekeeper, and the medical assistant robbed the patients, and of the old doctor, Andrey Yefimitch's predecessor, people declared that he secretly sold the hospital alcohol, and that he kept a regular harem consisting of nurses and female patients. These disorderly proceedings were perfectly well known in the town, and were even exaggerated, but people took them calmly; some justified them on the ground that there were only peasants and working men in the hospital, who could not be dissatisfied, since they were much worse off at home than in the hospital—they couldn't be fed on woodcocks! Others said in excuse that the town alone, without help from the Zemstvo, was not equal to maintaining a good hospital; thank God for having one at all, even a poor one. And the newly formed Zemstvo did not open infirmaries either in the town or the neighborhood, relying on the fact that the town already had its hospital.

After looking over the hospital Andrey Yefimitch came to the conclusion that it was an immoral institution and extremely prejudicial to the health of the townspeople. In his opinion the most sensible thing that could be done was to let out the patients and close the hospital. But he reflected that his will alone was not enough to do this, and that it would be useless; if physical and moral impurity were driven out of one place, they would only move to another; one must wait for it to wither away of itself. Besides, if people open a hospital and put up with having it, it must be because they need it; superstition and all the nastiness and abominations of daily life were necessary, since in process of time they worked out to something sensible, just as manure turns into black earth. There was nothing on earth so good that it had not something nasty about its first origin.

When Andrey Yefimitch undertook his duties he was apparently not greatly concerned about the irregularities at the hospital. He only asked the attendants and nurses not to sleep in the wards, and had two cupboards of instruments put up; the superintendent, the housekeeper, the medical assistant, and the erysipelas remained unchanged.

Andrey Yefimitch loved intelligence and honesty intensely, but he had no strength of will nor belief in his right to organize an intelligent and honest life about him. He was absolutely unable to give orders, to forbid things, and to insist. It seemed as though he had taken a vow never to raise his voice and never to make use of the imperative.

It was difficult for him to say "Fetch" or "Bring"; when he wanted his meals he would cough hesitatingly and say to the cook: "How about tea? . . ." or "How about dinner? . . ." To dismiss the superintendent or to tell him to leave off stealing, or to abolish the unnecessary parasitic post altogether, was absolutely beyond his powers. When Andrey Yefimitch was deceived or flattered, or accounts he knew to be crooked were brought him to sign, he would turn as red as a crab and feel guilty, but yet he would sign the accounts. When the patients complained to him of being hungry or of the roughness of the nurses, he would be confused and mutter guiltily: "Very well, very well, I will go into it later. . . . Most likely there is some misunderstanding. . . ."

At first Andrey Yefimitch worked very zealously. He saw patients every day from morning till dinner-time, performed operations, and even attended confinements. The ladies said of him that he was attentive and clever at diagnosing diseases, especially those of women and children. But in process of time the work unmistakably wearied him by its monotony and obvious uselessness. To-day one sees thirty patients, and to-morrow they have increased to thirty-five, the next day forty, and so on from day to day, from year to year, while the mortality in the town did not decrease and the patients did not leave off coming. To be any real help to forty patients between morning and dinner was not physically possible, so it could but lead to deception. If twelve thousand patients were seen in a year it meant, if one looked at it simply, that twelve thousand men were deceived. To put those who were seriously ill into wards, and to treat them according to the principles of science, was impossible, too, because though there were principles there was no science; if he were to put aside philosophy and pedantically follow the rules as other doctors did, the things above all necessary were cleanliness and ventilation instead of dirt, wholesome nourishment instead of broth made of stinking, sour cabbage, and good assistants instead of thieves; and, indeed, why hinder people dying if death is the normal and legitimate end of everyone? What is gained if some shopkeeper or clerk lives an extra five or ten years? If the aim of medicine is by drugs to alleviate suffering, the question forces itself on one: why alleviate it? In the first place, they say that suffering leads man to perfection; and in the second, if mankind really learns to alleviate its sufferings with pills and drops, it will completely abandon religion and philosophy, in which it has hitherto found not merely protection from all sorts of trouble, but even happiness. Pushkin suffered terrible agonies before his death, poor Heine lay paralyzed for several years; why, then, should not some Andrey Yefimitch or Matryona Savishna be ill, since their lives had nothing of importance in them, and would have been entirely empty and like the life of an amœba except for suffering?

Oppressed by such reflections, Andrey Yefimitch relaxed his efforts and gave up visiting the hospital every day.

6

His life was passed like this. As a rule he got up at eight o'clock in the morning, dressed, and drank his tea. Then he sat down in his study to read, or went to the hospital. At the hospital the out-patients were sitting in the dark, narrow little corridor waiting to be seen by the doctor. The nurses and the attendants, tramping with their boots over the brick floors, ran by them; gaunt-looking patients in dressing-gowns passed; dead bodies and vessels full of filth were carried by; the children were crying, and there was a cold draught. Andrey Yefimitch knew that such surroundings were torture to feverish, consumptive, and impressionable patients; but what could be done? In the consulting-room he was met by his assistant, Sergey Sergeyitch—a fat little man with a plump, well-washed shaven face, with soft, smooth manners, wearing a new loosely cut suit, and looking more like a senator than a medical assistant. He had an immense practice in the town, wore a white tie, and considered himself more proficient than the doctor, who had no practice. In the corner of the consulting-room there stood a huge ikon in a shrine with a heavy lamp in front of it, and near it a candle-stand with a white cover on it. On the walls hung portraits of bishops, a view of the Svyatogorsky Monastery, and wreaths of dried cornflowers. Sergey Sergeyitch was religious, and liked solemnity and decorum. The ikon had been put up at his expense; at his instructions some one of the patients read the hymns of praise in the consulting-room on Sundays, and after the reading Sergey Sergeyitch himself went through the wards with a censer and burned incense.

There were a great many patients, but the time was short, and so the work was confined to the asking of a few brief questions and the administration of some drugs, such as castor-oil or volatile ointment. Andrey Yefimitch would sit with his cheek resting in his hand, lost in thought and asking questions mechanically. Sergey Sergeyitch sat down too, rubbing his hands, and from time to time putting in his word.

"We suffer pain and poverty," he would say, "because we do not pray to the merciful God as we should. Yes!"

Andrey Yefimitch never performed any operations when he was seeing patients; he had long ago given up doing so, and the sight of blood upset him. When he had to open a child's mouth in order to look at its throat, and the child cried and tried to defend itself with its little hands, the noise in his ears made his head go round and brought tears into his eyes. He would make haste to prescribe a drug, and motion to the woman to take the child away.

He was soon wearied by the timidity of the patients and their incoherence, by the proximity of the pious Sergey Sergeyitch, by the portraits on the walls, and by his own questions which he had asked over and over again for twenty years. And he would go away after seeing five or six patients. The rest would be seen by his assistant in his absence.

With the agreeable thought that, thank God, he had no private practice now, and that no one would interrupt him, Andrey Yefimitch sat down to the table immediately on reaching home and took up a book. He read a great deal and always with enjoyment. Half his salary went on buying books, and of the six rooms that made up his abode three were heaped up with books and old magazines. He liked best of all works on history and philosophy; the only medical publication to which he subscribed was *The Doctor*, of which he always read the last pages first. He would always go on reading for several hours without a break and without being weary. He did not read as rapidly and impulsively as Ivan Dmitritch had done in the past, but slowly and with concentration, often pausing over a passage which he liked or did not find intelligible. Near the books there always stood a decanter of vodka, and a salted cu-

cumber or a pickled apple lay beside it, not on a plate, but
on the baize table-cloth. Every half-hour he would pour
himself out a glass of vodka and drink it without taking
his eyes off the book. Then without looking at it he would
feel for the cucumber and bite off a bit.

At three o'clock he would go cautiously to the kitchen
door, cough, and say: "Daryushka, what about dinner? . . ."

After his dinner—a rather poor and untidily served one
—Andrey Yefimitch would walk up and down his rooms
with his arms folded, thinking. The clock would strike four,
then five, and still he would be walking up and down thinking. Occasionally the kitchen door would creak, and the red
and sleepy face of Daryushka would appear.

"Andrey Yefimitch, isn't it time for you to have your
beer?" she would ask anxiously.

"No, it is not time yet . . ." he would answer. "I'll wait a
little. . . . I'll wait a little. . . ."

Towards the evening the postmaster, Mihail Averyanitch,
the only man in the town whose society did not bore Andrey
Yefimitch, would come in. Mihail Averyanitch had once
been a very rich land-owner, and had served in the cavalry,
but had come to ruin, and was forced by poverty to take a
job in the post office late in life. He had a hale and hearty
appearance, luxuriant grey whiskers, the manners of a well-
bred man, and a loud, pleasant voice. He was good-natured
and emotional, but hot-tempered. When anyone in the post
office made a protest, expressed disagreement, or even
began to argue, Mihail Averyanitch would turn crimson,
shake all over, and shout in a voice of thunder, "Hold your
tongue!" so that the post office had long enjoyed the reputation of an institution which it was terrible to visit. Mihail
Averyanitch liked and respected Andrey Yefimitch for his
culture and the loftiness of his soul; he treated the other inhabitants of the town superciliously, as though they were
his subordinates.

"Here I am," he would say, going in to Andrey Yefimitch. "Good-evening, my dear fellow! I'll be bound, you
are getting sick of me, aren't you?"

"On the contrary, I am delighted," said the doctor. "I
am always glad to see you."

The friends would sit down on the sofa in the study and
for some time would smoke in silence.

"Daryushka, what about the beer?" Andrey Yefimitch would say.

They would drink their first bottle still in silence, the doctor brooding and Mihail Averyanitch with a gay and animated face, like a man who has something very interesting to tell. The doctor was always the one to begin the conversation.

"What a pity," he would say quietly and slowly, not looking his friend in the face (he never looked anyone in the face)—"what a great pity it is that there are no people in our town who are capable of carrying on intelligent and interesting conversation, or care to do so. It is an immense privation for us. Even the educated class do not rise above vulgarity; the level of their development, I assure you, is not a bit higher than that of the lower orders."

"Perfectly true. I agree."

"You know, of course," the doctor went on quietly and deliberately, "that everything in this world is insignificant and uninteresting except the higher spiritual manifestations of the human mind. Intellect draws a sharp line between the animals and man, suggests the divinity of the latter, and to some extent even takes the place of the immortality which does not exist. Consequently the intellect is the only possible source of enjoyment. We see and hear of no trace of intellect about us, so we are deprived of enjoyment. We have books, it is true, but that is not at all the same as living talk and converse. If you will allow me to make a not quite apt comparison: books are the printed score, while talk is the singing."

"Perfectly true."

A silence would follow. Daryushka would come out of the kitchen and with an expression of blank dejection would stand in the doorway to listen, with her face propped on her fist.

"Eh!" Mihail Averyanitch would sigh. "To expect intelligence of this generation!"

And he would describe how wholesome, entertaining, and interesting life had been in the past. How intelligent the educated class in Russia used to be, and what lofty ideas it had of honor and friendship; how they used to lend money without an IOU, and it was thought a disgrace not to give a helping hand to a comrade in need; and what campaigns, what adventures, what skirmishes, what comrades, what women! And the Caucasus, what a marvellous country! The wife of a battalion commander, a queer woman, used to put on an officer's uniform and drive off into the mountains in the evening, alone, without a guide. It was said that she had a love affair with some princeling in a native village.

"Queen of Heaven, Holy Mother . . ." Daryushka would sigh.

"And how we drank! And how we ate! And what desperate liberals we were!"

Andrey Yefimitch would listen without hearing; he was musing as he sipped his beer.

"I often dream of intellectual people and conversation with them," he said suddenly, interrupting Mihail Averyanitch. "My father gave me an excellent education, but under the influence of the ideas of the sixties made me become a doctor. I believe if I had not obeyed him then, by now I should have been in the very centre of the intellectual movement. Most likely I should have become a member of some university. Of course, intellect, too, is transient and not eternal, but you know why I cherish a partiality for it. Life is a vexatious trap; when a thinking man reaches maturity and attains to full consciousness he cannot help feeling that he is in a trap from which there is no escape. Indeed, he is summoned without his choice by fortuitous circumstances from non-existence into life . . . what for? He tries to find out the meaning and object of his existence; he is told nothing, or he is told absurdities; he knocks and it is not opened to him; death comes to him— also without his choice. And so, just as in prison men held together by common misfortune feel more at ease when they are together, so one does not notice the trap in life when people with a bent for analysis and generalization meet together and pass their time in the interchange of proud and free ideas. In that sense the intellect is the source of an enjoyment nothing can replace."

"Perfectly true."

Not looking his friend in the face, Andrey Yefimitch would go on, quietly and with pauses, talking about intellectual people and conversation with them, and Mihail Averyanitch would listen attentively and agree: "Perfectly true."

"And you do not believe in the immortality of the soul?" he would ask suddenly.

"No, honored Mihail Averyanitch; I do not believe it, and have no grounds for believing it."

"I must own I doubt it too. And yet I have a feeling as though I should never die. Oh, I think to myself: 'Old fogey, it is time you were dead!' But there is a little voice in my soul says: 'Don't believe it; you won't die.' "

Soon after nine o'clock Mihail Averyanitch would go away. As he put on his fur coat in the entry he would say with a sigh:

"What a wilderness fate has carried us to, though, really! What's most vexatious of all is to have to die here. Ech! . . ."

7

After seeing his friend out Andrey Yefimitch would sit down at the table and begin reading again. The stillness of the evening, and afterwards of the night, was not broken by a single sound, and it seemed as though time were standing still and brooding with the doctor over the book, and as though there were nothing in existence but the books and the lamp with the green shade. The doctor's coarse peasant-like face was gradually lighted up by a smile of delight and enthusiasm over the progress of the human intellect. Oh, why is not man immortal? he thought. What is the good of the brain centres and convolutions, what is the good of sight, speech, self-consciousness, genius, if it is all destined to depart into the soil, and in the end to grow cold together with the earth's crust, and then for millions of years to fly with the earth round the sun with no meaning and no object? To do that there was no need at all to draw man with his lofty, almost godlike intellect out of non-existence, and then, as though in mockery, to turn him into clay. The transmutation of substances! But what cowardice to comfort oneself with that cheap substitute for immortality! The unconscious processes that take place in nature are lower even than the stupidity of man, since in stupidity there is, anyway, consciousness and will, while in those processes there is absolutely nothing. Only the coward who has more fear of death than dignity can comfort himself with the fact that his body will in time live again in the grass, in the

stones, in the toad. To find one's immortality in the transmutation of substances is as strange as to prophesy a brilliant future for the case after a precious violin has been
broken and become useless.

When the clock struck, Andrey Yefimitch would sink
back into his chair and close his eyes to think a little. And
under the influence of the fine ideas of which he had been
reading he would, unawares, recall his past and his present.
The past was hateful—better not to think of it. And it was
the same in the present as in the past. He knew that at the
very time when his thoughts were floating together with
the cooling earth round the sun, in the main building beside
his abode people were suffering in sickness and physical
impurity: someone perhaps could not sleep and was making
war upon the insects, someone was being infected by
erysipelas, or moaning over too tight a bandage; perhaps
the patients were playing cards with the nurses and drinking
vodka. According to the yearly return, twelve thousand
people had been deceived; the whole hospital rested as it
had done twenty years ago on thieving, filth, scandals,
gossip, on gross quackery, and, as before, it was an immoral
institution extremely injurious to the health of the inhabitants. He knew that Nikita knocked the patients about behind the barred windows of Ward No. 6, and that Moiseika
went about the town every day begging alms.

On the other hand, he knew very well that a magical
change had taken place in medicine during the last twenty-
five years. When he was studying at the university he had
fancied that medicine would soon be overtaken by the fate
of alchemy and metaphysics; but now when he was reading
at night the science of medicine touched him and excited
his wonder, and even enthusiasm. What unexpected bril-
liance, what a revolution! Thanks to the antiseptic system
operations were performed such as the great Pirogov had
considered impossible even *in spe*. Ordinary Zemstvo
doctors were venturing to perform the resection of the
kneecap; of abdominal operations only one per cent. was
fatal; while stone was considered such a trifle that they did
not even write about it. A radical cure for syphilis had been
discovered. And the theory of heredity, hypnotism, the
discoveries of Pasteur and of Koch, hygiene based on
statistics, and the work of our Zemstvo doctors!

Psychiatry with its modern classification of mental diseases, methods of diagnosis, and treatment, was a perfect Elborus in comparison with what had been in the past. They no longer poured cold water on the heads of lunatics nor put strait-waistcoats upon them; they treated them with humanity, and even, so it was stated in the papers, got up balls and entertainments for them. Andrey Yefimitch knew that with modern tastes and views such an abomination as Ward No. 6 was possible only a hundred and fifty miles from a railway in a little town where the mayor and all the town council were half-illiterate tradesmen who looked upon the doctor as an oracle who must be believed without any criticism even if he had poured molten lead into their mouths; in any other place the public and the newspapers would long ago have torn this little Bastille to pieces.

"But, after all, what of it?" Andrey Yefimitch would ask himself, opening his eyes. "There is the antiseptic system, there is Koch, there is Pasteur, but the essential reality is not altered a bit; ill-health and mortality are still the same. They get up balls and entertainments for the mad, but still they don't let them go free; so it's all nonsense and vanity, and there is no difference in reality between the best Vienna clinic and my hospital." But depression and a feeling akin to envy prevented him from feeling indifferent; it must have been owing to exhaustion. His heavy head sank on to the book, he put his hands under his face to make it softer, and thought: "I serve in a pernicious institution and receive a salary from people whom I am deceiving. I am not honest, but then, I of myself am nothing, I am only part of an inevitable social evil: all local officials are pernicious and receive their salary for doing nothing. . . . And so for my dishonesty it is not I who am to blame, but the times. . . . If I had been born two hundred years later I should have been different. . . ."

When it struck three he would put out his lamp and go into his bedroom; he was not sleepy.

8

Two years before, the Zemstvo in a liberal mood had decided to allow three hundred roubles a year to pay for additional medical service in the town till the Zemstvo hospital should be opened, and the district doctor, Yevgeny Fyodoritch Hobotov, was invited to the town to assist Andrey Yefimitch. He was a very young man—not yet thirty—tall and dark, with broad cheek-bones and little eyes; his forefathers had probably come from one of the many alien races of Russia. He arrived in the town without a farthing, with a small portmanteau, and a plain young woman whom he called his cook. This woman had a baby at the breast. Yevgeny Fyodoritch used to go about in a cap with a peak, and in high boots, and in the winter wore a sheepskin. He made great friends with Sergey Sergeyitch, the medical assistant, and with the treasurer, but held aloof from the other officials, and for some reason called them aristocrats. He had only one book in his lodgings, "The Latest Prescriptions of the Vienna Clinic for 1881." When he went to a patient he always took this book with him. He played billiards in the evening at the club: he did not like cards. He was very fond of using in conversation such expressions as "endless bobbery," "canting soft soap," "shut up with your finicking. . . ."

He visited the hospital twice a week, made the round of the wards, and saw out-patients. The complete absence of antiseptic treatment and the cupping roused his indignation, but he did not introduce any new system, being afraid of offending Andrey Yefimitch. He regarded his colleague as a sly old rascal, suspected him of being a man of large means, and secretly envied him. He would have been very glad to have his post.

9

On a spring evening towards the end of March, when there was no snow left on the ground and the starlings were singing in the hospital garden, the doctor went out to see his friend the postmaster as far as the gate. At that very moment the Jew Moiseika, returning with his booty, came into the yard. He had no cap on, and his bare feet were thrust into goloshes; in his hand he had a little bag of coppers.

"Give me a kopeck!" he said to the doctor, smiling, and shivering with cold. Andrey Yefimitch, who could never refuse anyone anything, gave him a ten-kopeck piece.

"How bad that is!" he thought, looking at the Jew's bare feet with their thin red ankles. "Why, it's wet."

And stirred by a feeling akin both to pity and disgust, he went into the lodge behind the Jew, looking now at his bald head, now at his ankles. As the doctor went in Nikita jumped up from his heap of litter and stood at attention.

"Good-day, Nikita," Andrey Yefimitch said mildly. "That Jew should be provided with boots or something, he will catch cold."

"Certainly, your honor. I'll inform the superintendent."

"Please do; ask him in my name. Tell him that I asked."

The door into the ward was open. Ivan Dmitritch, lying propped on his elbow on the bed, listened in alarm to the unfamiliar voice, and suddenly recognized the doctor. He trembled all over with anger, jumped up, and with a red and wrathful face, with his eyes starting out of his head, ran out into the middle of the road.

"The doctor has come!" he shouted, and broke into a laugh. "At last! Gentlemen, I congratulate you. The doctor is honoring us with a visit. Cursed reptile!" he shrieked, and stamped in a frenzy such as had never been seen in the ward before. "Kill the reptile! No, killing's too good. Drown him in the midden-pit!"

Andrey Yefimitch, hearing this, looked into the ward from the entry and asked gently: "What for?"

"What for?" shouted Ivan Dmitritch, going up to him with a menacing air and convulsively wrapping himself in his dressing-gown. "What for? Thief!" he said with a look of repulsion, moving his lips as though he would spit at him. "Quack! hangman!"

"Calm yourself," said Andrey Yefimitch, smiling guiltily. "I assure you I have never stolen anything; and as to the rest, most likely you greatly exaggerate. I see you are angry with me. Calm yourself, I beg, if you can, and tell me coolly what are you angry for?"

"What are you keeping me here for?"

"Because you are ill."

"Yes, I am ill. But you know dozens, hundreds of madmen are walking about in freedom because your ignorance is incapable of distinguishing them from the sane. Why am I and these poor wretches to be shut up here like scape-

goats for all the rest? You, your assistant, the superintendent, and all your hospital rabble, are immeasurably in-
ferior to every one of us morally; why then are we shut up
and you not? Where's the logic of it?"

"Morality and logic don't come in, it all depends on
chance. If anyone is shut up he has to stay, and if anyone is
not shut up he can walk about, that's all. There is neither
morality nor logic in my being a doctor and your being a
mental patient, there is nothing but idle chance."

"That twaddle I don't understand . . ." Ivan Dmitritch
brought out in a hollow voice, and he sat down on his bed.

Moiseika, whom Nikita did not venture to search in the
presence of the doctor, laid out on his bed pieces of bread,
bits of paper, and little bones, and, still shivering with cold,
began rapidly in a singsong voice saying something in
Yiddish. He most likely imagined that he had opened a
shop.

"Let me out," said Ivan Dmitritch, and his voice quivered.

"I cannot."

"But why, why?"

"Because it is not in my power. Think, what use will it
be to you if I do let you out? Go. The townspeople or the
police will detain you or bring you back."

"Yes, yes, that's true," said Ivan Dmitritch, and he rubbed
his forehead. "It's awful! But what am I to do, what?"

Andrey Yefimitch liked Ivan Dmitritch's voice and his
intelligent young face with its grimaces. He longed to be
kind to the young man and soothe him; he sat down on the
bed beside him, thought, and said:

"You ask me what to do. The very best thing in your
position would be to run away. But, unhappily, that is
useless. You would be taken up. When society protects itself from the criminal, mentally deranged, or otherwise
inconvenient people, it is invincible. There is only one thing
left for you: to resign yourself to the thought that your
presence here is inevitable."

"It is no use to anyone."

"So long as prisons and madhouses exist someone must
be shut up in them. If not you, I. If not I, some third person. Wait till in the distant future prisons and madhouses no

longer exist, and there will be neither bars on the windows nor hospital gowns. Of course, that time will come sooner or later."

Ivan Dmitritch smiled ironically.

"You are jesting," he said, screwing up his eyes. "Such gentlemen as you and your assistant Nikita have nothing to do with the future, but you may be sure, sir, better days will come! I may express myself cheaply, you may laugh, but the dawn of a new life is at hand; truth and justice will triumph, and—our turn will come! I shall not live to see it, I shall perish, but some people's great-grandsons will see it. I greet them with all my heart and rejoice, rejoice with them! Onward! God be your help, friends!"

With shining eyes Ivan Dmitritch got up, and stretching his hands towards the window, went on with emotion in his voice:

"From behind these bars I bless you! Hurrah for truth and justice! I rejoice!"

"I see no particular reason to rejoice," said Andrey Yefimitch, who thought Ivan Dmitritch's movement theatrical, though he was delighted by it. "Prisons and madhouses there will not be, and truth, as you have just expressed it, will triumph; but the reality of things, you know, will not change, the laws of nature will still remain the same. People will suffer pain, grow old, and die just as they do now. However magnificent a dawn lighted up your life, you would yet in the end be nailed up in a coffin and thrown into a hole."

"And immortality?"

"Oh, come, now!"

"You don't believe in it, but I do. Somebody in Dostoevsky or Voltaire said that if there had not been a God men would have invented him. And I firmly believe that if there is no immortality the great intellect of man will sooner or later invent it."

"Well said," observed Andrey Yefimitch, smiling with pleasure; "it's a good thing you have faith. With such a belief one may live happily even shut up within walls. You have studied somewhere, I presume?"

"Yes, I have been at the university, but did not complete my studies."

"You are a reflecting and a thoughtful man. In any

surroundings you can find tranquillity in yourself. Free and deep thinking which strives for the comprehension of life, and complete contempt for the foolish bustle of the world —those are two blessings beyond any that man has ever known. And you can possess them even though you lived behind threefold bars. Diogenes lived in a tub, yet he was happier than all the kings of the earth."

"Your Diogenes was a blockhead," said Ivan Dmitritch morosely. "Why do you talk to me about Diogenes and some foolish comprehension of life?" he cried, growing suddenly angry and leaping up. "I love life; I love it passionately. I have the mania of persecution, a continual agonizing terror; but I have moments when I am overwhelmed by the thirst for life, and then I am afraid of going mad. I want dreadfully to live, dreadfully!"

He walked up and down the ward in agitation, and said, dropping his voice:

"When I dream I am haunted by phantoms. People come to me, I hear voices and music, and I fancy I am walking through woods or by the seashore, and I long so passionately for movement, for interests. . . . Come, tell me, what news is there?" asked Ivan Dmitritch; "what's happening?"

"Do you wish to know about the town or in general?"

"Well, tell me first about the town, and then in general."

"Well, in the town it is appallingly dull. . . . There's no one to say a word to, no one to listen to. There are no new people. A young doctor called Hobotov has come here recently."

"He had come in my time. Well, he is a low cad, isn't he?"

"Yes, he is a man of no culture. It's strange, you know. . . . Judging by every sign, there is no intellectual stagnation in our capital cities; there is a movement—so there must be real people there too; but for some reason they always send us such men as I would rather not see. It's an unlucky town!"

"Yes, it is an unlucky town," sighed Ivan Dmitritch, and he laughed. "And how are things in general? What are they writing in the papers and reviews?"

It was by now dark in the ward. The doctor got up, and, standing, began to describe what was being written abroad and in Russia, and the tendency of thought that could be noticed now. Ivan Dmitritch listened attentively and put questions, but suddenly, as though recalling something terrible, clutched at his head and lay down on the bed with his back to the doctor.

"What's the matter?" asked Andrey Yefimitch.

"You will not hear another word from me," said Ivan Dmitritch rudely. "Leave me alone."

"Why so?"

"I tell you, leave me alone. Why the devil do you persist?"

Andrey Yefimitch shrugged his shoulders, heaved a sigh, and went out. As he crossed the entry he said: "You might clear up here, Nikita . . . there's an awfully stuffy smell."

"Certainly, your honor."

"What an agreeable young man!" thought Andrey Yefimitch, going back to his flat. "In all the years I have been living here I do believe he is the first I have met with whom one can talk. He is capable of reasoning and is interested in just the right things."

While he was reading, and afterwards, while he was going to bed, he kept thinking about Ivan Dmitritch, and when he woke next morning he remembered that he had the day before made the acquaintance of an intelligent and interesting man, and determined to visit him again as soon as possible.

10

Ivan Dmitritch was lying in the same position as on the previous day, with his head clutched in both hands and his legs drawn up. His face was not visible.

"Good-day, my friend," said Andrey Yefimitch. "You are not asleep, are you?"

"In the first place, I am not your friend," Ivan Dmitritch articulated into the pillow; "and in the second, your efforts are useless; you will not get one word out of me."

"Strange," muttered Andrey Yefimitch in confusion. "Yesterday we talked peacefully, but suddenly for some reason you took offence and broke off all at once. . . . Probably I expressed myself awkwardly, or perhaps gave utterance to some idea which did not fit in with your convictions. . . ."

"Yes, a likely idea!" said Ivan Dmitritch, sitting up and looking at the doctor with irony and uneasiness. His eyes were red. "You can go and spy and probe somewhere else, it's no use your doing it here. I knew yesterday what you had come for."

"A strange fancy," laughed the doctor. "So you suppose me to be a spy?"

"Yes, I do. . . . A spy or a doctor who has been charged to test me—it's all the same—"

"Oh, excuse me, what a queer fellow you are really!"

The doctor sat down on the stool near the bed and shook his head reproachfully.

"But let us suppose you are right," he said, "let us suppose that I am treacherously trying to trap you into saying something so as to betray you to the police. You would be arrested and then tried. But would you be any worse off being tried and in prison than you are here? If you are banished to a settlement, or even sent to penal servitude, would it be worse than being shut up in this ward? I imagine it would be no worse. . . . What, then, are you afraid of?"

These words evidently had an effect on Ivan Dmitritch. He sat down quietly.

It was between four and five in the afternoon—the time when Andrey Yefimitch usually walked up and down his rooms, and Daryushka asked whether it was not time for his beer. It was a still, bright day.

"I came out for a walk after dinner, and here I have come, as you see," said the doctor. "It is quite spring."

"What month is it? March?" asked Ivan Dmitritch.

"Yes, the end of March."

"Is it very muddy?"

"No, not very. There are already paths in the garden."

"It would be nice now to drive in an open carriage somewhere into the country," said Ivan Dmitritch, rubbing his red eyes as though he were just awake, "then to come home to a warm, snug study, and . . . and to have a decent doctor to cure one's headache. . . . It's so long since I have lived like a human being. It's disgusting here! Insufferably disgusting!"

After his excitement of the previous day he was exhausted and listless, and spoke unwillingly. His fingers twitched, and from his face it could be seen that he had a splitting headache.

"There is no real difference between a warm, snug study and this ward,'" said Andrey Yefimitch. "A man's peace and contentment do not lie outside a man, but in himself."

"What do you mean?"

"The ordinary man looks for good and evil in external things—that is, in carriages, in studies—but a thinking man looks for it in himself."

"You should go and preach that philosophy in Greece, where it's warm and fragrant with the scent of pomegranates, but here it is not suited to the climate. With whom was it I was talking of Diogenes? Was it with you?"

"Yes, with me yesterday."

"Diogenes did not need a study or a warm habitation; it's hot there without. You can lie in your tub and eat oranges and olives. But bring him to Russia to live: he'd be begging to be let indoors in May, let alone December. He'd be doubled up with the cold."

"No. One can be insensible to cold as to every other pain. Marcus Aurelius says: 'A pain is a vivid idea of pain; make an effort of will to change that idea, dismiss it, cease to complain, and the pain will disappear.' That is true. The wise man, or simply the reflecting, thoughtful man, is distinguished precisely by his contempt for suffering; he is always contented and surprised at nothing."

"Then I am an idiot, since I suffer and am discontented and surprised at the baseness of mankind."

"You are wrong in that; if you will reflect more on the subject you will understand how insignificant is all that external world that agitates us. One must strive for the comprehension of life, and in that is true happiness."

"Comprehension . . ." repeated Ivan Dmitritch frowning. "External, internal. . . . Excuse me, but I don't understand it. I only know," he said, getting up and looking angrily at the doctor—"I only know that God has created me of warm blood and nerves, yes, indeed! If organic tissue is capable of life it must react to every stimulus. And I do! To pain I respond with tears and outcries, to baseness with indignation, to filth with loathing. To my mind, that is just what is called life. The lower the organism, the less sensitive it is, and the more feebly it reacts to stimulus;

and the higher it is, the more responsively and vigorously it reacts to reality. How is it you don't know that? A doctor, and not know such trifles! To despise suffering, to be always contented, and to be surprised at nothing, one must reach this condition"—and Ivan Dmitritch pointed to the peasant who was a mass of fat—"or to harden oneself by suffering to such a point that one loses all sensibility to it—that is, in other words, to cease to live. You must excuse me, I am not a sage or a philosopher," Ivan Dmitritch continued with irritation, "and I don't understand anything about it. I am not capable of reasoning."

"On the contrary, your reasoning is excellent."

"The Stoics, whom you are parodying, were remarkable people, but their doctrine crystallized two thousand years ago and has not advanced, and will not advance, an inch forward, since it is not practical or living. It had a success only with the minority which spends its life in savoring all sort of theories and ruminating over them; the majority did not understand it. A doctrine which advocates indifference to wealth and to the comforts of life, and a contempt for suffering and death, is quite unintelligible to the vast majority of men, since that majority has never known wealth or the comforts of life; and to despise suffering would mean to it despising life itself, since the whole existence of man is made up of the sensations of hunger, cold, injury, loss, and a Hamlet-like dread of death. The whole of life lies in these sensations; one may be oppressed by it, one may hate it, but one cannot despise it. Yes, so, I repeat, the doctrine of the Stoics can never have a future; from the beginning of time up to to-day you see continually increasing the struggle, the sensibility to pain, the capacity of responding to stimulus."

Ivan Dmitritch suddenly lost the thread of his thoughts, stopped, and rubbed his forehead with vexation.

"I meant to say something important, but I have lost it," he said. "What was I saying? Oh, yes! This is what I mean: one of the Stoics sold himself into slavery to redeem his neighbor, so, you see, even a Stoic did react to stimulus, since, for such a generous act as the destruction of oneself for the sake of one's neighbor, he must have had a soul capable of pity and indignation. Here in prison I have forgotten everything I have learned, or else I could have recalled something else. Take Christ, for instance: Christ responded to reality by weeping, smiling, being sorrowful and moved to wrath, even overcome by misery. He did not go to meet His sufferings with a smile, He did not despise death, but prayed in the Garden of Gethesmane that this cup might pass Him by."

Ivan Dmitritch laughed and sat down.

"Granted that a man's peace and contentment lie not outside but in himself," he said, "granted that one must despise suffering and not be surprised at anything, yet on what ground do you preach the theory? Are you a sage? A philosopher?"

"No, I am not a philosopher, but everyone ought to preach it because it is reasonable."

"No, I want to know how it is that you consider yourself competent to judge of 'comprehension,' contempt for suffering, and so on. Have you ever suffered? Have you any idea of suffering? Allow me to ask you, were you ever thrashed in your childhood?"

"No, my parents had an aversion for corporal punishment."

"My father used to flog me cruelly; my father was a harsh, sickly Government clerk with a long nose and a yellow neck. But let us talk of you. No one has laid a finger on you all your life, no one has scared you nor beaten you; you are as strong as a bull. You grew up under your father's wing and studied at his expense, and then you dropped at once into a sinecure. For more than twenty years you have lived rent free with heating, lighting, and service all provided, and had the right to work how you pleased and as much as you pleased, even to do nothing. You were naturally a flabby, lazy man, and so you have tried to arrange your life so that nothing should disturb you or make you move. You have handed over your work to the assistant and the rest of the rabble while you sit in peace and warmth, save money, read, amuse yourself with reflections, with all sorts of lofty nonsense, and" (Ivan Dmitritch looked at the doctor's red nose) "with boozing; in fact, you have seen nothing of life, you know absolutely nothing of it, and are only theoretically acquainted with reality; you despise suffering and are surprised at nothing for a very simple reason: vanity of vanities, the external and the internal, contempt for life, for suffering and for death, comprehension, true happiness—that's the philosophy that suits the Russian sluggard best. You see a peasant beating his wife, for instance. Why interfere? Let him beat her, they will both die sooner or later, anyway; and, besides, he who beats injures by his blows, not the person he is beating, but himself. To get drunk is stupid and unseemly, but if you drink you die, and if you don't drink you die. A peasant woman comes with toothache . . . well, what of it? Pain is the idea of pain, and besides 'there is no living in this world without illness; we shall all die, and so, go away, woman, don't hinder me from thinking and drinking vodka.' A young man asks advice, what he is to do, how he is to live; anyone else would think before answering, but you have got the answer ready: strive for 'comprehension' or for true happiness. And what is that fantastic 'true happiness'? There's no answer, of course. We are kept here behind barred windows, tortured, left to rot; but that is very good and reasonable, because there is no difference at all between this ward and a warm, snug study. A convenient philosophy. You can do nothing, and your conscience is clear, and you feel you are wise. . . . No, sir, it is not philosophy, it's not thinking, it's not breadth of vision, but laziness, fakerism, drowsy stupefaction. Yes," cried Ivan Dmitritch, getting angry again, "you despise suffering, but I'll be bound if you pinch your finger in the door you will howl at the top of your voice."

"And perhaps I shouldn't howl," said Andrey Yefimitch, with a gentle smile.

"Oh, I dare say! Well, if you had a stroke of paralysis, or supposing some fool or bully took advantage of his position and rank to insult you in public, and if you knew he could do it with impunity, then you would understand what it means to put people off with comprehension and true happiness."

"That's original," said Andrey Yefimitch, laughing with pleasure and rubbing his hands. "I am agreeably struck by your inclination for drawing generalizations, and the sketch of my character you have just drawn is simply brilliant. I must confess that talking to you gives me great pleasure. Well, I've listened to you, and now you must graciously listen to me."

11

The conversation went on for about an hour longer, and apparently made a deep impression on Andrey Yefimitch. He began going to the ward every day. He went there in the mornings and after dinner, and often the dusk of evening found him in conversation with Ivan Dmitritch. At first Ivan Dmitritch held aloof from him, suspected him of evil designs, and openly expressed his hostility. But afterwards he got used to him, and his abrupt manner changed to one of condescending irony.

Soon it was all over the hospital that the doctor, Andrey Yefimitch, had taken to visiting Ward No. 6. No one—neither Sergey Sergeyitch, nor Nikita, nor the nurses—could conceive why he went there, why he stayed there for hours together, what he was talking about, and why he did not write prescriptions. His actions seemed strange. Often Mihail Averyanitch did not find him at home, which had never happened in the past, and Daryushka was greatly perturbed, for the doctor drank his beer now at no definite time, and sometimes was even late for dinner.

One day—it was at the end of June—Dr. Hobotov went to see Andrey Yefimitch about something. Not finding him at home, he proceeded to look for him in the yard; there he was told that the old doctor had gone to see the mental patients. Going into the lodge and stopping in the entry, Hobotov heard the following conversation:

"We shall never agree, and you will not succeed in converting me to your faith," Ivan Dmitritch was saying irritably; "you are utterly ignorant of reality, and you have never known suffering, but have only like a leech fed beside the sufferings of others, while I have been in continual suffering from the day of my birth till to-day. For that reason, I tell you frankly, I consider myself superior to you and more competent in every respect. It's not for you to teach me."

"I have absolutely no ambition to convert you to my faith," said Andrey Yefimitch gently, and with regret that the other refused to understand him. "And that is not what matters, my friend; what matters is not that you have suffered and I have not. Joy and suffering are passing; let us leave them, never mind them. What matters is that you and I think; we see in each other people who are capable of thinking and reasoning, and that is a common bond between us however different our views. If you knew, my friend, how sick I am of the universal senselessness, ineptitude, stupidity, and with what delight I always talk with you! You are an intelligent man, and I enjoy your company."

Hobotov opened the door an inch and glanced into the ward; Ivan Dmitritch in his nightcap and the doctor Andrey Yefimitch were sitting side by side on the bed. The madman was grimacing, twitching, and convulsively wrapping himself in his gown, while the doctor sat motionless with bowed head, and his face was red and looked helpless and sorrowful. Hobotov shrugged his shoulders, grinned, and glanced at Nikita. Nikita shrugged his shoulders too.

Next day Hobotov went to the lodge, accompanied by the assistant. Both stood in the entry and listened.

"I fancy our old man has gone clean off his chump!" said Hobotov as he came out of the lodge.

"Lord have mercy upon us sinners!" sighed the decorous Sergey Sergeyitch, scrupulously avoiding the puddles that he might not muddy his polished boots. "I must own, honored Yevgeny Fyodoritch, I have been expecting it for a long time."

12

After this Andrey Yefimitch began to notice a mysterious air in all around him. The attendants, the nurses, and the patients looked at him inquisitively when they met him, and then whispered together. The superintendent's little daughter Masha, whom he liked to meet in the hospital garden, for some reason ran away from him now when he went up with a smile to stroke her on the head. The postmaster no longer said, "Perfectly true," as he listened to him, but in unaccountable confusion muttered, "Yes, yes, yes . . ." and looked at him with a grieved and thoughtful expression; for some reason he took to advising his friend to give up vodka and beer, but as a man of delicate feeling he did not say this directly, but hinted it, telling him first about the commanding officer of his battalion, an excellent man, and then about the priest of the regiment, a capital fellow, both of whom drank and fell ill, but on giving up drinking completely regained their health. On two or three occasions Andrey Yefimitch was visited by his colleague Hobotov, who also advised him to give up spirituous liquors, and for no apparent reason recommended him to take bromide.

In August Andrey Yefimitch got a letter from the mayor of the town asking him to come on very important business. On arriving at the town hall at the time fixed, Andrey Yefimitch found there the military commander, the superintendent of the district school, a member of the town council, Hobotov, and a plump, fair gentleman who was introduced to him as a doctor. This doctor, with a Polish surname difficult to pronounce, lived at a pedigree stud-farm twenty miles away, and was now on a visit to the town.

"There's something that concerns you," said the member of the town council, addressing Andrey Yefimitch after they had all greeted one another and sat down to the table. "Here Yevgeny Fyodoritch says that there is not room for the dispensary in the main building, and that it ought to be transferred to one of the lodges. That's of no consequence —of course it can be transferred, but the point is that the lodge wants doing up."

"Yes, it would have to be done up," said Andrey Yefimitch after a moment's thought. "If the corner lodge, for instance, were fitted up as a dispensary, I imagine it would cost at least five hundred roubles. An unproductive expenditure!"

Everyone was silent for a space.

"I had the honor of submitting to you ten years ago," Andrey Yefimitch went on in a low voice, "that the hospital in its present form is a luxury for the town beyond its means. It was built in the forties, but things were different then. The town spends too much on unnecessary buildings and superfluous staff. I believe with a different system two model hospitals might be maintained for the same money."

"Well, let us have a different system, then!" the member of the town council said briskly.

"I have already had the honor of submitting to you that

the medical department should be transferred to the supervision of the Zemstvo."

"Yes, transfer the money to the Zemstvo and they will steal it," laughed the fair-haired doctor.

"That's what it always comes to," the member of the council assented, and he also laughed.

Andrey Yefimitch looked with apathetic, lusterless eyes at the fair-haired doctor and said: "One should be just."

Again there was silence. Tea was brought in. The military commander, for some reason much embarrassed, touched Andrey Yefimitch's hand across the table and said: "You have quite forgotten us, doctor. But of course you are a hermit: you don't play cards and don't like women. You would be dull with fellows like us."

They all began saying how boring it was for a decent person to live in such a town. No theater, no music, and at the last dance at the club there had been about twenty ladies and only two gentlemen. The young men did not dance, but spent all the time crowding round the refreshment bar or playing cards.

Not looking at anyone and speaking slowly in a low voice, Andrey Yefimitch began saying what a pity, what a terrible pity it was that the townspeople should waste their vital energy, their hearts, and their minds on cards and gossip, and should have neither the power nor the inclination to spend their time in interesting conversation and reading, and should refuse to take advantage of the enjoyments of the mind. The mind alone was interesting and worthy of attention, all the rest was low and petty. Hobotov listened to his colleague attentively and suddenly asked:

"Andrey Yefimitch, what day of the month is it?"

Having received an answer, the fair-haired doctor and he, in the tone of examiners conscious of their lack of skill, began asking Andrey Yefimitch what was the day of the week, how many days there were in the year, and whether it was true that there was a remarkable prophet living in Ward No. 6.

In response to the last question Andrey Yefimitch turned rather red and said: "Yes, he is mentally deranged, but he is an interesting young man."

They asked him no other questions.

When he was putting on his overcoat in the entry, the military commander laid a hand on his shoulder and said with a sigh:

"It's time for us old fellows to rest!"

As he came out of the hall, Andrey Yefimitch understood that it had been a committee appointed to enquire into his mental condition. He recalled the questions that had been asked him, flushed crimson, and for some reason, for the first time in his life, felt bitterly grieved for medical science.

"My God . . ." he thought, remembering how these doctors had just examined him; "why, they have only lately been hearing lectures on mental pathology; they had passed an examination—what's the explanation of this crass ignorance? They have not a conception of mental pathology!"

And for the first time in his life he felt insulted and moved to anger.

In the evening of the same day Mihail Averyanitch came to see him. The postmaster went up to him without waiting to greet him, took him by both hands, and said in an agitated voice:

"My dear fellow, my dear friend, show me that you believe in my genuine affection and look on me as your friend!" And preventing Andrey Yefimitch from speaking, he went on, growing excited: "I love you for your culture and nobility of soul. Listen to me, my dear fellow. The rules of their profession compel the doctors to conceal the truth from you, but I blurt out the plain truth like a soldier. You are not well! Excuse me, my dear fellow, but it is the truth; everyone about you has been noticing it for a long time. Dr. Yevgeny Fyodoritch has just told me that it is essential for you to rest and distract your mind for the sake of your health. Perfectly true! Excellent! In a day or two I am taking a holiday and am going away for a sniff of a different atmosphere. Show that you are a friend to me, let us go together! Let us go for a jaunt as in the good old days."

"I feel perfectly well," said Andrey Yefimitch after a moment's thought. "I can't go away. Allow me to show you my friendship in some other way."

To go off with no object, without his books, without his Daryushka, without his beer, to break abruptly through the routine of life, established for twenty years—the idea for the first minute struck him as wild and fantastic, but he remembered the conversation at the Zemstvo committee and the depressing feelings with which he had returned home, and the thought of a brief absence from the town in which stupid people looked on him as a madman was pleasant to him.

"And where precisely do you intend to go?" he asked.

"To Moscow, to Petersburg, to Warsaw. . . . I spent the five happiest years of my life in Warsaw. What a marvellous town! Let us go, my dear fellow!"

13

A week later it was suggested to Andrey Yefimitch that he should have a rest—that is, send in his resignation—a suggestion he received with indifference, and a week later still, Mihail Averyanitch and he were sitting in a posting carriage driving to the nearest railway station. The days were cool and bright, with a blue sky and a transparent distance. They were two days driving the hundred and fifty miles to the railway station, and stayed two nights on the way. When at the posting station the glasses given them for their tea had not been properly washed, or the drivers were slow in harnessing the horses, Mihail Averyanitch would turn crimson, and quivering all over would shout:

"Hold your tongue! Don't argue!"

And in the carriage he talked without ceasing for a moment, describing his campaigns in the Caucasus and in Poland. What adventures he had had, what meetings! He talked loudly and opened his eyes so wide with wonder that he might well be thought to be lying. Moreover, as he talked he breathed in Andrey Yefimitch's face and laughed into his ear. This bothered the doctor and prevented him from thinking or concentrating his mind.

In the train they travelled, from motives of economy, third-class in a non-smoking compartment. Half the passengers were decent people. Mihail Averyanitch soon made friends with everyone, and moving from one seat to another, kept saying loudly that they ought not to travel by these appalling lines. It was a regular swindle! A very different thing riding on a good horse: one could do over seventy miles a day and feel fresh and well after it. And our bad harvests were due to the draining of the Pinsk marshes; altogether, the way things were done was dreadful. He got excited, talked loudly, and would not let others speak. This endless chatter to the accompaniment of loud laughter and expressive gestures wearied Andrey Yefimitch.

"Which of us is the madman?" he thought with vexation. "I, who try not to disturb my fellow-passengers in any way, or this egoist who thinks that he is cleverer and more interesting than anyone here, and so will leave no one in peace?"

In Moscow Mihail Averyanitch put on a military coat without epaulettes and trousers with red braid on them. He wore a military cap and overcoat in the street, and soldiers saluted him. It seemed to Andrey Yefimitch, now, that his companion was a man who had flung away all that was good and kept only what was bad of all the characteristics of a country gentleman that he had once possessed. He liked to be waited on even when it was quite unnecessary. The matches would be lying before him on the table, and he would see them and shout to the waiter to give him the matches; he did not hesitate to appear before a maidservant in nothing but his underclothes; he used the familiar mode of address to all footmen indiscriminately, even old men, and when he was angry called them fools and blockheads. This, Andrey Yefimitch thought, was like a gentleman, but disgusting.

First of all Mihail Averyanitch led his friend to the Iversky Madonna. He prayed fervently, shedding tears and bowing down to the earth, and when he had finished, heaved a deep sigh and said:

"Even though one does not believe it makes one somehow easier when one prays a little. Kiss the ikon, my dear fellow."

Andrey Yefimitch was embarrassed and he kissed the image, while Mihail Averyanitch pursed up his lips and prayed in a whisper, and again tears came into his eyes. Then they went to the Kremlin and looked there at the Tsar-cannon and the Tsar-bell, and even touched them with their fingers, admired the view over the river, visited St. Saviour's and the Rumyantsev museum.

They dined at Tyestov's. Mihail Averyanitch looked a

long time at the menu, stroking his whiskers, and said in the
tone of a gourmand accustomed to dine in restaurants:

"We shall see what you give us to eat to-day, angel!"

14

The doctor walked about, looked at things, ate and drank,
but he had all the while one feeling: annoyance with Mihail Averyanitch. He longed to have a rest from his friend,
to get away from him, to hide himself, while the friend
thought it his duty not to let the doctor move a step away
from him, and to provide him with as many distractions as
possible. When there was nothing to look at he entertained
him with conversation. For two days Andrey Yefimitch
endured it, but on the third he announced to his friend
that he was ill and wanted to stay at home for the whole
day; his friend replied that in that case he would stay
too—that really he needed rest, for he was run off his legs
already. Andrey Yefimitch lay on the sofa, with his face to
the back, and clenching his teeth, listened to his friend,
who assured him with heat that sooner or later France
would certainly thrash Germany, that there were a great
many scoundrels in Moscow, and that it was impossible to
judge of a horse's quality by its outward appearance. The
doctor began to have a buzzing in his ears and palpitations
of the heart, but out of delicacy could not bring himself to
beg his friend to go away or hold his tongue. Fortunately
Mihail Averyanitch grew weary of sitting in the hotel room,
and after dinner he went out for a walk.

As soon as he was alone Andrey Yefimitch abandoned
himself to a feeling of relief. How pleasant to lie motionless
on the sofa and to know that one is alone in the room!
Real happiness is impossible without solitude. The fallen
angel betrayed God probably because he longed for solitude, of which the angels know nothing. Andrey Yefimitch
wanted to think about what he had seen and heard during
the last few days, but he could not get Mihail Averyanitch
out of his head.

"Why, he has taken a holiday and come with me out of
friendship, out of generosity," thought the doctor with
vexation; "nothing could be worse than this friendly super-

vision. I suppose he is good-natured and generous and a lively fellow, but he is a bore. An insufferable bore. In the same way there are people who never say anything but what is clever and good, yet one feels that they are dull-witted people."

For the following days Andrey Yefimitch declared himself ill and would not leave the hotel room; he lay with his face to the back of the sofa, and suffered agonies of weariness when his friend entertained him with conversation, or rested when his friend was absent. He was vexed with himself for having come, and with his friend, who grew every day more talkative and more free-and-easy; he could not succeed in attuning his thoughts to a serious and lofty level.

"This is what I get from the real life Ivan Dmitritch talked about," he thought, angry at his own pettiness. "It's of no consequence, though. . . . I shall go home, and everything will go on as before. . . ."

It was the same thing in Petersburg too; for whole days together he did not leave the hotel room, but lay on the sofa and only got up to drink beer.

Mihail Averyanitch was all haste to get to Warsaw.

"My dear man, what should I go there for?" said Andrey Yefimitch in an imploring voice. "You go alone and let me get home! I entreat you!"

"On no account," protested Mihail Averyanitch. "It's a marvellous town."

Andrey Yefimitch had not the strength of will to insist on his own way, and much against his inclination went to Warsaw. There he did not leave the hotel room, but lay on the sofa, furious with himself, with his friend, and with the waiters, who obstinately refused to understand Russian; while Mihail Averyanitch, healthy, hearty, and full of spirits as usual, went about the town from morning to night, looking for his old acquaintances. Several times he did not return home at night. After one night spent in some unknown haunt he returned home early in the morning, in a violently excited condition, with a red face and tousled hair. For a long time he walked up and down the rooms muttering something to himself, then stopped and said:

"Honor before everything."

After walking up and down a little longer he clutched
his head in both hands and pronounced in a tragic voice:
"Yes, honor before everything! Accursed be the moment
when the idea first entered my head to visit this Babylon!
My dear friend," he added, addressing the doctor, "you
may despise me, I have played and lost; lend me five hundred roubles!"

Andrey Yefimitch counted out five hundred roubles and
gave them to his friend without a word. The latter, still
crimson with shame and anger, incoherently articulated
some useless vow, put on his cap, and went out. Returning
two hours later he flopped into an easy-chair, heaved a
loud sigh, and said:

"My honor is saved. Let us go, my friend; I do not care
to remain another hour in this accursed town. Scoundrels!
Austrian spies!"

By the time the friends were back in their own town it
was November, and deep snow was lying in the streets. Dr.
Hobotov had Andrey Yefimitch's post; he was still living in
his old lodgings, waiting for Andrey Yefimitch to arrive
and clear out of the hospital apartments. The plain woman
whom he called his cook was already established in one of
the lodges.

Fresh scandals about the hospital were going the round
of the town. It was said that the plain woman had quarrelled
with the superintendent, and that the latter had crawled on
his knees before her begging forgiveness. On the very first
day he arrived Andrey Yefimitch had to look out for lodgings.

"My friend," the postmaster said to him timidly, "excuse an indiscreet question: what means have you at your
disposal?"

Andrey Yefimitch, without a word, counted out his
money and said: "Eighty-six roubles."

"I don't mean that," Mihail Averyanitch brought out in
confusion, misunderstanding him; "I mean, what have you
to live on?"

"I tell you, eighty-six roubles . . . I have nothng else."

Mihail Averyanitch looked upon the doctor as an honor-
able man, yet he suspected that he had accumulated a
fortune of at least twenty thousand. Now learning that

Andrey Yefimitch was a beggar, that he had nothing to live on he was for some reason suddenly moved to tears and embraced his friend.

15

Andrey Yefimitch now lodged in a little house with three windows. There were only three rooms besides the kitchen in the little house. The doctor lived in two of them which looked into the street, while Daryushka and the landlady with her three children lived in the third room and the kitchen. Sometimes the landlady's lover, a drunken peasant who was rowdy and reduced the children and Daryushka to terror, would come for the night. When he arrived and established himself in the kitchen and demanded vodka, they all felt very uncomfortable, and the doctor would be moved by pity to take the crying children into his room and let them lie on his floor, and this gave him great satisfaction.

He got up as before at eight o'clock, and after his morning tea sat down to read his old books and magazines: he had no money for new ones. Either because the books were old, or perhaps because of the change in his surroundings, reading exhausted him, and did not grip his attention as before. That he might not spend his time in idleness he made a detailed catalogue of his books and gummed little labels on their backs, and this mechanical, tedious work seemed to him more interesting than reading. The monotonous, tedious work lulled his thoughts to sleep in some unaccountable way, and the time passed quickly while he thought of nothing. Even sitting in the kitchen, peeling potatoes with Daryushka or picking over the buckwheat grain, seemed to him interesting. On Saturdays and Sundays he went to church. Standing near the wall and half closing his eyes, he listened to the singing and thought of his father, of his mother, of the university, of the religions of the world; he felt calm and melancholy, and as he went out of the church afterwards he regretted that the service was so soon over. He went twice to the hospital to talk to Ivan Dmitritch. But on both occasions Ivan Dmitritch was unusually excited and ill-humored; he bade the doctor leave him in peace, as he had long been sick of empty chatter, and declared, to make up for all his sufferings, he asked from the damned scoundrels only one favor—solitary confinement. Surely they would not refuse him even that? On both occasions when Andrey Yefimitch was taking leave of him and wishing him good-night, he answered rudely and said:

"Go to hell!"

And Andrey Yefimitch did not know now whether to go to him for the third time or not. He longed to go.

In old days Andrey Yefimitch used to walk about his rooms and think in the interval after dinner, but now from dinner-time till evening tea he lay on the sofa with his face to the back and gave himself up to trivial thoughts which he could not struggle against. He was mortified that after more than twenty years of service he had been given neither a pension nor any assistance. It is true he had not done his work honestly, but, then, all who are in the Service get a pension without distinction whether they are honest or not. Contemporary justice lies precisely in the bestowal of grades, orders, and pensions, not for moral qualities or capacities, but for service whatever it may have been like. Why was he alone to be an exception? He had no money at all. He was ashamed to pass by the shop and look at the woman who owned it. He owed thirty-two roubles for beer already. There was money owing to the landlady also. Daryushka sold old clothes and books on the sly, and told lies to the landlady, saying that the doctor was just going to receive a large sum of money.

He was angry with himself for having wasted on travelling the thousand roubles he had saved up. How useful that thousand roubles would have been now! He was vexed that people would not leave him in peace. Hobotov thought it his duty to look in on his sick colleague from time to time. Everything about him was revolting to Andrey Yefimitch—his well-fed face and vulgar, condescending tone, and his use of the word "colleague," and his high top-boots; the most revolting thing was that he thought it was his duty to treat Andrey Yefimitch, and thought that he really was treating him. On every visit he brought a bottle of bromide and rhubarb pills.

Mihail Averyanitch, too, thought it his duty to visit his friend and entertain him. Every time he went in to Andrey Yefimitch with an affectation of ease, laughed constrainedly, and began assuring him that he was looking very well to-day, and that, thank God, he was on the highroad to recovery, and from this it might be concluded that he looked on his friend's condition as hopeless. He had not yet repaid his Warsaw debt, and was overwhelmed by shame; he was constrained, and so tried to laugh louder and talk more amusingly. His anecdotes and descriptions seemed endless now, and were an agony both to Andrey Yefimitch and himself.

In his presence Andrey Yefimitch usually lay on the sofa with his face to the wall, and listened with his teeth clenched; his soul was oppressed with rankling disgust, and after every visit from his friend he felt as though this disgust had risen higher, and was mounting into his throat.

To stifle petty thoughts he made haste to reflect that he himself, and Hobotov, and Mihail Averyanitch, would all sooner or later perish without leaving any trace on the world. If one imagined some spirit flying by the earthly globe in space in a million years he would see nothing but clay and bare rocks. Everything—culture and the moral law—would pass away and not even a burdock would grow out of them. Of what consequence was shame in the presence of a shopkeeper, of what consequence was the insignificant Hobotov or the wearisome friendship of Mihail Averyanitch? It was all trivial and nonsensical.

But such reflections did not help him now. Scarcely had he imagined the earthly globe in a million years, when Hobotov in his high top-boots or Mihail Averyanitch with his forced laugh would appear from behind a bare rock, and he even heard the shamefaced whisper: "The Warsaw debt. . . . I will repay it in a day or two, my dear fellow, without fail. . . ."

16

One day Mihail Averyanitch came after dinner when Andrey Yefimitch was lying on the sofa. It so happened that Hobotov arrived at the same time with his bromide. Andrey Yefimitch got up heavily and sat down, leaning both arms on the sofa.

"You have a much better color to-day than you had

yesterday, my dear man," began Mihail Averyanitch. "Yes, you look jolly. Upon my soul, you do!"

"It's high time you were well, colleague," said Hobotov, yawning. "I'll be bound, you are sick of this bobbery."

"And we shall recover," said Mihail Averyanitch cheerfully. "We shall live another hundred years! To be sure!"

"Not a hundred years, but another twenty," Hobotov said reassuringly. "It's all right, all right, colleague; don't lose heart. . . . Don't go piling it on!"

"We'll show what we can do," laughed Mihail Averyanitch, and he slapped his friend on the knee. "We'll show them yet! Next summer, please God, we shall be off to the Caucasus, and we will ride all over it on horseback—trot, trot, trot! And when we are back from the Caucasus I shouldn't wonder if we will all dance at the wedding." Mihail Averyanitch gave a sly wink. "We'll marry you, my dear boy, we'll marry you. . . ."

Andrey Yefimitch felt suddenly that the rising disgust had mounted to his throat, his heart began beating violently.

"That's vulgar," he said, getting up quickly and walking away to the window. "Don't you understand that you are talking vulgar nonsense?"

He meant to go on softly and politely, but against his will he suddenly clenched his fists and raised them above his head.

"Leave me alone," he shouted in a voice unlike his own, flushing crimson and shaking all over. "Go away, both of you!"

Mihail Averyanitch and Hobotov got up and stared at him first with amazement and then with alarm.

"Go away, both!" Andrey Yefimitch went on shouting. "Stupid people! Foolish people! I don't want either your friendship or your medicines, stupid man! Vulgar! Nasty!"

Hobotov and Mihail Averyanitch, looking at each other in bewilderment, staggered to the door and went out. Andrey Yefimitch snatched up the bottle of bromide and flung it after them; the bottle broke with a crash on the door-frame.

"Go to the devil!" he shouted in a tearful voice, running out into the passage. "To the devil!"

When his guests were gone Andrey Yefimitch lay down

on the sofa, trembling as though in a fever, and went on for a long while repeating: "Stupid people! Foolish people!"

When he was calmer, what occurred to him first of all was the thought that poor Mihail Averyanitch must be feeling fearfully ashamed and depressed now, and that it was all dreadful. Nothing like this had ever happened to him before. Where was his intelligence and his tact? Where was his comprehension of things and his philosophical indifference?

The doctor could not sleep all night for shame and vexation with himself, and at ten o'clock next morning he went to the post office and apologized to the postmaster.

"We won't think again of what has happened," Mihail Averyanitch, greatly touched, said with a sigh, warmly pressing his hand. "Let bygones be bygones. Lyubavkin," he suddenly shouted so loud that all the postmen and other persons present started, "hand a chair; and you wait," he shouted to a peasant woman who was stretching out a registered letter to him through the grating. "Don't you see that I am busy? We will not remember the past," he went on, affectionately addressing Andrey Yefimitch; "sit down, I beg you, my dear fellow."

For a minute he stroked his knees in silence, and then said:

"I have never had a thought of taking offence. Illness is no joke, I understand. Your attack frightened the doctor and me yesterday, and we had a long talk about you afterwards. My dear friend, why won't you treat your illness seriously? You can't go on like this. . . . Excuse me speaking openly as a friend," whispered Mihail Averyanitch. "You live in the most unfavorable surroundings, in a crowd, in uncleanliness, no one to look after you, no money for proper treatment. . . . My dear friend, the doctor and I implore you with all our hearts, listen to our advice: go into the hospital! There you will have wholesome food and attendance and treatment. Though, between ourselves, Yevgeny Fyodoritch is *mauvais ton*, yet he does understand his work, you can fully rely upon him. He has promised me he will look after you."

Andrey Yefimitch was touched by the postmaster's genuine sympathy and the tears which suddenly glittered on his cheeks.

"My honored friend, don't believe it!" he whispered, laying his hand on his heart; "don't believe them. It's all a sham. My illness is only that in twenty years I have only found one intelligent man in the whole town, and he is mad. I am not ill at all, it's simply that I have got into an enchanted circle which there is no getting out of. I don't care; I am ready for anything."

"Go into the hospital, my dear fellow."

"I don't care if it were into the pit."

"Give me your word, my dear man, that you will obey Yevgeny Fyodoritch in everything."

"Certainly I will give you my word. But I repeat, my honored friend, I have got into an enchanted circle. Now everything, even the genuine sympathy of my friends, leads to the same thing—to my ruin. I am going to my ruin, and I have the manliness to recognize it."

"My dear fellow, you will recover."

"What's the use of saying that?" said Andrey Yefimitch with irritation. "There are few men who at the end of their lives do not experience what I am experiencing now. When you are told that you have something such as diseased kidneys or enlarged heart, and you begin being treated for it, or are told you are mad or a criminal—that is, in fact, when people suddenly turn their attention to you—you may be sure you have got into an enchanted circle from which you will not escape. You will try to escape and make things worse. You had better give in, for no human efforts can save you. So it seems to me."

Meanwhile the public was crowding at the grating. That he might not be in their way, Andrey Yefimitch got up and began to take leave. Mihail Averyanitch made him promise on his honor once more, and escorted him to the outer door. Towards evening on the same day Hobotov, in his sheepskin and his high top-boots, suddenly made his appearance and said to Andrey Yefimitch in a tone as though nothing had happened the day before:

"I have come on business, colleague. I have come to ask you whether you would not join me in a consultation. Eh?"

Thinking that Hobotov wanted to distract his mind with an outing, or perhaps really to enable him to earn something, Andrey Yefimitch put on his coat and hat, and went out with him into the street. He was glad of the opportunity to smooth over his fault of the previous day and to be reconciled, and in his heart thanked Hobotov, who did not even allude to yesterday's scene and was evidently sparing him. One would never have expected such delicacy from this uncultured man.

"Where is your invalid?" asked Andrey Yefimitch.

"In the hospital. . . . I have long wanted to show him to you. A very interesting case."

They went into the hospital yard, and going round the main building, turned towards the lodge where the mental cases were kept, and all this, for some reason, in silence. When they went into the lodge Nikita as usual jumped up and stood at attention.

"One of the patients here has a lung complication," Hobotov said in an undertone, going into the ward with Andrey Yefimitch. "You wait here, I'll be back directly. I am going for a stethoscope."

And he went away.

17

It was getting dusk. Ivan Dmitritch was lying on his bed with his face thrust into his pillow; the paralytic was sitting motionless, crying quietly and moving his lips. The fat peasant and the former sorter were asleep. It was quiet.

Andrey Yefimitch sat down on Ivan Dmitritch's bed and waited. But half an hour passed, and instead of Hobotov, Nikita came into the ward with a dressing-gown, some underlinen, and a pair of slippers in a heap on his arm.

"Please change your things, your honor," he said softly. "Here is your bed; come this way," he added, pointing to an empty bedstead which had obviously been recently brought into the ward. "It's all right; please God, you will recover."

Andrey Yefimitch understood it all. Without saying a word he crossed to the bed to which Nikita pointed and sat down; seeing that Nikita was standing waiting, he undressed entirely and he felt ashamed. Then he put on the hospital clothes; the drawers were very short, the shirt was long, and the dressing-gown smelt of smoked fish.

"Please God, you will recover," repeated Nikita, and he

gathered up Andrey Yefimitch's clothes into his arms, went out, and shut the door after him.

"No matter . . ." thought Andrey Yefimitch, wrapping himself in his dressing-gown in a shame-faced way and feeling that he looked like a convict in his new costume. "It's no matter. . . . It does not matter whether it's a dress-coat or a uniform or this dressing-gown. . . ."

But how about his watch? And the notebook that was in the side-pocket? And his cigarettes? Where had Nikita taken his clothes? Now perhaps to the day of his death he would not put on trousers, a waistcoat, and high boots. It was all somehow strange and even incomprehensible at first. Andrey Yefimitch was even now convinced that there was no difference between his landlady's house and Ward No. 6, that everything in this world was nonsense and vanity of vanities. And yet his hands were trembling, his feet were cold, and he was filled with dread at the thought that soon Ivan Dmitritch would get up and see that he was in a dressing-gown. He got up and walked across the room and sat down again.

Here he had been sitting already half an hour, an hour, and he was miserably sick of it: was it really possible to live here a day, a week, and even years like these people? Why, he had been sitting here, had walked about and sat down again; he could get up and look out of the window and walk from corner to corner again, and then what? Sit so all the time, like a post, and think? No, that was scarcely possible.

Andrey Yefimitch lay down, but at once got up, wiped the cold sweat from his brow with his sleeve, and felt that his whole face smelt of smoked fish. He walked about again.

"It's some misunderstanding . . ." he said, turning out the palms of his hands in perplexity. "It must be cleared up. There is a misunderstanding. . . ."

Meanwhile Ivan Dmitritch woke up; he sat up and propped his cheeks on his fists. He spat. Then he glanced lazily at the doctor, and apparently for the first minute did not understand; but soon his sleepy face grew malicious and mocking.

"Aha! so they have put you in here, too, old fellow?"

he said in a voice husky from sleepiness, screwing up one eye. "Very glad to see you. You sucked the blood of others, and now they will suck yours. Excellent!"

"It's a misunderstanding . . ." Andrey Yefimitch brought out, frightened by Ivan Dmitritch's words; he shrugged his shoulders and repeated: "It's some misunderstanding. . . ."

Ivan Dmitritch spat again and lay down.

"Cursed life," he grumbled, "and what's bitter and insulting, this life will not end in compensation for our sufferings, it will not end with apotheosis as it would in an opera, but with death; peasants will come and drag one's dead body by the arms and the legs to the cellar. Ugh! Well, it does not matter. . . . We shall have our good time in the other world. . . . I shall come here as a ghost from the other world and frighten these reptiles. I'll turn their hair grey."

Moiseika returned, and, seeing the doctor, held out his hand.

"Give me one little kopeck," he said.

18

Andrey Yefimitch walked away to the window and looked out into the open country. It was getting dark, and on the horizon to the right a cold crimson moon was mounting upwards. Not far from the hospital fence, not much more than two hundred yards away, stood a tall white house shut in by a stone wall. This was the prison.

"So this is real life," thought Andrey Yefimitch, and he felt frightened.

The moon and the prison, and the nails on the fence, and the far-away flames at the bone-charring factory were all terrible. Behind him there was the sound of a sigh. Andrey Yefimitch looked round and saw a man with glittering stars and orders on his breast, who was smiling and slily winking. And this, too, seemed terrible.

Andrey Yefimitch assured himself that there was nothing special about the moon or the prison, that even sane persons wear orders, and that everything in time will decay and turn to earth, but he was suddenly overcome with despair; he clutched at the grating with both hands and shook it with all his might. The strong grating did not yield.

Then that it might not be so dreadful he went to Ivan Dmitritch's bed and sat down.

"I have lost heart, my dear fellow," he muttered, trembling and wiping away the cold sweat, "I have lost heart."

"You should be philosophical," said Ivan Dmitritch ironically.

"My God, my God. ... Yes, yes. ... You were pleased to say once that there was no philosophy in Russia, but that all people, even the paltriest, talk philosophy. But you know the philosophizing of the paltriest does not harm anyone," said Andrey Yefimitch in a tone as if he wanted to cry and complain. "Why, then, that malignant laugh, my friend, and how can these paltry creatures help philosophizing if they are not satisfied? For an intelligent, educated man, made in God's image, proud and loving freedom, to have no alternative but to be a doctor in a filthy, stupid, wretched little town, and to spend his whole life among bottles, leeches, mustard plasters! Quackery, narrowness, vulgarity! Oh, my God!"

"You are talking nonsense. If you don't like being a doctor you should have gone in for being a statesman."

"I could not, I could not do anything. We are weak, my dear friend. ... I used to be indifferent. I reasoned boldly and soundly, but at the first coarse touch of life upon me I have lost heart. ... Prostration. ... We are weak, we are poor creatures ... and you, too, my dear friend, you are intelligent, generous, you drew in good impulses with your mother's milk, but you had hardly entered upon life when you were exhausted and fell ill. ... Weak, weak!"

Andrey Yefimitch was all the while at the approach of evening tormented by another persistent sensation besides terror and the feeling of resentment. At last he realized that he was longing for a smoke and for beer.

"I am going out, my friend," he said. "I will tell them to bring a light; I can't put up with this. ... I am not equal to it. ..."

Andrey Yefimitch went to the door and opened it, but at once Nikita jumped up and barred his way.

"Where are you going? You can't, you can't!" he said. "It's bedtime."

"But I'm only going out for a minute to walk about the yard," said Andrey Yefimitch.

"You can't, you can't; it's forbidden. You know that yourself."

"But what difference will it make to anyone if I do go out?" asked Andrey Yefimitch, shrugging his shoulders. "I don't understand. Nikita, I must go out!" he said in a trembling voice. "I must."

"Don't be disorderly, it's not right," Nikita said peremptorily.

"This is beyond everything," Ivan Dmitritch cried suddenly, and he jumped up. "What right has he not to let you out? How dare they keep us here? I believe it is clearly laid down in the law that no one can be deprived of freedom without trial! It's an outrage! It's tyranny!"

"Of course it's tyranny," said Andrey Yefimitch, encouraged by Ivan Dmitritch's outburst. "I must go out, I want to. He has no right! Open, I tell you."

"Do you hear, you dull-witted brute?" cried Ivan Dmitritch, and he banged on the door with his fist. "Open the door, or I will break it open! Torturer!"

"Open the door," cried Andrey Yefimitch, trembling all over; "I insist!"

"Talk away!" Nikita answered through the door, "talk away. . . ."

"Anyhow, go and call Yevgeny Fyodoritch! Say that I beg him to come for a minute!"

"His honor will come of himself to-morrow."

"They will never let us out," Ivan Dmitritch was going on meanwhile. "They will leave us to rot here! Oh, Lord, can there really be no hell in the next world, and will these wretches be forgiven? Where is justice? Open the door, you wretch! I am choking!" he cried in a hoarse voice, and flung himself upon the door. "I'll dash out my brains, murderers!"

Nikita opened the door quickly, and roughly with both his hands and his knee shoved Andrey Yefimitch back, then swung his arm and punched him in the face with his fist. It seemed to Andrey Yefimitch as though a huge salt wave enveloped him from his head downwards and dragged him to the bed; there really was a salt taste in his mouth: most likely the blood was running from his teeth. He waved his arms as though he were trying to swim out and clutch at a bedstead, and at the same moment felt Nikita hit him twice on the back.

Ivan Dmitritch gave a loud scream. He must have been beaten too.

Then all was still, the faint moonlight came through the grating, and a shadow like a net lay on the floor. It was terrible. Andrey Yefimitch lay and held his breath: he was expecting with horror to be struck again. He felt as though someone had taken a sickle, thrust it into him, and turned it round several times in his breast and bowels. He bit the pillow from pain and clenched his teeth, and all at once through the chaos in his brain there flashed the terrible unbearable thought that these people, who seemed now like black shadows in the moonlight, had to endure such pain day by day for years. How could it have happened that for more than twenty years he had not known it and had refused to know it? He knew nothing of pain, had no conception of it, so he was not to blame, but his conscience, as inexorable and as rough as Nikita, made him turn cold from the crown of his head to his heels. He leaped up, tried to cry out with all his might, and to run in haste to kill Nikita, and then Hobotov, the superintendent and the assistant, and then himself; but no sound came from his chest, and his legs would not obey him. Gasping for breath, he tore at the dressing-gown and the shirt on his breast, rent them, and fell senseless on the bed.

19

Next morning his head ached, there was a droning in his ears and a feeling of utter weakness all over. He was not ashamed at recalling his weakness the day before. He had been cowardly, had even been afraid of the moon, had openly expressed thoughts and feelings such as he had not expected in himself before; for instance, the thought that the paltry people who philosophized were really dissatisfied. But now nothing mattered to him.

He ate nothing, he drank nothing. He lay motionless and silent.

"It is all the same to me," he thought when they asked him questions. "I am not going to answer. . . . It's all the same to me."

After dinner Mihail Averyanitch brought him a quarter of a pound of tea and a pound of fruit pastilles. Daryushka came too and stood for a whole hour by the bed with an expression of dull grief on her face. Dr. Hobotov visited him. He brought a bottle of bromide and told Nikita to fumigate the ward with something.

Towards evening Andrey Yefimitch died of an apoplectic stroke. At first he had a violent shivering fit and a feeling of sickness; something revolting as it seemed, penetrating through his whole body, even to his finger-tips, strained from his stomach to his head and flooded his eyes and ears. There was a greenness before his eyes. Andrey Yefimitch understood that his end had come, and remembered that Ivan Dmitritch, Mihail Averyanitch, and millions of people believed in immortality. And what if it really existed? But he did not want immortality, and he thought of it only for one instant. A herd of deer, extraordinarily beautiful and graceful, of which he had been reading the day before, ran by him; then a peasant woman stretched out her hand to him with a registered letter. . . . Mihail Averyanitch said something, then it all vanished, and Andrey Yefimitch sank into oblivion for ever.

The hospital porters came, took him by his arms and his legs, and carried him away to the chapel.

There he lay on the table, with open eyes, and the moon shed its light upon him at night. In the morning Sergey Sergeyitch came, prayed piously before the crucifix, and closed his former chief's eyes.

Next day Andrey Yefimitch was buried. Mihail Averyanitch and Daryushka were the only people at the funeral.

1892

In Exile

OLD SEMYON, nicknamed Canny, and a young Tatar, whom no one knew by name, were sitting on the river-bank by the camp-fire; the other three ferrymen were in the hut. Semyon, an old man of sixty, lean and toothless, but broad-shouldered and still healthy-looking, was drunk; he would have gone in to sleep long before, but he had a bottle in his pocket and he was afraid that the fellows in the hut would ask him for vodka. The Tatar was ill and weary, and wrapping himself up in his rags was describing how once it was in the Simbirsk province, and what a beautiful and clever wife he had left behind at home. He was not more than twenty-five, and now by the light of the camp-fire, with his pale and sick, mournful face, he looked like a boy.

"To be sure, it is not paradise here," said Canny. "You can see for yourself, the water, the bare banks, clay, and nothing else. . . . Easter has long passed and yet there is ice on the river, and this morning there was snow. . . ."

"It's bad! it's bad!" said the Tatar, and looked round him in terror.

The dark, cold river was flowing ten paces away; it grumbled, lapped against the hollow clay banks and raced on swiftly towards the far-away sea. Close to the bank there was the dark blur of a big barge, which the ferrymen called a "karbos." Far away on the further bank, lights, dying down and flickering up again, zigzagged like little snakes; they were burning last year's grass. And beyond the little snakes there was darkness again. There little icicles could be heard knocking against the barge. It was damp and cold. . . .

The Tatar glanced at the sky. There were as many stars as at home, and the same blackness all round, but some-

thing was lacking. At home in the Simbirsk province the
stars were quite different, and so was the sky.

"It's bad! it's bad!" he repeated.

"You will get used to it," said Semyon, and he laughed.
"Now you are young and foolish, the milk is hardly dry on
your lips, and it seems to you in your foolishness that you
are more wretched than anyone; but the time will come
when you will say to yourself: 'I wish no one a better life
than mine.' You look at me. Within a week the floods will
be over and we shall set up the ferry; you will all go
wandering off about Siberia while I shall stay and shall
begin going from bank to bank. I've been going like that
for twenty-two years, day and night. The pike and the
salmon are under the water while I am on the water. And
thank God for it, I want nothing; God give everyone such
a life."

The Tatar threw some dry twigs on the camp-fire, lay
down closer to the blaze, and said:

"My father is a sick man. When he dies my mother and
wife will come here. They have promised."

"And what do you want your wife and mother for?"
asked Canny. "That's mere foolishness, my lad. It's the
devil confounding you, damn his soul! Don't you listen to
him, the cursed one. Don't let him have his way. He is at
you about the women, but you spite him; say, 'I don't
want them!' He is on at you about freedom, but you stand
up to him and say: 'I don't want it!' I want nothing, neither
father nor mother, nor wife, nor freedom, nor post, nor
paddock; I want nothing, damn their souls!"

Semyon took a pull at the bottle and went on:

"I am not a simple peasant, not of the working class, but
the son of a deacon, and when I was free I lived at Kursk;
I used to wear a frock-coat, and now I have brought myself
to such a pass that I can sleep naked on the ground and eat
grass. And I wish no one a better life. I want nothing and I
am afraid of nobody, and the way I look at it is that there
is nobody richer and freer than I am. When they sent me
here from Russia from the first day I stuck it out; I want
nothing! The devil was at me about my wife and about my
home and about freedom, but I told him: 'I want nothing.'
I stuck to it, and here you see I live well, and I don't complain, and if anyone gives way to the devil and listens to

him, if but once, he is lost, there is no salvation for him: he is sunk in the bog to the crown of his head and will never get out.

"It is not only a foolish peasant like you, but even gentlemen, well-educated people, are lost. Fifteen years ago they sent a gentleman here from Russia. He hadn't shared something with his brothers and had forged something in a will. They did say he was a prince or a baron, but maybe he was simply an official—who knows? Well, the gentleman arrived here, and first thing he bought himself a house and land in Muhortinskoe. 'I want to live by my own work,' says he, 'in the sweat of my brow, for I am not a gentleman now,' says he, 'but a settler.' 'Well,' says I, 'God help you, that's the right thing.' He was a young man then, busy and careful; he used to mow himself and catch fish and ride sixty miles on horseback. Only this is what happened: from the very first year he took to riding to Gyrino for the post; he used to stand on my ferry and sigh: 'Ech, Semyon, how long it is since they sent me any money from home!' 'You don't want money, Vassily Sergeyitch,' says I. 'What use is it to you? You cast away the past, and forget it as though it had never been at all, as though it had been a dream, and begin to live anew. Don't listen to the devil,' says I; 'he will bring you to no good, he'll draw you into a snare. Now you want money,' says I, 'but in a very little while you'll be wanting something else, and then more and more. If you want to be happy,' says I, 'the chief thing is not to want anything. Yes. . . . If,' says I, 'if Fate has wronged you and me cruelly, it's no good asking for her favor and bowing down to her, but you despise her and laugh at her, or else she will laugh at you.' That's what I said to him. . . .

"Two years later I ferried him across to this side, and he was rubbing his hands and laughing. 'I am going to Gyrino to meet my wife,' says he. 'She was sorry for me,' says he; 'she has come. She is good and kind.' And he was breathless with joy. So a day later he came with his wife. A beautiful young lady in a hat; in her arms was a baby girl. And lots of luggage of all sorts. And my Vassily Sergeyitch was fussing round her; he couldn't take his eyes off her and couldn't say enough in praise of her. 'Yes, brother Semyon, even in Siberia people can live!' 'Oh, all right,' thinks I, 'it will be a different tale presently.' And from that time forward he went almost every week to inquire whether money had not come from Russia. He wanted a lot of money. 'She is losing her youth and beauty here in Siberia for my sake,' says he, 'and sharing my bitter lot with me, and so I ought,' says he, 'to provide her with every comfort. . . .'

"To make it livelier for the lady he made acquaintance with the officials and all sorts of riff-raff. And of course he had to give food and drink to all that crew, and there had to be a piano and a shaggy lapdog on the sofa—plague take it! . . . Luxury, in fact, self-indulgence. The lady did not stay with him long. How could she? The clay, the water, the cold, no vegetables for you, no fruit. All around you ignorant and drunken people and no sort of manners, and she was a spoilt lady from Petersburg or Moscow. . . . To be sure she moped. Besides, her husband, say what you like, was not a gentleman now, but a settler—not the same rank.

"Three years later, I remember, on the eve of the Assumption, there was shouting from the further bank. I went over with the ferry, and what do I see but the lady, all wrapped up, and with her a young gentleman, an official. A sledge with three horses. . . . I ferried them across here, they got in and away like the wind. They were soon lost to sight. And towards morning Vassily Sergeyitch galloped down to the ferry. 'Didn't my wife come this way with a gentleman in spectacles, Semyon?' 'She did,' said I; 'you may look for the wind in the fields!' He galloped in pursuit of them. For five days and nights he was riding after them. When I ferried him over to the other side afterwards, he flung himself on the ferry and beat his head on the boards of the ferry and howled. 'So that's how it is,' says I. I laughed, and reminded him 'people can live even in Siberia!' And he beat his head harder than ever. . . .

"Then he began longing for freedom. His wife had slipped off to Russia, and of course he was drawn there to see her and to get her away from her lover. And he took, my lad, to galloping almost every day, either to the post or the town to see the commanding officer; he kept sending in petitions for them to have mercy on him and let him go back home; and he used to say that he had spent some two hundred roubles on telegrams alone. He sold his land and mortgaged his house to the Jews. He grew gray and bent, and yellow in the face, as though he was in consumption. If he talked to you he would go, khee—khee—khee, . . . and there were tears in his eyes. He kept rushing about like this with petitions for eight years, but now he has grown brighter and more cheerful again: he has found another whim to give way to. You see, his daughter has grown up. He looks at her, and she is the apple of his eye. And to tell the truth she is all right, good-looking, with black eyebrows and a lively disposition. Every Sunday he used to ride with her to church in Gyrino. They used to stand on the ferry, side by side, she would laugh and he could not take his eyes off her. 'Yes, Semyon,' says he, 'people can live even in Siberia. Even in Siberia there is happiness. Look,' says he, 'what a daughter I have got! I warrant you wouldn't find another like her for a thousand versts round.' 'Your daughter is all right,' says I, 'that's true, certainly.' But to myself I thought: 'Wait a bit, the wench is young, her blood is dancing, she wants to live, and there is no life here.' And she did begin to pine, my lad. . . . She faded and faded, and now she can hardly crawl about. Consumption.

"So you see what Siberian happiness is, damn its soul! You see how people can live in Siberia. . . . He has taken to going from one doctor to another and taking them home with him. As soon as he hears that two or three hundred miles away there is a doctor or a sorcerer, he will drive to fetch him. A terrible lot of money he spent on doctors, and to my thinking he had better have spent the money on drink. . . . She'll die just the same. She is certain to die, and then it will be all over with him. He'll hang himself from grief or run away to Russia—that's a sure thing. He'll run away and they'll catch him, then he will be tried, sent to prison, he will have a taste of the lash. . . ."

"Good! good!" said the Tatar, shivering with cold.

"What is good?" asked Canny.

"His wife, his daughter. . . . What of prison and what of sorrow!—anyway, he did see his wife and his daughter. . . . You say, want nothing. But 'nothing' is bad! His wife lived with him three years—that was a gift from God. 'Nothing' is bad, but three years is good. How not understand?"

Shivering and hesitating, with effort picking out the

Russian words of which he knew but few, the Tatar said that God forbid one should fall sick and die in a strange land, and be buried in the cold and dark earth; that if his wife came to him for one day, even for one hour, that for such happiness he would be ready to bear any suffering and to thank God. Better one day of happiness than nothing.

Then he described again what a beautiful and clever wife he had left at home. Then, clutching his head in both hands, he began crying and assuring Semyon that he was not guilty, and was suffering for nothing. His two brothers and an uncle had carried off a peasant's horses, and had beaten the old man till he was half dead, and the commune had not judged fairly, but had contrived a sentence by which all the three brothers were sent to Siberia, while the uncle, a rich man, was left at home.

"You will get used to it!" said Semyon.

The Tatar was silent, and stared with tear-stained eyes at the fire; his face expressed bewilderment and fear, as though he still did not understand why he was here in the darkness and the wet, beside strangers, and not in the Simbirsk province.

Canny lay near the fire, chuckled at something, and began humming a song in an undertone.

"What joy has she with her father?" he said a little later. "He loves her and he rejoices in her, that's true; but, mate, you must mind your ps and qs with him, he is a strict old man, a harsh old man. And young wenches don't want strictness. They want petting and ha-ha-ha! and ho-ho-ho! and scent and pomade. Yes. . . . Ech! life, life," sighed Semyon, and he got up heavily. "The vodka is all gone, so it is time to sleep. Eh? I am going, my lad. . . ."

Left alone, the Tatar put on more twigs, lay down and stared at the fire; he began thinking of his own village and of his wife. If his wife could only come for a month, for a day; and then if she liked she might go back again. Better a month or even a day than nothing. But if his wife kept her promise and came, what would he have to feed her on? Where could she live here?

"If there were not something to eat, how could she live?" the Tatar asked aloud.

He was paid only ten kopecks for working all day and all night at the oar; it is true that travelers gave him tips for tea and for vodka, but the men shared all they received among themselves, and gave nothing to the Tatar, but only laughed at him. And from poverty he was hungry, cold, and frightened. . . . Now, when his whole body was aching and shivering, he ought to go into the hut and lie down to sleep; but he had nothing to cover him there, and it was colder than on the river-bank; here he had nothing to cover him either, but at least he could make up the fire. . . .

In another week, when the floods were quite over and they set the ferry going, none of the ferrymen but Semyon would be wanted, and the Tatar would begin going from village to village begging for alms and for work. His wife was only seventeen; she was beautiful, spoilt, and shy; could she possibly go from village to village begging alms with her face unveiled? No, it was terrible even to think of that. . . .

It was already getting light; the barge, the bushes of willow on the water, and the waves could be clearly discerned, and if one looked round there was the steep clay slope; at the bottom of it the hut thatched with dingy brown straw, and the huts of the village lay clustered higher up. The cocks were already crowing in the village.

The rusty red clay slope, the barge, the river, the strange, unkind people, hunger, cold, illness, perhaps all that was not real. Most likely it was all a dream, thought the Tatar. He felt that he was asleep and heard his own snoring. . . . Of course he was at home in the Simbirsk province, and he had only to call his wife by name for her to answer; and in the next room was his mother. . . . What terrible dreams there are, though! What are they for? The Tatar smiled and opened his eyes. What river was this, the Volga?

Snow was falling.

"Boat!" was shouted on the further side. "Boat!"

The Tatar woke up, and went to wake his mates and row over to the other side. The ferrymen came on to the river-bank, putting on their torn sheepskins as they walked, swearing with voices husky from sleepiness and shivering from the cold. On waking from their sleep, the river, from which came a breath of piercing cold, seemed to strike them as revolting and horrible. They jumped into the barge without hurrying themselves. . . . The Tatar and the three ferrymen took the long, broad-bladed oars, which in the darkness looked like the claws of crabs; Semyon leaned his stomach against the tiller. The shout on the other side still continued, and two shots were fired from a revolver, probably with the idea that the ferrymen were asleep or had gone to the pothouse in the village.

"All right, you have plenty of time," said Semyon in the tone of a man convinced that there was no necessity in this world to hurry—that it would lead to nothing, anyway.

The heavy, clumsy barge moved away from the bank and floated between the willow-bushes, and only the willows slowly moving back showed that the barge was not standing still but moving. The ferrymen swung the oars evenly in time; Semyon lay with his stomach on the tiller and, describing a semicircle in the air, flew from one side to the other. In the darkness it looked as though the men were sitting on some antediluvian animal with long paws, and were moving on it through a cold, desolate land, the land of which one sometimes dreams in nightmares.

They passed beyond the willows and floated out into the open. The creak and regular splash of the oars was heard on the further shore, and a shout came: "Make haste! make haste!"

Another ten minutes passed, and the barge banged heavily against the landing-stage.

"And it keeps sprinkling and sprinkling," muttered Semyon, wiping the snow from his face; "and where it all comes from God only knows."

On the bank stood a thin man of medium height, in a jacket lined with fox-fur and in a white lambskin cap. He was standing at a little distance from his horses and not moving; he had a gloomy, concentrated expression, as though he were trying to remember something and angry with his untrustworthy memory. When Semyon went up to him and took off his cap, smiling, he said:

"I am hastening to Anastasyevka. My daughter's worse again, and they say that there is a new doctor at Anastasyevka."

They dragged the carriage on to the barge and floated back. The man whom Semyon addressed as Vassily Serge-yitch stood all the time motionless, tightly compressing his thick lips and staring off into space; when his coachman asked permission to smoke in his presence he made no answer, as though he had not heard. Semyon, lying with his stomach on the tiller, looked mockingly at him and said:

"Even in Siberia people can live—can li-ive!"

There was a triumphant expression on Canny's face, as though he had proved something and was delighted that things had happened as he had foretold. The unhappy help-lessness of the man in the foxskin coat evidently afforded him great pleasure.

"It's muddy driving now, Vassily Sergeyitch," he said when the horses were harnessed again on the bank. "You should have put off going for another fortnight, when it will be drier. Or else not have gone at all. . . . If any good would come of your going—but as you know yourself, people have been driving about for years and years, day and night, and it's always been no use. That's the truth."

Vassily Sergeyitch tipped him without a word, got into his carriage and drove off.

"There, he has galloped off for a doctor!" said Semyon, shrinking from the cold. "But looking for a good doctor is like chasing the wind in the fields or catching the devil by the tail, plague take your soul! What a queer chap, Lord forgive me a sinner!"

The Tatar went up to Canny, and, looking at him with hatred and repulsion, shivering, and mixing Tatar words with his broken Russian, said: "He is good . . . good; but you are bad! You are bad! The gentleman is a good soul, excellent, and you are a beast, bad! The gentleman is alive, but you are a dead carcass. . . . God created man to be alive, and to have joy and grief and sorrow; but you want nothing, so you are not alive, you are stone, clay! A stone wants nothing and you want nothing. You are a stone, and God does not love you, but He loves the gentleman!"

Everyone laughed; the Tatar frowned contemptuously, and with a wave of his hand wrapped himself in his rags and went to the camp-fire. The ferrymen and Semyon sauntered to the hut.

"It's cold," said one ferryman huskily as he stretched himself on the straw with which the damp clay floor was covered.

"Yes, it's not warm," another assented. "It's a dog's life. . . ."

They all lay down. The door was thrown open by the wind and the snow drifted into the hut; nobody felt inclined to get up and shut the door: they were cold, and it was too much trouble.

"I am all right," said Semyon as he began to doze. "I wouldn't wish anyone a better life."

"You are a tough one, we all know. Even the devils won't take you!"

Sounds like a dog's howling came from outside.

"What's that? Who's there?"

"It's the Tatar crying."

"I say. . . . He's a queer one!"

"He'll get u-used to it!" said Semyon, and at once fell asleep.

The others were soon asleep too. The door remained unclosed.

1892

My Life

THE SUPERINTENDENT said to me: "I only keep you out of regard for your worthy father; but for that you would have been sent flying long ago." I replied to him: "You flatter me too much, Your Excellency, in assuming that I am capable of flying." And then I heard him say: "Take that gentleman away; he gets upon my nerves."

Two days later I was dismissed. And in this way I have, during the years I have been regarded as grown-up, lost nine situations, to the great mortification of my father, the architect of our town. I have served in various departments, but all these nine jobs have been as alike as one drop of water is to another: I had to sit, write, listen to rude or stupid observations, and go on doing so till I was dismissed.

When I came in to my father he was sitting buried in a low armchair with his eyes closed. His dry, emaciated face, with a shade of dark blue where it was shaved (he looked like an old Catholic organist), expressed meekness and resignation. Without responding to my greeting or opening his eyes, he said:

"If my dear wife and your mother were living, your life would have been a source of continual distress to her. I see the Divine Providence in her premature death. I beg you, unhappy boy," he continued, opening his eyes, "tell me: what am I to do with you?"

In the past when I was younger my friends and relations had known what to do with me: some of them used to advise me to volunteer for the army, others to get a job in a pharmacy, and others in the telegraph department; now that I am over twenty-five, that grey hairs are beginning to show on my temples, and that I have been already in the army, and in a pharmacy, and in the telegraph department, it would seem that all earthly possibilities have been exhausted, and people have given up advising me, and merely sigh or shake their heads.

"What do you think about yourself?" my father went on. "By the time they are your age, young men have a secure social position, while look at you: you are a proletarian, a beggar, a burden on your father!"

And as usual he proceeded to declare that the young people of today were on the road to perdition through infidelity, materialism, and self-conceit, and that amateur theatricals ought to be prohibited, because they seduced young people from religion and their duties.

"Tomorrow we shall go together, and you shall apologise to the superintendent and promise to work conscientiously," he said in conclusion. "You ought not to remain one single day with no regular position in society."

"I beg you to listen to me," I said sullenly, expecting nothing good from this conversation. "What you call a position in society is the privilege of capital and education. Those who have neither wealth nor education earn their daily bread by manual labour, and I see no grounds for my being an exception."

"When you begin talking about manual labour it is always stupid and vulgar!" said my father with irritation. "Understand, you dense fellow—understand, you addlepate, that besides coarse physical strength you have the divine spirit, a spark of the holy fire, which distinguishes you in the most striking way from the ass or the reptile, and brings you nearer to the Deity! This fire is the fruit of the efforts of the best of mankind during thousands of years. Your great-grandfather Poloznev, the general, fought at Borodino; your grandfather was a poet, an orator, and a Marshal of Nobility; your uncle is a schoolmaster; and lastly, I, your father, am an architect! All the Poloznevs have guarded the sacred fire for you to put it out!"

"One must be just," I said. "Millions of people put up with manual labour."

"And let them put up with it! They don't know how to do anything else! Anybody, even the most abject fool or criminal, is capable of manual labour; such labour is the distinguishing mark of the slave and the barbarian, while the holy fire is vouchsafed only to a few!"

To continue this conversation was unprofitable. My father worshipped himself, and nothing was convincing to him but what he said himself. Besides, I knew perfectly well that the disdain with which he talked of physical toil was founded not so much on reverence for the sacred fire as on a secret dread that I should become a workman and should set the whole town talking about me; what was worse, all my contemporaries had long ago taken their degrees and were getting on well, and the son of the manager of the State Bank was already a collegiate assessor, while I, my father's only son, was nothing! To continue the conversation was unprofitable and unpleasant, but I still sat on and feebly retorted, hoping that I might at last be understood. The whole question, of course, was clear and simple, and only concerned with the means of my earning my living; but the simplicity of it was not seen, and I was talked to in mawkishly rounded phrases of Borodino, of the sacred fire, of my uncle a forgotten poet, who had once written poor and artificial verses; I was rudely called an addlepate and a dense fellow. And how I longed to be understood! In spite of everything, I loved my father and my sister and it had been my habit from childhood to consult them—a habit so deeply rooted that I doubt whether I could ever have got rid of it; whether I were in the right or the wrong, I was in constant dread of wounding them, constantly afraid that my father's thin neck would turn crimson and that he would have a stroke.

"To sit in a stuffy room," I began, "to copy, to compete with a typewriter, is shameful and humiliating for a man of my age. What can the sacred fire have to do with it?"

"It's intellectual work, anyway," said my father. "But that's enough; let us cut short this conversation, and in any case I warn you: if you don't go back to your work again, but follow your contemptible propensities, then my daughter and I will banish you from our hearts. I shall strike you out of my will, I swear by the living God!"

With perfect sincerity to prove the purity of the motives by which I wanted to be guided in all my doings, I said:

"The question of inheritance does not seem very important to me. I shall renounce it all beforehand."

For some reason or other, quite to my surprise, these words were deeply resented by my father. He turned crimson.

"Don't dare to talk to me like that, stupid!" he shouted in a thin, shrill voice. "Wastrel!" and with a rapid, skilful, and habitual movement he slapped me twice in the face. "You are forgetting yourself."

When my father beat me as a child I had to stand up straight, with my hands held stiffly to my trouser seams, and look him straight in the face. And now when he hit me I was utterly overwhelmed, and, as though I were still a child, drew myself up and tried to look him in the face. My father was old and very thin, but his delicate muscles must have been as strong as leather, for his blows hurt a good deal.

I staggered back into the passage, and there he snatched up his umbrella, and with it hit me several times on the head and shoulders; at that moment my sister opened the drawing-room door to find out what the noise was, but at once turned away with a look of horror and pity without uttering a word in my defence.

My determination not to return to the government office, but to begin a new life of toil, was not to be shaken. All that was left for me to do was to fix upon the special employment, and there was no particular difficulty about that, as it seemed to me that I was very strong and fitted for the very heaviest labour. I was faced with a monotonous life of toil in the midst of hunger, coarseness, and stench, continually preoccupied with earning my daily bread. And— who knows?—as I returned from my work along Great Dvoryansky Street, I might very likely envy Dolzhikov, the engineer, who lived by intellectual work, but, at the moment, thinking over all my future hardships made me lighthearted. At times I had dreamed of spiritual activity, imagining myself a teacher, a doctor, or a writer, but these dreams remained dreams. The taste for intellectual pleasures—for the theatre, for instance, and for reading—was a passion with me, but whether I had any ability for intellectual work I don't know. At school I had had an unconquerable aversion for Greek, so that I was only in the fourth class when they had to take me from school. For a long while I had coaches preparing me for the fifth class. Then

I served in various government offices, spending the greater part of the day in complete idleness, and I was told that was intellectual work. My activity in the scholastic and official sphere had required neither mental application nor talent, nor special qualifications, nor creative impulse; it was mechanical. Such intellectual work I put on a lower level than physical toil; I despise it, and I don't think that for one moment it could serve as a justification for an idle, careless life, as it is indeed nothing but a sham, one of the forms of that same idleness. Real intellectual work I have in all probability never known.

Evening came on. We lived in Great Dvoryansky Street; it was the principal street in the town, and in the absence of decent public gardens our *beau monde* used to use it as a promenade in the evenings. This charming street did to some extent take the place of a public garden, as on each side of it there was a row of poplars which smelled sweet, particularly after rain, and acacias, tall bushes of lilac, wild cherries and apple trees hung over the fences and palings. The May twilight, the tender young greenery with its shifting shades, the scent of the lilac, the buzzing of the insects, the stillness, the warmth—how fresh and marvellous it all is, though spring is repeated every year! I stood at the garden gate and watched the passers-by. With most of them I had grown up and at one time played pranks; now they might have been disconcerted by my being near them, for I was poorly and unfashionably dressed, and they used to say of my very narrow trousers and huge, clumsy boots that they were like sticks of macaroni stuck in boats. Besides, I had a bad reputation in the town because I had no decent social position, and used often to play billiards in cheap taverns, and also, perhaps, because I had on two occasions been hauled up before an officer of the police, though I had done nothing whatever to account for this.

In the big house opposite someone was playing the piano at Dolzhikov's. It was beginning to get dark, and stars were twinkling in the sky. Here my father, in an old top hat with wide upturned brim, walked slowly by with my sister on his arm, bowing in response to greetings.

"Look up," he said to my sister, pointing to the sky with the same umbrella with which he had beaten me that afternoon. "Look up at the sky! Even the tiniest stars are all worlds! How insignificant is man in comparison with the universe!"

And he said this in a tone that suggested that it was particularly agreeable and flattering to him that he was so insignificant. How absolutely devoid of talent and imagination he was! Sad to say, he was the only architect in the town, and in the fifteen to twenty years that I could remember not one single decent house had been built in it. When anyone asked him to plan a house, he usually drew first the reception hall and drawing-room: just as in old days the boarding-school misses always started from the stove when they danced, so his artistic ideas could only begin and develop from the hall and drawing-room. To them he tacked on a dining-room, a nursery, a study, linking the rooms together with doors, and so they all inevitably turned into passages, and every one of them had two or even three unnecessary doors. His imagination must have been lacking in clearness, extremely muddled, curtailed. As though feeling that something was lacking, he invariably had recourse to all sorts of outbuildings, planting one beside another; and I can see now the narrow entries, the pokey little passages, the crooked staircases leading to half landings where one could not stand upright, and where, instead of a floor, there were three huge steps like the shelves of a bathhouse; and the kitchen was invariably in the basement with a brick floor and vaulted ceilings. The front of the house had a harsh, stubborn expression; the lines of it were stiff and timid; the roof was low-pitched and, as it were, squashed down; and the fat, well-fed-looking chimneys were invariably crowned by wire caps with squeaking black cowls. And for some reason all these houses, built by my father exactly like one another, vaguely reminded me of his top hat and the back of his head, stiff and stubborn-looking. In the course of years they have grown used in the town to the poverty of my father's imagination. It has taken root and become our local style.

This same style my father had brought into my sister's life also, beginning with christening her Kleopatra (just as he had named me Misail). When she was a little girl he scared her by references to the stars, to the sages of ancient times, to our ancestors, and discoursed at length on the nature of life and duty; and now, when she was twenty-six, he kept up the same habits, allowing her to walk arm in arm with no one but himself, and imagining for some reason that sooner or later a suitable young man would be sure to appear, and desire to enter into matrimony with her from respect for her father's personal qualities. She adored my father, feared him, and believed in his exceptional intelligence.

It was quite dark, and gradually the street grew empty. The music had ceased in the house opposite; the gate was thrown wide open, and a team with three horses trotted frolicking along our street with a soft tinkle of little bells. That was the engineer going for a drive with his daughter. It was bedtime.

I had my own room in the house, but I lived in a shed in the yard, under the same roof as a brick barn which had been built some time or other, probably to keep harness in; great hooks were driven into the wall. Now it was not wanted, and for the last thirty years my father had stowed away in it his newspapers, which for some reason he had bound in half-yearly volumes and allowed nobody to touch. Living here, I was less liable to be seen by my father and his visitors, and I fancied that if I did not live in a real room, and did not go into the house every day to dinner, my father's words that I was a burden upon him did not sound so offensive.

My sister was waiting for me. Unseen by my father, she had brought me some supper: not a very large slice of cold veal and a piece of bread. In our house such sayings as: "A penny saved is a penny gained," and "Take care of the pence and the pounds will take care of themselves," and so on, were frequently repeated, and my sister, weighed down by these vulgar maxims, did her utmost to cut down the expenses, and so we fared badly. Putting the plate on the table, she sat down on my bed and began to cry.

"Misail," she said, "what a way to treat us!"

She did not cover her face; her tears dropped on her bosom and hands, and there was a look of distress on her face. She fell back on the pillow, and abandoned herself to her tears, sobbing and quivering all over.

"You have left the service again . . ." she articulated. "Oh, how awful it is!"

"But do understand, Sister, do understand . . ." I said, and I was overcome with despair because she was crying.

As ill luck would have it, the kerosene in my little lamp was exhausted; it began to smoke and was on the point of going out, and the old hooks on the walls looked down sullenly, and their shadows flickered.

"Have mercy on us," said my sister, sitting up. "Father is in terrible distress and I am ill; I shall go out of my mind. What will become of you?" she said, sobbing and stretching out her arms to me. "I beg you, I implore you, for our dear mother's sake, I beg you to go back to the office!"

"I can't, Kleopatra!" I said, feeling that a little more and I should give way. "I cannot!"

"Why not?" my sister went on. "Why not? Well, if you can't get on with the head, look out for another post. Why shouldn't you get a situation on the railway, for instance? I have just been talking to Anyuta Blagovo; she declares they would take you on the railway line and even promised to try and get a post for you. For God's sake, Misail, think a little! Think a little, I implore you."

We talked a little longer and I gave way. I said that the thought of a job on the railway that was being constructed had never occurred to me, and that if she liked I was ready to try it.

She smiled joyfully through her tears and squeezed my hand, and then went on crying because she could not stop, while I went to the kitchen for some kerosene.

2

Among the devoted supporters of amateur theatricals, concerts, and *tableaux vivants* for charitable objects the Azhogins, who lived in their own house in Great Dvoryansky Street, took a foremost place; they always provided the room and took upon themselves all the troublesome arrangements and the expenses. They were a family of wealthy landowners who had an estate of some nine thousand acres in the district and a capital house, but they did not care for the country and lived winter and summer alike in the town. The family consisted of the mother, a tall, spare, refined lady, with short hair, a short jacket, and a flat-looking skirt in the English fashion, and three daughters who, when they were spoken of, were called not by their names but simply: the eldest, the middle, and the youngest. They all had ugly sharp chins, and were short-sighted and round-shouldered. They were dressed like their mother, they lisped disagreeably, and yet, in spite of that, infallibly took part in every performance and were continually doing something with a charitable object—acting, reciting, singing. They were very serious and never smiled, and even in a musical comedy they played without the faintest trace of gaiety, with a businesslike air, as though they were engaged in bookkeeping.

I loved our theatricals, especially the numerous, noisy, and rather incoherent rehearsals, after which they always gave a supper. In the choice of the plays and the distribution of the parts I had no hand at all. The post assigned to me lay behind the scenes. I painted the scenes, copied out the parts, prompted, made up the actors' faces; and I was entrusted, too, with various stage effects such as thunder, the singing of nightingales, and so on. Since I had no proper social position and no decent clothes, at the rehearsals I held aloof from the rest in the shadows of the wings and maintained a shy silence.

I painted the scenes at the Azhogins' either in the barn or in the yard. I was assisted by Andrei Ivanov, a house painter, or, as he called himself, a contractor for all kinds of house decorations, a tall, very thin, pale man of fifty, with a hollow chest, with sunken temples, with blue rings round his eyes, rather terrible to look at in fact. He was afflicted with some internal malady, and every autumn and spring people said that he wouldn't recover, but after being laid up for a while he would get up and say afterwards with surprise: "I have escaped dying again."

In the town he was called Radish, and they declared that this was his real name. He was as fond of the theatre as I was, and as soon as rumours reached him that a performance was being got up he threw aside all his work and went to the Azhogins' to paint scenes.

The day after my talk with my sister, I was working at the Azhogins' from morning till night. The rehearsal was fixed for seven o'clock in the evening, and an hour before it began all the amateurs were gathered together in the hall, and the eldest, the middle, and the youngest Azhogins were pacing about the stage, reading from manuscript books. Radish, in a long rusty-red overcoat and a scarf muffled round his neck, already stood leaning with his head against the wall, gazing with a devout expression at the stage. Madam Azhogin went up first to one and then to another guest, saying something agreeable to each. She had a way of gazing into one's face and speaking softly as though telling a secret.

"It must be difficult to paint scenery," she said softly, coming up to me. "I was just talking to Madam Mufke about superstitions when I saw you come in. My goodness, my whole life I have been waging war against superstitions! To convince the servants what nonsense all their terrors are, I always light three candles, and begin all my important undertakings on the thirteenth of the month."

Dolzhikov's daughter came in, a plump, fair beauty, dressed, as people said, in everything from Paris. She did not act, but a chair was set for her on the stage at the rehearsals, and the performances never began till she had appeared in the front row, dazzling and astounding everyone with her fine clothes. As a product of the capital she was allowed to make remarks during the rehearsals; and she did so with a sweet indulgent smile, and one could see that she looked upon our performance as a childish amusement. It was said she had studied singing at the Petersburg Conservatoire, and even sang for a whole winter in a private opera. I thought her very charming, and I usually watched her through the rehearsals and performances without taking my eyes off her.

I had just picked up the manuscript book to begin prompting when my sister suddenly made her appearance. Without taking off her cloak or hat, she came up to me and said:

"Come along, I beg you."

I went with her. Anyuta Blagovo, also in her hat and wearing a dark veil, was standing behind the scenes at the door. She was the daughter of the assistant president of the court, who had held that office in our town almost ever since the establishment of the circuit court. Since she was tall and had a good figure, her assistance was considered indispensable for *tableaux vivants,* and when she represented a fairy or something like Glory her face burned with

shame; but she took no part in dramatic performances, and
came to the rehearsals only for a moment on some special
errand and did not go into the hall. Now, too, it was evident
that she had only looked in for a minute.

"My father was speaking about you," she said drily,
blushing and not looking at me. "Dolzhikov has promised
you a post on the railway line. Apply to him tomorrow; he
will be at home."

I bowed and thanked her for the trouble she had taken.

"And you can give up this," she said, indicating the exercise book.

My sister and she went up to Madam Azhogin and for
two minutes they were whispering with her looking towards
me; they were consulting about something.

"Yes, indeed," said Madam Azhogin, softly coming up
to me and looking intently into my face. "Yes, indeed, if
this distracts you from serious pursuits"—she took the
manuscript book from my hands—"you can hand it over
to someone else; don't distress yourself, my friend, go home,
and good luck to you."

I said good-bye to her and went away overcome with
confusion. As I went down the stairs I saw my sister and
Anyuta Blagovo going away; they were hastening along,
talking eagerly about something, probably about my going
into the railway service. My sister had never been at a rehearsal before, and now she was most likely conscience-
stricken and afraid her father might find out that, without
his permission, she had been to the Azhogins'!

I went to Dolzhikov's next day between twelve and one.
The footman conducted me into a very beautiful room,
which was the engineer's drawing-room, and, at the same
time, his working study. Everything here was soft and elegant, and, for a man so unaccustomed to luxury as I was, it
seemed strange. There were costly rugs, huge armchairs,
bronzes, pictures, gold and plush frames; among the photo-
graphs scattered about the walls there were very beautiful
women, clever, lovely faces, easy attitudes; from the drawing-room there was a door leading straight into the garden
on to a veranda: one could see lilac trees; one could see a
table laid for lunch, a number of bottles, a bouquet of roses;
there was a fragrance of spring and expensive cigars, a
fragrance of happiness—and everything seemed as though

it would say: "Here is a man who has lived and laboured and has attained at last the happiness possible on earth." The engineer's daughter was sitting at the writing table, reading a newspaper.

"You have come to see my father?" she asked. "He is having a shower bath; he will be here directly. Please sit down and wait."

I sat down.

"I believe you live opposite?" she questioned me, after a brief silence.

"Yes."

"I am so bored that I watch you every day out of the window; you must excuse me," she went on, looking at the newspaper. "And I often see your sister; she always has such a look of kindness and concentration."

Dolzhikov came in. He was rubbing his neck with a towel.

"Papa, Monsieur Poloznev," said his daughter.

"Yes, yes, Blagovo was telling me." He turned briskly to me without giving me his hand. "But listen, what can I give you? What sort of posts have I got? You are a queer set of people!" he went on aloud in a tone as though he were giving me a lecture. "A score of you keep coming to me every day; you imagine I am the head of a department! I am constructing a railway line, my friends; I have employment for heavy labour: I need mechanics, smiths, navvies, carpenters, well sinkers, and none of you can do anything but sit and write! You are all clerks."

And he seemed to me to have the same air of happiness as his rugs and easy chairs. He was stout and healthy, ruddy-cheeked and broad-chested, in a print cotton shirt and full trousers like a toy china sledge driver. He had a curly, round beard—and not a single grey hair—a hooked nose, and clear, dark, guileless eyes.

"What can you do?" he went on. "There is nothing you can do! I am an engineer. I am a man of an assured position, but before they gave me a railway line I was for years in harness; I have been a practical mechanic. For two years I worked in Belgium as an oiler. You can judge for yourself, my dear fellow; what kind of work can I offer you?"

"Of course that is so . . ." I muttered in extreme confusion, unable to face his clear, guileless eyes.

"Can you work the telegraph, anyway?" he asked, after a moment's thought.

"Yes, I have been a telegraph clerk."

"Hm! Well, we will see then. Meanwhile, go to Dubech-nya. I have got a fellow there, but he is a wretched creature."

"And what will my duties consist of?" I asked.

"We shall see. Go there; meanwhile I will make arrangements. Only please don't get drunk, and don't worry me with requests of any sort, or I shall send you packing."

He turned away from me without even a nod.

I bowed to him and his daughter, who was reading a newspaper, and went away. My heart felt so heavy that when my sister began asking me how the engineer had received me, I could not utter a single word.

I got up early in the morning, at sunrise, to go to Dubech-nya. There was not a soul in out Great Dvoryansky Street; everyone was asleep, and my footsteps rang out with a solitary, hollow sound. The poplars, covered with dew, filled the air with soft fragrance. I was sad and did not want to go away from the town. I was fond of my native town. It seemed to be so beautiful and so snug! I loved the fresh greenery, the still, sunny morning, the chiming of our bells; but the people with whom I lived in this town were boring, alien to me, sometimes even repulsive. I did not like them nor understand them.

I did not understand what these sixty-five thousand people lived for and by. I knew that Kimry lived by boots, that Tula made samovars and guns, that Odessa was a sea-port, but what our town was, and what it did, I did not know. Great Dvoryansky Street and the two other smartest streets lived on the interest of capital, or on salaries received by officials from the public treasury; but what the other eight streets, which ran parallel for over two miles and vanished beyond the hills, lived upon was always an insoluble riddle to me. And the way those people lived one is ashamed to describe! No garden, no theatre, no decent band; the public library and the club library were only visited by Jewish youths, so that the magazines and new books lay for months uncut; rich and well-educated people slept in close, stuffy bedrooms, on wooden bedsteads in-

fested with bugs; their children were kept in revoltingly dirty
rooms called nurseries, and the servants, even the old and
respected ones, slept on the floor in the kitchen, covered
with rags. On ordinary days the houses smelled of beetroot
soup, and on fast days of sturgeon cooked in sun-flower
oil. The food was not good, and the drinking water was
unwholesome. In the town council, at the governor's, at
the head priest's, on all sides in private houses, people had
been saying for years and years that our town had not a
good and cheap water supply, and that it was necessary to
obtain a loan of two hundred thousand from the Treasury
for laying on water; very rich people, of whom three dozen
could have been counted up in our town, and who at times
lost whole estates at cards, drank the polluted water, too,
and talked all their lives with great excitement of a loan for
the water supply—and I did not understand that; it seemed
to me it would have been simpler to take the two hundred
thousand out of their own pockets and lay it out on that
object.

I did not know one honest man in the town. My father
took bribes and imagined that they were given him out of
respect for his moral qualities; at the high school, in order
to be moved up rapidly from class to class, the boys went
to board with their teachers, who charged them exorbitant
sums; the wife of the military commander took bribes from
the recruits when they were called up before the board and
even deigned to accept refreshments from them, and on one
occasion could not get up from her knees in church because
she was drunk; the doctors took bribes, too, when the recruits came up for examination, and the town doctor and
the veterinary surgeon levied a regular tax on the butchers'
shops and the restaurants; at the district school they did a
trade in certificates, qualifying for partial exemption from
military service; the higher clergy took bribes from the
humbler priests and from the church elders; at the municipal, the artisans', and all the other boards every petitioner
was pursued by a shout: "Don't forget your thanks!" and
the petitioner would turn back to give sixpence or a shilling.
And those who did not take bribes, such as the higher
officials of the Department of Justice, were haughty, offered
two fingers instead of shaking hands, were distinguished by
the frigidity and narrowness of their judgments, spent a

great deal of time over cards, drank to excess, married heiresses, and undoubtedly had a pernicious corrupting influence on those around them. It was only the girls who had still the fresh fragrance of moral purity; most of them had higher impulses, pure and honest hearts; but they had no understanding of life and believed that bribes were given out of respect for moral qualities, and after they were married grew old quickly, let themselves go completely, and sank hopelessly in the mire of vulgar, petty bourgeois existence.

3

A railway line was being constructed in our neighbourhood. On the eve of feast days the streets were thronged with ragged fellows whom the townspeople called "navvies," and of whom they were afraid. And more than once I had seen one of these tatterdemalions, with a bloodstained countenance, being led to the police station, while a samovar or some linen, wet from the wash, was carried behind by way of material evidence. The navvies usually congregated about the taverns and the market place; they drank, ate, and used bad language, and pursued with shrill whistles every woman of light behaviour who passed by. To entertain this hungry rabble our shopkeepers made cats and dogs drunk with vodka, or tied an old kerosene can to a dog's tail; a hue and cry was raised, and the dog dashed along the street, jingling the can, squealing with terror; it fancied some monster was close upon its heels; it would run far out of the town into the open country and there sink exhausted. There were in the town several dogs who went about trembling with their tails between their legs; and people said this diversion had been too much for them and had driven them mad.

A station was being built four miles from the town. It was said that the engineers asked for a bribe of fifty thousand roubles for bringing the line right up to the town, but the town council would only consent to give forty thousand; they could not come to an agreement over the difference, and now the townspeople regretted it, as they had to make a road to the station and that, it was reckoned, would cost more. The sleepers and rails had been laid throughout the whole length of the line, and trains ran up and down it,

bringing building materials and labourers, and further progress was only delayed on account of the bridges which
Dolzhikov was building, and some of the stations were not
yet finished.

Dubechnya, as our first station was called, was a little
under twelve miles from the town. I walked. The cornfields,
bathed in the morning sunshine, were bright green. It was a
flat, cheerful country, and in the distance there were the
distinct outlines of the station, of ancient barrows, and far-
away homesteads. . . . How nice it was out there in the
open! And how I longed to be filled with the sense of freedom, if only for that one morning, that I might not think of
what was being done in the town, not think of my needs, not
feel hungry! Nothing has so marred my existence as an
acute feeling of hunger, which made images of buckwheat
porridge, *rissoles,* and baked fish mingle strangely with my
best thoughts. Here I was, standing alone in the open
country, gazing upward at a lark which hovered in the air
at the same spot, trilling as though in hysterics, and meanwhile I was thinking: "How nice it would be to eat a piece
of bread and butter!" Or I would sit down by the roadside
to rest, and shut my eyes to listen to the delicious sounds
of May, and what haunted me was the smell of hot potatoes.
Though I was tall and strongly built, I had as a rule little
to eat, and so the predominant sensation throughout the
day was hunger, and perhaps that was why I knew so well
how it is that such multitudes of people toil merely for their
daily bread and can talk of nothing but things to eat.

At Dubechnya they were plastering the inside of the station and building a wooden upper storey to the pumping
shed. It was hot; there was a smell of lime, and the workmen sauntered listlessly between the heaps of shavings and
mortar rubble. The pointsman lay asleep near his sentry
box, and the sun was blazing full on his face. There was not
a single tree. The telegraph wire hummed faintly and hawks
were perching on it here and there. I, wandering, too,
among the heaps of rubbish, and not knowing what to do,
recalled how the engineer, in answer to my question what
my duties would consist in, had said: "We shall see when
you are there"; but what could one see in that wilderness?

The plasterers spoke of the foreman, and of a certain
Fyodot Vasilyev. I did not understand, and gradually I

was overcome by depression—the physical depression in which one is conscious of one's arms and legs and huge body and does not know what to do with them or where to put them.

After I had been walking about for at least a couple of hours, I noticed that there were telegraph poles running off to the right from the station, and that they ended a mile or a mile and a half away at a white stone wall. The workmen told me the office was there, and at last I reflected that that was where I ought to go.

It was a very old manor house, deserted long ago. The wall round it, of porous white stone, was mouldering and had fallen away in places, and the lodge, the blank wall of which looked out on the open country, had a rusty roof with patches of tin plate gleaming here and there on it. Within the gates could be seen a spacious courtyard overgrown with rough weeds, and an old manor house with sun blinds on the windows, and a high roof red with rust. Two lodges, exactly alike, stood one on each side of the house to right and to left: one had its windows nailed up with boards; near the other, of which the windows were open, there was washing on the line, and there were calves moving about. The last of the telegraph poles stood in the courtyard, and the wire from it ran to the window of that lodge whose blank wall looked out into the open country. The door stood open; I went in. By the telegraph apparatus a gentleman with a curly dark head, wearing a reefer coat made of sailcloth, was sitting at a table; he glanced at me morosely from under his brows but immediately smiled and said:

"Hullo, Better-than-nothing!"

It was Ivan Cheprakov, an old schoolfellow of mine, who had been expelled from the second class for smoking. We used at one time, during autumn, to catch goldfinches, finches, and linnets together, and to sell them in the market early in the morning, while our parents were still in their beds. We watched for flocks of migrating starlings and shot at them with small shot; then we picked up those that were wounded, and some of them died in our hands in terrible agonies (I remember to this day how they moaned in the cage at night); those that recovered we sold and swore with the utmost effrontery that they were all cocks. On one occasion at the market I had only one starling left, which I had offered to purchasers in vain, till at last I sold it for a farthing. "Anyway, it's better than nothing," I said to comfort myself, as I put the farthing in my pocket, and from that day the street urchins and the schoolboys called after me: "Better-than-nothing"; and to this day the street boys and the shopkeepers mock at me with the nickname, though no one remembers how it arose.

Cheprakov was not of robust constitution: he was narrow-chested, round-shouldered, and long-legged. He wore a silk cord for a tie, had no trace of a waistcoat, and his boots were worse than mine, with the heels trodden down on one side. He stared, hardly even blinking, with a strained expression, as though he were just going to catch something, and he was always in a fuss.

"You wait a minute," he would say fussily. "You listen. . . . Whatever was I talking about?"

We got into conversation. I learned that the estate on which I now was had until recently been the property of the Cheprakovs, and had only the autumn before passed into the possession of Dolzhikov, who considered it more profitable to put his money into land than to keep it in notes, and had already bought up three good-sized mortaged estates in our neighbourhood. At the sale Cheprakov's mother has reserved for herself the right to live for the next two years in one of the lodges at the side and had obtained a post for her son in the office.

"I should think he could buy!" Cheprakov said of the engineer. "See what he fleeces out of the contractors alone! He fleeces everyone!"

Then he took me to dinner, deciding fussily that I should live with him in the lodge and have my meals from his mother.

"She is a bit stingy," he said, "but she won't charge you much."

It was very cramped in the little rooms in which his mother lived; they were all, even the passage and the entry, piled up with furniture which had been brought from the big house after the sale; and the furniture was all old-fashioned mahogany. Madam Cheprakov, a very stout middle-aged lady with slanting Chinese eyes, was sitting in a big armchair by the window, knitting a stocking. She received me ceremoniously.

"This is Poloznev, Mamma," Cheprakov introduced me. "He is going to serve here."

"Are you a nobleman?" she asked in a strange, disagreeable voice: it seemed to me to sound as though fat were bubbling in her throat.

"Yes," I answered.

"Sit down."

The dinner was a poor one. Nothing was served but pies filed with bitter curd, and milk soup. Elena Nikiforovna, who presided, kept blinking in a queer way, first with one eye and then with the other. She talked, she ate, but yet there was something deathly about her whole figure, and one almost fancied the faint smell of a corpse. There was only a glimmer of life in her, a glimmer of consciousness that she had been a lady who had once had her own serfs, that she was the widow of a general whom the servants had to address as "Your Excellency"; and when these feeble relics of life flickered up in her for an instant she would say to her son:

"Jean, you are not holding your knife properly!"

Or she would say to me, drawing a deep breath, with the mincing air of a hostess trying to entertain a visitor:

"You know we have sold our estate. Of course, it is a pity, we are used to the place, but Dolzhikov has promised to make Jean stationmaster of Dubechnya, so we shall not have to go away; we shall live here at the station, and that is just the same as being on our own property! The engineer is so nice! Don't you think he is very handsome?"

Until recently the Cheprakovs had lived in a wealthy style, but since the death of the general everything had been changed. Elena Nikiforovna had taken to quarrelling with the neighbours, to going to law, and to not paying her bailiffs or her labourers; she was in constant terror of being robbed, and in some ten years Dubechnya had become unrecognisable.

Behind the great house was an old garden which had already run wild, and was overgrown with rough weeds and bushes. I walked up and down the verandah, which was still solid and beautiful; through the glass doors one could see a room with parqueted floor, probably the drawing-room; an old-fashioned piano and pictures in deep mahogany frames—there was nothing else. In the old flower beds all that remained were peonies and poppies, which lifted their white and bright red heads above the grass. Young maples and elms, already nibbled by the cows, grew beside the paths, drawn up and hindering each other's growth. The garden was thickly overgrown and seemed impassable, but this was only near the house where there stood poplars, fir trees, and old lime trees, all of the same age, relics of the former avenues. Further on, beyond them, the garden had been cleared for the sake of hay, and here it was not moist and stuffy, and there were no spiders' webs in one's mouth and eyes. A light breeze was blowing. The further one went the more open it was, and here in the open space were cherries, plums, and spreading apple trees, disfigured by props and by canker, and pear trees so tall that one could not believe they were pear trees. This part of the garden was let to some shopkeepers of the town, and it was protected from thieves and starlings by a feeble-minded peasant who lived in a shanty in it.

The garden, growing more and more open, till it became definitely a meadow, sloped down to the river, which was overgrown with green weeds and osiers. Near the milldam was the millpond, deep and full of fish; a little mill with a thatched roof was working away with a wrathful sound, and frogs croaked furiously. Circles passed from time to time over the smooth, mirrorlike water, and the water lilies trembled, stirred by the lively fish. On the further side of the river was the little village Dubechnya. The still, blue millpond was alluring with its promise of coolness and peace. And now all thi. the millpond and the mill and the snug-looking banks—belonged to the engineer!

And so my new work began. I received and forwarded telegrams, wrote various reports, and made fair copies of the notes of requirements, the complaints, and the reports sent to the office by the illiterate foremen and workmen. But for the greater part of the day I did nothing but walk about the room waiting for telegrams, or made a boy sit in the lodge while I went for a walk in the garden, until the boy ran to tell me that there was a tapping at the operating machine. I had dinner at Madam Cheprakov's. Meat we had very rarely: our dishes were all made of milk, and Wednesdays and Fridays were fast days, and on those days we had pink plates which were called Lenten plates.

Madam Cheprakov was continually blinking—it was her invariable habit, and I always felt ill at ease in her presence.

As there was not enough work in the lodge for one, Cheprakov did nothing, but simply dozed, or went with his gun to shoot ducks on the millpond. In the evenings he drank too much in the village or the station, and, before going to bed, stared in the looking glass and said: "Hullo, Ivan Cheprakov."

When he was drunk he was very pale and kept rubbing his hands and laughing with a sound like a neigh: "Hee-hee-hee!" By way of bravado he used to strip and run about the country naked. He used to eat flies and say they were rather sour.

4

One day, after dinner, he ran breathless into the lodge and said: "Go along, your sister has come."

I went out, and there I found a hired brake from the town standing before the entrance of the great house. My sister had come in it with Anyuta Blagovo and a gentleman in a military tunic. Going up closer I recognised the latter: it was the brother of Anyuta Blagovo, the army doctor.

"We have come to you for a picnic," he said; "is that all right?"

My sister and Anyuta wanted to ask how I was getting on here, but both were silent and simply gazed at me. I was silent too. They saw that I did not like the place, and tears came into my sister's eyes, while Anyuta Blagovo turned crimson.

We went into the garden. The doctor walked ahead of us all and said enthusiastically:

"What air! Holy Mother, what air!"

In appearance he was still a student. And he walked and talked like a student, and the expression of his grey eyes was as keen, honest, and frank as a nice student's. Beside his tall and handsome sister he looked frail and thin; and his beard was thin too, and his voice, too, was a thin but rather agreeable tenor. He was serving in a regiment somewhere and had come home to his people for a holiday, and said he was going in the autumn to Petersburg for his examination as a doctor of medicine. He was already a family man, with a wife and three children; he had married very young, in his second year at the university, and now people in the town said he was unhappy in his family life and was not living with his wife.

"What time is it?" my sister asked uneasily. "We must get back in good time. Papa let me come to see my brother on condition I was back at six."

"Oh, bother your papa!" sighed the doctor.

I set the samovar. We put down a carpet before the verandah of the great house and had our tea there, and the doctor knelt down, drank out of his saucer, and declared that he now knew what bliss was. Then Cheprakov came with the key and opened the glass door, and we all went into the house. There it was half dark and mysterious, and smelled of mushrooms, and our footsteps had a hollow sound as though there were cellars under the floor. The doctor stopped and touched the keys of the piano, and it responded faintly with a husky, quivering, but melodious chord; he tried his voice and sang a song, frowning and tapping impatiently with his foot when some note was mute. My sister did not talk about going home but walked about the rooms and kept saying:

"How happy I am! How happy I am!"

There was a note of astonishment in her voice, as though it seemed to her incredible that she, too, could feel light-hearted. It was the first time in my life I had seen her so happy. She actually looked prettier. In profile she did not look nice; her nose and mouth seemed to stick out and had an expression as though she were pouting, but she had beautiful dark eyes, a pale, very delicate complexion, and a touching expression of goodness and melancholy, and when she talked she seemed charming and even beautiful. We both, she and I, took after our mother, were broad-shouldered, strongly built, and capable of endurance, but her pallor was a sign of ill-health; she often had a cough, and I sometimes caught in her face that look one sees in people who are seriously ill, but for some reason conceal the fact. There was something naïve and childish in her gaiety now, as though the joy that had been suppressed and smothered in our childhood by harsh education had now suddenly awakened in her soul and found a free outlet.

But when evening came on and the horses were brought

round, my sister sank into silence and looked thin and shrunken, and she got into the brake as though she were going to the scaffold.

When they had all gone, and the sound had died away . . . I remembered that Anyuta Blagovo had not said a word to me all day.

"She is a wonderful girl!" I thought. "Wonderful girl!"

St. Peter's fast came, and we had nothing but Lenten dishes every day. I was weighed down by physical depression due to idleness and my unsettled position, and dissatisfied with myself. Listless and hungry, I lounged about the garden and only waited for a suitable mood to go away.

Towards evening one day, when Radish was sitting in the lodge, Dolzhikov, very sunburnt and grey with dust, walked in unexpectedly. He had been spending three days on his land, and had come now to Dubechnya by the steamer, and walked to us from the station. While waiting for the carriage, which was to come for him from the town, he walked round the grounds with his bailiff, giving orders in a loud voice, then sat for a whole hour in our lodge, writing letters. While he was there telegrams came for him, and he himself tapped off the answers. We three stood in silence at attention.

"What a muddle!" he said, glancing contemptuously at a record book. "In a fortnight I am transferring the office to the station, and I don't know what I am to do with you, my friends."

"I do my best, your honour," said Cheprakov.

"To be sure, I see how you do your best. The only thing you can do is to take your salary." The engineer went on, looking at me, "You keep relying on patronage to *faire la carrière* as quickly and as easily as possible. Well, I don't care for patronage. No one took any trouble on my behalf. Before they gave me a railway contract I went about as a mechanic and worked in Belgium as an oiler. And you, Pantelei, what are you doing here?" he asked, turning to Radish. "Drinking with them?"

He, for some reason, always called humble people Pantelei, and such as me and Cheprakov he despised, and called them drunkards, beasts, and rabble to their faces. Altogether he was cruel to humble subordinates and used to fine them and turn them off coldly without explanations.

At last the horses came for him. As he said good-bye he promised to turn us all off in a fortnight; he called his bailiff a blockhead; and then, lolling at ease in his carriage, drove back to the town.

"Andrei Ivanich," I said to Radish, "take me on as a workman."

"Oh, all right!"

And we set off together in the direction of the town. When the station and the big house with its buildings were left behind I asked: "Andrei Ivanich, why did you come to Dubechnya this evening?"

"In the first place my fellows are working on the line, and in the second place I came to pay the general's lady my interest. Last year I borrowed fifty roubles from her, and I pay her now a rouble a month interest."

The painter stopped and took me by the button.

"Misail Alexeyich, our angel," he went on. "The way I look at it is that if any man, gentle or simple, takes even the smallest interest, he is doing evil. There cannot be truth and justice in such a man."

Radish, lean, pale, dreadful-looking, shut his eyes, shook his head, and, in the tone of a philosopher, pronounced:

"Lice consume the grass, rust consumes the iron, and lying the soul. Lord, have mercy upon us sinners."

5

Radish was not practical and was not at all good at forming an estimate; he took more work than he could get through, and when calculating he was agitated, lost his head, and so was almost always out of pocket over his jobs. He undertook painting, glazing, paper hanging, and even tiling roofs, and I can remember his running about for three days to find tilers for the sake of a paltry job. He was a first-rate workman; he sometimes earned as much as ten roubles a day; and if it had not been for the desire at all costs to be a master, and to be called a contractor, he would probably have had plenty of money.

He was paid by the job, but he paid me and the other workmen by the day, from one and twopence to two shillings a day. When it was fine and dry we did all kinds of outside work, chiefly painting roofs. When I was new to the

work it made my feet burn as though I were walking on hot
bricks, and when I put on felt boots they were hotter than
ever. But this was only at first; later on I got used to it, and
everything went swimmingly. I was living now among
people to whom labour was obligatory, inevitable, and who
worked like cart horses, often with no idea of the moral
significance of labour, and, indeed, never using the word
"labour" in conversation at all. Beside them I, too, felt like a
cart horse, growing more and more imbued with the feeling
of the obligatory and inevitable character of what I was doing, and this made my life easier, setting me free from all
doubt and uncertainty.

At first everything interested me, everything was new, as
though I had been born again. I could sleep on the ground
and go about barefoot, and that was extremely pleasant;
I could stand in a crowd of the common people and be no
constraint to anyone, and when a cab horse fell down in the
street I ran to help it up without being afraid of soiling
my clothes. And the best of it all was, I was living on my
own account and no burden to anyone!

Painting roofs, especially with our own oil and colours,
was regarded as a particularly profitable job, and so this
rough, dull work was not disdained, even by such good
workmen as Radish. In short breeches, and wasted, purple-
looking legs, he used to go about the roofs, looking like a
stork, and I used to hear him, as he plied his brush, breathing heavily and saying: "Woe, woe to us sinners!"

He walked about the roofs as freely as though he were
upon the ground. In spite of his being ill and pale as a
corpse, his agility was extraordinary: he used to paint the
domes and cupolas of the churches without scaffolding, like
a young man, with only the help of a ladder and a rope,
and it was rather horrible when standing on a height far
from the earth; he would draw himself up erect, and for
some unknown reason pronounce:

"Lice consume grass, rust consumes iron, and lying the
soul!"

Or, thinking about something, would answer his thoughts
aloud:

"Anything may happen! Anything may happen!"

When I went home from my work, all the people who
were sitting on benches by the gates, all the shopmen and

boys and their employers, made sneering and spiteful remarks after me, and this upset me at first and seemed to be simply monstrous.

"Better-than-nothing!" I heard on all sides. "House painter! Yellow ochre!"

And none behaved so ungraciously to me as those who had only lately been humble people themselves and had earned their bread by hard manual labour. In the streets full of shops I was once passing an ironmonger's when water was thrown over me as though by accident, and on one occasion someone darted out with a stick at me, while a fishmonger, a grey-headed old man, barred my way and said, looking at me angrily:

"I am not sorry for you, you fool! It's your father I am sorry for."

And my acquaintances were for some reason overcome with embarrassment when they met me. Some of them looked upon me as a queer fish and a comic fool; others were sorry for me; others did not know what attitude to take up to me, and it was difficult to make them out. One day I met Anyuta Blagovo in a side street near Great Dvoryansky Street. I was going to work, and was carrying two long brushes and a pail of paint. Recognising me, Anyuta flushed crimson.

"Please do not bow to me in the street," she said nervously, harshly, and in a shaking voice, without offering me her hand, and tears suddenly gleamed in her eyes. "If to your mind all this is necessary, so be it . . . so be it, but I beg you not to meet me!"

I no longer lived in Great Dvoryansky Street, but in the suburb with my old nurse Karpovna, a good-natured but gloomy old woman, who always foreboded some harm, was afraid of all dreams, and even in the bees and wasps that flew into her room saw omens of evil, and the fact that I had become a workman, to her thinking, boded nothing good.

"Your life is ruined," she would say, mournfully shaking her head, "ruined."

Her adopted son Prokofy, a huge, uncouth, redheaded fellow of thirty, with bristling moustaches, a butcher by trade, lived in the little house with her. When he met me in the passage he would make way for me in respectful silence and if he was drunk he would salute me with all five fingers at once. He used to have supper in the evening, and through the partition wall of boards I could hear him clear his throat and sigh as he drank off glass after glass.

"Mamma," he would call in an undertone.

"Well," Karpovna, who was passionately devoted to her adopted son, would respond: "What is it, Sonny?"

"I can show you a testimony of my affection, Mamma. All this earthly life I will cherish you in your declining years in this vale of tears, and when you die I will bury you at my expense; I have said it, and you can believe it."

I got up every morning before sunrise and went to bed early. We house painters ate a great deal and slept soundly; the only thing amiss was that my heart used to beat violently at night. I did not quarrel with my mates. Violent abuse, desperate oaths, and wishes such as, "Blast your eyes," or "Cholera take you," never ceased all day, but, nevertheless, we lived on very friendly terms. The other fellows suspected me of being some sort of religious sectary and made good-natured jokes at my expense, saying that even my own father had disowned me, and thereupon would add that they rarely went into the temple of God themselves, and that many of them had not been to confession for ten years. They justified this laxity on their part by saying that a painter among men was like a jackdaw among birds.

The men had a good opinion of me, and treated me with respect; it was evident that my not drinking, not smoking, but leading a quiet, steady life pleased them very much. It was only an unpleasant shock to them that I took no hand in stealing oil and did not go with them to ask for tips from people on whose property we were working. Stealing oil and paints from those who employed them was a house painter's custom and was not regarded as theft, and it was remarkable that even so upright a man as Radish would always carry away a little white lead and oil as he went home from work. And even the most respectable old fellows, who owned the houses in which they lived in the suburb, were not ashamed to ask for a tip, and it made me feel vexed and ashamed to see the men go in a body to congratulate some nonentity on the commencement or the completion of the job and thank him with degrading servility when they had received a few coppers.

With people on whose work they were engaged they behaved like wily courtiers, and almost every day I was reminded of Shakespeare's Polonius.

"I fancy it is going to rain," the man whose house was being painted would say, looking at the sky.

"It is, there is not a doubt it is," the painters would agree.

"I don't think it is a rain cloud, though. Perhaps it won't rain after all."

"No, it won't, your honour! I am sure it won't."

But their attitude to their patrons behind their backs was usually one of irony, and when they saw, for instance, a gentleman sitting in the verandah reading a newspaper, they would observe:

"He reads the paper, but I daresay he has nothing to eat."

I never went home to see my own people. When I came back from work I often found waiting for me little notes, brief and anxious, in which my sister wrote to me about my father; that he had been particularly preoccupied at dinner and had eaten nothing, or that he had been giddy and staggering, or that he had locked himself in his room and had not come out for a long time. Such items of news troubled me; I could not sleep, and at times even walked up and down Great Dvoryansky Street at night by our house, looking in at the dark windows and trying to guess whether everything was well at home. On Sundays my sister came to see me, but came in secret, as though it were not to see me but our nurse. And if she came in to see me she was very pale, with tear-stained eyes, and she began crying at once.

"Our father will never live through this," she would say. "If anything should happen to him—God grant it may not —your conscience will torment you all your life. It's awful, Misail; for our mother's sake I beseech you: reform your ways."

"My darling sister," I would say, "how can I reform my ways if I am convinced that I am acting in accordance with my conscience? Do understand!"

"I know you are acting on your conscience, but perhaps it could be done differently, somehow, so as not to wound anybody."

"Ah, holy Saints!" the old woman sighed through the

door. "Your life is ruined! There will be trouble, my dears, there will be trouble!"

6

One Sunday Dr. Blagovo turned up unexpectedly. He was wearing a military tunic over a silk shirt and high boots of patent leather.

"I have come to see you," he began, shaking my hand heartily like a student. "I am hearing about you every day, and I have been meaning to come and have a heart-to-heart talk, as they say. The boredom in the town is awful, there is not a living soul, no one to say a word to. It's hot, Holy Mother," he went on, taking off his tunic and sitting in his silk shirt. "My dear fellow, let me talk to you."

I was dull myself and had for a long time been craving for the society of someone not a house painter. I was genuinely glad to see him.

"I'll begin by saying," he said, sitting down on my bed, "that I sympathise with you from the bottom of my heart and deeply respect the life you are leading. They don't understand you here in the town, and, indeed, there is no one to understand, seeing that, as you know, they are all, with very few exceptions, regular Gogolesque pig faces here. But I saw what you were at once that time at the picnic. You are a noble soul, an honest, high-minded man! I respect you and feel it a great honour to shake hands with you!" he went on enthusiastically. "To have made such a complete and violent change of life as you have done, you must have passed through a complicated spiritual crisis, and to continue this manner of life now, and to keep up to the high standard of your convictions continually, must be a strain on your mind and heart from day to day. Now to begin our talk, tell me, don't you consider that if you had spent your strength of will, this strained activity, all these powers on something else, for instance, on gradually becoming a great scientist, or artist, your life would have been broader and deeper and would have been more productive?"

We talked, and when we got upon manual labour I expressed this idea: that what is wanted is that the strong should not enslave the weak, that the minority should not be a parasite on the majority, nor a vampire for ever sucking its vital sap; that is, all, without exception, strong and weak, rich and poor, should take part equally in the struggle for existence, each one on his own account, and that there was no better means for equalising things in that way than manual labour, in the form of universal service, compulsory for all.

"Then do you think everyone without exception ought to engage in manual labour?" asked the doctor.

"Yes."

"And don't you think that if everyone, including the best men, the thinkers and great scientists, taking part in the struggle for existence, each on his own account, is going to waste his time breaking stones and painting roofs, may not that threaten a grave danger to progress?"

"Where is the danger?" I asked. "Why, progress is in deeds of love, in fulfilling the moral law; if you don't enslave anyone, if you don't oppress anyone, what further progress do you want?"

"But, excuse me," Blagovo suddenly fired up, rising to his feet. "But, excuse me! If a snail in its shell busies itself over perfecting its own personality and muddles about with the moral law, do you call that progress?"

"Why muddles?" I said, offended. "If you don't force your neighbour to feed and clothe you, to transport you from place to place, and defend you from your enemies, surely in the midst of a life entirely resting on slavery, that is progress, isn't it? To my mind it is the most important progress, and perhaps the only one possible and necessary for man."

"The limits of universal world progress are in infinity, and to talk of some 'possible' progress limited by our needs and temporary theories is, excuse my saying so, positively strange."

"If the limits of progress are in infinity as you say, it follows that its aims are not definite," I said. "To live without knowing definitely what you are living for!"

"So be it! But that 'not knowing' is not so dull as your 'knowing.' I am going up a ladder which is called progress, civilisation, culture; I go on and up without knowing definitely where I am going, but really it is worth living for the sake of that delightful ladder; while you know what you are living for, you live for the sake of some people's not enslaving others, that the artist and the man who rubs his paints may dine equally well. But you know that's the petty, bourgeois, kitchen, grey side of life, and surely it is revolting to live for that alone? If some insects do enslave others, bother them, let them devour each other! We need not think about them. You know they will die and decay just the same, however zealously you rescue them from slavery. We must think of that great millennium which awaits humanity in the remote future."

Blagovo argued warmly with me, but at the same time one could see he was troubled by some irrelevant idea.

"I suppose your sister is not coming?" he said, looking at his watch. "She was at our house yesterday, and said she would be seeing you today. You keep saying slavery, slavery . . ." he went on. "But you know that is a special question, and all such questions are solved by humanity gradually."

We began talking of doing things gradually. I said that "the question of doing good or evil everyone settles for himself, without waiting till humanity settles it by the way of gradual development. Moreover, this gradual process has more than one aspect. Side by side with the gradual development of human ideas the gradual growth of ideas of another order is observed. Serfdom is no more, but the capitalist system is growing. And in the very heyday of emancipating ideas, just as in the days of Baty, the majority feeds, clothes, and defends the minority while remaining hungry, inadequately clad, and defenceless. Such an order of things can be made to fit in finely with any tendencies and currents of thought you like, because the art of enslaving is also gradually being cultivated. We no longer flog our servants in the stable, but we give to slavery refined forms, at least, we succeed in finding a justification for it in each particular case. Ideas are ideas with us, but if now, at the end of the nineteenth century, it were possible to lay the burden of the most unpleasant of our physiological functions upon the working class, we should certainly do so, and afterwards, of course, justify ourselves by saying that if the best people, the thinkers and great scientists, were to waste their precious time on these functions, progress might be menaced with great danger."

But at this point my sister arrived. Seeing the doctor, she

was flustered and troubled, and began saying immediately that it was time for her to go home to her father.

"Kleopatra Alexyevna," said Blagovo earnestly, pressing both hands to his heart, "what will happen to your father if you spend half an hour or so with your brother and me?"

He was frank and knew how to communicate his liveliness to others. After a moment's thought, my sister laughed, and all at once became suddenly gay as she had been at the picnic. We went out into the country, and, lying in the grass, went on with our talk, and looked towards the town where all the windows facing west were like glittering gold because the sun was setting.

After that, whenever my sister was coming to see me Blagovo turned up too, and they always greeted each other as though their meeting in my room was accidental. My sister listened while the doctor and I argued, and at such times her expression was joyfully enthusiastic, full of tenderness and curiosity, and it seemed to me that a new world she had never dreamed of before, and which she was now striving to fathom, was gradually opening before her eyes. When the doctor was not there she was quiet and sad, and now if she sometimes shed tears as she sat on my bed it was for reasons of which she did not speak.

In August Radish ordered us to be ready to go to the railway line. Two days before we were "banished" from the town my father came to see me. He sat down and in a leisurely way, without looking at me, wiped his red face, then took out of his pocket our town *Messenger*, and deliberately, with emphasis on each word, read out the news that the son of the branch manager of the State Bank, a young man of my age, had been appointed head of a department in the Exchequer.

"And now look at you," he said, folding up the newspaper; "a beggar, in rags, good for nothing! Even working-class people and peasants obtain education in order to become men, while you, a Poloznev, with ancestors of rank and distinction, aspire to the gutter! But I have not come here to talk to you; I have washed my hands of you——" he added in a stifled voice, getting up. "I have come to find out where your sister is, you worthless fellow. She left home after dinner, and here it is nearly eight and she is not back. She has taken to going out frequently without telling me;

she is less dutiful—and I see in it your evil and degrading influence. Where is she?"

In his hand he had the umbrella I knew so well, and I was already flustered and drew myself up like a schoolboy, expecting my father to begin hitting me with it, but he noticed my glance at the umbrella and most likely that restrained him.

"Live as you please!" he said. "I shall not give you my blessing!"

"Holy Saints!" my nurse muttered behind the door. "You poor, unlucky child! Ah, my heart bodes ill!"

I worked on the railway line. It rained without stopping all August; it was damp and cold; they had not carried the corn in the fields, and on big farms where the wheat had been cut by machines it lay not in sheaves but in heaps, and I remember how those luckless heaps of wheat turned blacker every day and the grain was sprouting in them. It was hard to work; the pouring rain spoiled everything we managed to do. We were not allowed to live or to sleep in the railway buildings, and we took refuge in the damp and filthy mud huts in which the navvies had lived during the summer, and I could not sleep at night for the cold and the wood lice crawling on my face and hands. And when we worked near the bridges the navvies used to come in the evenings in a gang, simply in order to beat the painters—it was a form of sport to them. They used to beat us, to steal our brushes. And to annoy us and rouse us to fight they used to spoil our work; they would, for instance, smear over the signal boxes with green paint. To complete our troubles, Radish took to paying us very irregularly. All the painting work on the line was given out to a contractor; he gave it out to another; and this subcontractor gave it to Radish after subtracting twenty per cent for himself. The job was not a profitable one in itself, and the rain made it worse; time was wasted; we could not work while Radish was obliged to pay the fellows by the day. The hungry painters almost came to beating him, called him a cheat, a bloodsucker, a Judas, while he, poor fellow, sighed, lifted up his hand to heaven in despair, and was continually going to Madam Cheprakov for money.

7

Autumn came on, rainy, dark, and muddy. The season of unemployment set in, and I used to sit at home out of work for three days at a stretch, or did various little jobs, not in the painting line. For instance, I wheeled earth, earning about fourpence a day by it. Dr. Blagovo had gone away to Petersburg, my sister had given up coming to see me. Radish was laid up at home ill, expecting death from day to day.

And my mood was autumnal too. Perhaps because, having become a workman, I saw our town life only from the seamy side, it was my lot almost every day to make discoveries which reduced me almost to despair. Those of my fellow citizens, about whom I had no opinion before, or who had externally appeared perfectly decent, turned out now to be base, cruel people, capable of any dirty action. We common people were deceived, cheated, and kept waiting for hours together in the cold entry or the kitchen; we were insulted and treated with the utmost rudeness. In the autumn I papered the reading-room and two other rooms at the club; I was paid a penny three-farthings the piece, but had to sign a receipt at the rate of twopence halfpenny, and when I refused to do so, a gentleman of benevolent appearance in gold-rimmed spectacles, who must have been one of the club committee, said to me:

"If you say much more, you blackguard, I'll pound your face into a jelly!"

And when the flunkey whispered to him who I was, the son of Poloznev, the architect, he became embarrassed, turned crimson, but immediately recovered himself and said: "Devil take him."

In the shops they palmed off on us workmen putrid meat, musty flour, and tea that had been used and dried again; the police hustled us in church, the assistants and nurses in the hospital plundered us, and if we were too poor to give them a bribe they revenged themselves by bringing us food in dirty vessels. In the post office the pettiest official considered he had a right to treat us like animals, and to shout with coarse insolence: "You wait!" "Where are you shoving to?" Even the house dogs were unfriendly to us and fell upon us with peculiar viciousness. But the thing that struck me most of all in my new position was the complete lack of justice, what is defined by the peasants in the words: "They have forgotten God." Rarely did a day pass without swindling. We were swindled by the merchants who sold us oil, by the contractors and the workmen and the people who employed us. I need not say that there could never be a question of our rights, and we always had to ask for the money we earned as though it were a charity, and to stand waiting for it at the back door, cap in hand.

I was papering a room at the club next to the reading-room; in the evening, when I was just getting ready to go, the daughter of Dolzhikov, the engineer, walked into the room with a bundle of books under her arm.

I bowed to her.

"Oh, how do you do!" she said, recognising me at once, and holding out her hand. "I'm very glad to see you."

She smiled and looked with curiosity and wonder at my smock, my pail of paste, the paper stretched on the floor; I was embarrassed, and she, too, felt awkward.

"You must excuse my looking at you like this," she said. "I have been told so much about you. Especially by Dr. Blagovo; he is simply in love with you. And I have made the acquaintance of your sister too; a sweet, dear girl, but I can never persuade her that there is nothing awful about your adopting the simple life. On the contrary, you have become the most interesting man in the town."

She looked again at the pail of paste and the wallpaper, and went on:

"I asked Dr. Blagovo to make me better acquainted with you, but apparently he forgot, or had not time. Anyway, we are acquainted all the same, and if you would come to see me quite simply I should be extremely indebted to you. I so long to have a talk. I am a simple person," she added, holding out her hand to me, "and I hope that you will feel no constraint with me. My father is not here, he is in Petersburg."

She went off into the reading-room, rustling her skirts, while I went home, and for a long time could not get to sleep.

That cheerless autumn some kind soul, evidently wishing to alleviate my existence, sent me from time to time tea and lemons, or biscuits, or roast game. Karpovna told me that they were always brought by a soldier, and from whom they came she did not know; and the soldier used to enquire whether I was well, and whether I dined every day, and whether I had warm clothing. When the frosts began I was presented in the same way in my absence with a soft knitted scarf brought by the soldier. There was a faint elusive smell of scent about it, and I guessed who my good fairy was. The scarf smelled of lilies of the valley, the favourite scent of Anyuta Blagovo.

Towards winter there was more work and it was more cheerful. Radish recovered, and we worked together in the cemetery church, where we were putting the groundwork on the ikon stand before gilding. It was a clean, quiet job, and, as our fellows used to say, profitable. One could get through a lot of work in a day, and the time passed quickly, imperceptibly. There was no swearing, no laughter, no loud talk. The place itself compelled one to quietness and decent behaviour, and disposed one to quiet, serious thoughts. Absorbed in our work we stood or sat motionless like statues; there was a deathly silence in keeping with the cemetery, so that if a tool fell, or a flame spluttered in the lamp, the noise of such sounds rang out abrupt and resonant and made us look round. After a long silence we would hear a buzzing like the swarming of bees: it was the requiem of a baby being chanted slowly in subdued voices in the porch; or an artist, painting a dove with stars round it on a cupola would begin softly whistling, and, recollecting himself with a start, would at once relapse into silence; or Radish, answering his thoughts, would say with a sigh: "Anything is possible! Anything is possible!" or a slow disconsolate bell would begin ringing over our heads, and the painters would observe that it must be for the funeral of some wealthy person. . . .

My days I spent in this stillness in the twilight of the church, and in the long evenings I played billiards or went to the theatre in the gallery wearing the new trousers I had bought out of my own earnings. Concerts and performance had already begun at the Azhogins'; Radish used to paint the scenes alone now. He used to tell me the plot of the plays and describe the *tableaux vivants* which he witnessed I listened to him with envy. I felt greatly drawn to the re hearsals, but I could not bring myself to go to the Azhogins'.

A week before Christmas Dr. Blagovo arrived. And again we argued and played billiards in the evenings. When he played he used to take off his coat and unbutton his shirt over his chest, and for some reason tried altogether to assume the air of a desperate rake. He did not drink much but made a great uproar about it, and had a special faculty for getting through twenty roubles in an evening at such a poor cheap tavern as the Volga.

My sister began coming to see me again; they both expressed surprise every time on seeing each other, but from her joyful, guilty face it was evident that these meetings were not accidental. One evening, when we were playing billiards, the doctor said to me:

"I say, why don't you go and see Miss Dolzhikov? You don't know Marya Viktorovna; she is a clever creature, a charmer, a simple, good-natured soul."

I described how her father had received me in the spring.

"Nonsense!" laughed the doctor, "the engineer's one thing and she's another. Really, my dear fellow, you mustn't be nasty to her; go and see her sometimes. For instance, let's go and see her tomorrow evening. What do you say?"

He persuaded me. The next evening I put on my new serge trousers, and in some agitation I set off to Mademoiselle Dolzhikov's. The footman did not seem so haughty and terrible, nor the furniture so gorgeous, as on that morning when I had come to ask a favour. Marya Viktorovna was expecting me, and she received me like an old acquaintance, shaking hands with me in a friendly way. She was wearing a grey cloth dress with full sleeves, and had her hair done in the style which we used to call "dogs' ears," when it came into fashion in the town a year before. The hair was combed down over the ears, and this made Marya Viktorovna's face look broader, and she seemed to me this time very much like her father, whose face was broad and red, with something in its expression like a sledge driver. She was handsome and elegant, but not youthful looking; she looked thirty, though in reality she was not more than twenty-five.

"Dear Doctor, how grateful I am to you," she said, making me sit down. "If it hadn't been for him you wouldn't have come to see me. I am bored to death! My father has gone away and left me alone, and I don't know what to do with myself in this town."

Then she began asking me where I was working now, how much I earned, where I lived.

"Do you spend on yourself nothing but what you earn?" she asked.

"No."

"Happy man!" she sighed. "All the evil in life, it seems to me, comes from idleness, boredom, and spiritual emptiness, and all this is inevitable when one is accustomed to living at other people's expense. Don't think I am showing off. I tell you truthfully: it is not interesting or pleasant to be rich. 'Make to yourself friends of the mammon of unrighteousness' is said because there is not and cannot be a mammon that's righteous."

She looked round at the furniture with a grave, cold expression, as though she wanted to count it over, and went on:

"Comfort and luxury have a magical power; little by little they draw into their clutches even strong-willed people. At one time Father and I lived simply, not in a rich style, but now you see how! It is something monstrous," she said, shrugging her shoulders; "we spent up to twenty thousand a year! In the provinces!"

"One comes to look at comfort and luxury as the invariable privilege of capital and education," I said, "and it seems to me that the comforts of life may be combined with any sort of labour, even the hardest and dirtiest. Your father is rich, and yet he says himself that it has been his lot to be a mechanic and an oiler."

She smiled and shook her head doubtfully: "My father sometimes eats bread dipped in kvass," she said. "It's a fancy, a whim!"

At that moment there was a ring and she got up.

"The rich and well-educated ought to work like everyone else," she said, "and if there is comfort it ought to be equal for all. There ought not to be any privileges. But that's enough philosophising. Tell me something amusing. Tell me about the painters. What are they like? Funny?"

The doctor came in; I began telling them about the painters, but, being unaccustomed to talking, I was constrained, and described them like an ethnologist, gravely and tediously. The doctor, too, told us some anecdotes of working-men: he staggered about, shed tears, dropped on his knees, and, even, mimicking a drunkard, lay on the floor; it was as good as a play, and Marya Viktorovna laughed till she cried as she looked at him. Then he played on the piano and sang in his thin, pleasant tenor, while Marya Viktorovna stood by and picked out what he was to sing and corrected him when he made a mistake.

"I've heard that you sing, too?" I enquired.

"Sing, too!" cried the doctor in horror. "She sings exquisitely, a perfect artist, and you talk of her 'singing too'! What an idea!"

"I did study in earnest at one time," she said, answering my question, "but now I have given it up."

Sitting on a low stool she told us of her life in Petersburg and mimicked some celebrated singers, imitating their voices and manner of singing. She made a sketch of the doctor in her album, then of me; she did not draw well, but both the portraits were like us. She laughed and was full of mischief and charming grimaces, and this suited her better than talking about the mammon of unrighteousness, and it seemed to me that she had been talking just before about wealth and luxury, not in earnest, but in imitation of someone. She was a superb comic actress. I mentally compared her with our young ladies, and even the handsome, dignified Anyuta Blagovo could not stand comparison with her; the difference was immense, like the difference between a beautiful, cultivated rose and a wild briar.

We had supper together, the three of us. The doctor and Marya Viktorovna drank red wine, champagne, and coffee with brandy in it; they clinked glasses and drank to friendship, to enlightenment, to progress, to liberty, and they did not get drunk but only flushed, and were continually, for no reason, laughing till they cried. So as not to be tiresome I drank claret too.

"Talented, richly endowed natures," said Mademoiselle Dolzhikov, "know how to live, and go their own way; mediocre people, like myself for instance, know nothing and can do nothing of themselves; there is nothing left for them but to discern some deep social movement, and to float where they are carried by it."

"How can one discern what doesn't exist?" asked the doctor.

"We think so because we don't see it."

"Is that so? The social movements are the invention of the new literature. There are none among us."

An argument began.

"There are no deep social movements among us and never have been," the doctor declared loudly. "There is no end to what the new literature has invented! It has invented intellectual workers in the country, and you may search through all our villages and find at the most some lout in a reefer jacket or a black frockcoat who will make four mistakes in spelling a word of three letters. Cultured life has not yet begun among us. There's the same savagery, the same uniform boorishness, the same triviality, as five hundred years ago. Movements, currents there have been, but it has all been petty, paltry, bent upon vulgar and mercenary interests—and one cannot see anything important in them. If you think you have discerned a deep social movement, and, in following it, you devote yourself to tasks in the modern taste, such as the emancipation of insects from slavery or abstinence from beef *rissoles*, I congratulate you, madam. We must study, and study, and study, and we must wait a bit with our deep social movements; we are not mature enough for them yet; and to tell the truth, we don't know anything about them."

"You don't know anything about them, but I do," said Marya Viktorovna. "Goodness, how tiresome you are to-day!"

"Our duty is to study and to study, to try to accumulate as much knowledge as possible, for genuine social movements arise where there is knowledge; and the happiness of mankind in the future lies only in knowledge. I drink to science!"

"There is no doubt about one thing: one must organise one's life somehow differently," said Marya Viktorovna, after a moment's silence and thought. "Life, such as it has been hitherto, is not worth having. Don't let us talk about it."

As we came away from her the cathedral clock struck two.

"Did you like her?" asked the doctor; "she's nice, isn't she?"

On Christmas Day we dined with Marya Viktorovna, and all through the holidays we went to see her almost every day. There was never anyone there but ourselves, and she was right when she said that she had no friends in the town but the doctor and me. We spent our time for the most part in conversation; sometimes the doctor brought some book or magazine and read aloud to us. In reality he was the first well-educated man I had met in my life: I cannot judge whether he knew a great deal, but he always displayed his knowledge as though he wanted other people to share it. When he talked about anything relating to medicine he was not like any one of the doctors in our town, but made a fresh, peculiar impression upon me, and I fancied that if he liked he might have become a real man of science. And he was perhaps the only person who had a real influence upon me at that tme. Seeing him, and reading the books he gave me, I began little by little to feel a thirst for the knowledge which would have given significance to my cheerless labour. It seemed strange to me, for instance, that I had not known till then that the whole world was made up of sixty elements, I had not known what oil was, what paints were, and that I could have got on without knowing these things. My acquaintance with the doctor elevated me morally too. I was continually arguing with him and, though I usually remained of my own opinion, yet, thanks to him, I began to perceive that everything was not clear to me, and I began trying to work out as far as I could definite convictions in myself that the dictates of conscience might be definite, and that there might be nothing vague in my mind. Yet, though he was the most cultivated and best man in the town, he was nevertheless far from perfection. In his manners, in his habit of turning every conversation into an argument, in his pleasant tenor, even in his friendliness, there was something coarse, like a divinity student, and when he took off his coat and sat in his silk shirt, or flung a tip to a waiter in the restaurant, I always fancied that culture might be all very well, but the Tatar was fermenting in him still.

At Epiphany he went back to Petersburg. He went off in

the morning, and after dinner my sister came in. Without taking off her fur coat and her cap, she sat down in silence, very pale, and kept her eyes fixed on the same spot. She was chilled by the frost and one could see that she was upset by it.

"You must have caught cold," I said.

Her eyes filled with tears; she got up and went out to Karpovna without saying a word to me, as though I had hurt her feelings. And a little later I heard her saying, in a tone of bitter reproach:

"Nurse, what have I been living for till now? What? Tell me, haven't I wasted my youth? All the best years of my life to know nothing but keeping accounts, pouring out tea, counting the halfpence, entertaining visitors, and thinking there was nothing better in the world! Nurse, do understand, I have the cravings of a human being, and I want to live, and they have turned me into something like a housekeeper. It's horrible, horrible!"

She flung her keys towards the door, and they fell with a jingle into my room. They were the keys of the sideboard, of the kitchen cupboard, of the cellar, and of the tea caddy, the keys which my mother used to carry.

"Oh, merciful heavens!" cried the old woman in horror. "Holy Saints above!"

Before going home, my sister came into my room to pick up the keys, and said:

"You must forgive me. Something queer has happened to me lately."

8

On returning home late one evening from Marya Viktorovna's, I found waiting in my room a young police inspector in a new uniform; he was sitting at my table, looking through my books.

"At last," he said, getting up and stretching himself. "This is the third time I have been to you. The governor commands you to present yourself before him at nine o'clock in the morning. Without fail."

He took from me a signed statement that I would act upon His Excellency's command, and went away. This late visit of the police inspector and unexpected invitation to the governor's had an overwhelmingly oppressive effect upon me. From my earliest childhood I have felt terror stricken in the presence of gendarmes, policemen, and law-court officials, and now I was tormented by uneasiness, as though I were really guilty in some way. And I could not get to sleep. My nurse and Prokofy were also upset and could not sleep. My nurse had earache too; she moaned, and several times began crying with pain. Hearing that I was awake, Prokofy came into my room with a lamp and sat down at the table.

"You ought to have a drink of pepper cordial," he said, after a moment's thought. "If one does have a drink in this vale of tears it does no harm. And if Mamma were to pour a little pepper cordial in her ear it would do her a lot of good."

Between two and three he was going to the slaughter-house for the meat. I knew I should not sleep till morning now, and to get through the time till nine o'clock I went with him. We walked with a lantern, while his shopboy Nikolka, aged thirteen, with blue patches on his cheeks from frostbites, a regular young brigand to judge by his expression, drove after us in the sledge, urging on the horse in a husky voice.

"I suppose they will punish you at the governor's." Prokofy said to me on the way. "There are rules of the trade for governors, and rules for the higher clergy, and rules for the officers, and rules for the doctors, and every class has its rules. But you haven't kept to your rules, and you can't be allowed."

The slaughterhouse was behind the cemetery, and till then I had only seen it in the distance. It consisted of three gloomy barns, surrounded by a grey fence, and when the wind blew from that quarter on hot days in summer, it brought a stifling stench from them. Now, going into the yard in the dark, I did not see the barns; I kept coming across horses and sledges, some empty, some loaded up with meat. Men were walking about with lanterns, swearing in a disgusting way. Prokofy and Nikolka swore just as revoltingly, and the air was in a continual uproar with swearing, coughing, and the neighing of horses.

There was a smell of dead bodies and of dung. It was thawing, the snow was changing into mud; and in the darkness it seemed to me that I was walking through pools of blood.

Having piled up the sledges full of meat, we set off to the butcher's shop in the market. It began to get light. Cooks with baskets and elderly ladies in mantles came along one after another. Prokofy, with a chopper in his hand, in a white apron spattered with blood, swore fearful oaths, crossed himself at the church, shouted aloud for the whole market to hear that he was giving away the meat at cost price and even at a loss to himself. He gave short weight and short change, the cooks saw that, but, deafened by his shouts, did not protest and only called him a hangman. Brandishing and bringing down his terrible chopper he threw himself into picturesque attitudes, and each time uttered the sound "Geck" with a ferocious expression, and I was afraid he really would chop off somebody's head or hand.

I spent all the morning in the butcher's shop, and when at last I went to the governor's, my overcoat smelled of meat and blood. My state of mind was as though I were being sent spear in hand to meet a bear. I remember the tall staircase with a striped carpet on it, and the young official, with shiny buttons, who mutely motioned me to the door with both hands, and ran to announce me. I went into a hall luxuriously but frigidly and tastelessly furnished, and the high, narrow mirrors in the spaces between the walls, and the bright yellow window curtains, struck the eye particularly unpleasantly. One could see that the governors were changed, but the furniture remained the same. Again the young official motioned me with both hands to the door, and I went up to a big green table at which a military general, with the Order of Vladimir on his breast, was standing.

"Monsieur Poloznev, I have asked you to come," he began, holding a letter in his hand, and opening his mouth like a round "o," "I have asked you to come here to inform you of this. Your highly respected father has appealed by letter and by word of mouth to the Marshal of Nobility begging him to summon you and to lay before you the inconsistency of your behaviour with the rank of the nobility to which you have the honour to belong. His excellency Alexandr Pavlovich, justly supposing that your conduct might serve as a bad example, and considering that mere persuasion on his part would not be sufficient, but that official intervention in earnest was essential, presents me here in this letter with his views in regard to you, which I share."

He said this, quietly, respectfully, standing erect, as though I were his superior officer and looking at me with no trace of severity. His face looked worn and wizened and was all wrinkles; there were bags under his eyes, his hair was dyed, and it was impossible to tell from his appearance how old he was—forty or sixty.

"I trust," he went on, "that you appreciate the delicacy of our honoured Alexandr Pavlovich, who has addressed himself to me not officially, but privately. I, too, have asked you to come here unofficially, and I am speaking to you, not as a governor, but from a sincere regard for your father. And so I beg you either to alter your line of conduct and return to duties in keeping with your rank, or, to avoid setting a bad example, remove to another district where you are not known, and where you can follow any occupation you please. In the other case, I shall be forced to take extreme measures."

He stood for half a minute in silence, looking at me with his mouth open.

"Are you a vegetarian?" he asked.

"No, Your Excellency, I eat meat."

He sat down and drew some papers towards him. I bowed and went out.

It was not worth while now to go to work before dinner. I went home to sleep, but could not sleep from an unpleasant, sickly feeling, induced by the slaughterhouse and my conversation with the governor; and when the evening came I went, gloomy and out of sorts, to Marya Viktorovna. I told her how I had been at the governor's, while she stared at me in perplexity as though she did not believe it, then suddenly began laughing gaily, loudly, irrepressibly, as only good-natured laughter-loving people can.

"If only one could tell that in Petersburg!" she brought out, almost falling over with laughter, and propping herself against the table. "If one could tell that in Petersburg!"

9

Now we used to see each other often, sometimes twice a day. She used to come to the cemetery almost every day after dinner, and read the epitaphs on the crosses and tomb-stones while she waited for me. Sometimes she would come into the church, and, standing by me, would look on while I worked. The stillness, the naïve work of the painters and gilders, Radish's sage reflections, and the fact that I did not differ externally from the other workmen, and worked just as they did in my waistcoat with no socks on, and that I was addressed familiarly by them—all this was new to her and touched her. One day a workman, who was painting a dove on the ceiling, called out to me in her presence:

"Misail, hand me up the white paint."

I took him the white paint, and afterwards, when I let myself down by the frail scaffolding, she looked at me, touched to tears and smiling.

"What a dear you are!" she said.

I remembered from my childhood how a green parrot, belonging to one of the rich men of the town, had escaped from its cage, and how for quite a month afterwards the beautiful bird had haunted the town, flying from garden to garden, homeless and solitary. Marya Viktorovna reminded me of that bird.

"There is positively nowhere for me to go now but the cemetery," she said to me with a laugh. "The town has become disgustingly dull. At the Azhogins' they are still reciting, singing, lisping. I have grown to detest them of late; your sister is an unsociable creature; Mademoiselle Blagovo hates me for some reason. I don't care for the theatre. Tell me where am I to go?"

When I went to see her I smelled of paint and turpentine, and my hands were stained—and she liked that; she wanted me to come to her in my ordinary working clothes; but in her drawing-room those clothes made me feel awk-ward. I felt embarrassed, as though I were in uniform, so I always put on my new serge trousers when I went to her. And she did not like that.

"You must own you are not quite at home in your new character," she said to me one day. "Your workman's dress does not feel natural to you; you are awkward in it. Tell me, isn't that because you haven't a firm conviction and are not satisfied? The very kind of work you have chosen—your painting—surely it does not satisfy you, does it?" she asked, laughing. "I know paint makes things look nicer and last longer, but those things belong to rich people who live in towns, and after all they are luxuries. Besides, you have often said yourself that everybody ought to get his bread by the work of his own hands, yet you get money and not bread. Why shouldn't you keep to the literal sense of your words? You ought to be getting bread, that is, you ought to be ploughing, sowing, reaping, threshing, or doing something which has a direct connection with agriculture, for instance, looking after cows, digging, building huts of logs. . . ."

She opened a pretty cupboard that stood near her writing table, and said:

"I am saying all this to you because I want to let you into my secret. *Voilà!* This is my agricultural library. Here I have fields, kitchen garden and orchard, and cattle yard and beehives. I read them greedily and have already learned all the theory to the tiniest detail. My dream, my darling wish, is to go to our Dubechnya as soon as March is here. It's marvellous there, exquisite, isn't it? The first year I shall have a look round and get into things, and the year after I shall begin to work properly myself, putting my back into it as they say. My father has promised to give me Dubechnya and I shall do exactly what I like with it."

Flushed, excited to tears, and laughing, she dreamed aloud how she would live at Dubechnya, and what an interesting life it would be! I envied her. March was near, the days were growing longer and longer, and on bright sunny days water dripped from the roofs at midday, and there was a fragrance of spring; I, too, longed for the country.

And when she said that she should move to Dubechnya, I realised vividly that I should remain in the town alone, and I felt that I envied her with her cupboard of books and her agriculture. I knew nothing of work on the land and did not like it, and I should have liked to have told her that work on the land was slavish toil, but I remembered that something similar had been said more than once by my father, and I held my tongue.

Lent began. Viktor Ivanich, whose existence I had begun to forget, arrived from Petersburg. He arrived unexpectedly, without even a telegram to say he was coming. When I went in, as usual in the evening, he was walking about the drawing-room, telling some story, with his face freshly washed and shaven, looking ten years younger: his daughter was kneeling on the floor, taking out of his trunks boxes, bottles, and books, and handing them to Pavel, the footman. I involuntarily drew back a step when I saw the engineer, but he held out both hands to me and said, smiling, showing his strong white teeth that looked like a sledge driver's:

"Here he is, here he is! Very glad to see you, Monsieur House-painter! Masha has told me all about it; she has been singing your praises. I quite understand and approve," he went on, taking my arm. "To be a good workman is ever so much more honest and more sensible than wasting government paper and wearing a cockade on your head. I myself worked in Belgium with these very hands and then spent two years as a mechanic. . . ."

He was wearing a short reefer jacket and indoor slippers; he walked like a man with the gout, rolling slightly from side to side and rubbing his hands. Humming something, he softly purred and hugged himself with satisfaction at being at home again at last, and able to have his beloved shower bath.

"There is no disputing," he said to me at supper, "there is no disputing; you are all nice and charming people, but for some reason, as soon as you take to manual labour, or go in for saving the peasants, in the long run it all comes to no more than being a dissenter. Aren't you a dissenter? Here you don't take vodka. What's the meaning of that if it is not being a dissenter?"

To satisfy him I drank some vodka and I drank some wine, too. We tasted the cheese, the sausage, the *pâtés,* the pickles, and the savouries of all sorts that the engineer had brought with him, and the wine that had come in his absence from abroad. The wine was first-rate. For some reason the engineer got wine and cigars from abroad without paying duty; the caviare and the dried sturgeon someone sent him for nothing; he did not pay rent for his flat as the owner of the house provided the kerosene for the line;

and altogether he and his daughter produced on me the impression that all the best in the world was at their service and provided for them for nothing.

I went on going to see them, but not with the same eagerness. The engineer made me feel constrained. I could not face his clear, guileless eyes, his reflections wearied and sickened me; I was sickened, too, by the memory that so lately I had been in the employ of this red-faced, well-fed man, and that he had been brutally rude to me. It is true that he put his arm round my waist, slapped me on the shoulder in a friendly way, approved my manner of life, but I felt that, as before, he despised my insignificance, and only put up with me to please his daughter, and I couldn't now laugh and talk as I liked, and I behaved unsociably and kept expecting that in another minute he would address me at Pantelei as he did his footman Pavel. How my pride as a provincial and a workingman was revolted. I, a proletarian, a house painter, went every day to rich people who were alien to me, and whom the whole town regarded as though they were foreigners, and every day I drank costly wines with them and ate unusual dainties—my conscience refused to be reconciled to it! On my way to the house I sullenly avoided meeting people, and looked at them from under my brows as though I really were a dissenter, and when I was going home from the engineer's I was ashamed of my well-fed condition.

Above all I was afraid of being carried away. Whether I was walking along the street, or working, or talking to the other fellows, I was all the time thinking of one thing only, of going in the evening to see Marya Viktorovna and was picturing her voice, her laugh, her movements. When I was getting ready to go to her, I always spent a long time before my nurse's warped looking glass as I fastened my tie; my serge trousers were detestable in my eyes, and I suffered torments, and at the same time despised myself for being so trivial. When she called to me out of the other room that she was not dressed and asked me to wait, I listened to her dressing; it agitated me, I felt as though the ground were giving way under my feet. And when I saw a woman's figure in the street, even at a distance, I invariably compared it. It seemed to me that all our girls and women were vulgar, that they were absurdly dressed and did not know how to hold themselves; and these comparisons aroused a feeling of pride in me: Marya Viktorovna was the best of them all! And I dreamed of her and myself at night.

One evening at supper with the engineer we ate a whole lobster. As I was going home afterwards I remembered that the engineer twice called me "My dear fellow" at supper, and I reflected that they treated me very kindly in that house, as they might an unfortunate big dog that had been kicked out by its owners, that they were amusing themselves with me, and that when they were tired of me they would turn me out like a dog. I felt ashamed and wounded, wounded to the point of tears as though I had been insulted, and, looking up at the sky, I took a vow to put an end to all this.

The next day I did not go to the Dolzhikovs'. Late in the evening, when it was quite dark and raining, I walked along Great Dvoryansky Street, looking up at the windows. Everyone was asleep at the Azhogins', and the only light was in one of the furthest windows. It was Madam Azhogin in her own room, sewing by the light of three candles, imagining that she was combating superstition. Our house was in darkness, but at the Dolzhikovs', on the contrary, the windows were lighted up, but one could distinguish nothing through the flowers and the curtains. I kept walking up and down the street; the cold March rain drenched me through. I heard my father come home from the club; he stood knocking at the gate. A minute later a light appeared at the window, and I saw my sister, who was hastening down with a lamp, while with the other hand she was twisting her thick hair together as she went. Then my father walked about the drawing-room, talking and rubbing his hands, while my sister sat in a low chair, thinking and not listening to what he said.

But then they went away; the light went out. . . . I glanced round at the engineer's, and there, too, all was darkness now. In the dark and the rain I felt hopelessly alone, abandoned to the whims of destiny; I felt that all my doings, my desires, and everything I had thought and said till then were trivial in comparison with my loneliness, in comparison with my present suffering, and the suffering that lay before me in the future. Alas, the thoughts and doings of living creatures are not nearly so significant as their sufferings! And without clearly realising what I was doing, I pulled at the bell of the Dolzhikovs' gate, broke it, and ran along the street like some naughty boy, with a feeling of terror in my heart, expecting every moment that they would come out and recognise me. When I stopped at the end of the street to take breath I could hear nothing but the sound of the rain, and somewhere in the distance a watchman striking on a sheet of iron.

For a whole week I did not go to the Dolzhikovs'. My serge trousers were sold. There was nothing doing in the painting trade. I knew the pangs of hunger again and earned from twopence to fourpence a day where I could, by heavy and unpleasant work. Struggling up to my knees in the cold mud, straining my chest, I tried to stifle my memories, and, as it were, to punish myself for the cheeses and preserves with which I had been regaled at the engineer's. But all the same, as soon as I lay in bed, wet and hungry, my sinful imagination immediately began to paint exquisite, seductive pictures, and with amazement I acknowledged to myself that I was in love, passionately in love, and I fell into a sound, heavy sleep, feeling that hard labour only made my body stronger and younger.

One evening snow began falling most inappropriately, and the wind blew from the north as though winter had come back again. When I returned from work that evening I found Marya Viktorovna in my room. She was sitting in her fur coat and had both hands in her muff.

"Why don't you come to see me?" she asked, raising her clear, clever eyes, and I was utterly confused with delight and stood stiffly upright before her, as I used to stand facing my father when he was going to beat me; she looked into my face and I could see from her eyes that she understood why I was confused.

"Why don't you come to see me?" she repeated. "If you don't want to come, you see, I have come to you."

She got up and come close to me.

"Don't desert me," she said, and her eyes filled with tears. "I am alone, utterly alone."

She began crying and, hiding her face in her muff, articulated:

"Alone! My life is hard, very hard, and in all the world I have no one but you. Don't desert me!"

Looking for a handkerchief to wipe her tears she smiled; we were silent for some time, then I put my arms round her and kissed her, scratching my cheek till it bled with her hatpin as I did it.

And we began talking to each other as though we had been on the closest terms for ages and ages.

10

Two days later she sent me to Dubechnya and I was unutterably delighted to go. As I walked towards the station and afterwards, as I was sitting in the train, I kept laughing from no apparent cause, and people looked at me as though I were drunk. Snow was falling, and there were still frosts in the mornings, but the roads were already dark-coloured and rooks hovered over them, cawing.

At first I had intended to fit up an abode for us two, Masha and me, in the lodge at the side opposite Madam Cheprakov's lodge, but it appeared that the doves and the ducks had been living there for a long time, and it was impossible to clean it without destroying a great number of nests. There was nothing for it but to live in the comfortless rooms of the big house with the sun blinds. The peasants called the house the palace; there were more than twenty rooms in it, and the only furniture was a piano and a child's armchair lying in the attic. And if Masha had brought all her furniture from the town we should even then have been unable to get rid of the impression of immense emptiness and cold. I picked out three small rooms with windows looking into the garden, and worked from early morning till night, setting them to rights, putting in new panes, papering the walls, filling up the holes and chinks in the floors. It was easy, pleasant work. I was continually running to the river to see whether the ice were not going; I kept fancying that starlings were flying. And at night, thinking of Masha, I listened with an unutterably sweet feeling, with clutching delight, to the noise of the rats and the wind droning and knocking above the ceiling. It seemed as though some old house spirit were coughing in the attic.

The snow was deep; a great deal had fallen even at the end of March, but it melted quickly, as though by magic, and the spring floods passed in a tumultuous rush, so that by the beginning of April the starlings were already noisy, and yellow butterflies were flying in the garden. It was exquisite weather. Every day, towards evening, I used to walk to the town to meet Masha, and what a delight it was to walk with bare feet along the gradually drying, still soft road. Halfway I used to sit down and look towards the town, not venturing to go near it. The sight of it troubled me. I kept wondering how the people I knew would behave when they heard of my love. What would my father say? What troubled me particularly was the thought that my life was more complicated, and that I had completely lost all power to set it right, and that, like a balloon, it was bearing me away, God knows whither. I no longer considered the problem how to earn my daily bread, how to live, but thought about—I really don't know what.

Masha used to come in a carriage; I used to get in with her, and we drove to Dubechnya, feeling lighthearted and free. Or, after waiting till the sun had set, I would go back dissatisfied and dreary, wondering why Masha had not come; at the gate or in the garden I would be met by a sweet, unexpected apparition—it was she! It would turn out that she had come by rail and had walked from the station. What a festival it was! In a simple woollen dress with a kerchief on her head, with a modest sunshade, but laced in, slender, in expensive foreign boots—it was a talented actress playing the part of a little workgirl. We looked round our domain and decided which should be her room, and which mine, where we would have our avenue, our kitchen garden, our beehives.

We already had hens, ducks, and geese, which we loved because they were ours. We had, all ready for sowing, oats, clover, timothy grass, buckwheat, and vegetable seeds, and we always looked at all these stores and discussed at length the crop we might get; and everything Masha said to me seemed extraordinarily clever and fine. This was the happiest time of my life.

Soon after St. Thomas's week we were married at our parish church in the village of Kurilovka, two miles from Dubechnya. Masha wanted everything to be done quietly; at her wish our "best men" were peasant lads, the sacristan sang alone, and we came back from the church in a small, jolting chaise which she drove herself. Our only guest from the town was my sister Kleopatra, to whom Masha sent a note three days before the wedding. My sister came in a white dress and wore gloves. During the wedding she cried quietly from joy and tenderness. Her expression was motherly and infinitely kind. She was intoxicated with our happiness and smiled as though she were absorbing a sweet delirium; and, looking at her during our wedding, I realised that for her there was nothing in the world higher than love, earthly love, and that she was dreaming of it secretly, timidly, but continually and passionately. She embraced and kissed Masha, and, not knowing how to express her rapture, said to her of me: "He is good! He is very good!"

Before she went away she changed into her ordinary dress and drew me into the garden to talk to me alone.

"Father is very much hurt," she said, "that you have written nothing to him. You ought to have asked for his blessing. But in reality he is very much pleased. He says that this marriage will raise you in the eyes of all society and that under the influence of Marya Viktorovna you will begin to take a more serious view of life. We talk of nothing but you in the evenings now, and yesterday he actually used the expression: 'Our Misail.' That pleased me. It seems as though he had some plan in his mind, and I fancy he wants to set you an example of magnanimity and be the first to speak of reconciliation. It is very possible he may come here to see you in a day or two."

She hurriedly made the sign of the cross over me several times and said:

"Well, God be with you. Be happy. Anyuta Blagovo is a very clever girl; she says about your marriage that God is sending you a fresh ordeal. To be sure—married life does not bring only joy but suffering too. That's bound to be so."

Masha and I walked a couple of miles to see her on her way; we walked back slowly and in silence, as though we were resting. Masha held my hand, my heart felt light, and I had no inclination to talk about love; we had become closer and more akin now that we were married, and we felt that nothing now could separate us.

"Your sister is a nice creature," said Masha, "but it seems as though she had been tormented for years. Your father must be a terrible man."

I began telling her how my sister and I had been brought up, and what a senseless torture our childhood had really been. When she heard how my father had so lately beaten me, she shuddered and drew closer to me.

"Don't tell me any more," she said. "It's horrible!"

Now she never left me. We lived together in the three rooms in the big house, and in the evenings we bolted the door which led to the empty part of the house, as though someone were living there whom we did not know and were afraid of. I got up early, at dawn, and immediately set to work of some sort. I mended the carts, made paths in the garden, dug the flower beds, painted the roof of the house. When the time came to sow the oats I tried to plough the ground over again, to harrow and to sow, and I did it all conscientiously, keeping up with our labourer; I was worn out, the rain and the cold wind made my face and feet burn for hours afterwards. I dreamed of ploughed land at night. But field labour did not attract me. I did not understand farming, and I did not care for it; it was perhaps because my forefathers had not been tillers of the soil, and the very blood that flowed in my veins was purely of the city. I loved nature tenderly; I loved the fields and meadows and kitchen gardens, but the peasant who turned up the soil with his plough and urged on his pitiful horse, wet and tattered, with his craning neck, was to me the expression of coarse, savage, ugly force, and every time I looked at the peasant's uncouth movements I involuntarily began thinking of the legendary life of the remote past, before men knew the use of fire. The fierce bull that ran with the peasants' herd, and the horses, when they dashed about the village, stamping their hoofs, moved me to fear, and everything rather big, strong, and angry, whether it was the ram with its horns, the gander, or the yard dog, seemed to me the expression of the same coarse, savage force. This mood was particularly strong in me in bad weather, when heavy clouds were hanging over the black ploughed land. Above all, when I was ploughing or sowing, and two or three people stood looking at how I was doing it, I had not the feeling that this work was inevitable and obligatory, and it seemed to me that I was amusing myself. I preferred doing something in the yard, and there was nothing I liked so much as painting the roof.

I used to walk through the garden and the meadow to

our mill. It was let to a peasant of Kurilovka called Stepan, a handsome, dark fellow with a thick black beard, who looked very strong. He did not like the miller's work, and looked upon it as dreary and unprofitable, and only lived at the mill in order not to live at home. He was a leather-worker and was always surrounded by a pleasant smell of tar and leather. He was not fond of talking; he was listless and sluggish and was always sitting in the doorway or on the riverbank, humming "oo-loo-loo." His wife and mother-in-law, both white-faced, languid, and meek, used some-times to come from Kurilovka to see him; they made low bows to him and addressed him formally, "Stepan Petro-vich," while he went on sitting on the riverbank, softly humming "oo-loo-loo," without responding by word or movement to their bows. One hour and then a second would pass in silence. His mother-in-law and wife, after whispering together, would get up and gaze at him for some time, ex-pecting him to look round; then they would make a low bow, and in sugary, chanting voices, say:

"Good-bye, Stepan Petrovich!"

And they would go away. After that Stepan, picking up the parcel they had left, containing cracknels or a shirt, would heave a sigh and say, winking in their direction:

"The female sex!"

The mill with two sets of millstones worked day and night. I used to help Stepan; I liked the work, and when he went off I was glad to stay and take his place.

11

After bright warm weather came a spell of wet; all May it rained and was cold. The sound of the mill wheels and of the rain disposed one to indolence and slumber. The floor trembled, there was a smell of flour, and that, too, induced drowsiness. My wife in a short fur-lined jacket, and in men's high galosh boots, would make her appearance twice a day, and she always said the same thing:

"And this is called summer! Worse than it was in Oc-tober!"

We used to have tea and make the porridge together, or we would sit for hours at a stretch without speaking, waiting for the rain to stop. Once, when Stepan had gone off to the fair, Masha stayed all night at the mill. When we got up we could not tell what time it was, as the rain clouds covered the whole sky; but sleepy cocks were crowing at Dubech-nya, and landrails were calling in the meadows; it was still very, very early. . . . My wife and I went down to the mill-pond and drew out the net which Stepan had thrown in overnight in our presence. A big pike was struggling in it, and a crayfish was twisting about, clawing upwards with its pincers.

"Let them go," said Masha. "Let them be happy too."

Because we got up so early and afterwards did nothing, that day seemed very long, the longest day in my life. To-wards evening Stepan came back and I went home.

"Your father came today," said Masha.

"Where is he?" I asked.

"He has gone away. I would not see him."

Seeing that I remained standing and silent, that I was sorry for my father, she said:

"One must be consistent. I would not see him and sent word to him not to trouble to come and see us again."

A minute later I was out at the gate and walking to the town to explain things to my father. It was muddy, slippery, cold. For the first time since my marriage I felt suddenly sad, and in my brain, exhausted by that long, grey day, there was stirring the thought that perhaps I was not living as I ought. I was worn out; little by little I was overcome by despondency and indolence, I did not want to move or think, and after going on a little I gave it up with a wave of my hand and turned back.

The engineer in a leather overcoat with a hood was standing in the middle of the yard.

"Where's the furniture? There used to be lovely furniture in the Empire style: there used to be pictures, there used to be vases, while now you could play ball in it! I bought the place with the furniture. The devil take her!"

Moisei, a thin, pock-marked fellow of twenty-five, with insolent little eyes, who was in the service of the general's widow, stood near him crumpling up his cap in his hands; one of his cheeks was bigger than the other, as though he had lain too long on it.

"Your honour was graciously pleased to buy the place without the furniture," he brought out irresolutely; "I remember."

"Hold your tongue!" shouted the engineer; he turned crimson and shook with anger . . . and the echo in the garden loudly repeated his shout.

12

When I was doing anything in the garden or the yard, Moisei would stand beside me, and, folding his arms behind his back, he would stand lazily and impudently staring at me with his little eyes. And this irritated me to such a degree that I threw up my work and went away.

From Stepan we heard that Moisei was Madam Cheprakov's lover. I noticed that when people came to her to borrow money they addressed themselves first to Moisei, and once I saw a peasant, black from head to foot—he must have been a coal heaver—bow down at Moisei's feet. Sometimes, after a little whispering, he gave out money himself, without consulting his mistress, from which I concluded that he did a little business on his own account.

He used to shoot in our garden under our windows, carried off victuals from our cellar, borrowed our horses without asking permission, and we were indignant and began to feel as though Dubechnya were not ours; and Masha would say, turning pale:

"Can we really have to go on living with these reptiles another year?"

Madam Cheprakov's son, Ivan, was serving as a guard on our railway line. He had grown much thinner and feebler during the winter, so that a single glass was enough to make him drunk, and he shivered out of the sunshine. He wore the guard's uniform with aversion and was ashamed of it, but considered his post a good one, as he could steal the candles and sell them. My new position excited in him a mixed feeling of wonder, envy, and a vague hope that something of the same sort might happen to him. He used to watch Masha with ecstatic eyes, ask me what had for dinner now, and his lean and ugly face wore a sad and sweetish expression, and he moved his fingers as though he were feeling my happiness with them.

"Listen, Better-than-nothing," he said fussily, relighting his cigarette at every instant; there was always a litter where he stood, for he wasted dozens of matches lighting one cigarette. "Listen, my life now is the nastiest possible. The worst of it is any subaltern can shout: 'Hi, there, guard!' I have overheard all sorts of things in the train, my boy, and do you know, I have learned that life's a beastly thing! My mother has been the ruin of me! A doctor in the train told me that if parents are immoral, their children are drunkards or criminals. Think of that!"

Once he came into the yard, staggering; his eyes gazed about blankly, his breathing was laboured; he laughed and cried and babbled as though in a high fever, and the only words I could catch in his muddled talk were, "My mother! Where's my mother?" which he uttered with a wail like a child who has lost his mother in a crowd. I led him into our garden and laid him down under a tree, and Masha and I took turns to sit by him all that day and all night. He was very sick, and Masha looked with aversion at his pale, wet face, and said:

"Is it possible these reptiles will go on living another year in our yard? It's awful! It's awful!"

And how many mortifications the peasants caused us! How many bitter disappointments in those early days in the spring months, when we so longed to be happy. My wife built a school. I drew a plan of a school for sixty boys, and the Zemstvo Board approved of it but advised us to build the school at Kurilovka, the big village which was only two miles from us. Moreover, the school at Kurilovka in which children—from four villages, our Dubechnya being one of the number—were taught, was old and too small, and the floor was scarcely safe to walk upon. At the end of March, at Masha's wish, she was appointed guardian of the Kurilovna school, and at the beginning of April we three times summoned the village assembly and tried to persuade the peasants that their school was old and overcrowded, and that it was essential to build a new one. A member of the Zemstvo Board and the inspector of peasant schools came, and they, too, tried to persuade them. After each meeting the peasants surrounded us, begging for a bucket of vodka; we were hot in the crowd; we were soon exhausted and returned home dissatisfied and a little ill at ease. In the end the peasants set apart a plot of ground for the school and were obliged to bring all the building material from the town with their own horses. And the very first Sunday after the spring corn was sown carts set off from Kurilovka and Dubechnya to fetch bricks for the foundations. They set off as soon as it was light and came back late in the evening; the peasants were drunk and said they were worn out.

As ill luck would have it, the rain and the cold persisted all through May. The road was in an awful state: it was deep in mud. The carts drove into our yard when they came back from the town—and what a horrible ordeal it was. A potbellied horse would appear at the gate, setting its front legs wide apart; it would stumble forward before coming into the yard; a beam, nine yards long, wet and slimy-looking, crept in on a waggon. Beside it, muffled up against the rain, strode a peasant with the skirts of his coat tucked up in his belt, not looking where he was going, but stepping through the puddles. Another cart would appear with boards, then a third with a beam, a fourth . . . and the space before our house was gradually crowded up with horses, beams, and planks. Men and women, with their heads muffled and their skirts tucked up, would stare angrily at our windows, make an uproar, and clamour for the mistress to come out to them; coarse oaths were audible. Meanwhile Moisei stood at one side, and we fancied he was enjoying our discomfiture.

"We are not going to cart any more," the peasants would shout. "We are worn out! Let her go and get the stuff herself."

Masha, pale and flustered, expecting every minute that they would break into the house, would send them out a half pail of vodka; after that the noise would subside and the long beams, one after another, would crawl slowly out of the yard.

When I was setting off to see the building my wife was worried and said:

"The peasants are spiteful; I only hope they won't do you a mischief. Wait a minute, I'll come with you."

We drove to Kurilovka together, and there the carpenters asked us for a drink. The framework of the house was ready. It was time to lay the foundation, but the masons had not come; this caused delay, and the carpenters complained. And when at last the masons did come, it appeared that there was no sand; it had been somehow overlooked that it would be needed. Taking advantage of our helpless position, the peasants demanded thirty kopecks for each cartload, though the distance from the building to the river where they got the sand was less than a quarter of a mile, and more than five hundred cartloads were found to be necessary. There was no end to the misunderstandings, swearing, and importunity; my wife was indignant, and the foreman of the masons, Tit Petrov, an old man of seventy, took her by the arm, and said:

"You look here! You look here! You only bring me the sand; I set ten men on at once, and in two days it will be done! You look here!"

But they brought the sand and two days passed, and four, and a week, and instead of the promised foundation there was still a yawning hole.

"It's enough to drive one out of one's senses," said my wife, in distress. "What people! What people!"

In the midst of these disorderly doings the engineer arrived; he brought with him parcels of wine and savouries, and after a prolonged meal lay down for a nap in the verandah and snored so loudly that the labourers shook their heads and said: "Well!"

Masha was not pleased at his coming; she did not trust him, though at the same time she asked his advice. When, after sleeping too long after dinner, he got up in a bad humour and said unpleasant things about our management of the place, or expressed regret that he had bought Dubechnya, which had already been a loss to him, poor Masha's face wore an expression of misery. She would complain to him, and he would yawn and say that the peasants ought to be flogged.

He called our marriage and our life a farce and said it was a caprice, a whim.

"She has done something of the sort before," he said about Masha. "She once fancied herself a great opera singer and left me; I was looking for her for two months, and, my dear soul, I spent a thousand roubles on telegrams alone."

He no longer called me a dissenter or Monsieur Painter, and did not as in the past express approval of my living like a workman, but said:

"You are a strange person! You are not a normal person! I won't venture to prophesy, but you will come to a bad end!"

And Masha slept badly at night and was always sitting at our bedroom window thinking. There was no laughter at supper now, no charming grimaces. I was wretched, and when it rained every drop that fell seemed to pierce my heart, like small shot, and I felt ready to fall on my knees before Masha and apologise for the weather. When the peasants made a noise in the yard I felt guilty also. For hours at a time I sat still in one place, thinking of nothing but what a splendid person Masha was, what a wonderful person. I loved her passionately, and I was fascinated by everything she did, everything she said. She had a bent for quiet, studious pursuits; she was fond of reading for hours together, of studying. Although her knowledge of farming was only from books she surprised us all by what she knew; and every piece of advice she gave was of value; not one was ever thrown away; and, with all that, what nobility, what taste, what graciousness, that graciousness which is only found in well-educated people.

To this woman, with her sound, practical intelligence, the disorderly surroundings with petty cares and sordid anxieties in which we were living now were an agony: I saw that and could not sleep at night; my brain worked feverishly and I had a lump in my throat. I rushed about not knowing what to do.

I galloped to the town and brought Masha books, newspapers, sweets, flowers; with Stepan I caught fish, wading for hours up to my neck in the cold water in the rain to catch eelpout to vary our fare; I demeaned myself to beg the peasants not to make a noise; I plied them with vodka, bought them off, made all sorts of promises. And how many other foolish things I did!

At last the rain ceased, the earth dried. One would get up at four o'clock in the morning; one would go out into the garden—where there was dew sparkling on the flowers, the twitter of birds, the hum of insects, not one cloud in the sky; and the garden, the meadows, and the river were

so lovely, yet there were memories of the peasants, of their
carts, of the engineer. Masha and I drove out together in
the racing droshky to the fields to look at the oats. She used
to drive, I sat behind; her shoulders were raised and the
wind played with her hair.

"Keep to the right!" she shouted to those she met.

"You are like a sledge driver," I said to her one day.

"Maybe! Why, my grandfather, the engineer's father, was
a sledge driver. Didn't you know that?" she asked, turning
to me, and at once she mimicked the way sledge drivers
shout and sing.

"And thank God for that," I thought as I listened to her.
"Thank God."

And again memories of the peasants, of the carts, of the
engineer . . .

13

Dr. Blagovo arrived on his bicycle. My sister began coming
often. Again there were conversations about manual labour,
about progress, about a mysterious millennium awaiting
mankind in the remote future. The doctor did not like our
farm-work because it interfered with arguments, and said
that ploughing, reaping, grazing calves were unworthy of
a free man, and all these coarse forms of the struggle for
existence men would in time relegate to animals and machines, while they would devote themselves exclusively to
scientific investigation. My sister kept begging them to let
her go home earlier, and if she stayed on till late in the
evening, or spent the night with us, there would be no end
to the agitation.

"Good heavens, what a baby you are still!" said Masha
reproachfully. "It is positively absurd."

"Yes, it is absurd," my sister agreed, "I know it's absurd; but what is to be done if I haven't the strength to get
over it? I keep feeling as though I were doing wrong."

At haymaking I ached all over from the unaccustomed
labour; in the evening, sitting on the verandah and talking
with the others, I suddenly dropped asleep, and they
laughed aloud at me. They waked me up and made me sit
down to supper; I was overpowered with drowsiness and I
saw the lights, the faces, and the plates as it were in a

dream, heard the voices, but did not understand them. And getting up early in the morning, I took up the scythe at once, or went to the building and worked hard all day.

When I remained at home on holidays I noticed that my sister and Masha were concealing something from me and even seemed to be avoiding me. My wife was tender to me as before, but she had thoughts of her own apart, which she did not share with me. There was no doubt that her exasperation with the peasants was growing, the life was becoming more and more distasteful to her, and yet she did not complain to me. She talked to the doctor now more readily than she did to me, and I did not understand why it was so.

It was the custom in our province at haymaking and harvest time for the labourers to come to the manor house in the evening and be regaled with vodka; even young girls drank a glass. We did not keep up this practice; the mowers and the peasant women stood about in our yard till late in the evening expecting vodka and then departed abusing us. And all the time Masha frowned grimly and said nothing, or murmured to the doctor with exasperation: "Savages! Pechenyegs!"

In the country newcomers are met ungraciously, almost with hostility, as they are at school. And we were received in this way. At first we were looked upon as stupid, silly people, who had bought an estate simply because we did not know what to do with our money. We were laughed at. The peasants grazed their cattle in our wood and even in our garden; they drove away our cows and horses to the village and then demanded money for the damage done by them. They came in whole companies into our yard and loudly clamoured that at the mowing we had cut some piece of land that did not belong to us; and as we did not yet know the boundaries of our estate very accurately, we took their word for it and paid damages. Afterwards it turned out that there had been no mistake at the mowing. They barked the lime trees in our wood. One of the Dubechnya peasants, a regular shark, who did a trade in vodka without a licence, bribed our labourers and in collaboration with them cheated us in a most treacherous way. They took the new wheels off our carts and replaced them with old ones, stole our ploughing harness and actually sold them to us, and so on. But what was most mortifying of all was what happened at the building; the peasant women stole by night boards, bricks, tiles, pieces of iron. The village elder with witnesses made a search in their huts; the village meeting fined them two roubles each, and afterwards this money was spent on drink by the whole commune.

When Masha heard about this, she would say to the doctor or my sister indignantly:

"What beasts! It's awful! awful!"

And I heard her more than once express regret that she had ever taken it into her head to build the school.

"You must understand," the doctor tried to persuade her, "that if you build this school and do good in general, it's not for the sake of the peasants, but in the name of culture, in the name of the future; and the worse the peasants are the more reason for building the school. Understand that!"

But there was a lack of conviction in his voice, and it seemed to me that both he and Masha hated the peasants.

Masha often went to the mill, taking my sister with her, and they both said, laughing, that they went to have a look at Stepan, he was so handsome. Stepan, it appeared, was torpid and taciturn only with men; in feminine society his manners were free and easy, and he talked incessantly. One day, going down to the river to bathe, I accidentally overheard a conversation. Masha and Kleopatra, both in white dresses, were sitting on the bank in the spreading shade of a willow, and Stepan was standing by them with his hands behind his back, and was saying:

"Are peasants men? They are not men, but, asking your pardon, wild beasts, impostors. What life has a peasant? Nothing but eating and drinking; all he cares for is victuals to be cheaper and swilling liquor at the tavern like a fool; and there's no conversation, no manners, no formality, nothing but ignorance! He lives in filth, his wife lives in filth, and his children live in filth. What he stands up in, he lies down to sleep in; he picks the potatoes out of the soup with his fingers; he drinks kvass with a cockroach in it and doesn't bother to blow it away!"

"It's their poverty, of course," my sister put in.

"Poverty? There is want to be sure, there's different sorts of want, madam. If a man is in prison, or let us say blind or crippled, that really is trouble I wouldn't wish anyone,

but if a man's free and has all his senses, if he has his eyes
and his hands and his strength and God, what more does he
want? It's cockering themselves, and it's ignorance, madam,
it's not poverty. If you, let us suppose, good gentlefolk, by
your education, wish out of kindness to help him, he will
drink away your money in his low way; or, what's worse,
he will open a drinkshop, and with your money start robbing the people. You say poverty, but does the rich peasant
live better? He, too, asking your pardon, lives like a swine:
coarse, loud-mouthed, cudgel-headed, broader than he is
long, fat, red-faced mug, I'd like to swing my fist and send
him flying, the scoundrel. There's Larion, another rich one
at Dubechnya, and I bet he strips the bark off your trees as
much as any poor one; and he is a foul-mouthed fellow;
his children are the same, and when he has had a drop too
much he'll topple with his nose in a puddle and sleep there.
They are all a worthless lot, madam. If you live in a village
with them it is like hell. It has stuck in my teeth, that village
has, and thank the Lord, the King of Heaven, I've plenty to
eat and clothes to wear, I served out my time in the dra-
goons, I was village elder for three years, and now I am a
free Cossack, I live where I like. I don't want to live in the
village, and no one has the right to force me. They say—
my wife. They say you are bound to live in your cottage
with your wife. But why so? I am not her hired man."

"Tell me, Stepan, did you marry for love?" asked Masha.

"Love among us in the village!" answered Stepan, and
he gave a laugh. "Properly speaking, madam, if you care to
know, this is my second marriage. I am not a Kurilovka
man, I am from Zalegoshcho, but afterwards I was taken
into Kurilovka when I married. You see my father did not
want to divide the land among us. There were five of us
brothers. I took my leave and went to another village to live
with my wife's family, but my first wife died when she was
young."

"What did she die of?"

"Of foolishness. She used to cry and cry and cry for no
reason, and so she pined away. She was always drinking
some sort of herbs to make her better-looking, and I suppose she damaged her inside. And my second wife is a
Kurilovka woman too, there is nothing in her. She's a
village woman, a peasant woman, and nothing more. I was

taken in when they plighted me to her. I thought she was young and fair-skinned, and that they lived in a clean way. Her mother was just like a Flagellant and she drank coffee, and the chief thing, to be sure, they were clean in their ways. So I married her, and next day we sat down to dinner; I bade my mother-in-law give me a spoon, and she gives me a spoon, and I see her wipe it out with her finger. So much for you, thought I; nice sort of cleanliness yours is. I lived a year with them and then I went away. I might have married a girl from the town," he went on after a pause. "They say a wife is a helpmate to her husband. What do I want with a helpmate? I help myself; I'd rather she talked to me, and not clack, clack, clack, but circumstantially, feelingly. What is life without good conversation?"

Stepan suddenly paused, and at once there was the sound of his dreary, monotonous "oo-loo-loo." This meant that he had seen me.

Masha used often to go to the mill and evidently found pleasure in her conversations with Stepan. Stepan abused the peasants with such sincerity and conviction, and she was attracted to him. Every time she came back from the mill the feeble-minded peasant, who looked after the garden, shouted at her:

"Wench Palashka! Hulla, wench Palashka!" and he would bark like a dog: "Ga! Ga!"

And she would stop and look at him attentively, as though in that idiot's barking she found an answer to her thoughts, and probably he attracted her in the same way as Stepan's abuse. At home some piece of news would await her, such, for instance, as that the geese from the village had ruined our cabbage in the garden, or that Larion had stolen the reins; and shrugging her shoulders, she would say with a laugh:

"What do you expect of these people?"

She was indignant, and there was rancour in her heart, and meanwhile I was growing used to the peasants, and I felt more and more drawn to them. For the most part they were nervous, irritable, downtrodden people; they were people whose imagination had been stifled, ignorant, with a poor, dingy outlook on life, whose thoughts were ever the same—of the grey earth, of grey days, of black bread, people who cheated, but like birds hiding nothing but their heads behind the tree—people who could not count. They would not come to mow for us for twenty roubles, but they came for half a pail of vodka, though for twenty roubles they could have bought four pails. There really was filth and drunkenness and foolishness and deceit, but with all that one yet felt that the life of the peasants rested on a firm, sound foundation. However uncouth a wild animal the peasant following the plough seemed, and however he might stupefy himself with vodka, still, looking at him more closely, one felt that there was in him what was needed, something very important, which was lacking in Masha and in the doctor, for instance, and that was that he believed the chief thing on earth was truth and justice, and that his salvation, and that of the whole people, was only to be found in truth and justice, and so more than anything in the world he loved just dealing. I told my wife she saw the spots on the glass, but not the glass itself; she said nothing in reply, or hummed like Stepan "oo-loo-loo." When this goodhearted and clever woman turned pale with indignation, and with a quiver in her voice spoke to the doctor of the drunkenness and dishonesty, it perplexed me, and I was struck by the shortness of her memory. How could she forget that her father the engineer drank too, and drank heavily, and that the money with which Dubechnya had been bought had been acquired by a whole series of shameless, impudent dishonesties? How could she forget it?

14

My sister, too, was leading a life of her own which she carefully hid from me. She was often whispering with Masha. When I went up to her she seemed to shrink into herself, and there was a guilty, imploring look in her eyes; evidently there was something going on in her heart of which she was afraid or ashamed. So as to avoid meeting me in the garden, or being left alone with me, she always kept close to Masha, and I rarely had an opportunity of talking to her except at dinner.

One evening I was walking quietly through the garden on my way back from the building. It was beginning to ge dark. Without noticing me, or hearing my step, my sister was walking near a spreading old apple tree, absolutely noiselessly as though she were a phantom. She was dressed in black and was walking rapidly backwards and forwards on the same track, looking at the ground. An apple fell from the tree; she started at the sound, stood still and pressed her hands to her temples. At that moment I went up to her.

In a rush of tender affection which suddenly flooded my heart, with tears in my eyes, suddenly remembering my mother and our childhood, I put my arm round her shoulders and kissed her.

"What is the matter?" I asked her. "You are unhappy; I have seen it for a long time. Tell me what's wrong?"

"I am frightened," she said, trembling.

"What is it?" I insisted. "For God's sake, be open!"

"I will, I will be open; I will tell you the whole truth. To hide it from you is so hard, so agonising. Misail, I love . . ." she went on in a whisper, "I love him . . . I love him. . . . I am happy, but why am I so frightened?"

There was the sound of footsteps; between the trees appeared Dr. Blagovo in his silk shirt with his high top boots. Evidently they had arranged to meet near the apple tree. Seeing him, she rushed impulsively towards him with a cry of pain as though he were being taken from her.

"Vladimir! Vladimir!"

She clung to him and looked greedily into his face, and only then I noticed how pale and thin she had become of late. It was particularly noticeable from her lace collar which I had known for so long, and which now hung more loosely than ever before about her thin, long neck. The doctor was disconcerted, but at once recovered himself, and, stroking her hair, said:

"There, there. . . . Why so nervous? You see, I'm here."

We were silent, looking with embarrassment at each other, then we walked on, the three of us together, and I heard the doctor say to me:

"Civilised life has not yet begun among us. Old men console themselves by making out that if there is nothing now, there was something in the forties or the sixties; that's the old: you and I are young; our brains have not yet been

touched by *marasmus senilis;* we cannot comfort ourselves
with such illusions. The beginning of Russia was in 862,
but the beginning of civilised Russia has not come yet."

But I did not grasp the meaning of these reflections. It
was somehow strange, I could not believe it, that my sister
was in love, that she was walking with and holding the arm
of a stranger and looking tenderly at him. My sister, this
nervous, frightened, crushed, fettered creature, loved a
man who was married and had children! I felt sorry for
something, but what exactly I don't know; the presence of
the doctor was for some reason distasteful to me now, and
I could not imagine what would come of this love of theirs.

15

Masha and I drove to Kurilovka to the dedication of the
school.

"Autumn, autumn, autumn . . ." said Masha softly, looking away. "Summer is over. There are no birds and nothing
is green but the willows."

Yes, summer was over. There were fine, warm days, but
it was fresh in the morning, and the shepherds went out in
their sheepskins already; and in our garden the dew did not
dry off the asters all day long. There were plaintive sounds
all the time, and one could not make out whether they came
from the shutters creaking on their rusty hinges, or from the
flying cranes—and one's heart felt light, and one was eager
for life.

"The summer is over," said Masha. "Now you and I can
balance our accounts. We have done a lot of work, a lot
of thinking; we are the better for it—all honour and glory to
us—we have succeeded in self-improvement; but have our
successes had any perceptible influence on the life around
us, have they brought any benefit to anyone whatever? No.
Ignorance, physical uncleanliness, drunkenness, an appallingly high infant mortality, everything remains as it was,
and no one is the better for your having ploughed and sown,
and my having wasted money and read books. Obviously we
have been working only for ourselves and have had advanced ideas only for ourselves." Such reasonings perplexed me, and I did not know what to think.

"We have been sincere from beginning to end," said I, "and if anyone is sincere he is right."

"Who disputes it? We were right, but we haven't succeeded in properly accomplishing what we were right in. To begin with, our external methods themselves—aren't they mistaken? You want to be of use to men, but by the very fact of your buying an estate, from the very start you cut yourself off from any possibility of doing anything useful for them. Then if you work, dress, eat like a peasant, you sanctify, as it were, by your authority, their heavy, clumsy dress, their horrible huts, their stupid beards. . . . On the other hand, if we suppose that you work for long, long years, your whole life, that in the end some practical results are obtained, yet what are they, your results, what can they do against such elemental forces as wholesale ignorance, hunger, cold, degeneration? A drop in the ocean! Other methods of struggle are needed, strong, bold, rapid! If one really wants to be of use one must get out of the narrow circle of ordinary social work, and try to act direct upon the mass! What is wanted, first of all, is a loud, energetic propaganda. Why is it that art—music, for instance—is so living, so popular, and in reality so powerful? Because the musician or the singer affects thousands at once. Precious, precious art!" she went on, looking dreamily at the sky. "Art gives us wings and carries us far, far away! Anyone who is sick of filth, of petty, mercenary interests, anyone who is revolted, wounded, and indignant can find peace and satisfaction only in the beautiful."

When we drove into Kurilovka the weather was bright and joyous. Somewhere they were threshing; there was a smell of rye straw. A mountain ash was bright red behind the hurdle fences, and all the trees wherever one looked were ruddy or golden. They were ringing the bells, they were carrying the ikons to the school, and we could hear them sing: "Holy Mother, our Defender," and how limpid the air was, and how high the doves were flying.

The service was being held in the classroom. Then the peasants of Kurilovka brought Masha the ikon, and the peasants of Dubechnya offered her a big loaf and a gilt saltcellar. And Masha broke into sobs.

"If anything has been said that shouldn't have been or

anything done not for your liking, forgive us," said an old man, and he bowed down to her and to me.

As we drove home, Masha kept looking round at the school; the green roof, which I had painted, and which was glistening in the sun, remained in sight for a long while. And I felt that the look Masha turned upon it now was one of farewell.

16

In the evening she got ready to go to the town. Of late she had taken to going often to the town and staying the night there. In her absence I could not work, my hands felt weak and limp; our huge courtyard seemed a dreary, repulsive, empty hole. The garden was full of angry noises, and without her the house, the trees, the horses were no longer "ours."

I did not go out of the house, but went on sitting at her table beside her bookshelf with the books on land work, those old favourites no longer wanted and looking at me now so shamefacedly. For whole hours together, while it struck seven, eight, nine, while the autumn night, black as soot, came on outside, I kept examining her old glove, or the pen with which she always wrote, or her little scissors. I did nothing and realised clearly that all I had done before, ploughing, mowing, chopping, had only been because she wished it. And if she had sent me to clean a deep well, where I had to stand up to my waist in deep water, I should have crawled into the well without considering whether it was necessary or not. And now when she was not near, Dubechnya, with its ruins, its untidiness, its banging shutters, with its thieves by day and by night, seemed to me a chaos in which any work would be useless. Besides, what had I to work for here, why anxiety and thought about the future, if I felt that the earth was giving way under my feet, that I had played my part in Dubechnya, and that the fate of the books on farming was awaiting me too? Oh what misery it was at night, in hours of solitude, when I was listening every minute in alarm, as though I were expecting someone to shout that it was time for me to go away! I did not grieve for Dubechnya. I grieved for my love, which, too, was threatened with its autumn. What a immense happiness it is to love and be loved, and how awful to feel that one is slipping down from that high pinnacle!

Masha returned from the town towards the evening of the next day. She was displeased with something, but she concealed it, and only said, why was it all the window frames had been put in for the winter; it was enough to suffocate one. I took out two frames. We were not hungry, but we sat down to supper.

"Go and wash your hands," said my wife; "you smell of putty."

She had brought some new illustrated papers from the town, and we looked at them together after supper. There were supplements with fashion plates and patterns. Masha looked through them casually and was putting them aside to examine them properly later on, but one dress, with a flat skirt as full as a bell and large sleeves, interested her, and she looked at it for a minute gravely and attentively.

"That's not bad," she said.

"Yes, that dress would suit you beautifully," I said, "beautifully."

And looking with emotion at the dress, admiring that patch of grey simply because she liked it, I went on tenderly:

"A charming, exquisite dress! Splendid, glorious, Masha! My precious Masha!"

And tears dropped on the fashion plate.

"Splendid Masha . . ." I muttered; "sweet, precious Masha . . ."

She went to bed, while I sat another hour looking at the illustrations.

"It's a pity you took out the window frames," she said from the bedroom, "I am afraid it may be cold. Oh dear, what a draught there is!"

I read something out of the column of odds and ends, a receipt for making cheap ink, and an acount of the biggest diamond in the world. I came again upon the fashion plate of the dress she liked, and I imagined her at a ball, with a fan, bare shoulders, brilliant, splendid, with a full understanding of painting, music, literature, and how small and how brief my part seemed!

Our meeting, our marriage, had been only one of the

episodes of which there would be many more in the life of this vital, richly gifted woman. All the best in the world, as I have said already, was at her service, and she received it absolutely for nothing, and even ideas and the intellectual movement in vogue served simply for her recreation, giving variety to her life, and I was only the sledge driver who drove her from one entertainment to another. Now she did not need me. She would take flight, and I should be alone.

And as though in response to my thought, there came a despairing scream from the garden.

"He-e-elp!"

It was a shrill, womanish voice, and as though to mimic it the wind whistled in the chimney on the same shrill note. Half a minute passed, and again through the noise of the wind, but coming, it seemed, from the other end of the yard:

"He-e-elp!"

"Misail, do you hear?" my wife asked me softly. "Do you hear?"

She came out from the bedroom in her nightgown, with her hair down, and listened, looking at the dark window.

"Someone is being murdered," she said. "That is the last straw."

I took my gun and went out. It was very dark outside, the wind was high, and it was difficult to stand. I went to the gate and listened, the trees roared, the wind whistled, and, probably at the feeble-minded peasant's, a dog howled lazily. Outside the gates the darkness was absolute, not a light on the railway line. And near the lodge, which a year before had been the office, suddenly sounded a smothered scream:

"He-e-elp!"

"Who's there?" I called.

There were two people struggling. One was thrusting the other out, while the other was resisting, and both were breathing heavily.

"Leave go," said one, and I recognised Ivan Cheprakov; it was he who was shrieking in a shrill, womanish voice: "Let go, you damned brute, or I'll bite your hand off."

The other I recognised as Moisei. I separated them, and as I did so I could not resist hitting Moisei two blows in the

face. He fell down, then got up again, and I hit him once
more.

"He tried to kill me," he muttered. "He was trying to get
at his mamma's chest. . . . I want to lock him up in the
lodge for security."

Cheprakov was drunk and did not recognise me; he kept
drawing deep breaths, as though he were just going to shout
"help" again.

I left them and went back to the house; my wife was lying
on her bed; she had dressed. I told her what had happened
in the yard and did not conceal the fact that I had hit
Moisei.

"It's terrible to live in the country," she said. "And what
a long night it is. Oh dear, if only it were over!"

"He-e-elp!" we heard again, a little later.

"I'll go and stop them," I said.

"No, let them bite each other's throats," she said with an
expression of disgust.

She was looking up at the ceiling, listening, while I sat
beside her, not daring to speak to her, feeling as though I
were to blame for their shouting "help" in the yard and for
the night's seeming so long.

We were silent, and I waited impatiently for a gleam of
light at the window, and Masha looked all the time as
though she had awakened from a trance and now was
marvelling how she, so clever and well-educated, so elegant,
had come into this pitiful, provincial, empty hole among a
crew of petty, insignificant people, and how she could have
so far forgotten herself as ever to be attracted by one of
these people, and for more than six months to have been his
wife. It seemed to me that at that moment it did not matter
to her whether it was I, or Moisei, or Cheprakov; everything
for her was merged in that savage drunken "help"—I and
our marriage, and our work together, and the mud and
slush of autumn, and when she sighed or moved into a more
comfortable position I read in her face: "Oh, that morning
would come quickly!"

In the morning she went away. I spent another three days
at Dubechnya expecting her, then I packed all our things in
one room, locked it, and walked to the town. It was already
evening when I rang at the engineer's, and the street lamps

were burning in Great Dvoryansky Street. Pavel told me there was no one at home; Viktor Ivanich had gone to Petersburg, and Marya Viktorovna was probably at the rehearsal at the Azhogins'. I remember with what emotion I went on to the Azhogins', how my heart throbbed and fluttered as I mounted the stairs and stood waiting a long while on the landing at the top, not daring to enter that temple of the muses! In the big room there were lighted candles everywhere, on a little table, on the piano, and on the stage, everywhere in threes; and the first performance was fixed for the thirteenth, and now the first rehearsal was on a Monday, an unlucky day. All part of the war against superstition! All the devotees of the scenic art were gathered together; the eldest, the middle, and the youngest sisters were walking about the stage, reading their parts in exercise books. Apart from all the rest stood Radish, motionless, with the side of his head pressed to the wall as he gazed with adoration at the stage, waiting for the rehearsal to begin. Everything as it used to be.

I was making my way to my hostess; I had to pay my respects to her, but suddenly everyone said "Hush!" and waved me to step quietly. There was a silence. The lid of the piano was raised; a lady sat down at it, screwing up her shortsighted eyes at the music, and my Masha walked up to the piano, in a low-necked dress, looking beautiful, but with a special, new sort of beauty not in the least like the Masha who used to come and meet me in the spring at the mill. She sang: "Why do I love the radiant night?"

It was the first time during our whole acquaintance that I had heard her sing. She had a fine, mellow, powerful voice, and while she sang I felt as though I were eating a ripe, sweet, fragrant melon. She ended, the audience applauded, and she smiled, very much pleased, making play with her eyes, turning over the music, smoothing her skirts, like a bird that has at last broken out of its cage and preens its wings in freedom. Her hair was arranged over her ears, and she had an unpleasant, defiant expression in her face, as though she wanted to throw down a challenge to us all, or to shout to us as she did to her horses: "Hey, there, my beauties!"

And she must at that moment have been very much like her grandfather the sledge driver.

"You here too?" she said, giving me her hand. "Did you hear me sing? Well, what did you think of it?" and without waiting for my answer she went on: "It's a very good thing you are here. I am going tonight to Petersburg for a short time. You'll let me go, won't you?"

At midnight I went with her to the station. She embraced me affectionately, probably feeling grateful to me for not asking unnecessary questions, and she promised to write to me, and I held her hands a long time, and kissed them, hardly able to restrain my tears and not uttering a word.

And when she had gone I stood watching the retreating lights, caressing her in imagination and softly murmuring: "My darling Masha, glorious Masha . . ."

I spent the night at Karpovna's, and next morning I was at work with Radish, re-covering the furniture of a rich merchant who was marrying his daughter to a doctor.

17

My sister came after dinner on Sunday and had tea with me.

"I read a great deal now," she said, showing me the books which she had fetched from the public library on her way to me. "Thanks to your wife and to Vladimir, they have awakened me to self-realisation. They have been my salvation; they have made me feel myself a human being. In old days I used to lie awake at night with worries of all sorts, thinking what a lot of sugar we had used in the week, or hoping the cucumbers would not be too salt. And now, too, I lie awake at night, but I have different thoughts. I am distressed that half my life has been passed in such a foolish, cowardly way. I despise my past; I am ashamed of it. And I look upon our father now as my enemy. Oh, how grateful I am to your wife! And Vladimir! He is such a wonderful person! They have opened my eyes!"

"That's bad that you don't sleep at night," I said.

"Do you think I am ill? Not at all. Vladimir sounded me, and said I was perfectly well. But health is not what matters, it is not so important. . . . Tell me: am I right?"

She needed moral support, that was obvious. Masha had gone away. Dr. Blagovo was in Petersburg, and there was no one left in the town but me to tell her she was right.

She looked intently into my face, trying to read my secret thoughts, and if I were absorbed or silent in her presence, she thought this was on her account and was grieved. I always had to be on my guard, and when she asked me whether she was right I hastened to assure that she was right, and that I had a deep respect for her.

"Do you know they have given me a part at the Azhogins'?" she went on. "I want to act on the stage, I want to live—in fact, I mean to drain the full cup. I have no talent, none, and the part is only ten lines, but still this is immeasurably finer and loftier than pouring out tea five times a day, and looking to see if the cook has eaten too much. Above all, let my father see I am capable of protest."

After tea she lay down on my bed, and lay for a little while with her eyes closed, looking very pale.

"What weakness," she said, getting up. "Vladimir says all city-bred women and girls are anaemic from doing nothing. What a clever man Vladimir is! He is right, absolutely right. We must work!"

Two days later she came to the Azhogins' with her manuscript for the rehearsal. She was wearing a black dress with a string of coral round her neck, and a brooch that in the distance was like a pastry puff, and in her ears earrings sparkling with brilliants. When I looked at her I felt uncomfortable. I was struck by her lack of taste. That she had very inappropriately put on earrings and brilliants, and that she was strangely dressed, was remarked by other people too; I saw smiles on people's faces, and heard someone say with a laugh: "Kleopatra of Egypt."

She was trying to assume society manners, to be unconstrained and at her ease, and so seemed artificial and strange. She had lost simplicity and sweetness.

"I told Father just now that I was going to the rehearsal," she began, coming up to me, "and he shouted that he would not give me his blessing, and actually almost struck me. Only fancy, I don't know my part," she said, looking at her manuscript. "I am sure to make a mess of it. So be it, the die is cast," she went on in intense excitement. "The die is cast. . . ."

It seemed to her that everyone was looking at her, and

that all were amazed at the momentous step she had taken, that everyone was expecting something special of her, and it would have been impossible to convince her that no one was paying attention to people so petty and insignificant as she and I were.

She had nothing to do till the third act, and her part, that of a visitor, a provincial crony, consisted only in standing at the door as though listening, and then delivering a brief monologue. In the interval before her appearance, an hour and a half at least, while they were moving about on the stage reading their parts, drinking tea and arguing, she did not leave my side, and was all the time muttering her part and nervously crumpling up the manuscript. And, imagining that everyone was looking at her and waiting for her appearance, with a trembling hand she smoothed back her hair and said to me:

"I shall certainly make a mess of it. . . . What a load on my heart, if only you knew! I feel frightened, as though I were just going to be led to execution."

At last her turn came.

"Kleopatra Alexyevna, it's your cue!" said the stage manager.

She came forward into the middle of the stage with an expression of horror on her face, looking ugly and angular, and for half a minute stood as though in a trance, perfectly motionless, and only her big earrings shook in her ears.

"The first time you can read it," said someone.

It was clear to me that she was trembling, and trembling so much that she could not speak, and could not unfold her manuscript, and that she was incapable of acting her part; and I was already on the point of going to her and saying something, when she suddenly dropped on her knees in the middle of the stage and broke into loud sobs.

All was commotion and hubbub. I alone stood still, leaning against the side scene, overwhelmed by what had happened, not understanding and not knowing what to do. I saw them lift her up and lead her away. I saw Anyuta Blagovo come up to me; I had not seen her in the room before, and she seemed to have sprung out of the earth. She was wearing her hat and veil, and, as always, had an air of having come only for a moment.

"I told her not to take a part," she said angrily, jerking out each word abruptly and turning crimson. "It's insanity! You ought to have prevented her!"

Madam Azhogin, in a short jacket with short sleeves, with cigarette ash on her breast, looking thin and flat, came rapidly towards me.

"My dear, this is terrible," she brought out, wringing her hands, and, as her habit was, looking intently into my face. "This is terrible! Your sister is in a condition. . . . She is with child. Take her away, I implore you. . . ."

She was breathless with agitation, while on one side stood her three daughters, exactly like her, thin and flat, huddling together in a scared way. They were alarmed, overwhelmed, as though a convict had been caught in their house. What a disgrace, how dreadful! And yet this estimable family had spent its life waging war on superstition; evidently they imagined that all the superstition and error of humanity was limited to the three candles, the thirteenth of the month, and to the unluckiness of Monday!

"I beg you . . . I beg," repeated Madam Azhogin, pursing up her lips in the shape of a heart on the syllable "you." "I beg you to take her home."

18

A little later my sister and I were walking along the street. I covered her with the skirts of my coat; we hastened, choosing back streets where there were no street lamps, avoiding passers-by; it was as though we were running away. She was no longer crying, but looked at me with dry eyes. To Karpovna's, where I took her, it was only twenty minutes' walk, and, strange to say, in that short time we succeeded in thinking of our whole life; we talked over everything, considered our position, reflected. . . .

We decided we could not go on living in this town, and that when I had earned a little money we would move to some other place. In some houses everyone was asleep, in others they were playing cards; we hated these houses; we were afraid of them. We talked of the fanaticism, the coarseness of feeling, the insignificance of these respectable families, these amateurs of dramatic art whom we had so alarmed, and I kept asking in what way these stupid, cruel, lazy, and dishonest people were superior to the drunken and superstitious peasants of Kurilovka, or in what way they were better than animals, who in the same way are thrown into a panic when some incident disturbs the monotony of their life limited by their instincts. What would have happened to my sister now if she had been left to live at home?

What moral agonies would she have experienced, talking with my father, meeting every day with acquaintances? I imagined this to myself, and at once there came into my mind people, all people I knew, who had been slowly done to death by their nearest relations. I remembered the tortured dogs, driven mad, the live sparrows plucked naked by boys and flung into the water, and a long, long series of obscure lingering miseries which I had looked on continually from early childhood in that town; and I could not understand what these sixty-five thousand people lived for, what they read the gospel for, why they prayed, why they read books and magazines. What good had they gained from all that had been said and written hitherto if they were still possessed by the same spiritual darkness and hatred of liberty, as they were a hundred and three hundred years ago? A master carpenter spends his whole life building houses in the town, and always, to the day of his death, calls a "gallery" a "galdery." So these sixty-five thousand people have been reading and hearing of truth, of justice, of mercy, of freedom for generations, and yet from morning till night, till the day of their death, they are lying, and tormenting each other, and they fear liberty and hate it as a deadly foe.

"And so my fate is decided," said my sister, as we arrived home. "After what has happened I cannot go back *there*. Heavens, how good that is! My heart feels lighter."

She went to bed at once. Tears were glittering on her eyelashes, but her expression was happy; she fell into a sound sweet sleep, and one could see that her heart was lighter and that she was resting. It was a long, long time since she had slept like that.

And so we began our life together. She was always singing and saying that her life was very happy, and the books I brought her from the public library I took back unread, as now she could not read; she wanted to do nothing but dream and talk of the future, mending my linen, or helping Karpovna near the stove; she was always singing, or talking of her Vladimir, of his cleverness, of his charming manners, of his kindness, of his extraordinary learning, and I assented to all she said, though by now I disliked her doctor. She wanted to work, to lead an independent life on her own account, and she used to say that she would become a schoolteacher or a doctor's assistant as soon as her health would permit her and would herself do the scrubbing and the washing. Already she was passionately devoted to her child; he was not yet born, but she knew already the colour of his eyes, what his hands would be like, and how he would laugh. She was fond of talking about education, and as her Vladimir was the best man in the world, all her discussion of education could be summed up in the question how to make the boy as fascinating as his father. There was no end to her talk, and everything she said made her intensely joyful. Sometimes I was delighted, too, though I could not have said why.

I suppose her dreaminess infected me. I, too, gave up reading and did nothing but dream. In the evenings, in spite of my fatigue, I walked up and down the room, with my hands in my pockets, talking of Masha.

"What do you think?" I would ask of my sister. "When will she come back? I think she'll come back at Christmas, not later; what has she to do there?"

"As she doesn't write to you, it's evident she will come back very soon."

"That's true," I assented, though I knew perfectly well that Masha would not return to our town.

I missed her fearfully, and could no longer deceive myself, and tried to get other people to deceive me. My sister was expecting her doctor, and I—Masha; and both of us talked incessantly, laughed, and did not notice that we were preventing Karpovna from sleeping. She lay on the stove and kept muttering:

"The samovar hummed this morning, it did hum! Oh, it bodes no good, my dears, it bodes no good!"

No one ever came to see us but the postman, who brought my sister letters from the doctor, and Prokofy, who sometimes came in to see us in the evening, and, after looking at my sister, without speaking went away, and when he was in the kitchen said:

"Every class ought to remember its rules, and anyone who is so proud that he won't understand that will find it a vale of tears."

He was very fond of the phrase "a vale of tears." One day —it was in Christmas week, when I was walking by the bazaar—he called me into the butcher's shop, and, not shaking hands with me, announced that he had to speak to me about something very important. His face was red from the frost and vodka; near him, behind the counter, stood Nikolka, with the expression of a brigand, holding a blood-stained knife in his hand.

"I desire to express my word to you," Prokofy began. "This incident cannot continue, because, as you understand yourself that for such a vale, people will say nothing good of you or of us. Mamma, through pity, cannot say something unpleasant to you, that your sister should move into another lodging on account of her condition, but I won't have it any more, because I can't approve of her behaviour."

I understood him, and I went out of the shop. The same day my sister and I moved to Radish's. We had no money for a cab, and we walked on foot; I carried a parcel of our belongings on my back; my sister had nothing in her hands, but she gasped for breath and coughed and kept asking whether we should get there soon.

19

At last a letter came from Masha.

"Dear, good M.A." (she wrote), "our kind, gentle 'angel,' as the old painter calls you, farewell; I am going with my father to America for the exhibition. In a few days I shall see the ocean—so far from Dubechnya, it's dreadful to think! It's far and unfathomable as the sky, and I long to be there in freedom. I am triumphant, I am mad, and you see how incoherent my letter is. Dear, good one, give me my freedom, make haste to break the thread, which still holds, binding you and me together. My meeting and knowing you was a ray from heaven that lighted up my existence; but my becoming your wife was a mistake, you understand that, and I am oppressed now by the consciousness of the mistake, and I beseech you, on my knees, my generous friend, quickly, quickly, before I start for the ocean, telegraph that you consent to correct our common mistake, to remove the solitary stone from my wings, and my father, who will undertake all the arrangements, promised me not to burden you too much with formalities. And so I am free to fly whither I will? Yes?

"Be happy, and God bless you; forgive me, a sinner.

"I am well, I am wasting money, doing all sorts of silly things, and I thank God every minute that such a bad woman as I has no children. I sing and have success, but it's not an infatuation; no, it's my haven, my cell to which I go for peace. King David had a ring with an inscription on it: 'All things pass.' When one is sad those words make one cheerful, and when one is cheerful it makes one sad. I have got myself a ring like that with Hebrew letters on it, and this talisman keeps me from infatuations. All things pass, life will pass, one wants nothing. Or at least one wants nothing but the sense of freedom, for when anyone is free, he wants nothing, nothing, nothing. Break the thread. A warm hug to you and your sister. Forgive and forget your M."

My sister used to lie down in one room, and Radish, who had been ill again and was now better, in another. Just at the moment when I received this letter my sister went softly into the painter's room, sat down beside him and began reading aloud. She read to him every day. Ostrovsky or Gogol, and he listened, staring at one point, not laughing, but shaking his head and muttering to himself from time to time:

"Anything may happen! Anything may happen!"

If anything ugly or unseemly were depicted in the play he would say as though vindictively, thrusting his finger into the book:

"There it is, lying! That's what it does, lying does."

The plays fascinated him, both from their subjects and their moral, and from their skilful, complex construction, and he marvelled at "him," never calling the author by his name. How neatly *he* has put it all together.

This time my sister read softly only one page and could

read no more: her voice would not last out. Radish took her hand and, moving his parched lips, said, hardly audibly, in a husky voice:

"The soul of a righteous man is white and smooth as chalk, but the soul of a sinful man is like pumice stone. The soul of a righteous man is like clear oil, but the soul of a sinful man is gas tar. We must labour, we must sorrow, we must suffer sickness," he went on, "and he who does not labour and sorrow will not gain the Kingdom of Heaven. Woe, woe to them that are well fed, woe to the mighty, woe to the rich, woe to the moneylenders! Not for them is the Kingdom of Heaven. Lice eat grass, rust eats iron . . ."

"And lying the soul," my sister added laughing.

I read the letter through once more. At that moment there walked into the kitchen a soldier who had been bringing us twice a week parcels of tea, French bread, and game, which smelled of scent, from some unknown giver. I had no work. I had had to sit at home idle for whole days together, and probably whoever sent us the French bread knew that we were in want.

I heard my sister talking to the soldier and laughing gaily. Then, lying down, she ate some French bread and said to me:

"When you wouldn't go into the service, but became a house painter, Anyuta Blagovo and I knew from the beginning that you were right, but we were frightened to say so aloud. Tell me what force is it that hinders us from saying what one thinks? Take Anyuta Blagovo now, for instance. She loves you, she adores you, she knows you are right, she loves me too, like a sister, and knows that I am right, and I daresay in her soul envies us, but some force prevents her from coming to see us, she shuns us, she is afraid."

My sister crossed her arms over her breast, and said passionately:

"How she loves you, if only you knew! She has confessed her love to no one but me, and then very secretly in the dark. She led me into a dark avenue in the garden and began whispering how precious you were to her. You will see, she'll never marry, because she loves you. Are you sorry for her?"

"Yes."

"It's she who has sent the bread. She is absurd really,

what is the use of being so secret? I used to be absurd and foolish, but now I have got away from that and am afraid of nobody. I think and say aloud what I like and am happy. When I lived at home I hadn't a conception of happiness, and now I wouldn't change with a queen."

Dr. Blagovo arrived. He had taken his doctor's degree, and was now staying in our town with his father; he was taking a rest, and said that he would soon go back to Petersburg again. He wanted to study anti-toxins against typhus, and, I believe, cholera; he wanted to go abroad to perfect his training, and then to be appointed a professor. He had already left the army service, and wore a roomy serge reefer jacket, very full trousers, and magnificent neckties. My sister was in ecstasies over his scarf pin, his studs, and the red silk handkerchief which he wore, I suppose from foppishness, sticking out of the breast pocket of his jacket. One day, having nothing to do, she and I counted up all the suits we remembered him wearing, and came to the conclusion that he had at least ten. It was clear that he still loved my sister as before, but he never once even in jest spoke of taking her with him to Petersburg or abroad, and I could not picture to myself clearly what would become of her if she remained alive and what would become of her child. She did nothing but dream endlessly and never thought seriously of the future; she said he might go where he liked and might abandon her even, so long as he was happy himself; that what had been was enough for her.

As a rule he used to sound her very carefully on his arrival and used to insist on her taking milk and drops in his presence. It was the same on this occasion. He sounded her and made her drink a glass of milk, and there was a smell of creosote in our room afterwards.

"That's a good girl," he said, taking the glass from her. "You mustn't talk too much now; you've taken to chattering like a magpie of late. Please hold your tongue."

She laughed. Then he came into Radish's room where I was sitting and affectionately slapped me on the shoulder.

"Well, how goes it, old man?" he said, bending down to the invalid.

"Your honour," said Radish, moving his lips slowly, "your honour, I venture to submit. . . . We all walk in the fear of God, we all have to die. . . . Permit me to tell you the truth. . . . Your honour, the Kingdom of Heaven will not be for you!"

"There's no help for it," the doctor said jestingly; "there must be somebody in hell, you know."

And all at once something happened with my consciousness; as though I were in a dream, as though I were standing on a winter night in the slaughterhouse yard, and Prokofy beside me, smelling of pepper cordial; I made an effort to control myself, and rubbed my eyes, and at once it seemed to me that I was going along the road to the interview with the governor. Nothing of the sort had happened to me before, or has happened to me since, and these strange memories that were like dreams I ascribed to overexhaustion of my nerves. I lived through the scene at the slaughterhouse, and the interview with the governor, and at the same time was dimly aware that it was not real.

When I came to myself I saw that I was no longer in the house, but in the street, and was standing with the doctor near a lamppost.

"It's sad, it's sad," he was saying, and tears were trickling down his cheeks. "She is in good spirits, she's always laughing and hopeful, but her position's hopeless, dear boy. Your Radish hates me and is always trying to make me feel that I have treated her badly. He is right from his standpoint, but I have my point of view too; and I shall never regret all that has happened. One must love; we ought all to love—oughtn't we? There would be no life without love; anyone who fears and avoids love is not free."

Little by little he passed to other subjects, began talking of science, of his dissertation which had been liked in Petersburg. He was carried away by his subject, and no longer thought of my sister, nor of his grief, nor of me. Life was of absorbing interest to him. She has America and her ring with the inscription on it, I thought, while this fellow has his doctor's degree and a professor's chair to look forward to, and only my sister and I are left with the old things.

When I said good-bye to him, I went up to the lamppost and read the letter once more. And I remembered, I remembered vividly how that spring morning she had come to me at the mill, lain down and covered herself with her jacket—she wanted to be like a simple peasant woman. And how, another time—it was in the morning also—we drew the net out of the water, and heavy drops of rain fell upon us from the riverside willows, and we laughed. . . .

It was dark in our house in Great Dvoryansky Street. I got over the fence and, as I used to do in the old days, went by the back way to the kitchen to borrow a lantern. There was no one in the kitchen. The samovar hissed near the stove, waiting for my father. "Who pours out my father's tea now?" I thought. Taking the lantern I went out to the shed, built myself up a bed of old newspapers and lay down. The hooks on the walls looked forbidding, as they used to of old, and their shadows flickered. It was cold. I felt that my sister would come in in a minute and bring me supper, but at once I remembered that she was ill and was lying at Radish's, and it seemed to me strange that I should have climbed over the fence and be lying here in this unheated shed. My mind was in a maze, and I saw all sorts of absurd things.

There was a ring. A ring familiar from childhood: first the wire rustled against the wall, then a short plaintive ring in the kitchen. It was my father come back from the club. I got up and went into the kitchen. Axinya, the cook, clasped her hands on seeing me and for some reason burst into tears.

"My own!" she said softly. "My precious! O Lord!"

And she began crumpling up her apron in her agitation. In the window there were standing jars of berries in vodka. I poured myself out a teacupful and greedily drank it off, for I was intensely thirsty. Axinya had quite recently scrubbed the table and benches, and there was that smell in the kitchen which is found in bright, snug kitchens kept by tidy cooks. And that smell and the chirp of the cricket used to lure us as children into the kitchen and put us in the mood for hearing fairy tales and playing at "kings."

"Where's Kleopatra?" Axinya asked softly, in a fluster, holding her breath; "and where is your cap, my dear? Your wife, you say, has gone to Petersburg?"

She had been our servant in our mother's time and used once to give Kleopatra and me our baths, and to her we were still children who had to be talked to for their good. For a quarter of an hour or so she laid before me all the reflections which she had with the sagacity of an old serv ant been accumulating in the stillness of that kitchen, all the time since we had seen each other. She said that the doctor could be forced to marry Kleopatra; he only needed to be thoroughly frightened; and that if an appeal were promptly written the bishop would annul the first marriage; that it would be a good thing for me to sell Dubechnya without my wife's knowledge and put the money in the bank in my own name; that if my sister and I were to bow down at my father's feet and ask him properly, he might perhaps forgive us; that we ought to have a service sung to the Queen of Heaven. . . .

"Come, go along, my dear, and speak to him," she said, when she heard my father's cough. "Go along, speak to him; bow down, your head won't drop off."

I went in. My father was sitting at the table sketching a plan of a summer villa, with Gothic windows, and with a fat turret like a fireman's watchtower—something peculiarly stiff and tasteless. Going into the study I stood still where I could see his drawing. I did not know why I had gone in to my father, but I remember that when I saw his lean face, his red neck, and his shadow on the wall, I wanted to throw myself on his neck, and as Axinya had told me, bow down at his feet; but the sight of the summer villa with the Gothic windows, and the fat turret, restrained me.

"Good evening," I said.

He glanced at me and at once dropped his eyes to his drawing.

"What do you want?" he asked, after waiting a little.

"I have come to tell you my sister's very ill. She can't live very long," I added in a hollow voice.

"Well," sighed my father, taking off his spectacles and laying them on the table. "What thou sowest that shalt thou reap. What thou sowest," he repeated, getting up from the table, "that shalt thou reap. I ask you to remember how you came to me two years ago, and on this very spot I begged you, I besought you to give up your errors; I reminded you of your duty, of your honour, of what you owed to your forefathers whose traditions we ought to preserve as sacred. Did you obey me? You scorned my counsels and obstinately persisted in clinging to your false ideals; worse still you drew your sister into the path of error with you and led her to lose her moral principles and sense of shame. Now you are both in a bad way. Well, as thou sowest, so shalt thou reap!"

As he said this we walked up and down the room. He probably imagined that I had come to him to confess my wrong doings, and he probably expected that I should begin begging him to forgive my sister and me. I was cold, I was shivering as though I were in a fever and spoke with difficulty in a husky voice.

"And I beg you, too, to remember," I said, "on this very spot I besought you to understand me, to reflect, to decide with me how and for what we should live, and in answer you began talking about our forefathers, about my grandfather who wrote poems. One tells you now that your only daughter is hopelessly ill, and you go on again about your forefathers, your traditions. . . . And such frivolity in your old age, when death is close at hand, and you haven't more than five or ten years left!"

"What have you come here for?" my father asked sternly, evidently offended at my reproaching him for his frivolity.

"I don't know. I love you, I am unutterably sorry that we are so far apart—so you see I have come. I love you still, but my sister has broken with you completely. She does not forgive you and will never forgive you now. Your very name arouses her aversion for the past, for life."

"And who is to blame for it?" cried my father. "It's your fault, you scoundrel!"

"Well, suppose it is my fault," I said. "I admit I have been to blame in many things, but why is it that this life of yours, which you think binding upon us, too—why is it so dreary, so barren? How is it that in not one of these houses you have been building for the last thirty years has there been anyone from whom I might have learned how to live, so as not to be to blame? There is not one honest man in the whole town! These houses of yours are nests of damnation, where mothers and daughters are made away with, where children are tortured. . . . My poor mother!" I went on in despair. "My poor sister! One has to stupefy oneself with vodka, with cards, with scandal; one must become a scoundrel, a hypocrite, or go on drawing plans for years and years, so as not to notice all the horrors that lie hidden in these houses. Our town has existed for hundreds of years and all that time it has not produced one man of service to our country—not one. You have stifled in the germ everything in the least living and bright. It's a town of shopkeepers, publicans, countinghouse clerks, canting hypocrites; it's a useless, unnecessary town, which not one soul would regret if it suddenly sank through the earth."

"I don't want to listen to you, you scoundrel!" said my father, and he took up his ruler from the table. "You are drunk. Don't dare come and see your father in such a state! I tell you for the last time, and you can repeat it to your depraved sister, that you'll get nothing from me, either of you. I have torn my disobedient children out of my heart, and if they suffer for their disobedience and obstinacy I do not pity them. You can go whence you came. It has pleased God to chastise me with you, but I will bear the trial with resignation, and, like Job, I will find consolation in my sufferings and in unremitting labour. You must not cross my threshold till you have mended your ways. I am a just man, all I tell you is for your benefit, and if you desire your own good you ought to remember all your life what I say and have said to you. . . ."

I waved my hand in despair and went away. I don't remember what happened afterwards, that night and next day.

I am told that I walked about the streets bareheaded, staggering, and singing aloud, while a crowd of boys ran after me, shouting:

"Better-than-nothing!"

20

If I wanted to order a ring for myself, the inscription I should choose would be: "Nothing passes away." I believe that nothing passes away without leaving a trace, and that every step we take, however small, has significance for our present and our future existence.

What I have been through has not been for nothing. My great troubles, my patience, have touched people's hearts, and now they don't call me "Better-than-nothing," they don't laugh at me, and when I walk by the shops they don't throw water over me. They have grown used to my being a workman, and see nothing strange in my carrying a pail of paint and putting in windows, though I am of noble rank;

on the contrary, people are glad to give me orders, and I am now considered a first-rate workman, and the best foreman after Radish, who, though he has regained his health, and though, as before, he paints the cupola on the belfry without scaffolding, has no longer the force to control the workmen; instead of him I now run about the town looking for work, I engage the workmen and pay them, borrow money at a high rate of interest, and now that I myself am a contractor, I understand how it is that one may have to waste three days racing about the town in search of tilers on account of some twopenny-halfpenny job. People are civil to me, they address me politely, and in the houses where I work they offer me tea and send to enquire whether I wouldn't like dinner. Children and young girls often come and look at me with curiosity and compassion.

One day I was working in the governor's garden, painting an arbour there to look like marble. The governor, walking in the garden, came up to the arbour and, having nothing to do, entered into conversation with me, and I reminded him how he had once summoned me to an interview with him. He looked into my face intently for a minute, then made his mouth like a round "O," flung up his hands, and said: "I don't remember!"

I have grown older, have become silent, stern, and austere; I rarely laugh, and I am told that I have grown like Radish, and that like him I bore the workmen by my useless exhortations.

Marya Viktorovna, my former wife, is living now abroad, while her father is constructing a railway somewhere in the eastern provinces, and is buying estates there. Dr. Blagovo is also abroad. Dubechnya has passed again into the possession of Madam Cheprakov, who has bought it after forcing the engineer to knock the price down twenty per cent. Moisei goes about now in a bowler hat; he often drives into the town in a racing droshky on business of some sort and stops near the bank. They say he has already bought up a mortgaged estate and is constantly making enquiries at the bank about Dubechnya, which he means to buy too. Poor Ivan Cheprakov was for a long while out of work, staggering about the town and drinking. I tried to get him into our work, and for a time he painted roofs and put in window-panes in our company, and even got to like it, and stole oil, asked for tips, and drank like a regular painter. But he soon got sick of the work and went back to Dubechnya, and afterwards the workmen confessed to me that he had tried to persuade them to join him one night and murder Moisei and rob Madam Cheprakov.

My father has greatly aged; he is very bent, and in the evenings walks up and down near his house. I never go to see him.

During an epidemic of cholera Prokofy doctored some of the shopkeepers with pepper cordial and pitch, and took money for doing so, and, as I learned from the newspapers, was flogged for abusing the doctors as he sat in his shop. His shopboy Nikolka died of cholera. Karpovna is still alive and, as always, she loves and fears her Prokofy. When she sees me, she always shakes her head mournfully, and says with a sigh: "Your life is ruined."

On working days I am busy from morning till night. On holidays, in fine weather, I take my tiny niece (my sister reckoned on a boy, but the child is a girl) and walk in a leisurely way to the cemetery. There I stand or sit down, and stay a long time gazing at the grave that is so dear to me, and tell the child that her mother lies here.

Sometimes, by the graveside, I find Anyuta Blagovo. We greet each other and stand in silence, or talk of Kleopatra, of her child, of how sad life is in this world; then, going out of the cemetery, we walk along in silence and she slackens her pace on purpose to walk beside me a little longer. The little girl, joyous and happy, pulls at her hand, laughing and screwing up her eyes in the bright sunlight, and we stand still and join in caressing the dear child.

When we reach the town, Anyuta Blagovo, agitated and flushing crimson, says good-bye to me and walks on alone, austere and respectable. . . . And no one who met her could, looking at her, imagine that she had just been walking beside me and even caressing the child.

1896

Peasants

NIKOLAY CHIKILDEYEV, a waiter in the Moscow hotel, Slavyansky Bazar, had been taken ill. His legs went numb and his gait became unsteady, so that one day as he was going along the corridor, carrying an order of ham and peas on a tray, he stumbled and fell. He had to give up his job. Whatever money he and his wife had was spent on doctors and medicines; they had nothing left to live on; idleness weighed heavily upon him and he decided to go back to the village from which he had come. It was easier to be ill at home, and it was cheaper living there; and not for nothing is it said that there is help in the walls of home.

He arrived in his native Zhukovo toward evening. In his childhood the house in which he was born figured as a bright, cosy, comfortable place. But now, going into the log cabin, he was positively frightened: it was so dark and crowded and squalid. His wife Olga and his daughter Sasha, who had come with him, stared in bewilderment at the big dirty stove, which occupied almost half the room and was black with soot and flies. What a lot of flies! The stove was lopsided, the logs in the walls sloped, and it looked as though the cabin were about to collapse. In the corner, near the icons, bottle labels and scraps of newspaper were pasted on the walls instead of pictures. The poverty, the poverty! None of the grown-ups were at home; all were at work, reaping. On the stove sat a flaxen-haired girl of eight, unwashed, apathetic; she did not even look up at the newcomers. Below, a white cat was rubbing itself against the oven fork.

"Pussy, pussy!" Sasha called to it coaxingly. "Pussy!"

"It can't hear," said the little girl; "it's gone deaf."

"Why?"

"Oh, it was hit."

Nikolay and Olga realized at first glance what life was like here, but said nothing to each other; silently they put down their bundles, and silently went out into the village street. Their cabin was the third from the end and seemed the poorest and oldest-looking; the second was not much better; but the last one had an iron roof and curtains at the windows. That cottage stood apart, and was not enclosed; it was a tavern. The cabins were all in a single row, and the entire little village—quiet and pensive, with willows, elders, and mountain ash peeping out from the courtyards—had a pleasant look.

Behind the peasant homesteads the ground sloped down to the river steeply and precipitously, so that huge boulders jutted out here and there through the clay. On the steep slope paths wound among the stones and pits dug by the potters; pieces of broken pottery, brown and red, lay about in heaps, and below there stretched a broad, level, bright-green meadow, already mown, over which the peasants' cattle were now wandering. The river, two thirds of a mile from the village, ran, twisting and turning, between beautiful wooded banks. Beyond it was another broad meadow, a herd of cattle, long files of white geese; then, just as on the hither side, there was a steep rise, and at the top of it, on a ridge, a village with a church that had five domes, and, at a little distance, a manor house.

"It's nice here!" said Olga, crossing herself at the sight of the church. "Lord, what space!"

Just at that moment the bells began ringing for vespers (it was Saturday evening). Two little girls, down below, who were carrying a pail of water, looked round at the church to listen to the chimes.

"About this time they are serving the dinners at the Slavyansky Bazar," said Nikolay dreamily.

Sitting on the edge of the ravine, Nikolay and Olga watched the sunset, and saw how the gold and crimson sky was reflected in the river, in the church windows, and in the very air, which was soft and still and inexpressibly pure, as it never was in Moscow. And when the sun had set, the herds went past, bleating and bellowing; geese flew across from the other side of the river, and then all was hushed; the soft light faded from the air, and dusk began its rapid descent.

Meanwhile Nikolay's father and mother, two gaunt, bent, toothless old people, of the same height, had returned. The daughters-in-law, Marya and Fyokla, who had been working on the estate across the river, came home, too. Marya, the wife of Nikolay's brother Kiryak, had six children, and Fyokla, the wife of his brother Denis, who was in the army, had two; and when Nikolay, stepping into the cabin, saw the whole family, all those bodies big and little stirring on the sleeping platforms, in the cradles and in all the corners, and when he saw the greed with which his old father and the women ate the black bread, dipping it in water, it was borne in upon him that he had made a mistake in coming here, sick, penniless, and with a family, too—a mistake!

"And where is brother Kiryak?" he asked, when they had greeted each other.

"He works as a watchman for a merchant," answered his father; "he stays there in the woods. He ain't a bad worker, but he's too fond of the drink."

"He's no breadwinner," said the old woman tearfully. "Our men are a poor lot; they bring nothing into the house, but take plenty out. Kiryak drinks, and the old man too knows his way to the tavern—it's no use hiding the sin. The wrath of the Queen of Heaven is on us."

On account of the guests they heated the samovar. The tea smelt of fish; the sugar was gray and had been nibbled; cockroaches ran about over the bread and the crockery. It was disgusting to drink the tea, and the conversation was disgusting, too—about nothing but poverty and sickness. And before they had emptied their first cups there came a loud, long-drawn-out, drunken shout from the courtyard:

"Ma-arya!"

"Looks like Kiryak's coming," said the old man. "Talk of the devil—"

Silence fell. And after a little while, the shout sounded again, coarse and long-drawn-out, as though it came from under the ground:

"Ma-arya!"

Marya, the elder daughter-in-law, turned pale and huddled against the stove, and it was odd to see the look of terror on the face of this strong, broad-shouldered, homely woman. Her daughter, the apathetic-looking little girl who had been sitting on the stove, suddenly broke into loud weeping.

"What are you bawling for, you pest?" Fyokla, a handsome woman, also strong and broad-shouldered, shouted at her. "He won't kill her, no fear!"

From the old man Nikolay learned that Marya was afraid to live in the woods with Kiryak, and that whenever he was drunk he came for her, raised Cain, and beat her mercilessly.

"Ma-arya!" the shout sounded at the very door.

"Help me, for Christ's sake, good people," stammered Marya, breathing as though she were being plunged into icy water. "Help me, good people—"

All the children in the cabin began crying, and affected by their example, Sasha, too, began to cry. A drunken cough was heard, and a tall, black-bearded peasant wearing a winter cap came into the cabin, and because his face could not be seen in the dim light of the little lamp, he looked terrifying. It was Kiryak. Going up to his wife, he swung his arm and punched her in the face; stunned by the blow, she did not utter a sound, but sank down, and her nose instantly began bleeding.

"What a shame! What a shame!" muttered the old man, clambering up onto the stove. "Before guests, too! What a sin!"

The old woman sat silent, hunched, lost in thought; Fyokla rocked the cradle.

Evidently aware of inspiring terror, and pleased by it, Kiryak seized Marya by the arm, dragged her toward the door, and growled like a beast in order to seem still more terrible; but at that moment he suddenly caught sight of the guests and halted.

"Oh, they have come . . ." he said, letting go of his wife; "my own brother with his family . . ."

Staggering and opening his blood-shot, drunken eyes wide, he muttered a prayer before the icon and went on:

"My dear brother and his family, come to the parental house—from Moscow, I mean. The ancient capital city of Moscow, I mean, mother of cities— Excuse me."

He sank down on the bench near the samovar and began drinking tea, sipping it loudly from the saucer amid general silence. He drank a dozen cups, then lay down on the bench and began to snore.

They started going to bed. Nikolay, being ill, was to sleep on the stove with the old man; Sasha lay down on the floor, while Olga went into the shed with the other women.

"Now, now, dearie," she said, lying down on the hay beside Marya; "tears won't help. Bear your cross, that's all. It says in Scripture: 'Whosoever shall smite thee on thy right cheek, turn to him the other also.' . . . Now, now, dearie."

Then, speaking under her breath in a singsong, she told them about Moscow, about her life, how she had been a chambermaid in furnished rooms.

"And in Moscow the houses are big, made of stone," she said; "and there are many, many churches, forty times forty, dearie; and in the houses they're all gentry, so goodlooking and so proper!"

Marya said that not only had she never been to Moscow, but had not even been in their own district town; she could neither read nor write, and knew no prayers, not even "Our Father." Both she and Fyokla, her sister-in-law, who was sitting a little way off listening, were exceedingly backward and dull-witted. They both disliked their husbands; Marya was afraid of Kiryak, and whenever he stayed with her she shook with fear, and always got a headache from the fumes of vodka and tobacco of which he reeked. And in response to the question whether she did not miss her husband, Fyokla replied sourly:

"Deuce take him!"

They talked a while and then grew silent.

It was cool, and a cock was crowing at the top of his voice near the shed, interfering with sleep. When the bluish morning light was already showing through every crack, Fyokla got up quietly and went out, and then they heard her hurry off somewhere, her bare feet thumping as she ran.

2

Olga went to church, and took Marya with her. As they went down the path toward the meadow both were cheerful. Olga liked the open country, and Marya felt that in her sister-in-law she had found someone near and dear to her

The sun was rising. Low over the meadow hovered a drowsy hawk; the river looked dull; wisps of mist were floating here and there, but on the farther shore a streak of light already lay across the hill; the church was shining, and in the garden attached to the manor the rooks were cawing frantically.

"The old man ain't bad," Marya told her, "but Granny is strict, and is free with her hand. Our own flour lasted till Carnival, and now we buy it at the tavern; so she's cross; she says we eat too much."

"Now, now, dearie! Bear your cross, that's all. It's written: 'Come unto me, all ye that labor and are heavy laden.' "

Olga spoke sedately, in a singsong, and her gait was that of a pilgrim woman, rapid and fidgety. Every day she read the gospel, read it aloud like a deacon; a great deal of it she did not understand, but the sacred phrases moved her to tears, and such words as "behold" and "whosoever" she pronounced with a sweet faintness at her heart. She believed in God, in the Holy Virgin, in the saints; she believed that it was wrong to harm anyone—whether simple folk, or Germans, or gypsies, or Jews—and that misfortune awaited even those who did not pity animals. She believed that this was written in the Scriptures; and so when she pronounced words from Holy Writ, even though she did not understand them, her face softened with emotion, grew compassionate and radiant.

"Where do you come from?" Marya asked her.

"I am from the province of Vladimir. But I was taken to Moscow long ago, when I was eight years old."

They reached the river. On the other side a woman stood at the water's edge, taking off her clothes.

"That's our Fyokla," said Marya, recognizing her. "She's been across the river to the manor yard. She's been with the squire's men. She's a hussy and foul-mouthed—she is that!"

Black-browed Fyokla, her hair undone, still young and with the firm flesh of a girl, jumped off the bank and began thrashing the water with her feet, sending waves in all directions.

"A hussy—she is that!" repeated Marya.

The river was spanned by a rickety little bridge of logs,

and below in the clean, clear water shoals of broad-headed
chub were swimming. The dew was glistening on the green
shrubs that were mirrored in the water. Then the air grew
warmer; it was pleasant. What a glorious morning it was!
And how glorious life would probably be in this world, were
it not for want, horrible, inescapable want, from which you
cannot hide anywhere! Only to look round at the village
was to remember all that had happened the day before, and
the spell of the happiness that they thought they felt around
them vanished instantly.

They went into the church. Marya stood in the entrance
and did not dare to go farther. Nor did she dare to sit down
either, though they only began ringing for Mass after eight
o'clock. She remained standing the whole time.

While the gospel was being read the crowd suddenly
parted to make way for the squire's family. Two young
ladies in white frocks and wide-brimmed hats walked in,
and with them was a chubby, rosy boy in a sailor suit.
Their appearance moved Olga; she concluded at first glance
that they were decent, elegant, cultivated people. But
Marya glared at them from under her brows, sullenly,
dejectedly, as though they were not human beings but mon-
sters who might crush her if she did not move aside.

And every time the deacon intoned in his bass voice,
she imagined that she heard the cry, "Ma-arya!" and she
shuddered.

3

The arrival of the guests became known in the village, and
directly after Mass a great many people assembled in the
cabin. The Leonychevs and the Matveichevs and the
Ilyichovs came to make inquiries about relatives of their
who had situations in Moscow. All the lads of Zhukov
who could read and write were packed off to Moscow an
hired out as bellboys or waiters (just as the lads from th
village on the other side of the river all apprenticed
bakers), and this had been the custom from the days c
serfdom, long ago, when a certain Luka Ivanych, a peasa
from Zhukovo, now a legendary figure, who had been
bartender in one of the Moscow clubs, would take no
but his fellow villagers into his service, and these in tur

as they got up in the world, sent for their kinsfolk and found jobs for them in taverns and restaurants; and from that time on the village of Zhukovo was known throughout the countryside round about as Flunkeyville or Toadytown. Nikolay had been taken to Moscow when he was eleven, and gotten a situation by Ivan Makarych, a Matveichev, who was then an attendant at the Hermitage garden restaurant. And now, addressing the Matveichevs, Nikolay said unctuously:

"Ivan Makarych is my benefactor, and I am bound to pray for him day and night, because it was he who set me on the right path."

"God bless you!" a tall old woman, the sister of Ivan Makarych, said tearfully, "and not a word have we heard about him, the dear man."

"Last winter he was in service at Omon's, and there was a rumor that this season he was somewhere out of town, in a garden restaurant. He has aged! Why, it used to be that he would bring home as much as ten rubles a day in the summertime, but now things are very quiet everywhere. It's hard on the old man."

The women and the old crones looked at Nikolay's feet, shod in felt boots, and at his pale face, and said mournfully:

"You're no breadwinner, Nikolay Osipych; you're no breadwinner! No, indeed!"

And they all fondled Sasha. She was going on eleven, but she was small and very thin, and she looked no more than seven. Among the other little girls, with their sunburnt faces and roughly cropped hair, and their long, faded shifts, she, with her pallor, her big dark eyes and the red ribbon in her hair, looked droll, as though she were some little wild thing that had been caught in the fields and brought into the cabin.

"She can read, too," said Olga, looking tenderly at her daughter and showing her off. "Read a little, child!" she said, taking the Gospels from the corner. "You read, and the good Christian folk will listen."

It was an old, heavy volume in a leather binding with dog-eared edges, and it gave off a smell as though monks had come into the house. Sasha raised her eyebrows and began in a loud singsong:

" 'And when they were departed, behold, the angel of the Lord . . . appeareth to Joseph in a dream, saying, Arise, and take the young child and his mother . . .' "

" 'The young child and his mother,' " Olga repeated, and flushed all over with emotion.

" 'And flee into Egypt, and be thou there until I bring thee word: for Herod will seek the young child, to destroy him . . .' "

At these words Olga could not contain herself and burst into tears. Affected by her example, Marya began to whimper, and then Ivan Makarych's sister followed suit. The old man coughed and bustled about looking for a present for his granddaughter, but finding nothing, gave it up with a wave of his hand. And when the reading was over the neighbors dispersed to their homes, deeply moved and very much pleased with Olga and Sasha.

Because of the holiday, the family stayed home all day. The old woman, whom her husband, her daughters-in-law, her grandchildren, all alike called Granny, always tried to do everything herself; she lit the stove and heated the samovar with her own hands, even carried the midday meal to the men in the fields, and then complained that she was worn out with work. And all the time she fretted for fear that someone should eat a bite too much or that her husband and daughters-in-law should sit idle. Now she would hear the tavernkeeper's geese making for her kitchen garden by the back way, and she would run out of the cabin with a long stick and spend half an hour screaming beside her cabbages which were as meager and flabby as herself; again she would imagine that a crow was after her chickens and would rush at it with loud words of abuse. She was cross and full of complaints from morning till night, and often raised such a hubbub that passers-by stopped in the street.

She treated the old man roughly, calling him a lazybones and a plague. He was a shiftless, undependable man and perhaps if she had not been prodding him continually he would not have worked at all, but would just have sat on the stove and talked. He told his son at great length about certain enemies of his, complained of the injuries he suffered every day at the hands of the neighbors, and it was tedious to listen to him.

"Yes," he would hold forth, with his arms akimbo, "Yes— A week after the Exaltation of the Cross I sold my hay at thirty kopecks a pood, of my own free will. Yes, well and good. So you see I was taking the hay in the morning of my own free will; I wasn't doing no one no harm. In an unlucky hour I see the village headman, Antip Sedelnikov, coming out of the tavern. 'Where are you taking it, you blank blank?' says he, and fetches me a box on the ear."

Kiryak had a terrible hangover and was ashamed to face his brother.

"What vodka will do! Oh, my God!" he muttered as he shook his throbbing head. "For Christ's sake, forgive me, dear brother and sister; I'm not happy about it myself."

Because it was a holiday, they bought a herring at the tavern and made a soup of the herring head. At midday they sat down to have tea and went on drinking it until they were all perspiring; they looked actually swollen with tea; and then they attacked the soup, all helping themselves out of one pot. The herring itself Granny hid away.

In the evening a potter was firing pots on the slope. Down below in the meadow the girls got up a round dance and sang songs. Someone played an accordion. On the other side of the river, too, one kiln was going, and the girls sang songs, and in the distance the singing sounded soft and melodious. In and about the tavern the peasants were making a racket. They sang with drunken voices, discordantly, and swore at one another so filthily that Olga could only shudder and repeat:

"Oh, holy saints!"

What amazed her was that the swearing was incessant, and that the old men who were near their end were the loudest and most persistent in using this foul language. And the girls and children listened to the swearing without turning a hair; it was evident that they had been used to it from their cradles.

It got to be past midnight, the fire in the kilns on both sides of the river died down, but in the meadow below and in the tavern the merrymaking continued. The old man and Kiryak, both drunk, walking arm in arm, their shoulders jostling, went up to the shed where Olga and Marya were lying.

"Let her be," the old man pleaded; "let her be— She's a harmless woman— It's a sin—"

"Ma-arya!" shouted Kiryak.

"Let her be— It's a sin— She's not a bad woman."

Both stood there for a minute and then went on.

"I lo-ove the flowers of the fi-ield," the old man burst forth in a high, piercing tenor. "I lo-ove to pick them in the meadows!"

Then he spat, swore filthily, and went into the cabin.

4

Granny stationed Sasha near her kitchen garden and ordered her to see to it that the geese did not get in. It was a hot August day. The tavernkeeper's geese could get into the kitchen garden by the back way, but at the moment they were seriously engaged: they were picking up oats near the tavern, peacefully chatting together, and only the gander craned his neck as though to see if the old woman were not coming with a stick. Other geese from down below might have trespassed, but they were now feeding far away on the other side of the river, stretching across the meadow in a long white garland. Sasha stood about a while, grew bored, and, seeing that the geese were not coming, went up to the brink of the slope.

There she saw Marya's eldest daughter Motka, who was standing motionless on a huge boulder, staring at the church. Marya had been brought to bed thirteen times, but she had only six living children, all girls, not one boy, and the eldest was eight. Motka, barefoot and wearing a long shift, was standing in the full sunshine; the sun was blazing down right on her head, but she did not notice it, and seemed as though turned to stone. Sasha stood beside her and said, looking at the church:

"God lives in the church. People have lamps and candles, but God has little green and red and blue icon-lamps like weeny eyes. At night God walks about the church, and with Him the Holy Mother of God and Saint Nicholas— clump, clump, clump they go! And the watchman is scared so scared! Now, now, dearie," she added, imitating her mother. "And when the end of the world comes, all the churches will fly up to heaven."

"With the be-elfri-ies?" Motka asked in a deep voice, drawling the syllables.

"With the belfries. And when the end of the world comes, the good people will go to Paradise, but the wicked will burn in fire eternal and unquenchable, dearie. To my mama and to Marya, too, God will say: 'You never harmed anyone, and so you go to the right, to Paradise'; but to Kiryak and Granny He will say: 'You go to the left, into the fire.' And the ones who ate forbidden food on fast days will be sent into the fire, too."

She looked up at the sky, opening her eyes wide, and said:

"Look at the sky and don't blink and you will see angels."

Motka began looking at the sky, too, and a minute passed in silence.

"Do you see them?" asked Sasha.

"I don't," said Motka in her deep voice.

"But I do. Little angels are flying about the sky and go flap, flap with their little wings like midges."

Motka thought for a while, with her eyes on the ground, and asked:

"Will Granny burn?"

"She will, dearie."

From the boulder down to the very bottom there was a smooth, gentle slope, covered with soft green grass, which one longed to touch with one's hands or to lie upon.

Sasha lay down and rolled to the bottom. Motka, with a grave, stern face, and breathing heavily, followed suit, and as she did so, her shift rolled up to her shoulders.

"What fun!" said Sasha, delighted.

They walked up to the top to roll down again, but just then they heard the familiar, shrill voice. Oh, how awful it was! Granny, toothless, bony, hunched, her short gray hair flying in the wind, was driving the geese out of the kitchen garden with a long stick, screaming.

"They have trampled all the cabbages, the cursed creatures! May you croak, you thrice accursed plagues! Why don't the devil take you!"

She saw the little girls, threw down the stick, picked up a switch, and, seizing Sasha by the neck with her fingers, dry and hard as spikes, began whipping her. Sasha cried with pain and fear, while the gander, waddling and craning his neck, went up to the old woman and hissed something, and when he went back to his flock all the geese greeted him approvingly with a "Ga-ga-ga!" Then Granny proceeded to whip Motka, and so Motka's shift was rolled up again. In despair and crying loudly, Sasha went to the cabin to complain. Motka followed her; she, too, was crying, but on a deeper note, without wiping her tears, and her face as wet as though it had been dipped in water.

"Holy Fathers!" cried Olga, dismayed, as the two came into the cabin. "Queen of Heaven!"

Sasha began telling her story, when Granny walked in with shrill cries and abuse; then Fyokla got angry, and there was a hubbub in the house.

"Never mind, never mind!" Olga, pale and distressed, tried to comfort the children, stroking Sasha's head. "She's your grandmother; it's a sin to be cross with her. Never mind, child."

Nikolay, who was already worn out by the continual clamor, the hunger, the sickening fumes, the stench, who already hated and despised the poverty, who was ashamed of his father and mother before his wife and daughter, swung his legs off the stove and said to his mother in an irritable, tearful voice:

"You shouldn't beat her! You have no right to beat her!"

"You're ready to croak there on the stove, you loafer!" Fyokla snapped at him spitefully. "The devil has brought you here, you spongers!"

Sasha and Motka and all the little girls in the household huddled into a corner on top of the stove behind Nikolay's back, and from there listened to all this in silence and terror, and one could hear the beating of their little hearts. When there is someone in a family who has long been ill, and hopelessly ill, there come terrible moments when all those close to him timidly, secretly, at the bottom of their hearts wish for his death, and only the children fear the death of someone close to them, and always feel horrified at the thought of it. And now the little girls, with bated breath and a mournful look on their faces, stared at Nikolay and thought that he would soon die; and they wanted to cry and to say something friendly and compassionate to him.

He was pressing close to Olga, as though seeking her protection, and saying to her softly in a shaking voice:

"Olga dear, I can't bear it here any longer. I haven't the strength. For Christ's sake, for the sake of God in heaven, write to your sister, Klavdia Abramovna. Let her sell and pawn everything she has; let her send us the money, and we'll go away from here. Oh, Lord," he went on with anguish, "to have one peep at Moscow! To see mother Moscow, if only in my dreams!"

And when evening came, and it was dark in the cabin, it got so dismal that it was hard to bring out a word. Granny, cross as ever, soaked some crusts of rye bread in a cup, and was a whole hour sucking at them. Marya, having milked the cow, brought in a pail of milk and set it on a bench; then Granny poured it from the pail into jugs slowly and deliberately, evidently pleased that it was now the Fast of Assumption, so that no one would drink milk and all of it would be left untouched. And she only poured out just a little into a saucer for Fyokla's baby. When she and Marya carried the jugs down to the cellar, Motka suddenly came to life, slipped down from the stove, and going to the bench where the wooden cup full of crusts was standing, splashed some milk from the saucer into it.

Granny, coming back into the cabin, attacked her soaked crusts again, while Sasha and Motka sat on the stove, staring at her, and were glad that she had taken forbidden food and now was sure to go to hell. They were comforted and lay down to sleep, and as she dozed off, Sasha pictured the Last Judgment to herself: a fire was burning in a stove something like a potter's kiln, and the Evil One, with horns like a cow's and black all over, was driving Granny into the fire with a long stick, just as Granny herself had driven the geese.

5

On the Feast of Assumption, after ten o'clock at night, the girls and boys who were making merry down in the meadow suddenly began to scream and shout, and ran in the direction of the village; and those who were sitting on the brink of the slope at first could not make out what was the matter.

"Fire! Fire!" desperate shouts sounded from below. "The place is on fire!"

Those who were sitting above looked back and a terrible and extraordinary spectacle presented itself to them. From the thatched roof of one of the last cabins in the village rose a pillar of flame, seven feet high, which coiled and scattered sparks in all directions as though it were a fountain playing. And all at once the whole roof burst into bright flame, and the crackling of the fire was heard.

The moonlight was dimmed, and now the whole village was enveloped in a quivering red glow: black shadows moved over the ground, there was a smell of burning, and those who ran up from below were all gasping and trembling so that they could not speak; they jostled each other, fell down, and, unaccustomed to the bright light, could hardly see and did not recognize each other. It was terrifying. What was particularly frightening was that pigeons were flying in the smoke above the flames, and that in the tavern, where they did not yet know of the fire, people were still singing and playing the accordion as though nothing was wrong.

"Uncle Semyon's place is on fire," someone shouted in a loud, coarse voice.

Marya was rushing about near her cabin, weeping and wringing her hands, her teeth chattering, though the fire was a long way off, at the other end of the village. Nikolay came out in felt boots, the children ran about in their little shifts. Near the village policeman's cabin an iron sheet was struck. Boom, boom, boom! floated through the air, and this rapid, incessant sound sent a pang to the heart and turned one cold. The old women stood about, holding the icons. Sheep, calves, cows were driven out of the courtyards into the street; chests, sheepskins, tubs were carried out. A black stallion, that was kept apart from the drove of horses because he kicked and injured them, was set free and ran back and forth through the village once or twice, neighing and pawing the ground, then suddenly stopped short near a cart and started kicking it with his hind legs.

The bells in the church on the other side of the river began ringing.

Near the burning cabin it was so hot and so bright that every blade of grass on the ground was distinctly visible. On one of the chests that they had managed to carry out sat Semyon, a carrot-haired peasant with a long nose, wearing a jacket and a cap pulled down over his ears; his wife was lying face down, unconscious and moaning. A little old man of eighty with a big beard, who looked like a gnome, a stranger to the village, but apparently connected in some way with the fire, walked about near it, bareheaded, with a white bundle in his arms. The flames were reflected on his bald spot. The village headman, Antip Sedelnikov, as swarthy and black-haired as a gypsy, went up to the cabin with an ax, and hacked out the windows one after another—no one knew why—and then began chopping up the porch.

"Women, water!" he shouted. "Bring the engine! Shake a leg!"

The peasants who had just been carousing in the tavern were dragging up the engine. They were all drunk; they kept stumbling and falling down, and all had a helpless expression and tears in their eyes.

"Girls, water!" shouted the headman, who was drunk, too. "Shake a leg, girls!"

The women and the girls ran downhill to a spring, and hauled pails and tubs of water up the hill, and, after pouring it into the engine, ran down again. Olga and Marya and Sasha and Motka, too, all carried water. The women and the boys pumped the water; the hose hissed, and the headman, directing it now at the door, now at the windows, held back the stream with his finger, which made it hiss yet more sharply.

"He's a top-notcher, Antip is!" voices shouted approvingly. "Keep it up!"

Antip dove into the burning cabin and shouted from within.

"Pump! Lend a hand, good Orthodox folk, on the occasion of such a terrible accident!"

The peasants stood round in a crowd, doing nothing and staring at the fire. No one knew what to do, no one knew how to do anything, and there were stacks of grain and hay, piles of faggots, and sheds all about. Kiryak and old Osip, his father, both tipsy, stood there, too. And, as though to justify his inaction, old Osip said to the woman lying on the ground:

"Why carry on so, friend? The cabin's insured—why worry?"

Semyon, addressing himself now to one person, now to another, kept telling how the fire had started.

"That same old man, the one with the bundle, a house-serf of General Zhukov's— He was cook at our general's, God rest his soul! He came over this evening: 'Let me stay the night,' says he. Well, we had a glass, to be sure. The wife got busy with the samovar—we were going to give the old man some tea, and in an unlucky hour she set the samovar in the entry. And the sparks from the chimney blew straight up to the thatch; well, that's how it was. We were nearly burnt up ourselves. And the old man's cap got burnt up; it's a shame!"

And the sheet of iron was struck tirelessly, and the bells of the church on the other side of the river kept ringing. Ruddy with the glow, and breathless, Olga, looking with horror at the red sheep and at the pink pigeons flying through the smoke, kept running down the slope and up again. It seemed to her that the ringing had entered her soul like a sharp thorn, that the fire would never be over, that Sasha was lost. . . . And when the ceiling of the cabin fell in with a crash, the thought that now the whole village was sure to burn down made her faint, and she could no longer go on carrying water, but sat down on the edge of the slope, setting the buckets near her; beside her and below her, the peasant women sat wailing as though at a wake.

Then, from the village across the river, came men in two carts, bringing a fire-engine with them. A very young student, his white tunic wide open, rode up on horseback. There was the sound of axes. A ladder was placed against the burning frame of the house, and five men ran up it at once, led by the student, who was red in the face and shouted in a harsh, hoarse voice, and in the tone of one who was used to putting out fires. They pulled the house to pieces, a log at a time; they took apart the stable and the wattled fence, and removed the near-by stack of hay.

"Don't let them smash things!" cried stern voices in the crowd. "Don't let them."

Kiryak made his way to the cabin with a resolute air, as though he meant to prevent the newcomers from smashing things, but one of the workmen turned him round and hit him on the neck. There was the sound of laughter, the workman struck him again, Kiryak fell and crawled back into the crowd on all fours.

Two pretty girls in hats, probably the student's sisters, came from the other side of the river. They stood at a distance, looking at the fire. The logs that had been pulled away were no longer burning, but were smoking badly; the student, who was working the hose, turned the stream first on the logs, then on the peasants, then on the women who were hauling the water.

"Georges!" the girls called to him reproachfully and anxiously, "Georges!"

The fire was over. And only when the crowd began to disperse they noticed that day was breaking, that all were pale and rather dark in the face, as people always appear in the early morning when the last stars are fading. As they separated, the peasants laughed and cracked jokes about General Zhukov's cook and his cap which had been burnt, they already wanted to turn the fire into a jest, and even seemed sorry that it had been put out so soon.

"You were good at putting out the fire, sir!" said Olga to the student. "You ought to come to us in Moscow: there we have a fire 'most every day."

"Why, do you come from Moscow?" asked one of the young ladies.

"Yes, miss. My husband was employed at the Slavyansky Bazar. And this is my daughter," she said, pointing to Sasha, who was chilly and huddled up to her. "She is a Moscow girl, too."

The two young ladies said something in French to the student and he gave Sasha a twenty-kopeck piece.

Old Osip noticed this, and a gleam of hope came into his face.

"We must thank God, your honor, there was no wind," he said, addressing the student, "or else we should have been all burnt out in no time. Your honor, kind gentlefolk," he added, with embarrassment in a lower tone, "the dawn's chilly . . . something to warm a man . . . half a bottle to your honor's health."

He was given nothing, and clearing his throat, he shuffled off towards home. Afterwards Olga stood on the edge of the slope and watched the two carts fording the river and the gentlefolk walking across the meadow; a carriage was waiting for them on the other side of the river. Going into the cabin, she said to her husband with enthusiasm:

"Such kind people! And so good-looking! The young ladies were like cherubs!"

"May they burst!" Fyokla, who was sleepy, said spitefully.

6

Marya thought herself unhappy, and often said that she longed to die; Fyokla, on the contrary, found everything in this life to her taste: the poverty, the filth, the incessant cursing. She ate whatever was given her indiscriminately, slept anywhere and on whatever came to hand. She would empty the slops just at the porch, would splash them out from the doorsill, and then walk barefoot through the puddle. And from the very first day she conceived a hatred for Olga and Nikolay just because they did not like this life.

"I'll see what you'll eat here, you Moscow gentry!" she would say maliciously. "I'll see!"

One morning at the beginning of September Fyokla, vigorous, good-looking, and rosy from the cold, brought up two pails of water from down below on a yoke; Marya and Olga were just then sitting at the table, having tea.

"Enjoy your tea!" said Fyokla sarcastically. "The fine ladies!" she added, setting down the pails. "They've gotten into the habit of tea every day. You'd better look out you don't swell up with your tea-drinking," she went on, looking at Olga with hatred. "She's come by her fat mug in Moscow, the tub of lard!"

She swung the yoke and hit Olga a blow on the shoulder so that the two sisters-in-law could only strike their hands together and say:

"Oh, holy saints!"

Then Fyokla went down to the river to wash the clothes, swearing all the time so loudly that she could be heard in the house.

The day passed and then came the long autumn evening. They wound silk in the cabin; everyone did it except Fyokla; she had gone across the river. They got the silk from a factory near by, and the whole family working together earned a mere trifle, some twenty kopecks a week.

"Under the masters things were better," said the old man as he wound silk. "You worked and ate and slept, everything in its turn. At dinner you had *shchi* and *kasha,* and at supper the same again. Cucumbers and cabbage galore: you could eat to your heart's content, as much as you liked. And there was more strictness. Everyone knew his place."

The cabin was lighted by a single little lamp, which burned dimly and smoked. When someone stood in front of the lamp and a large shadow fell across the window, one noticed the bright moonlight. Speaking unhurriedly, old Osip related how people used to live before the Emancipation; how in these very parts, where life was now so poverty-stricken and dreary, they used to hunt with harriers, greyhounds, and specially trained stalkers, and the peasants who were employed as beaters got vodka; how caravans loaded with slaughtered fowls were sent to Moscow for the young masters; how the serfs that were bad were beaten with rods or sent off to the Tver estate, while those who were good were rewarded. And Granny, too, had something to tell. She remembered everything, absolutely everything. She told about her mistress, a kind, God-fearing woman, whose husband was a boozer and a rake, and all of whose daughters made wretched marriages: one married a drunkard, another a commoner, a third eloped (Granny herself, a young girl at the time, had helped with the elopement), and they had all three soon died of grief, as did their mother. And remembering all this, Granny actually shed a tear.

Suddenly someone knocked at the door, and they all started.

"Uncle Osip, put me up for the night."

The little bald old man, General Zhukov's cook, the very one whose cap had been burnt, walked in. He sat

down and listened. Then he, too, began to reminisce and
tell stories. Nikolay, sitting on the stove with his legs hanging down, listened and asked questions about the dishes
that were prepared for the gentry in the old days. They
talked about chops, cutlets, various soups and sauces, and
the cook, who remembered everything very well, mentioned
dishes that are no longer prepared; there was one, for instance—a dish made of bulls' eyes, that was called "Waking
up in the morning."

"And did you have cutlets *maréchal* then?" asked
Nikolay.

"No."

Nikolay shook his head scornfully and said:

"Ah-h! Fine cooks you were!"

The little girls, who were sitting or lying on the stove,
stared down without blinking; there seemed to be a lot of
them, like cherubs in the clouds. They liked the stories;
they sighed and shuddered and turned pale with rapture or
terror, and to Granny, whose stories were the most interesting of all, they listened breathlessly, afraid to stir.

They lay down to sleep in silence; and the old people,
stirred up and troubled by their reminiscences, thought
what a fine thing it was to be young: youth, whatever it
may have been like, left nothing in the memory but what
was buoyant, joyful, touching; and death, they thought,
how terribly cold was death, which was not far off—better
not think of it! The little lamp went out. The darkness,
and the two little windows brightly lit by the moon, and the
stillness and the creak of the cradle, for some reason made
them think of nothing but that life was over and that there
was no way of bringing it back. You doze off, you sink into
obliviousness, and suddenly someone touches your shoulder or breathes on your cheek—and sleep is gone; your
body feels numb, as though circulation had stopped, and
thoughts of death keep coming into your head. You turn
on the other side: you forget about death, but old, dull,
dismal thoughts of want, of fodder, of how dear flour is
getting, stray through the mind, and a little later you remember again that life is over and there is no way of bringing it back. . . .

"Oh, Lord!" sighed the cook.

Someone rapped gently, ever so gently, at the window. It

must have been Fyokla, come back. Olga got up, and yawning and whispering a prayer, unlocked the door, then pulled the bolt of the outer door. But no one came in; only there was a cold draft of air from the street and the entry suddenly grew bright with moonlight. Through the open door could be seen the silent, deserted street, and the moon itself floating across the sky.

"Who's there?" called Olga.

"Me," came the answer, "it's me."

Near the door, hugging the wall, stood Fyokla, stark naked. She was shivering with cold, her teeth were chattering, and in the bright moonlight she looked very pale, strange, and beautiful. The shadows and the bright spots of moonlight on her skin stood out sharply, and her dark eyebrows and firm, young breasts were defined with peculiar distinctness.

"The ruffians over there stripped me and turned me out like this," she muttered. "I had to go home without my clothes—mother-naked. Bring me something to put on."

"But come inside," Olga said softly, beginning to shiver, too.

"I don't want the old folks to see." Granny was, in fact, already stirring and grumbling, and the old man asked: "Who's there?" Olga brought out her own shift and skirt, dressed Fyokla, and then both went softly into the house, trying to close the door noiselessly.

"Is that you, you slick one?" Granny grumbled angrily, guessing who it was. "Curse you, you nightwalker! Why don't the devil take you!"

"It's all right, it's all right," whispered Olga, wrapping Fyokla up; "it's all right, dearie."

All was quiet again. They always slept badly; each one was kept awake by something nagging and persistent: the old man by the pain in his back, Granny by anxiety and malice, Marya by fear, the children by itch and hunger. Now, too, their sleep was restless; they kept turning from one side to the other, they talked in their sleep, they got up for a drink.

Fyokla suddenly burst out into a loud, coarse howl, but checked herself at once, and only sobbed from time to time, her sobs growing softer and more muffled until she was still. Occasionally from the other side of the river came the sound of the striking of the hours; but the clock struck oddly—first five and then three.

"Oh, Lord!" sighed the cook.

Looking at the windows, it was hard to tell whether the moon was still shining or whether it was already dawn. Marya got up and went out, and could be heard milking the cows and saying, "Stea-dy!" Granny went out, too. It was still dark in the cabin, but already one could distinguish all the objects in it.

Nikolay, who had not slept all night, got down from the stove. He took his dress-coat out of a green chest, put it on, and going to the window, stroked the sleeves, fingered the coat-tails—and smiled. Then he carefully removed the coat, put it away in the chest, and lay down again.

Marya came in again and started to light the stove. She was evidently half asleep and was waking up on her feet. She must have had some dream, or perhaps the stories of the previous night came into her mind, for she stretched luxuriously before the stove and said:

"No, freedom is better!"

7

"The master" arrived—that was what they called the district police inspector. When he would come and what he was coming for had been known for a week. There were only forty households in Zhukovo, but they had accumulated more than two thousand rubles of arrears in Zemstvo and other taxes.

The police inspector stopped at the tavern. There he drank two glasses of tea, and then went on foot to the headman's house, near which a crowd of tax defaulters stood waiting. The headman, Antip Sedelnikov, in spite of his youth—he was only a little over thirty—was strict and always sided with the authorities, though he himself was poor and remiss in paying his taxes. Apparently he enjoyed being headman, and liked the sense of power, which he could only display by harshness. At the village meetings he was feared and obeyed. Occasionally he would pounce on a drunken man in the street or near the tavern, tie his hands behind him, and put him in jail. Once he even put

Granny under arrest and kept her in the lock-up for a whole day and a night because, coming to the village meeting instead of Osip, she started to curse. He had never lived in a city or read a book, but somewhere or other he had picked up various bookish expressions, and loved to employ them in conversation, and people respected him for this although they did not always understand him.

When Osip came into the headman's cabin with his tax book, the inspector, a lean old man with long gray side-whiskers, who wore a gray tunic, was sitting at a table in a corner writing something down. The cabin was clean; all the walls were bright with pictures clipped from magazines, and in the most conspicuous place near the icons there was a portrait of Prince Battenberg of Bulgaria. Beside the table stood Antip Sedelnikov with his arms folded.

"He owes one hundred and nineteen rubles, Your Honor," he said, when Osip's turn came. "Before Easter he paid a ruble, and he's not paid a kopeck since."

The inspector looked up at Osip and asked:

"Why is this, brother?"

"Show heavenly mercy, Your Honor," began Osip, growing agitated. "Allow me to say, last year the master from Lutoretzk said to me, 'Osip,' says he, 'sell me your hay . . . you sell it,' says he. Well, why not? I had a hundred *poods*[1] for sale; the women mowed it on the water-meadow. Well, we struck a bargain. It was all right and proper."

He complained of the headman, and kept turning round to the peasants as though inviting them to bear witness; his face got red and sweaty and his eyes grew sharp and angry.

"I don't know why you're saying all this," said the inspector. "I am asking you—I am asking you why you don't pay your arrears. You don't pay, any of you, and am I to answer for you?"

"I just can't."

"These words are of no consequence, Your Honor," said the headman. "The Chikildeyevs certainly are of the needy class, but please just inquire of the others, the root of it all is vodka, and they are a disorderly lot. With no understanding at all."

[1] *Pood* is a unit of weight, a little over 36 pounds.

The inspector wrote something down, and then said to Osip quietly, in an even tone, as though he were asking him for a drink of water:

"Get out."

Soon he drove off; and as he was climbing into his cheap buggy, coughing as he did so, it could be seen from the very look of his long lean back that he no longer remembered Osip or the village headman or the Zhukovo arrears, but was thinking of his own affairs. Before he had gone two thirds of a mile Antip was already carrying off the samovar from the Chikildeyevs' cabin, while Granny followed him, screaming shrilly, straining her lungs:

"I won't let you have it! I won't let you have it, god-damn you!"

He walked rapidly with long strides, and she ran after him, panting, almost falling down, a hunched infuriated creature; her kerchief slipped onto her shoulders, her gray hair with a greenish tint to it blew in the wind. She suddenly stood still, and like a real insurgent, fell to thumping her breast with her fists and shouting louder than ever in a singsong voice, seeming to sob:

"Christians, all you who believe in God! Dear friends, they have wronged me! Darlings, they're trampling on me! Oh, oh, darlings, come and help me!"

"Granny, Granny!" said the village headman sternly, "get some sense into your head!"

With no samovar it was hopelessly dismal in the Chikildeyevs' cabin. There was something humiliating in this deprivation, something insulting, as though the honor of the house were lost. It would have been better, had the headman carried off the table, all the benches, all the pots—the place would not have seemed so bare. Granny screamed, Marya cried, and the little girls, seeing her tears, cried too. The old man, feeling guilty, sat in the corner, silent, with hanging head. Nikolay too was silent. Granny loved him and was sorry for him, but now, forgetting her pity, she fell upon him with abuse, with reproaches, shaking her fist right in his face. She screamed that it was all his fault; indeed, why had he sent them so little when he bragged in his letters that he was earning fifty rubles a month at the Slavyansky Bazar? Why had he come, and with his family, too? If he died, where would the money come from for his funeral? And it was pitiful to look at Nikolay, Olga, and Sasha.

The old man sighed hoarsely, took his cap, and went off to the headman. It was getting dark. Antip was soldering something by the stove, puffing out his cheeks; the air was full of fumes. His children, thin and unwashed, no better than the Chikildeyev brood, were scrambling about on the floor; his wife, an ugly, freckled, big-bellied woman, was winding silk. They were a wretched, unlucky family, and Antip was the only one who looked sturdy and handsome. On a bench stood five samovars in a row. The old man muttered a prayer to Battenberg and then said:

"Antip, show heavenly mercy, give me back the samovar! For Christ's sake!"

"Bring three rubles, then you can have it."

"I just can't."

Antip puffed out his cheeks, the fire hummed and hissed, and was reflected in the samovars. The old man kneaded his cap and said after a moment's thought:

"You give it back to me."

The dark-skinned headman looked quite black and resembled a magician; he turned round to Osip and said sternly, speaking rapidly:

"It all depends on the district magistrate. On the twenty-sixth instant you can state the grounds of your dissatisfaction before the administrative session, verbally or in writing."

Osip did not understand a word, but he was satisfied with that and went home.

Some ten days later the police inspector came again, stayed for an hour and drove away. During those days it had been cold and windy; the river had been frozen for a long time, but still there was no snow, and people were worn to a frazzle because the roads were impassable. On the eve of a holiday some of the neighbors came in to Osip's to sit and have a chat. They talked in the dark, because it was a sin to work and so they did not light the lamp. There were some scraps of news, all rather unpleasant. In two or three households hens had been taken for the arrears and had been sent to the district office, and there they had died because no one had fed them; sheep had been taken, and while they were being carted away tied to one another, and shifted into another cart at each village, one of them had died. And now the question was being discussed: who was to blame?

"The Zemstvo," said Osip. "Who else?"

"Of course, the Zemstvo."

The Zemstvo was blamed for everything—for the arrears, the unjust exactions, the failure of the crops, though no one of them knew what was meant by the Zemstvo. And this dated from the time when well-to-do peasants who had factories, shops, and inns of their own served as members of the Zemstvo boards, were dissatisfied with them, and took to berating the Zemstvos in their factories and taverns.

They talked about how God was not sending the snow; wood had to be hauled for fuel, yet there was no driving or walking over the frozen ruts. In former days, fifteen to twenty years ago, talk had been much more interesting in Zhukovo. In those days every old man looked as though he were guarding some secret; as though he knew something and were waiting for something. They used to talk about a charter with a golden seal, about the division of acreage, about new lands, about treasure troves; they hinted at something. Now the folk of Zhukovo had no secrets at all; their whole life lay bare and clear to all, as though on the palm of your hand, and they could talk of nothing but want, food and fodder, the absence of snow.

There was a lull. Then they recalled the hens again, and the sheep, and began arguing once more as to who was at fault.

"The Zemstvo," said Osip dejectedly. "Who else?"

8

The parish church was nearly four miles away at Kosogorovo, and the peasants only attended it when they had to do so, for christenings, weddings, or funerals; for regular services they went to the church across the river. On holidays in fine weather the girls dressed up in their best and went to Mass in a crowd, and it was a cheering sight to see them walk across the meadow in their red, yellow, and green frocks; when the weather was bad they all stayed home. To confess and to take the communion they went to the parish church. The priest, making the

round of the cabins with the cross at Easter, took fifteen
kopecks from each of those who had not managed to take
the sacrament during Lent.

The old man did not believe in God, for he had hardly
ever given Him a thought; he acknowledged the super-
natural, but felt that it could be of concern to women only,
and when religion or miracles were discussed in his
presence, and a question about these matters was put to
him, he would say reluctantly, scratching himself:

"Who can tell!"

Granny did believe, but somehow her faith was hazy;
everything was mixed up in her memory, and no sooner
did she begin to think of sins, of death, of the salvation of
the soul, than want and cares took possession of her mind,
and she instantly forgot what she had started to think about.
She remembered no prayers at all, and usually in the evenings, before lying down to sleep, she would stand before
the icons and whisper:

"Virgin Mother of Kazan, Virgin Mother of Smolensk,
Virgin Mother of the Three Arms. . . ."

Marya and Fyokla crossed themselves regularly, fasted,
and took communion every year, but quite ignorantly. The
children were not taught any prayers, nothing was told
them about God, and no moral precepts were given them;
they were merely forbidden to take certain foods on fast
days. In other families it was much the same: there were
few who believed, few who had any understanding. At the
same time all loved the Holy Scripture, loved it tenderly,
reverently; but they had no books, there was no one to
read the Bible and explain it, and because Olga sometimes
read them the Gospels, they respected her, and they all
addressed her and Sasha in the deferential second-person
plural.

For local holidays and special services Olga often went
to neighboring villages and to the county seat, in which
there were two monasteries and twenty-seven churches.
She was abstracted, and when she went on these pilgrimages
she quite forgot her family, and only when she was on her
way home would suddenly make the joyful discovery that
she had a husband and daughter, and then she would say,
smiling and radiant:

"God has blessed me!"

What went on in the village seemed to her revolting and was a source of torment to her. On St. Elijah's Day they drank, at the Assumption they drank, at the Exaltation of the Cross they drank. The Feast of the Intercession was the parish holiday for Zhukovo, and on that occasion the peasants drank for three days on end; they drank up fifty rubles belonging to the communal fund, and on top of that collected money for vodka from each household. On the first day the Chikildeyevs slaughtered a sheep and ate mutton in the morning, at noon, and in the evening; they ate large amounts of it, and the children got up at night to eat some more. Those three days Kiryak was fearfully drunk; he drank up all his belongings, even his cap and boots, and beat Marya so terribly that they had to pour water over her to revive her. Afterwards they were all ashamed and felt sick.

However, even in Zhukovo, in this "Flunkeyville," once a year there was a genuine religious event. It was in August, when they carried the icon of the Life-Bearing Mother of God from village to village throughout the district. The day on which it was expected at Zhukovo was windless and the sky was overcast. The girls, in their bright holiday frocks, set off in the morning to meet the icon, and they brought it to the village towards evening, in solemn procession, singing, while the bells pealed in the church across the river. A huge crowd of villagers and strangers blocked the street; there was noise, dust, a crush of people . . . The old man and Granny and Kiryak all stretched out their hands to the icon, gazed at it greedily and cried weeping:

"Intercede for us! Mother! Intercede!"

All seemed suddenly to grasp that there was no void between earth and heaven, that the rich and powerful had not seized everything, that there was still protection from abuse, from bondage, from crushing, unbearable want, from the terrible vodka.

"Intercede for us! Mother!" sobbed Marya. "Mother!"

But the service ended, the icon was carried away, and everything went on as before; and again the sound of coarse, drunken voices came from the tavern.

Only the well-to-do peasants were afraid of death; the richer they grew the less they believed in God and in the salvation of the soul, and only through fear of their earthly end did they light candles and have Masses said, in order to be on the safe side. The poorer peasants did not fear death. The old man and Granny were told to their faces that they had lived too long, that it was time they were dead, and they did not mind. They did not scruple to tell Fyokla in Nikolay's presence that when Nikolay died her husband Denis would be discharged from the army and returned home. And Marya, far from dreading death, regretted that it was so long in coming, and was glad when her children died.

Death they did not fear, but they had an exaggerated terror of every disease. The merest trifle—an upset stomach, a slight chill, and Granny would lie down on the stove, wrap herself up, and start moaning loudly and incessantly: "I am dy-ing!" the old man would hurry off for the priest, and Granny would receive the sacrament and extreme unction. They often talked of colds, of worms, of tumors that shifted about in the stomach and moved up close to the heart. Most of all they feared catching cold, and so dressed in heavy clothes even in summer and warmed themselves on the stove. Granny was fond of doctoring herself and often drove to the dispensary, where she always said she was fifty-eight instead of seventy; she supposed that if the doctor knew her real age he would not treat her, but would say it was time she died instead of doctoring herself. She usually went to the dispensary early in the morning, taking with her two or three of the little girls, and came back in the evening, hungry and cross, with drops for herself and salves for the little girls. Once she had Nikolay go along with her, too, and for a fortnight afterwards he took drops, and said he felt better.

Granny knew all the doctors, medical assistants, and quacks for twenty miles round, and not one of them she liked. At the Feast of the Intercession, when the priest made the round of the cabins with the cross, the deacon told her that in the town near the prison lived an old man who had been an army surgeon's assistant and who worked many cures, and advised her to turn to him. Granny took his advice. After the first snowfall she drove to the town and fetched a little bearded old man, in a long coat, a converted Jew, whose face was covered with a network of tiny blue veins. Just then there were people working in the house: an old tailor, in terrifying spectacles, was cutting a waistcoat out of some rags, and two young men were making felt boots out of wool; Kiryak, who had been sacked for drunkenness and now lived at home, was sitting beside the tailor mending a horse-collar. And the place was crowded, stuffy, and evil-smelling. The converted Jew examined Nikolay and said that it was necessary to cup the patient.

He put on the cups, and the old tailor, Kiryak, and the little girls stood round and looked on, and it seemed to them that they saw the disease coming out of Nikolay; and Nikolay, too, watched how the cups sucking at his breast gradually filled with dark blood, and felt as though there really were something coming out of him, and smiled with pleasure.

"That's fine," said the tailor. "Please God, it will do you good."

The convert put on twelve cups and then another twelve, had tea, and drove away. Nikolay began shivering; his face took on a drawn look, and, as the women put it, shrank up into a little fist; his fingers turned blue. He wrapped himself up in a quilt and a sheepskin coat, but felt colder and colder. Towards evening he began to feel very ill, asked to be laid on the floor, begged the tailor not to smoke; then he grew quiet under the coat, and towards morning he died.

9

Oh, what a hard, what a long, winter it was!

Already by Christmas their own flour had given out and they started buying flour. Kiryak, who lived at home now, was disorderly in the evenings, terrifying everyone, and in the mornings he was tormented by headache and shame, and it was pitiful to look at him. Day and night the bellowing of the starved cow came from the barn—breaking the hearts of Granny and Marya. And as though out of spite, the frosts were bitter the whole time and the snow-drifts high; and the winter dragged on. At Annunciation there was a regular blizzard, and snow fell at Easter.

But after all, the winter did end. At the beginning of April there were warm days and frosty nights; winter would not yield, but one warm day overpowered it at last, and the streams began to flow and the birds to sing. The whole meadow and the shrubs that fringed the river were submerged by the spring floods, and the area between Zhukovo and the farther bank was one vast sheet of water, from which wild ducks rose up in flocks here and there. Every evening a fiery spring sunset, with superb clouds, offered new, extraordinary, incredible sights, just the sort of thing that one does not credit afterwards, when one sees those very colors and those very clouds in a painting.

The cranes flew swiftly, swiftly, uttering mournful sounds, and there seemed to be a summoning note in their cries. Standing on the edge of the slope, Olga stared for a long time at the flooded meadow, at the sunshine, at the church, which looked bright and rejuvenated, as it were; and her tears flowed and she gasped for breath: so passionate was her longing to go away, anywhere, to the end of the world. It was already decided that she should return to Moscow to go into service as a chambermaid, and that Kiryak should set off with her to get a job as a gatekeeper or something of the sort. Oh, to get away quickly!

As soon as the ground was dry and it was warm, they made ready to leave. Olga and Sasha, with bundles on their backs and sandals of plaited bast on their feet, left at daybreak: Marya came out, too, to see them off. Kiryak was not well and remained at home for another week. For the last time Olga, looking at the church, crossed herself and murmured a prayer; thought of her husband, and though she did not cry, her face puckered up and turned ugly, like an old woman's. During the winter she had grown thinner and plainer, her hair had gone a little gray, and instead of her former attractive appearance and pleasant smile, her face now had the sad, resigned expression left by the sorrows she had experienced, and there was something obtuse and wooden about her gaze, as though she were deaf.

She was sorry to leave the village and the peasants. She kept remembering how they had carried Nikolay down the street, and how a Mass for the repose of his soul had been said at every cabin, and how all had wept in sympathy with her grief. During the summer and the winter there had been hours and days when it seemed as though these people lived worse than cattle, and it was terrible to be with them; they were coarse, dishonest, dirty, and drunken; they did not live at peace with one another but quarreled continually, because they feared, suspected, and despised each other. Who keeps the tavern and encourages drunkenness? The peasant. Who embezzles and drinks up the funds that belong to the community, the schools, the church? The peasant. Who steals from his neighbors, sets fire to their property, bears false witness at court for a bottle of vodka? At meetings of the Zemstvo and other local bodies, who is the first to raise his voice against the peasants? The peasant. Yes, to live with them was terrible; but yet, they were human beings, they suffered and wept like human beings, and there was nothing in their lives for which one could not find justification. Crushing labor that made the whole body ache at night, cruel winters, scanty crops, overcrowding; and no help, and nowhere to look for help. Those who were stronger and better-off could give no assistance, as they were themselves coarse, dishonest, drunken, and swore just as foully. The most insignificant little clerk or official treated the peasants as though they were tramps, and addressed even the village elders and church wardens as inferiors, and as though they had a right to do so. And indeed, can any sort of help or good example be given by lazy, grasping, greedy, dissolute men who only visit the village in order to outrage, to despoil, to terrorize? Olga recalled the wretched, humiliated look of the old folks when in the winter Kiryak had been led off to be flogged. . . . And now she felt sorry for all these people, it hurt her, and as she walked on she kept looking back at the cabins.

After walking two miles with them Marya said goodby, then she knelt, and pressing her face against the earth began wailing:

"Again I am left alone. Poor me! Poor unhappy sou that I am!"

And for a long time she went on wailing like this, an for a long time Olga and Sasha could see her still on he knees, as she kept bowing sideways, clutching her head i her hands, while the rooks flew over her.

The sun rose high; it turned hot. Zhukovo was left fa behind. Walking was pleasant; Olga and Sasha soon forg both the village and Marya; they were cheerful and ever thing entertained them: an ancient burial-mound; a row telegraph posts marching one after another into the distance and disappearing on the horizon, the wires humming mysteriously; a farmhouse, half hidden by green foliage, and with a scent of dampness and hemp coming from it, a place that for some reason seemed inhabited by happy people; a horse's skeleton making a lonely white spot in the open fields. And the larks trilled tirelessly, quails called to one another, and the corncrake cawed as though someone were jerking an old cramp-iron.

At noon Olga and Sasha came to a large village. There on the broad street they encountered the little old man who had been General Zhukov's cook. He was hot, and his red, perspiring bald spot shone in the sun. At first he and Olga failed to recognize each other, then they looked round at the same moment, did recognize each other, and went their separate ways without saying a word. Stopping before the open windows of a cottage which looked newer and more prosperous than the rest, Olga bowed down and said in a loud, thin, singsong voice:

"Orthodox Christians, give alms, for Christ's sake, as much as you can, and in the Kingdom of Heaven may your parents know peace eternal."

"Orthodox Christians," Sasha echoed her chant, "give alms, for Christ's sake, as much as you can, and in the Kingdom of Heaven. . . ."

1897

The Darling

OLENKA, the daughter of the retired collegiate assessor, Plemyanniakov, was sitting in her back porch, lost in thought. It was hot, the flies were persistent and teasing, and it was pleasant to reflect that it would soon be evening. Dark rain-clouds were gathering from the east, and bringing from time to time a breath of moisture in the air.

Kukin, who was the manager of an open-air theatre called the Tivoli, and who lived in the lodge, was standing in the middle of the garden looking at the sky.

"Again!" he observed despairingly. "It's going to rain again! Rain every day, as though to spite me! I might as well hang myself! It's ruin! Fearful loses every day."

He flung up his hands, and went on, addressing Olenka: "There! that's the life we lead, Olga Semyonovna. It's enough to make one cry. One works and does one's utmost; one wears oneself out, getting no sleep at night, and racks one's brain what to do for the best. And then what happens? To begin with, one's public is ignorant, boorish. I give them the very best operetta, a dainty masque, first-rate music-hall artists. But do you suppose that's what they want! They don't understand anything of that sort. They want a clown; what they ask for is vulgarity. And then look at the weather! Almost every evening it rains. It started on the tenth of May, and it's kept it up all May and June. It's simply awful! The public doesn't come, but I've to pay the rent just the same, and pay the artists."

The next evening the clouds would gather again, and Kukin would say with an hysterical laugh:

"Well, rain away, then! Flood the garden, drown me! Damn my luck in this world and the next! Let the artist have me up! Send me to prison!—to Siberia!—the scaffold! Ha, ha, ha!"

And next day the same thing.

Olenka listened to Kukin with silent gravity, and sometimes tears came into her eyes. In the end his misfortunes touched her; she grew to love him. He was a small thin man, with a yellow face, and curls combed forward on his forehead. He spoke in a thin tenor; as he talked his mouth worked on one side, and there was always an expression of despair on his face; yet he aroused a deep and genuine affection in her. She was always fond of someone, and could not exist without loving. In earlier days she had loved her papa, who now sat in a darkened room, breathing with difficulty; she had loved her aunt who used to come every other year from Bryansk; and before that, when she was at school, she had loved her French master. She was a gentle, soft-hearted, compassionate girl, with mild, tender eyes and very good health. At the sight of her full rosy cheeks, her soft white neck with a little dark mole on it, and the kind, naïve smile, which came into her face when she listened to anything pleasant, men thought, "Yes, not half bad," and smiled too, while lady visitors could not refrain from seizing her hand in the middle of a conversation, exclaiming in a gush of delight, "You darling!"

The house in which she had lived from her birth upwards, and which was left her in her father's will, was at the extreme end of the town, not far from the Tivoli. In the evenings and at night she could hear the band playing, and the crackling and banging of fireworks, and it seemed to her that it was Kukin struggling with his destiny, storming the entrenchments of his chief foe, the indifferent public; there was a sweet thrill at her heart, she had no desire to sleep, and when he returned home at daybreak, she tapped softly at her bedroom window, and showing him only her face and one shoulder through the curtain, she gave him a friendly smile. . . .

He proposed to her, and they were married. And when he had a closer view of her neck and her plump, fine shoulders, he threw up his hands, and said:

"You darling!"

He was happy, but as it rained on the day and night of his wedding, his face still retained an expression of despair.

They got on very well together. She used to sit in his office, to look after things in the Tivoli, to put down the accounts and pay the wages. And her rosy cheeks, her sweet, naïve, radiant smile, were to be seen now at the office window, now in the resfreshment bar or behind the scenes at the theatre. And already she used to say to her acquaintances that the theatre was the chief and most important thing in life, and that it was only through the drama that one could derive true enjoyment and become cultivated and humane.

"But do you suppose the public understands that?" she used to say. "What they want is a clown. Yesterday we gave 'Faust Inside Out,' and almost all the boxes were empty; but if Vanitchka and I had been producing some vulgar thing, I assure you the theatre would have been packed. To-morrow Vanitchka and I are doing 'Orpheus in Hell.' Do come."

And what Kukin said about the theatre and the actors she repeated. Like him she despised the public for their ignorance and their indifference to art; she took part in the rehearsals, she corrected the actors, she kept an eye on the behaviour of the musicians, and when there was an unfavourable notice in the local paper, she shed tears, and then went to the editor's office to set things right.

The actors were fond of her and used to call her "Vanitchka and I," and "the darling"; she was sorry for them and used to lend them small sums of money, and if they deceived her, she used to shed a few tears in private, but did not complain to her husband.

They got on well in the winter too. They took the theatre in the town for the whole winter, and let it for short terms to a Little Russian company, or to a conjurer, or to a local dramatic society. Olenka grew stouter, and was always beaming with satisfaction, while Kukin grew thinner and yellower, and continually complained of their terrible losses, although he had not done badly all the winter. He used to cough at night, and she used to give him hot raspberry tea or lime-flower water, to rub him with eau-de-Cologne and to wrap him in her warm shawls.

"You're such a sweet pet!" she used to say with perfect sincerity, stroking his hair. "You're such a pretty dear!"

Towards Lent he went to Moscow to collect a new troupe, and without him she could not sleep, but sat a night at her window, looking at the stars, and she compare herself with the hens, who are awake all night and uneasy when the cock is not in the hen-house. Kukin was detained in Moscow, and wrote that he would be back at Easter, adding some instructions about the Tivoli. But on the Sunday before Easter, late in the evening, came a sudden ominous knock at the gate; someone was hammering on the gate as though on a barrel—boom, boom, boom! The drowsy cook went flopping with her bare feet through the puddles, as she ran to open the gate.

"Please open," said someone outside in a thick bass. "There is a telegram for you."

Olenka had received telegrams from her husband before, but this time for some reason she felt numb with terror. With shaking hands she opened the telegram and read as follows:

"Ivan Petrovitch died suddenly to-day. Awaiting immate instructions fufuneral Tuesday."

That was how it was written in the telegram—"fufuneral," and the utterly incomprehensible word "immate." It was signed by the stage manager of the operatic company.

"My darling!" sobbed Olenka. "Vanitchka, my precious, my darling! Why did I ever meet you! Why did I know you and love you! Your poor heart-broken Olenka is all alone without you!"

Kukin's funeral took place on Tuesday in Moscow, Olenka returned home on Wednesday, and as soon as she got indoors she threw herself on her bed and sobbed so loudly that it could be heard next door, and in the street.

"Poor darling!" the neighbours said, as they crossed themselves. "Olga Semyonovna, poor darling! How she does take on!"

Three months later Olenka was coming home from mass, melancholy and in deep mourning. It happened that one of her neighbours, Vassily Andreitch Pustovalov, returning home from church, walked back beside her. He was the manager at Babakayev's, the timber merchant's. He wore straw hat, a white waistcoat, and a gold watch-chain, and looked more like a country gentleman than a man in trade.

"Everything happens as it is ordained, Olga Semyonovna," he said gravely, with a sympathetic note in his voice; "and if any of our dear ones die, it must be because it is the will of God, so we ought to have fortitude and bear it submissively."

After seeing Olenka to her gate, he said good-bye and went on. All day afterwards she heard his sedately dignified voice, and whenever she shut her eyes she saw his dark beard. She liked him very much. And apparently she had made an impression on him too, for not long afterwards an elderly lady, with whom she was only slightly acquainted, came to drink coffee with her, and as soon as she was seated at table began to talk about Pustovalov, saying that he was an excellent man whom one could thoroughly depend upon, and that any girl would be glad to marry him. Three days later Pustovalov came himself. He did not stay long, only about ten minutes, and he did not say much, but when he left, Olenka loved him—loved him so much that she lay awake all night in a perfect fever, and in the morning she sent for the elderly lady. The match was quickly arranged, and then came the wedding.

Pustovalov and Olenka got on very well together when they were married.

Usually he sat in the office till dinner-time, then he went out on business, while Olenka took his place, and sat in the office till evening, making up accounts and booking orders.

"Timber gets dearer every year; the price rises twenty per cent.," she would say to her customers and friends. "Only fancy we used to sell local timber, and now Vassitchka always has to go for wood to the Mogilev district. And the freight!" she would add, covering her cheeks with her hands in horror. "The freight!"

It seemed to her that she had been in the timber trade for ages and ages, and that the most important and necessary thing in life was timber; and there was something intimate and touching to her in the very sound of words such as "baulk," "post," "beam," "pole," "scantling," "batten," "lath," "plank," etc.

At night when she was asleep she dreamed of perfect mountains of planks and boards, and long strings of waggons, carting timber somewhere far away. She dreamed that a whole regiment of six-inch beams forty feet high, standing on end, was marching upon the timber-yard; tha logs, beams, and boards knocked together with the resounding crash of dry wood, kept falling and getting up again, piling themselves on each other. Olenka cried out in her sleep, and Pustovalov said to her tenderly: "Olenka, what's the matter, darling? Cross yourself!"

Her husband's ideas were hers. If he thought the room was too hot, or that business was slack, she thought the same. Her husband did not care for entertainments, and on holidays he stayed at home. She did likewise.

"You are always at home or in the office," her friends said to her. "You should go to the theatre, darling, or to the circus."

"Vassitchka and I have no time to go to theatres," she would answer sedately. "We have no time for nonsense. What's the use of these theatres?"

On Saturdays Pustovalov and she used to go to the evening service; on holidays to early mass, and they walked side by side with softened faces as they came home from church. There was a pleasant fragrance about them both, and her silk dress rustled agreeably. At home they drank tea, with fancy bread and jams of various kinds, and afterwards they ate pie. Every day at twelve o'clock there was a savoury smell of beet-root soup and of mutton or duck in their yard, and on fast-days of fish, and no one could pass the gate without feeling hungry. In the office the samovar was always boiling, and customers were regaled with tea and cracknels. Once a week the couple went to the baths and returned side by side, both red in the face.

"Yes, we have nothing to complain of, thank God," Olenka used to say to her acquaintances. "I wish everyone were as well off as Vassitchka and I."

When Pustovalov went away to buy wood in the Mogilev district, she missed him dreadfully, lay awake and cried. A young veterinary surgeon in the army, called Smirnin, to whom they had let their lodge, used sometimes to come in in the evening. He used to talk to her and play cards with her, and this entertained her in her husband's absence. She was particularly interested in what he told her of his home life. He was married and had a little boy, but was separated from his wife because she had been unfaithful to him, and now he hated her and used to send her forty roubles a month for the maintenance of their son. And hearing of all this, Olenka sighed and shook her head. She was sorry for him.

"Well, God keep you," she used to say to him at parting, as she lighted him down the stairs with a candle. "Thank you for coming to cheer me up, and may the Mother of God give you health."

And she always expressed herself with the same sedateness and dignity, the same reasonableness, in imitation of her husband. As the veterinary surgeon was disappearing behind the door below, she would say:

"You know, Vladimir Platonitch, you'd better make it up with your wife. You should forgive her for the sake of your son. You may be sure the little fellow understands."

And when Pustovalov came back, she told him in a low voice about the veterinary surgeon and his unhappy home life, and both sighed and shook their heads and talked about the boy, who, no doubt, missed his father, and by some strange connection of ideas, they went up to the holy ikons, bowed to the ground before them and prayed that God would give them children.

And so the Pustovalovs lived for six years quietly and peaceably in love and complete harmony.

But behold! one winter day after drinking hot tea in the office, Vassily Andreitch went out into the yard without his cap on to see about sending off some timber, caught cold and was taken ill. He had the best doctors, but he grew worse and died after four months' illness. And Olenka was a widow once more.

"I've nobody, now you've left me, my darling," she sobbed, after her husband's funeral. "How can I live without you, in wretchedness and misery! Pity me, good people, all alone in the world!"

She went about dressed in black with long "weepers," and gave up wearing hat and gloves for good. She hardly ever went out, except to church, or to her husband's grave and led the life of a nun. It was not till six months later that she took off the weepers and opened the shutters of the windows. She was sometimes seen in the mornings, going with her cook to market for provisions, but what went on in her house and how she lived now could only be surmised. People guessed, from seeing her drinking tea in her garden with the veterinary surgeon, who read the newspaper aloud to her, and from the fact that, meeting a lady she knew at the post-office, she said to her:

"There is no proper veterinary inspection in our town, and that's the cause of all sorts of epidemics. One is always hearing of people's getting infection from the milk supply, or catching diseases from horses and cows. The health of domestic animals ought to be as well cared for as the health of human beings."

She repeated the veterinary surgeon's words, and was of the same opinion as he about everything. It was evident that she could not live a year without some attachment, and had found new happiness in the lodge. In anyone else this would have been censured, but no one could think ill of Olenka; everything she did was so natural. Neither she nor the veterinary surgeon said anything to other people of the change in their relations, and tried, indeed, to conceal it, but without success, for Olenka could not keep a secret. When he had visitors, men serving in his regiment, and she poured out tea or served the supper, she would begin talking of the cattle plague, of the foot and mouth disease, and of the municipal slaughter-houses. He was dreadfully embarrassed, and when the guests had gone, he would seize her by the hand and hiss angrily:

"I've asked you before not to talk about what you don't understand. When we veterinary surgeons are talking among ourselves, please don't put your word in. It's really annoying."

And she would look at him with astonishment and dismay, and ask him in alarm: "But, Voloditchka, what *am* I to talk about?"

And with tears in her eyes she would embrace him, begging him not to be angry, and they were both happy.

But this happiness did not last long. The veterinary surgeon departed, departed for ever with his regiment, when it was transferred to a distant place—to Siberia, it may be. And Olenka was left alone.

Now she was absolutely alone. Her father had long been dead, and his arm-chair lay in the attic, covered with dust and lame of one leg. She got thinner and plainer, and when people met her in the street they did not look at her as they used to, and did not smile to her; evidently her best years were over and left behind, and now a new sort of life had begun for her, which did not bear thinking about. In the evening Olenka sat in the porch, and heard the band playing and the fireworks popping in the Tivoli, but now the sound stirred no response. She looked into her yard without interest, thought of nothing, wished for nothing, and afterwards, when night came on she went to bed and dreamed of her empty yard. She ate and drank as it were unwillingly.

And what was worst of all, she had no opinions of any sort. She saw the objects about her and understood what she saw, but could not form any opinion about them, and did not know what to talk about. And how awful it is not to have any opinions! One sees a bottle, for instance, or the rain, or a peasant driving in his cart, but what the bottle is for, or the rain, or the peasant, and what is the meaning of it, one can't say, and could not even for a thousand roubles. When she had Kukin, or Pustovalov, or the veterinary surgeon, Olenka could explain everything, and give her opinion about anything you like, but now there was the same emptiness in her brain and in her heart as there was in her yard outside. And it was as harsh and as bitter as wormwood in the mouth.

Little by little the town grew in all directions. The road became a street, and where the Tivoli and the timber-yard had been, there were new turnings and houses. How rapidly time passes! Olenka's house grew dingy, the roof got rusty, the shed sank on one side, and the whole yard was overgrown with docks and stinging-nettles. Olenka herself had grown plain and elderly; in summer she sat in the porch, and her soul, as before, was empty and dreary and full of bitterness. In winter she sat at her window and looked at the snow. When she caught the scent of spring, or heard the chime of the church bells, a sudden rush of memories from the past came over her, there was a tender ache in her heart, and her eyes brimmed over with tears, but this was only for a minute, and then came emptiness again and the sense of the futility of life. The black kitten, Briska, rubbed against her and purred softly, but Olenka was not touched by these feline caresses. That was not what she needed. She wanted a love that would absorb her whole being, her whole soul and reason—that would give her ideas and an object in life, and would warm her old blood. And she would shake the kitten off her skirt and say with vexation:

"Get along; I don't want you!"

And so it was, day after day and year after year, and no joy, and no opinions. Whatever Mavra, the cook, said she accepted.

One hot July day, towards evening, just as the cattle were being driven by, and the whole yard was full of dust, someone suddenly knocked at the gate. Olenka went to open it herself and was dumfounded when she looked out: she saw Smirnin, the veterinary surgeon, grey-headed, and dressed as a civilian. She suddenly remembered everything. She could not help crying and letting her head fall on his breast without uttering a word, and in the violence of her feeling she did not notice how they both walked into the house and sat down to tea.

"My dear Vladimir Platonitch! What fate has brought you?" she muttered, trembling with joy.

"I want to settle here for good, Olga Semyonovna," he told her. "I have resigned my post, and have come to settle down and try my luck on my own account. Besides, it's time for my boy to go to school. He's a big boy. I am reconciled with my wife, you know."

"Where is she?" asked Olenka.

"She's at the hotel with the boy, and I'm looking for lodgings."

"Good gracious, my dear soul! Lodgings! Why not have my house? Why shouldn't that suit you? Why, my goodness, I wouldn't take any rent!" cried Olenka in a flutter, beginning to cry again. "You live here, and the lodge will do nicely for me. Oh dear! how glad I am!"

Next day the roof was painted and the walls were whitewashed, and Olenka, with her arms akimbo, walked about the yard giving directions. Her face was beaming with her old smile, and she was brisk and alert as though she had waked from a long sleep. The veterinary's wife arrived—a thin, plain lady, with short hair and a peevish expression. With her was her little Sasha, a boy of ten, small for his age, blue-eyed, chubby, with dimples in his cheeks. And scarcely had the boy walked into the yard when he ran after the cat, and at once there was the sound of his gay, joyous laugh.

"Is that your puss, auntie?" he asked Olenka. "When she has little ones, do give us a kitten. Mamma is awfully afraid of mice."

Olenka talked to him, and gave him tea. Her heart warmed and there was a sweet ache in her bosom, as though the boy had been her own child. And when he sat at the table in the evening, going over his lessons, she looked at him with deep tenderness and pity as she murmured to herself:

"You pretty pet! . . . my precious! . . . Such a fair little thing, and so clever."

" 'An island is a piece of land which is entirely surrounded by water,' " he read aloud.

"An island is a piece of land," she repeated, and this was the first opinion to which she gave utterance with positive conviction after so many years of silence and dearth of ideas.

Now she had opinions of her own, and at supper she talked to Sasha's parents, saying how difficult the lessons were at the high schools, but that yet the high school was better than a commercial one, since with a high school education all careers were open to one, such as being a doctor or an engineer.

Sasha began going to the high school. His mother departed to Harkov to her sister's and did not return; his father used to go off every day to inspect cattle, and would often be away from home for three days together, and it seemed to Olenka as though Sasha was entirely abandoned, that he was not wanted at home, that he was being starved, and she carried him off to her lodge and gave him a little room there.

And for six months Sasha had lived in the lodge with her. Every morning Olenka came into his bedroom and found him fast asleep, sleeping noiselessly with his hand under his cheek. She was sorry to wake him.

"Sashenka," she would say mournfully. "get up, darling It's time for school."

He would get up, dress and say his prayers, and then sit down to breakfast, drink three glasses of tea, and eat two large cracknels and half a buttered roll. All this time he was hardly awake and a little ill-humoured in consequence.

"You don't quite know your fable, Sashenka," Olenka would say, looking at him as though he were about to set off on a long journey. "What a lot of trouble I have with you! You must work and do your best, darling, and obey your teachers."

"Oh, do leave me alone!" Sasha would say.

Then he would go down the street to school, a little figure, wearing a big cap and carrying a satchel on his shoulder. Olenka would follow him noiselessly.

"Sashenka!" she would call after him, and she would pop into his hand a date or a caramel. When he reached the street where the school was, he would feel ashamed of being followed by a tall, stout woman; he would turn round and say:

"You'd better go home, auntie. I can go the rest of the way alone."

She would stand still and look after him fixedly till he had disappeared at the school-gate.

Ah, how she loved him! Of her former attachments not one had been so deep; never had her soul surrendered to any feeling so spontaneously, so disinterestedly, and so joyously as now that her maternal instincts were aroused. For this little boy with the dimple in his cheek and the big school cap, she would have given her whole life, she would have given it with joy and tears of tenderness. Why? Who can tell why?

When she had seen the last of Sasha, she returned home, contented and serene, brimming over with love; her face, which had grown younger during the last six months, smiled and beamed; people meeting her looked at her with pleasure.

"Good-morning, Olga Semyonovna, darling. How are you, darling?"

"The lessons at the high school are very difficult now," she would relate at the market. "It's too much; in the first class yesterday they gave him a fable to learn by heart, and a Latin translation and a problem. You know it's too much for a little chap."

And she would begin talking about the teachers, the lessons, and the school books, saying just what Sasha said.

At three o'clock they had dinner together: in the evening they learned their lessons together and cried. When she put him to bed, she would stay a long time making the cross over him and murmuring a prayer; then she would go to bed and dream of that far-away misty future when Sasha would finish his studies and become a doctor or an engineer, would have a big house of his own with horses and a carriage, would get married and have children. . . . She would fall asleep still thinking of the same thing, and tears would run down her cheeks from her closed eyes, while the black cat lay purring beside her: "Mrr, mrr, mrr."

Suddenly there would come a loud knock at the gate.

Olenka would wake up breathless with alarm, her heart throbbing. Half a minute later would come another knock.

"It must be a telegram from Harkov," she would think, beginning to tremble from head to foot. "Shasha's mother is sending for him from Harkov. . . . Oh, mercy on us!"

She was in despair. Her head, her hands, and her feet would turn chill, and she would feel that she was the most unhappy woman in the world. But another minute would pass, voices would be heard: it would turn out to be the veterinary surgeon coming home from the club.

"Well, thank God!" she would think.

And gradually the load in her heart would pass off, and she would feel at ease. She would go back to bed thinking of Sasha, who lay sound asleep in the next room, sometimes crying out in his sleep:

"I'll give it you! Get away! Shut up!"

1898